Calculated
RISK

K S Ferguson

K S FERGUSON

ACKNOWLEDGMENTS

I would like to thank the many people who assisted with this novel. First, thanks to my daughter for her unfailing support and thoughtful suggestions. Then thanks to my writing partner, primary beta reader, and copy editor, James Grayson, for his sharp eye and dedication to quality storytelling. Thanks also to Brenda Windberg, professional editor for making the manuscript better. And I couldn't have done it without the cheerleading and morale boosting given by the FreyedCritters and the Maass Destruction lists.

I would also like to thank my readers. Your support is greatly appreciated. If you enjoy this book, please consider leaving a review at your favorite retailer or library site. Reviews help other readers find this work and keep food on the table so writers don't starve.

If you would like to be notified when the next book in the series is released, please sign up at http://www.ksferguson.net/sign-up-for-news.html. I won't sell your contact info to anyone for any reason.

Titles by K S Ferguson

Rafe & Kama series:

Calculated Risk

Hostile Takeover

Family Owned

River Madden series:

Touching Madness

Undercover Madness

The Hellhound series:

No Place Like Hell

Novella:

Puncher's Chance
(with James Grayson)

This is a work of fiction. Names, characters, places, and incidents either are the product of the author's imagination or are used fictitiously, and any resemblance to actual persons, living or dead, business establishments, events, or locales is entirely coincidental. The publisher does not have any control over and does not assume any responsibility for third-party websites or their content.

Calculated Risk

Contact the publisher: http://www.ksferguson.net

ISBN: 1938179188
ISBN-13: 9781938179181

1

The giant swordsman thrust Rafe's short sword aside, thumping the blade against the steel bulkhead. Rafe ducked another strike. His forehead glanced off his assailant's knee, blurring his vision. He'd thought he could take on two at once. He was better-trained, more experienced, and at thirty, still as quick as he'd ever be—and *damned* if he was going to lose this fight. But these guys were built like gorillas and quicker than he'd expected. Each topped six feet by several inches, while Rafe barely made a lithe five foot ten. They'd kill him.

Rafe shook stars from his eyes. He feinted to the left, dove into a forward roll down the EcoMech space yacht's companionway, spun, and thrust a killing strike to the kidneys of one of the men. The other surged forward, his shoulder taking Rafe in the chest. Rafe fell hard and rolled left as his adversary's sword crashed down. His opponent loomed over him. He kicked out, catching the man in the knee and unsettling his balance long enough for a last, desperate thrust to the throat.

"Ow!" shouted his opponent, clapping his hand to his neck.

Rafe scrambled to his feet. "Sorry, Cookie. I got carried away. You okay?"

The ship's cook laughed and placed the rubberized practice sword into Rafe's hand, then tapped on his nanocom gauntlet. "All right, Mr. McTavish, you've won the bet. I'll upload my chili recipe to your account."

"Rafe. Call me Rafe. Don't forget any secret ingredients." He grinned and pushed sweat-dampened hair off his forehead. His own nanocom chimed, and an unopened mail announcement replaced the date and time on the tiny screen—23:45, 11 March, 2040.

The cook's assistant handed over his sword and clapped Rafe on the shoulder. "Thanks for the sparring match. Haven't had so much fun since I left the service. You're strong for a little guy."

The backhanded compliment brought back fond memories from when Rafe led a squad of mercenaries in the field instead of languishing behind a CEO's desk. He couldn't remember now why he'd thought that running his own security company would be more satisfying than commanding a close-knit combat team for Earth Authority.

The vibration of the ship's engines changed pitch, and a second later, Rafe felt the bang of a docking collar. The other two registered the change and glanced down the companionway toward the cargo bays and airlock. They exchanged a wary look and turned away.

"What's up?" Rafe asked. "I thought once we cleared the Earth-to-asteroid-belt jump gate, we were going straight through to the mining station?"

Cookie spoke over his shoulder. "Captain Benson didn't tell you? We're picking up passengers at the jump gate station."

The men disappeared into the ship's galley. Little prickles raised the hairs on Rafe's arms. He could think of only one person with the authority to divert his borrowed ride. The hatch at the end of the companionway banged back.

As Rafe feared, Leon Goldman, the subject of his stealth investigation, stamped through. He looked fifteen years older than Rafe, even though only four years separated them. His brown hair was swept back and plastered with too much hair gel. A stylish business suit did nothing to enhance his pudgy shape. Even at a distance, the chunky gold wedding ring on his left hand and the diamond studded band on his right flashed in the light. His beefy cheeks and bulbous nose glowed pink, like he'd had one too many drinks, but his walk was sure and swift, and his hazel eyes promised trouble.

Captain Benson, the yacht's commander, trailed in Leon's wake, his normal upright posture slightly bent in deference to the EcoMech CEO. Rafe steeled himself for the coming confrontation, uncomfortable in Leon's presence, but confident he could suffer through.

Leon's wife, Amaya, clattered down the companionway next, the flared legs of a black pantsuit swishing around her swollen ankles, her skin more yellow than Rafe remembered. In the dim light, her slanted brown eyes appeared sunken, and her black hair hung straight and unadorned to her waist. Her expression made his breath catch; the same sour, judgmental air she'd had since she was ten.

The blood curdled in Rafe's veins, and the temperature in the companionway dropped ten degrees. He hadn't seen his sister-in-law since his wife's death, fourteen years ago. Amaya leaned on the arm of a young Adonis, Leon's eleven-year-old son, Gabe. His bright blue eyes darted around the ship, awe on his face. The sight of the boy chafed at old wounds in Rafe's heart. He forced his gaze back to his brother-in-law.

Leon slammed open the hatch to the executive suite and glanced inside. "Benson! Clear this room and get our things in here."

"Sir, Mr. McTavish is using—"

"This isn't a debate. Get it done."

Benson's eyes communicated apology, and Rafe shrugged. The captain flagged a crewman loaded with luggage into the suite.

Leon advanced along the companionway.

"Still playing pretend I see."

Rafe glanced at his practice swords. His cheeks warmed, the only source of heat in the suddenly chilly space. *Focus. Breathe. Speak.* He sucked in air, but his lungs seemed unwilling to inflate. "Hello, Leon."

"What brings you way out here, McTavish?" The man's smug eyes glittered like a crocodile's. He folded his arms across his chest.

Crap, he knows. So much for conducting a quiet investigation. Still, Rafe had an obligation to finish what he'd started. "I've been hired to check out this mining station EcoMech wants to purchase. The onsite inspection needs to be completed before the sale goes through."

"And you're such an expert on asteroid mining that you're qualified to do it?" Leon sneered. "Anyway, you're on a fool's errand. I signed the purchase papers yesterday. You can run along home now, back to your toy soldiers and war games."

Rafe counted a slow five and fought the urge to bunch his fists. "Sorry, I have a contract to fulfill, and this is my ride, provided by your father."

Leon's pink face reddened. He stepped closer and dropped his hands to his sides. "You think you're so hot building your little company from your momma's money, living the high life, fast women and faster flyers, a real playboy. Do those mercs you lead know what a coward you are? How you couldn't be bothered to show up for your wife's funeral? Don't tell me you don't break contracts."

Rafe's nerves burned like he'd been poked with a taser. He wanted to run from Leon's accusations, but his muscles wouldn't respond. Fourteen years vanished in a heartbeat, and he stood again in his wife's bedroom. Blood spattered the yellow walls and soaked the lacy white coverlet on the bed. Congealing blood oozed between his bare toes. The scent of slaughter poisoned the air. The memory made his stomach float as if he were in zero gravity. He thought he might vomit on Leon's fancy Italian shoes. The CEO's face glowed with victory.

Rafe jerked closer and smelled the bourbon on Leon's breath. "I follow your father's orders, not yours." His voice came out barely louder than a whisper.

Leon's muscles tensed, and he shook with the effort to maintain his composure. Rafe felt sure a punch was coming, almost hoped for it. His brother-in-law frowned, his control returning but his rage undimmed.

"You won't find anything." Leon grabbed Gabe by the shoulders and dragged him away, ruffling the boy's hair. "Come on, son. Let's go kill some orcs. I've got a new strategy I want to try in that *Galaxy at War* game."

Rafe stared after Leon. Amaya stood by the open door to the executive suite, an icy glare frosting the air between them. She waited. He didn't know what to say, still couldn't express the grief aloud, make the apology he should have made fourteen years ago. With a snort, she disappeared inside and slammed the hatch.

2

Kamala Bhatia slid silently along the empty mining station corridor in the dim half-light of the artificial night. If she hadn't lost her way, the administrative section was just around the corner. She'd spent the last hour trying to access the business server from the safety of her rat hole cabin before determining it was offline.

Damned administrators shutting off the computer at night. How was any self-respecting hacker supposed to crack it when they'd powered it down? She'd find the computer closet, pick the lock, and power it up. A few more minutes decoding the log-on credentials, and she'd plant her search-and-destroy program. Maybe she'd have time to go back to bed for an hour before that bear of a smelter supervisor, Browning, came for her. She hated managers, especially when she'd had less than four hours' sleep.

The lights brightened without warning, and chimes echoed. Kama's heart jumped. In the distance, she heard hinges creak, male voices mumble and complain, and the thump of boots on decks. She focused bleary eyes on the nanocom on her wrist. *Vishnu preserve us, they start at 5:00 a.m.?* She couldn't risk breaking into the computer now.

With all the aplomb she could muster, she slung her duffel bag of computer tools over her shoulder and strolled back the way she'd come. As she walked, she set her nanocom to play *They're Coming to Take Me Away* and chanted along under her breath. It didn't take long for a crowd of miners to gather up ahead. She chided herself for not paying more attention to the station layout and avoiding the living quarters. The wolf whistles and cat calls began at once.

Damn! These guys looked more desperate for female companionship than she'd anticipated, and here she was parading through the thick of them. She never wore makeup, always hid her shapely figure under baggy Oasis Corp coveralls, and pulled her hair back in a business-like ponytail at the base of her neck. And still men swarmed toward her like bees to a butterfly bush.

Kama embedded plugs in her ears. A touch to her nanocom and "heavy metal" droned from the speakers. Another touch and the volume rose loud enough to rattle her teeth. She hooted and stamped down the corridor to the grinding beat of the bass like some lunatic fresh from the asylum. The miners fled. Excellent. She hated using the backup plan: a little vial of *eau du road kill.*

A hand touched her shoulder, and she pivoted to see Edgar Browning, a short, black-skinned man with close-cropped hair, a pugnacious face, and an enormous upper body. He was dressed in work-stained overalls and thick boots. She guessed he was about forty-five—old for a miner. Two tattoos covered his dark forearm, one a crudely-drawn dragon, the other a stenciled prison serial number. He pointed to her nanocom and shouted something. Kama silenced the noise and removed her ear plugs.

"What didn't you understand about 'stay in your quarters until I come for you'?" his gravelly voice scolded. "The last thing I need is you distracting the guys or getting yourself lost. Out here, inattention can kill."

She bristled. Just because she hadn't gotten where she was going didn't mean she was lost. She did her best to feign contrition. "Sorry. My boss likes to know I'm earning my pay, so I thought I'd give him a shout."

"Long range com's down again. Miss Patty'll check it later." Browning gestured to the man beside him."This is Yuri Roshal, our shipping manager."

About forty, immensely tall and thin, with darting eyes and enormous bony hands, Roshal had dark hair and a Slavic cast to his face. He wore cargo pants and a garish yellow t-shirt emblazoned with a sports logo obscured by blotchy red stains. A fidgety man full of nervous energy, he didn't look much better rested than Browning.

Kama nodded and shook the cool hand he offered.

"Mr. Levine around?" she asked.

Browning grimaced. "Admin side don't start the same time as the rest of us. Got something to fill your time, though. Urgent job's come up, and we could use your help."

She froze. Buying Levine's silence and recovering that bloody lost contract was her mission, not helping the two hundred workers at this owner-operated startup.

"Can't start until I check in with the manager. Have to get a run-down of my duties, sign forms, yada, yada..."

Browning's brow furrowed. "Your duties are to do what I damn well need doing," he muttered, rubbing his temples. "Look, it won't take long. Yuri here can give you the lowdown, then you can see Mr. Levine once he's up and about."

"We've got a mass spectrometer array that's acting twitchy," Roshal put in. "We haven't got the tech skills to fix it."

Kama checked the time. She figured she could repair a mass spectrometer in about five minutes and be knocking on Levine's door within ten.

"It can't wait," Browning said. "We stand to strike out on an asteroid claim and can't afford to lose it."

"R. S. Steele's sniffing around it," Roshal added.

Browning's muscular shoulders quivered, and he got a worried look. "Those bloody cowboys. How the hell do they always know when we make a good find?"

Guilt rose in Kama's chest. Whatever her private objectives, however many faceless thousands counted on her, these people were counting on her right here, right now. They weren't powerful executives or company drones; they were independent people trying to make their own way on the backs of their skills. Just the kind of people she and Oasis said they wanted to help.

"All right," she said. "Just the one job. Then I'll need to see Mr. Levine."

Browning broke into a smile, all the more charming for his missing canine tooth. "Thanks, Miss Bhatia! Levine'll be flattered when he finds out how keen you are to meet him. Yuri here will ferry you out to the ship."

"No problem," Roshal chimed in. "I only stopped here to pick up some parts. I'll drop you off on the way to my tug."

Kama did a double-take. "Ship?"

Browning nodded. "Yeah. You know, the ship with the mass spec? Got a prospecting team heading out in a couple hours, and they won't be much good without a working mass spec."

Kama's stomach gnawed on itself, and she struggled not to swear. Five minutes' work, but probably half an hour's journey to and from some isolated ship, and no possibility of an early return. She hoped she wouldn't be too late getting to Levine, or the failure of the entire Sharma Network project might fall on her shoulders.

3

Rafe drilled the little rubber ball to the floor and caught it as it rico-cheted off the far wall. Someone tapped on his cabin door, but he ignored them and threw the ball again. No matter which way he turned the mining station purchase, it didn't add up. He'd traipse around the station with his brother-in-law, send his report to Aaron Goldman, Chairman of EcoMech and Leon's father, and take the first vessel headed home to Earth—as long as it wasn't this one. Not a satisfactory repayment of the debt he owed Aaron, but it would have to do.

The tapping became loud, insistent rapping. Rafe pocketed the ball and sighed. He took the two steps across the cramped cabin and opened the door.

His dead brother Miguel stood in the companionway. The sight stole his breath. On second reflection, he realized that this boy stood at least three inches taller and couldn't be more than seventeen or eighteen, not the twenty-five Miguel had been at his death. Endowed with the same curly black hair and cobalt blue eyes the McTavish men all shared, he wore an ill-fitting business suit and wiped one hand against his trouser leg. The other hand held a filmie.

"Uncle Rafe? I'm Greg." He shuffled his feet and ducked his head. When Rafe didn't step back to let him in, he continued. "You know, Shannon's kid? Your sister? Can I come in?"

Rafe gave the boy his best smile but didn't open the door. "Greg, yes, how nice to see you. Unfortunately, you've come at a bad time. We're arriving at the station soon, and I have to prepare. Perhaps we can talk later."

"Mom has a message for you." Greg glanced down the corridor and lowered his voice. "She doesn't want Mr. Goldman to know about it."

Rafe felt like a violin string—dug out of something's guts and stretched far too tight. He didn't want cryptic messages from his sister. He didn't want anything but for this trip to be over, for the mystery of Leon's inexplicable purchase to quit rattling around inside his head. He waved the boy inside.

Greg glanced around the interior, and Rafe saw it through his eyes. Untidy stacks of filmies tottered on the desk and bedside table, a few sheets already scattered on the floor. A pair of trousers and a shirt hung over the back of the chair. One workout shoe lay in the middle of the floor, and the other—where was the other? His canvas hold-all was kicked against one wall, the practice swords piled on top. Perhaps they should have used Greg's cabin.

Greg seized one of the swords and swished it through the air. "Wow, Gabe told me you had swords. You must go to those Renaissance fair reenactments. Do you have armor? You know, chainmail, or maybe real plate?"

Rafe grabbed the sword and put it back on the hold-all, glad he'd tucked the real sword and off-hand dueling dagger away at the bottom of the bag. "They aren't toys. In space, energy or projectile weapons are no one's friend. Soldiers on ships and orbital stations favor close quarter weapons—knives, swords, nunchucks, batons. Why are you here?"

"Gramps thought I should do an internship with Mr. Goldman. I didn't want to, but Mom said I could help her get information she need-ed. Goldman doesn't like me much."

Rafe lifted an eyebrow. He wondered if the boy used 'Gramps' to the old man's face. "I meant, what's the message?"

"Oh, yeah." He handed over the filmie. "Hey, I know you don't probably remember me, but maybe I could do an internship with you? I mean, with you being a CEO of your own company and all, I could work for you? I bet you're a better boss than Goldman any day. And besides, you're family."

Which is exactly why I'd never hire you. Rafe added Greg's filmie to the pile on the desk. He didn't intend to read it, at least not before he was in his own office on Earth, away from Leon, EcoMech, and his annoying nephew. He took the boy's arm and propelled him toward the door.

"Now isn't the best time. Let me think on it, and we'll talk later."

"You mean it? Thanks! But I can't go unless I have a reply for Mom. She said it was urgent."

Rafe bit back the response he wanted to make, resisted the urge to throw Greg into the corridor, and returned to the filmie:

Rafe,

I've found corporate documents crediting Dad with pushing through the purchase of this mining station you're visiting, as though it was all his idea. I've seen the figures. The purchase is a disaster with serious repercussions for EcoMech. When the whole venture fails, Dad will be blamed. He'll have to step down from his position on the board. That'll kill him.

We both know this is Leon's doing. I need your help.

Shannon

He crushed the filmie in his fist and dropped onto the bed, rage spreading like fire through his blood. Couldn't his family understand that he'd disowned them? Why should he rescue a man who hated him, for whom he'd never been good enough?

"Are you all right, Uncle Rafe? You look kind of pale." Greg shuffled his feet. "What should I tell Mom?"

"Tell her..."

He reread the filmie. The CEO's purpose for purchasing the station suddenly became clear: he didn't want to share power with the McTavish family anymore. With Cullen McTavish off the board, only the Goldmans would remain to control EcoMech. Had Aaron Goldman known—or at least suspected—that Leon intended to frame Cullen when he'd coerced Rafe to investigate the purchase? Rafe had questions. Leon had answers.

He pushed past Greg and strode down the cramped hallway. Anger boiling inside him, he swept the dimly lit lounge looking for his brother-in-law. View screens that emulated windows showed the tiny sparks of distant suns scattered over blackness. A thick green carpet damped the constant throb of the ship's engines. Comfortable armchairs or couches were bolted to the deck.

He found Leon seated alone in the corner on a wing-back chair, a tall glass of bourbon on a table by his elbow. From the rheumy look in the man's eyes, it wasn't his first drink. He didn't seem surprised to see Rafe.

"So Shannon's little mole has delivered her message." He smiled at Rafe's astonishment. "What, you thought you were the only one doing any spying?"

"You know the mining station is a white elephant, and you're using it to destroy my father. You want EcoMech all for yourself, you selfish, greedy bastard."

Leon reached for his drink and took a noisy sip. "Grow up, McTavish. Your family's influence at EcoMech is nil. Your father's only a figurehead, and a piece of piss to manipulate. Shannon won't speak to me, and you won't come within a light-year of the company. Miguel was the only one with both balls and brains. Too bad he splattered himself on a mountainside."

"Then why are you framing my father? Buying the station makes no sense in any other context."

Leon gave him a grim smile. "I'm in a war, and Cullen is collateral damage. I like your old man, I really do, but if I'm to win, he had to be sacrificed."

Rafe stepped back, perplexed by the easy admission. "What war?"

"One for family honor and position at EcoMech. But what would you know about that?" Leon drained the rest of the bourbon. "You disgraced your family long ago."

Before Rafe could drag Leon from the chair and pound the daylights out of him, Captain Benson knocked on the hatch frame and stepped in.

"Excuse me, gentlemen." Benson looked uncomfortable, his eyes flicking to Rafe before settling on Leon. "We've arrived at the station."

Leon rose. "I didn't hear the docking collar."

"There's been a communications snafu, sir. The station's long-range com has been down all night. We've just reached them via ship-to-ship radio."

The CEO straightened his jacket, ignoring Rafe. "Typical. Well, get on with the docking. We don't have all day."

"They won't allow us to dock, sir. They say they weren't expecting us." Benson fell back in Leon's wake as the pudgy man steamrolled through the hatch into the companionway, cussing out everyone and vowing to take care of the matter himself.

Rafe remained behind, sucking in deep breaths to regain his composure. Mind racing, he drew the ball from his pocket and bounced it against the deck. None of what Leon said made sense, nor did it give him any ideas for how to extricate his father from the mess he'd gotten himself into. Shannon wanted his help, but what could he do?

He needed to get inside his brother-in-law's thick skull to find out more about this war. Short of kidnapping and torture, the only way he could see to do that was to chain himself to the vile man until he got answers.

Rafe pocketed the ball and went after the CEO, who stormed around screaming at everyone. Benson ducked into the com room, presumably to convince the station to let them dock. Leon ordered Greg and his assistant, Bob, to wait for him at the airlock, then he disappeared into the executive suite.

When Leon emerged, he was the sharp, self-confident CEO ready to do business. He wore a fresh suit, and he'd rinsed his mouth with some minty product that masked the smell of the bourbon. As he headed for the airlock, Rafe grabbed his arm and kept his voice low.

"A good general knows not to fight a war on two fronts, Leon. Tell me what's going on. Or shut me out and have me on your flank. It's your choice."

Leon's eyes flashed. "What's this? The runt of the litter challenging the big dog? You're all bark and no bite, same as you always were."

The docking collar clanged against the ship, and the CEO pulled away. Rafe followed him to the airlock, seething from his rebuke. Leon bounced on the balls of his feet. Bob stood placidly behind his boss, and Greg fidgeted next to Rafe. The hatch opened with a squeal of metal.

The docking bay was just a metal cube with a bench along one wall, a rack of spacesuits, and a tool locker. Rows of indicator lights punctuated a non-slip floor, the bay number scrawled in yellow paint on each wall. Two men and a woman waited for them. No one smiled.

"Leon Goldman, CEO, EcoMech Corporation." Leon extended his hand to the one he'd somehow determined must be in charge, a short, black man with broad shoulders and a challenging gaze. He didn't bother introducing Rafe, Bob, or Greg.

The miner eyed Leon before extending a beefy hand of his own. "Edgar Browning, smelter supervisor. This is Miss Patty Hertzog, assistant to our manager, Donald Levine, and Yuri Roshal, shipping manager."

An unlikely team, Rafe thought. About sixty, blonde, and heavily made-up, Hertzog wore an old-fashioned, ankle-length dress and heels. Roshal reminded him of a scarecrow stirred by a breeze, in his garish yellow shirt splattered with a huge red stain and dirty black trousers bagging on a stick-figure frame. Distrust oozed from their tense faces and rigid postures. Rafe glanced around the docking bay, automatically evaluating its defensibility.

"And where is Mr. Levine?" asked Leon.

"He's not available," Roshal said, his gaze sliding to the entrance of the docking bay. Rafe followed his lead and spotted a security camera above the door.

"Before we continue, can you give us any proof of who you are or your claims to ownership of this facility?" Browning stood, hands on hips, blocking their passage. His belligerent, bull-necked posture reminded Rafe of the troll under the bridge in the children's story.

Leon stared at Browning as though he were a naked madman spouting Shakespeare. "The Galaxy Mining home office has informed Mr. Levine of the transfer of ownership."

"And that's a problem, Mr. Goldman, because we believe that we own this station, not Galaxy. Or you," Browning said, huffing up. His biceps strained against the material of his shirt. Rafe's unease ratcheted up.

Leon shifted to a more aggressive stance, while Greg wandered over to peer up at the security camera. Boots drummed on the deck outside the docking bay.

A gruff voice shouted, "In here. Get em, boys!"

A rough-looking man dressed in an old work shirt, worn-out jeans, and heavy boots stepped through the door. He carried an enormous wrench. Behind him, another lout swung a length of pipe against the door frame, testing its strength. More men crowded behind the first two. Browning's dark face morphed from a scowl to naked aggression.

Rafe shoved Leon toward the spaceship hatch. "Run!"

Leon sprinted across the decking, followed by Bob. Greg froze. Rafe grabbed him by the collar and half threw him toward the airlock before turning to meet the attack of the man wielding the wrench. The manager's assistant, Miss Hertzog, screamed.

Rafe sidestepped a crunching overhead swing and paid the over-eager miner with an uppercut under the ribs. The man had a stomach like a steel plate, but the blow still doubled him over. A knee to the miner's face finished the job.

He stepped inside a swing from the lout with the pipe, locked the man's arm, and rammed a thumb into his Adam's apple. The miner went down, choking, and the pipe was Rafe's.

The mob fought their way through the doorway, but it was too tight for them to rush him *en masse*. A fist swung at Rafe, then the owner howled as knuckles landed full-force on the unyielding pipe. Two miners dashed past him, lunging for Greg who lay terrified a few yards from the hatch. Rafe landed a boot on one's kneecap, then jabbed the end of the pipe into the other's groin and sent him tumbling with a shove.

Someone picked up the fallen wrench, and Rafe was driven to his knees as he parried a massive swing with the pipe braced above his head. His counterblow with an elbow to another rock-solid gut didn't cause so much as an eyebrow twitch. He lowered his weapon to invite a horizontal swing at his skull, wormed his way under it, and used the pipe as a lever to send the miner tumbling under the feet of his fellows, scattering them.

Rafe grabbed Greg's belt and hauled him across the deck, slinging him through the yawning hatchway as something cannoned into the back of his legs. The deck rushed up to meet him. He landed hard, smacking his head against the unyielding surface. Fear sent fresh energy coursing through him, and he scrambled to rise.

The metal hatchway sang as Rafe's escape route slammed closed. Dazed and terrified, he rolled into a ball while the group of men kicked and punched him. He wondered briefly how long it would take them to beat him to death and what he'd done to deserve it. Then something heavy and unforgiving connected with his skull, and the world went black.

4

Kama ran the diagnostic program again, hoping it would be the last time. She'd finished the mass spec work hours ago and had been crawling around the scanner arrays on this rust bucket ever since, tightening bolts and measuring tolerances, for lack of anything better to do. Management should be up by now, and she wanted to be back on the station, but strolling through vacuum in a spacesuit wasn't her idea of a good time. Her fingers drummed a rapid tattoo on the console, out of sync with the music playing in her ear bud. Roshal better come back for her soon.

Down the corridor, feet clattered on the deck. Probably the ship's pilot, Davy Todd, headed her way again. She turned toward the sound; leaving her backside unguarded wasn't advisable with this guy. He wore a loud, Hawaiian-print shirt unbuttoned halfway to his navel, and the reek of his cologne filled the little ship. He'd deliberately bumped against her once already, pretending he'd tripped. His first mate, Juan Rodriguez, was no better. Being alone on the ship with the two of them creeped her out.

To her relief, it wasn't Todd or Rodriguez, but Roshal.

"About time," she said. "Give me half a sec to finish this up."

"All hell's broke loose on the station," the shipping manager said. "Bunch of corporate tossers think they can bully us off our turf. Browning wants everyone on station now."

He put her in mind of a cheap video recording set at Pause; all shivers and squirms and jiggles. He had a nervous energy that crackled like static, putting her on edge.

"Browning? What's Mr. Levine doing?" She wanted to get her confrontation with the manager over. The last thing she needed was for him to be distracted by some crisis.

Roshal shrugged. "Browning's running the show. Todd and Rodriguez are waiting. Hustle up."

Kama picked up an adjustable spanner to close the valve she'd been working on. Her hand slipped, and blood-red hydraulic fluid sprayed out onto her coveralls. She swore, recovered the spanner, and closed the valve. A huge oily stain spread over her heart, and speckles of scarlet fluid reached up her arms. She wiped at it uselessly.

"Sorry," she said, seeing splashes of red on Roshal's t-shirt as well.

He shrugged, making it seem like four movements instead of one, and brushed at his own stained shirt front. "Missed me. Got these repairing a thruster control on my tug last night. Occupational hazard. Come on, let's go."

Kama put away her tools and followed him to the docking bay. She gripped the edge of her seat, convinced they'd overshoot the docking point and crash into the station as Roshal made record time for the return trip. Once the vehicle settled, Todd, Rodriguez, and Roshal leaped out and vanished, leaving her to fend for herself.

Miners milled everywhere. She approached one standing post outside the bay.

"What's going on?"

"Buncha pirates docked, trying to take the station by force."

Another miner interrupted them. "Not pirates. Some big corp claiming they own the place. I hear they have an army of mercs standing by to throw us off. They'll space us if we don't surrender."

"Let 'em try." The first miner smacked a hammer against the palm of his hand. "We kicked their butts in the first assault."

Kama didn't like what she heard. Forcible boarding, questionable ownership? Oasis' plans for the Sharma Network relied on this station's output of wassonite. Damn Browning and his 'high priority' repairs. She should have stayed here and spoken with the station manager first thing.

"Where's Mr. Levine?"

"Don't know. Whole place has gone to hell in a black hole this morning. Long range com's down, and there's a search on for Levine. I was going with Roshal to check hydroponics when Browning stationed me here."

"Anyone try Levine's quarters? Maybe he's sick or injured."

"We ain't stupid, lady. Somebody musta. Probably he's hiding under the covers with the door locked. Anyway, repelling pirates is more important than finding that wimp, so who cares where he is?"

An airlock clanged open down the corridor. The miner looked past her and grinned. "Hey, Swede, about time. How long you been gone?"

"Not long enough, I guess," said a tall blond.

Kama left them to it, heading for the executive quarters at a jog. She had a window of opportunity and wouldn't waste it. No wolf whistles this time. Every miner she passed showed a grim face and hurried by her without so much as a glance. Tension filled the air like a build-up of static before a lightning strike, and it scared her.

When she got to Levine's door, it stood open. Frowning, she stepped inside an empty living room. Regulation company-issue furniture filled the space—padded plastic couch and lounge chair, well-worn plasteel coffee table. A scratched and dented vid screen took up a big chunk of one wall, with a paltry rack of entertainment disks next to it.

Everything looked scrupulously clean and neat, like Levine was a compulsive tidier: pictures on the walls right-angle straight, ornaments perfectly spaced and facing forward, video disks organized alphabetically. Spartan and orderly; her kind of place. She spent a moment drinking in the look and feel of the room. She'd need to leave it in exactly the state she'd found it, and she didn't have much time.

She started her search with the rack of videos, connecting the first one into her nanocom. It contained what the label claimed—Levine, it seemed, liked twentieth century romantic comedies. Behind her, soft footsteps approached from the bedroom. She spun to face an elderly woman dressed in dowdy clothes and wearing make-up from the previous century. They'd seen one another when Kama arrived on the mail ship the night before, but Browning hadn't introduced them.

"What are you doing in here?" the woman asked.

"I'm Kamala Bhatia, the tech upgrading your computer systems," she replied, side-stepping the question. "Where's Mr. Levine?"

"There's nothing for you to upgrade in here. Now get out before I report you for pilfering."

Kama raised her brows. "And you would be...?"

"Miss Patty, Mr. Levine's assistant." She frowned at Kama, snatched the video back, and replaced it in the rack.

"Did you find Levine?"

The woman's frown deepened. "He's a very busy man. What do you want with him?"

"I need his thumbprint on my work order," Kama lied. "Mr. Levine must think very highly of you to give you override permissions for his quarters."

Pink crawled up Miss Patty's checks. "Someone has to have override permissions... in case of emergencies. You need to go. I have to get back to the admin offices."

Frustrated, Kama let Miss Patty usher her out the door. She paused in the hallway and unzipped her duffel to dig out a ration bar while she waited for the old bat to leave. Unfortunately, the nosy old lady stopped with her, making sure to lock Levine's door behind them.

"You should go to your quarters, dearie, and wait there until Mr. Browning comes for you. It's not safe for strangers on the station right now. The men are pretty stirred up over this group from EcoMech coming. There's been violence already."

Kama stared at Miss Patty, thinking that the old hag must have misunderstood. Why would a big ag corporation be interested in this scrap heap of an asteroid mining station? "Are you sure they're from EcoMech?"

Miss Patty sniffed and did her best to look down her nose, even though she was a good three inches too short to pull it off. "I was there when they tried to board. That unfortunate man was nearly beaten to death in the lock, not that he didn't deserve it. What do they take us for, deep space yokels?"

"What are they doing here?"

"I'm sorry, dearie, I have things to do and can't stand here chatting all day. You get to your quarters and lock yourself in. We'll let you know when it's safe to come out."

Miss Patty hurried away, and Kama strode off in the opposite direction. At the first cross-corridor, she made a right and stopped. She counted to fifty, checked that Miss Patty was gone, and then retraced her steps to Levine's door. She waited while a miner hurried past, then placed the unusual violet stone of the ring on her left hand against the thumbprint reader next to the door.

The light on the lock clicked, beeped, and changed from red to green. Kama kissed the ring. Like many of its discoveries, Oasis didn't trumpet the technology in the bauble, which read the print on the lock pad left by the previous user and broadcast it back to the lock. She eased the door open and slipped inside, closing the door behind her.

She checked the remainder of the video disks to be sure none of them contained data other than their labels stated. Then she moved into the bedroom. The comfortable mattress held no secrets. The wardrobe contained a pair of polished shoes, two suits, and a collection of starched shirts on hangers; the drawers held a wad of crumpled socks and underwear. The bedside table sported a reading light and a filmie of a mining report.

Kama was speed-reading through the report when it suddenly hit her. She dropped the report and went back to the drawers. *What kind of man starches his shirts and arranges his movies by title, but shoves his underwear into the drawer like a teenager?* She looked around, seeing the room with new eyes. Someone had already searched the place. Miss Patty?

She walked the rooms again and saw other telltales: an error in the order of the videos; slippers stacked the wrong way around. Her eye caught on a fresh scratch near the edge of the video screen. She teased the plastic rectangle off.

The wiring had been bundled and taped aside, leaving a small space to hide objects. A clever hiding place containing a treasure—a bank chip good for fifty thousand credits. She clenched the chip as though she could crush it and muttered a curse. She was too late. Levine had already sold the secret of the Sharma Network and received his payment.

But who had he sold it to, and where was he now? She had to find him and get the name of the purchaser. Her heart raced. She'd notify Samir first, and then go after Levine. Maybe they had time for damage control if they acted quickly.

5

I must be dead and this is Hell, because I feel like I'm on fire, Rafe thought. If he could just slip back into the cool blackness, everything would be better.

The devil's voice intruded on his solitude. "How long until he comes around?"

Although his jaw ached and he could still taste the blood from a split lip, he muttered, "If it's my soul you want, I'm sure we can come to a gentlemanly agreement."

"He's hallucinating," a minion's voice said. "Probably the speed heal. Or maybe his concussion is worse than I thought."

With great effort, Rafe opened his eyes a fraction and saw only grey shapes moving in whiteness. He'd never imagined Hell as white. Wasn't it black in all those old paintings and engravings? The fire ravaging his skin changed to an annoying prickling sensation, like a porcupine waltzed the length of his body. The cot supporting him had about as much give as a slab of granite. Maybe it was an autopsy table, not a cot. His eyelids sagged closed.

"Stay with me, man. You can't drift off. Talk to me."

He felt the pressure and heard the whoosh of a hypospray pushed against his arm. His chest seemed to rise and fall faster, even though he didn't want it to. The porcupine stopped its dance. He blinked his eyes open, surprised at how much lighter his lids had become. The grey blobs in the fog resolved into two anxious faces against a background of dingy white walls.

A young, scrawny guy in a lab coat studied him. "How many fingers am I holding up?"

Rafe blinked a few times before the man's hand came into focus. "Three."

"What's your name?"

He opened his mouth to speak and closed it again. Did they know who he was? Better to put off formal introductions until he had the lay of the land. "Where are the men I boarded with?"

A burly man leaned in, glowering down at him. "They're back on their ship, which is standing about two clicks off the station. Tell me what you're doing here."

The name Browning floated back to Rafe. The man in charge? "Do you usually offer such a warm reception to your visitors?" he countered, flooded with relief that Greg had gotten away safe.

Browning frowned and crossed his massive arms. "Look, I don't know who you are, but you better have a damn good explanation for why you showed up claiming you own this station."

Rafe did his best to look young, innocent, and not too bright. He wasn't sure how well that came across considering the beating his face had taken. "Hey, I'm just doing a job, same's you. I was hired to make a pre-purchase inspection tour. I don't make no claims to owning this place."

"That right?" The smelter supervisor snorted. "They teach you how to fight at inspecting school?"

Damn. He managed a diffident half-shrug, hard to do flat on his back. "All I know is we're supposed to meet some manager name of Levine."

Browning exchanged a look with the medic in the lab coat, and then he ran his eyes down Rafe's body, refusing to meet his eyes. "Mr. Levine's been detained."

"Ah." Rafe thought about that one for a minute, giving the man a chance to say more. When he didn't, he asked, "Detained as in locked up?"

"No, of course not," Browning snapped, too quickly. "He's just not available at the moment."

Since the Devil wouldn't look at him, Rafe tried the minion. "How bad is it, Doc?"

The medic raised an eyebrow. "You think we'd have a doctor at a godforsaken place like this? Maybe I better take another look at your head."

The scarecrow man from the docking bay stuck his head in the door. "That CEO is screaming his head off on the radio. Wants proof that his man is okay."

"Tell him to go to hell! I'll deal with him when I know what's going on. No, wait, don't tell him that." Browning wiped a meaty fist across his brow and addressed the medic. "Think we can get him to the com center?"

The medic rolled his eyes. "Sure, if you don't mind that he's dead when he gets there. He needs to stay prone and let the drugs work."

"That asshole big shot is bound to do something stupid if we don't let him see this guy's in one piece, and we need time to get organized in case they make a strike against us."

The medic suppressed a laugh. "Yeah, seeing him like this is gonna be great reassurance, eh?"

Browning looked like he might explode, and the medic drew back. Instead, he turned to Roshal. "Get Miss Patty's supply cart."

Rafe closed his eyes, hoping that Browning wouldn't continue the interrogation while they waited. He needed time to assess the situation and think about what he'd say to Leon—and maybe catch a nap. Why did the miners think they were under attack? Couldn't they all behave like businessmen and talk? But the medic poked him each time his eyes closed, insisting that he stay awake.

He swept his eyes around the room, taking in the glass-fronted cupboards filled with a sparse collection of medical supplies and equipment. His home first aid cabinet was better stocked. Two vacant cots stood against the far wall. If this was the extent of the station's medical facility, Rafe hoped his injuries weren't as severe as the medic implied. Loaded on drugs, he felt pretty good, if drifty. Roshal reappeared five minutes later, pushing a narrow, flatbed cart with a squeaky wheel.

Together, the three miners hoisted Rafe's cot onto the cart and maneuvered it toward the door. The cot overhung both sides and the end of the cart. He felt like he'd be dumped on the deck any minute. A group of hostile-looking miners loitered in the corridor. They grumbled when Browning ordered them to disperse but followed his command.

Seeing the naked anger in their faces, Rafe decided he'd be safer if he disavowed any affiliation with Leon and EcoMech, and safer still if he could get off the station before anyone found out otherwise. Whatever was going on, it wasn't his fight. Let Leon deal with it. He wouldn't become a disposable pawn in the CEO's game. The debt he owed Aaron Goldman wasn't worth his life.

They navigated a series of corridors and levels, the force that pushed Rafe against the hard cot lessening as they rose closer to the central axis of the station. The older woman with the frilly dress came toward them. She glanced at Rafe and sucked in her breath, before squaring off with Browning.

"The com tech tells me that our long-range com was vandalized overnight. We don't have a replacement part in stock, and I can't order one if the com isn't working. Besides, I'd need Mr. Levine's approval.

Have you found him yet?"

Browning puffed out his cheeks and exhaled hard. "I've been a little busy this morning, Miss Patty. We'll need that com working if we're going to call in reinforcements. Isn't there something the tech can jury-rig?"

"Not according to him." She pulled a lace handkerchief from her sleeve and dabbed at her lips. "Besides, who'd dare anger big corps like Galaxy or EcoMech to help us?"

"Give 'em a run for their money, I say. Make 'em pay in blood if they try to take the station," Roshal said, his hands flapping in the air like injured birds.

Rafe tried to remember his attackers. Had Roshal been among them? A little shiver ran down his spine.

Miss Patty blanched, and long fingers went to her throat. "That's barbaric. How can you suggest such a thing? We should contact a lawyer, get an injunction or something."

Roshal looked ready to wring the woman's scrawny neck.

Browning shoved the cart forward sharply. "We'll deal with it later. Right now, I have other things to take care of."

Eventually, they jockeyed through a narrow hatch into a cluttered communications center. Against the medic's recommendation, Browning transferred Rafe to a chair in front of a vid screen. His head swam, and his stomach pirouetted with it. Browning drew up a chair and positioned himself so he shared the screen. Then he flagged a miner sitting at a nearby console, and the screen in front of Rafe lit up to show Captain Benson bent over a control board.

Benson's eyes lifted to his own screen and registered shock bordering on horror.

"Mr. McTavish, are you all right?"

"He's doing okay," Browning said before Rafe could open his mouth. "Put the fat guy on."

Benson disappeared off screen. Rafe looked at Browning, Roshal, and the technician. None of them gave any indication that they'd recognized his name. A miner or two drifted up to hover near the com room door, joined by a slim Indian goddess as tall as him. Her good looks were spoiled by an expression of worry and a stained pair of unfashionable gray coveralls. In her mid-twenties perhaps, she had eyes like bottomless pools of dark chocolate, a honey-brown complexion, and lustrous henna-colored hair pulled back from her face. The sight of her improved his cardiac output. If he could get off the station, he'd take her with him. This place was too dangerous for a lady.

Movement on the vid screen drew Rafe's wandering mind. Leon stared back at him, face purpled with rage. Benson stood in the background. Concern flicked on the CEO's features for the barest instant before they set in a hard mask.

Rafe jumped in before either Browning or Leon could speak.

"Mr. Goldman, I quit. I came here to do a simple inspection. No one said anything about getting in the middle of some war. I'm taking the first ship out of here, and I'm sending you a bill for any medical services I require."

Leon's eyes narrowed and focused on Browning's face. Rafe held his breath and prayed the CEO would go along with the deception.

"Be assured that the people responsible for your injuries will be held accountable, Mr. McTavish."

His brother-in-law seemed unwilling to look at him. Rafe remembered the hatch slamming closed and wondered whether Leon felt guilty for leaving him behind now that he saw the results of his actions. Behind Leon, Greg slipped into view. His mouth dropped open, and for a moment, Rafe thought the boy might faint; not a bad thing if it kept the kid quiet.

Browning leaned into him, smelling of sweat and fear. "As you can see, your man's alive. We're the legal owners of this station, so unless you're willing to fight us for it, you better back off until the courts tell us otherwise."

"You'll put that man on a shuttle and send him to my ship immediately," Leon said. "In the meantime, I'm reporting this incident to Earth Authority. Whoever beat him will be prosecuted to the full extent of the law."

"Do I look stupid?" Browning asked. "No way I'm sending a shuttle to your ship."

Greg stepped toward the vid screen, but Benson yanked him away and shoved him off camera. Leon barely glanced around at the commotion. "If you don't surrender him, I'll remove him and the culprits by force. You'll all be charged with aiding and abetting."

Trust pig-headed Leon to make a bad situation worse. "Look, Mr. Goldman, I think I'd rather find my own way home, okay? I'm not interested in getting mixed up with EA. You guys can let your lawyers hash this out. I want no part of it."

Leon seemed on the verge of an angry retort when Benson placed a hand on his shoulder and bent to mutter something in his ear. He turned back toward the vid screen. "Captain Benson tells me there's a cargo ship parked near the station, some kind of independent merchant."

"That's Jay Maltraw's ship," Browning said. "What of it?"

"Send Mr. McTavish there as a first step on his journey home. When he's arrived, I'll provide a copy of our documentation proving that EcoMech owns the station." Leon stared hard at Browning, daring the miner to disagree.

"Excellent idea. Then when he dies because he was moved too soon, it won't be on our heads, eh?" the medic muttered.

Rafe had thought the medic was exaggerating the extent of his injuries earlier, but the drugs were wearing off. His head throbbed and his back and legs ached. He kept his breathing shallow to avoid a stabbing pain in his ribs and wondered how close to death he might be.

Browning rubbed a hand over his jowls. He glanced at the com center door, and Rafe followed his gaze. The group of miners listening in had grown to a crowd jamming the corridor, the pretty woman at their forefront. She stood very still and contained, like a cat about to pounce. The miners looked even more unhappy, if that was possible.

Browning frowned at the sight of them.

"All right, if McTavish and Maltraw agree, we'll transport him to Maltraw's ship."

"Contact me again when he's been delivered." Leon cut the connection.

Rafe slumped against his chair. He'd be out of there soon, and no longer under threat from the miners. The whole situation was a sun ready to go supernova. The woman stepped into the room, and he gave her his most charming smile. It bounced off her like a laser off a mirror.

"You filthy liar. You'd say anything to cheat these people, wouldn't you? They're just so much dirt beneath your feet."

Browning rose and faced her. "Ms. Bhatia, what is this about?"

Her eyes smoldered, and Rafe couldn't help thinking it made her all the more attractive, but he didn't like where the conversation was going. He tried to slide his chair back from the communications console so he could stand, as good manners dictated, but he was blocked by the medic.

"He's Rafael McTavish, not some lackey working for Leon Goldman."

Browning gave her a blank look. "Is that supposed to mean something to me?"

"McTavish, as in his father was a co-founder of EcoMech. That same father sits on the board of directors." She glared down at Rafe. "Just look at him. Do you really think a common inspector would wear a five thousand-credit suit and custom-tailored silk shirt? He's the CEO of Security Partners, a company that vends mercenaries to the highest bidder."

"Mercs!" one of the miners in the crowd at the door said. The others all started talking at the same time, an ominous rumbling of angry voices.

"Are you sure that's who he is?" Browning asked.

"He's been on the news vids enough, touting the EA contracts his company has won."

Browning turned to Rafe, and the look on his face warned of an impending storm. "Is that true?"

The room seemed to tilt, and Rafe felt sick. "Yes, I'm Rafael McTavish, but I have nothing to do with EcoMech."

"Then why are you here?" the woman challenged.

"I'm on contract to inspect the station. There's nothing sinister involved." He put a hand on the com table to steady himself, but the room spun faster.

The miners shoved in through the door, and one of them muttered, "We don't believe you, you lying SOB. You're part of that corporate scum trying to steal our property."

Roshal stepped forward. "Have you got forces on your ship? How many men?"

"Back off!" Browning shouted. "Get out of here and let me handle this."

The woman turned to face the miners. Rafe saw fear on her face in place of the anger of a moment ago. The medic and Browning stepped in front of him to block the mob.

Browning thrust his chest out and punched his fist into the palm of his other hand.

"I gave you an order. Now move!"

For one tense moment, the miners in the front of the mob stared back at the smelter supervisor, their faces getting blurry. Then eyes dropped and men turned away. They seemed very far away, almost as though they floated into clouds.

At a great distance, Rafe heard the medic's voice.

"Oh, shit! He's crashing."

6

Kama looked on as the medic and Browning transferred McTavish to his cot. What was he doing here? He was the last person she expected to see. Six months ago, his geek rangers nearly caught her hacking into the Wandermere Consortium computers. Unknown to her, they'd employed Security Partners—McTavish's company—to upgrade their internal and external security. She'd needed all her considerable skill to dump their network trace in a dead-end. No one had ever come so close to nailing her. Just thinking about it made her twitch.

From his reputation in the security community, she'd credited him with more sense than to blow his cover by wearing expensive custom clothing while pretending to be some lowly inspector, but maybe he was just the pretty face of Security Partners while the smart people worked behind the scenes. Or maybe not-so-smart people if they allowed their brainless figurehead to go on a dangerous mission unprepared.

Had his handlers really let him run off alone to play bodyguard to the CEO of EcoMech? Shouldn't he have his own bodyguards? All rich corporate types did. And mercenaries were brawny giants, not wiry guys like him. What did he say to provoke the beating, and why hadn't he gotten away with the rest of the boarding party? Maybe he'd been frozen with fear when the miners responded.

She chewed her lip and frowned. She'd been proud of blowing the whistle on his little game until she'd seen the murderous looks on the miners' faces. She didn't like thinking she'd put some helpless desk jockey in jeopardy even if he was a corporate slimeball.

His skin shaded a sickly gray, and the medic pumped one hypospray after another into his neck, checking the electronic medical stats bracelet strapped to his wrist after each one. Dead or alive, he meant trouble. If he survived, he'd be underfoot, and if he didn't, Earth Authority would come down on the station with a vengeance, bringing more attention her direction than she liked. She wanted him gone, but not dead. She couldn't wish that for him, even if he was a smarmy corporate liar. *Vishnu watch over him.* A dull ache crept up the back of her skull, and she rolled her shoulders, willing herself to relax.

"He needs a doctor," the medic said. He looked up at Browning, the fear plain on his face. "A real doctor."

"God damn it." Browning stared down at the medic, then broke eye contact. He looked around the cramped com room. "Where's Roshal?"

Kama glanced over her shoulder, but the shipping manager had disappeared with the disgruntled miners. Only the com tech remained in the room, and he played deaf, dumb, and blind.

"God damn it," Browning swore again. "Get him back to the infirmary and do what you can."

The smelter supervisor rushed from the room as the medic flagged the com tech over, and together they maneuvered the squeaking hand trolley carrying McTavish away down the corridor. Kama shut the door behind them and took a deep breath.

What in the name of Shiva was going on here? If EcoMech had bought the secret of the Sharma Network from Levine, it explained their sudden interest in acquiring the station. What corporation wouldn't jump at the chance to supply materials for the building of jump gates? They cost a bloody fortune, ate materials like a black hole swallowed light, and had the potential to make billions in revenue.

Had Galaxy and EcoMech colluded against the miners after learning about the Sharma Network? Did Galaxy have some legal trick up their sleeve to negate the miners' purchase? Judging by events, EcoMech hadn't expected a hostile welcome, which seemed to belie a conspiracy. Regardless, the miners wouldn't stand a chance in an ownership war with two bully mega-corps like Galaxy and EcoMech.

Where was Levine? Was he party to the scam? And why had the CEO of a giant corp like EcoMech come all the way out here with the masquerading CEO of a security company? Far-flung expeditions were typically left to lackeys. Pondering so many unanswered questions made her head throb.

She had to get a message to Samir right away, let him notify Oasis management that their secret plans weren't so secret anymore. Maybe they could speed up their timetable to purchase the materials for the Sharma Network jump gates before speculators heard about it. Without the network, the poor would stagnate on Earth for more untold generations. She couldn't let that happen on her watch.

Besides, if the station was about to be overrun with corporate executives, EA law enforcement investigators, and mercs, she wanted an escape hatch. She'd get Samir to send a ship and return to her students at the computer tech training school on Earth. She didn't want to be on Security Partners' radar, or EA's either. They made her skin crawl.

Settling in at the console, she activated the long range com software, one nail tapping the desk while she waited. Instead of the usual sending interface, a series of error messages scrolled down the screen. Hissing at the errors, she flicked the system off, counted to ten, and switched it on again. Rebooting didn't cure the problem, so she turned to the bank of archaic equipment behind her.

An access panel stood ajar. Kama opened it and had her answer—an empty slot where the modulation board should be. Then she remembered Browning's comments about the system being down. Maybe the board had finally failed and the tech had removed it intending to replace it, but what horrible timing. She wouldn't feel safe until she knew she had a backdoor available for a quick escape, and she couldn't arrange that without access to communications.

Thwarted by the missing board, she returned to the com console. The com tech would return any moment, but maybe she could find the correspondence between Levine and EcoMech or Galaxy where he coughed up the Sharma Network. It might provide information crucial to delaying leakage of Oasis' secrets.

With a few hurried keystrokes, she brought up the message queue. All but one of the previous night's messages had gone out in a single batch at midnight. The final message had gone out nearly two and a half hours later: 2:18 a.m. Levine's name was in the Sender category. She pressed more keys with shaking fingers. The list vanished, and the full text of the message popped up.

EcoMech arriving, no time to waste. Meet me as before.

She switched back to the message list and scanned the address bar of Levine's message; it looked like a ship identification code: SD321-44321. Was Levine making a run for it? Before she could check more of the message queue, something thumped against the com room door, and she jumped. She quickly exited the software. The door lock clicked, and the scrawny, sallow tech glared at her.

"Can I help you, Miss?"

Kama scrambled up from the chair, heart racing. "I wanted to send a message to Oasis, let them know I arrived."

"Don't hold your breath, lady. The equipment's down, and I have no ETA for new parts. Miss Patty says we don't have a replacement, and with the long-range down, we can't order anything." The tech reclaimed his seat at the console.

Kama tugged the zipper of her coveralls down enough to expose a triangle of honey skin that hinted at cleavage beyond and widened her eyes. "Warm in here, isn't it? Hey, maybe I could help with the repairs. What's wrong exactly?"

The tech's eyes lingered on her chest before slipping to the open access panel. "Someone stole a part."

"Wow," Kama said, wheels turning furiously in her mind. *Blatant theft?* "Who's got access to this room?"

"We don't lock the door," the tech said. His eyes flickered between her face and her chest like a strobe light gone mad.

She pursed her lips and asked for more with a questioning brow.

"A lot of the guys come in here to record their messages home whenever they get a spare minute, and then Miss Patty sends them out in a daily batch," he explained. "It was a nuisance having to unlock the place at all hours. Besides, we know our guys. Something happens, it's not too hard to figure out who it might be when you live this close together."

Kama didn't point out the obvious fallacy of that statement. Instead, she leaned over the console, giving the tech a beguiling smile and a peek down her coveralls. "Isn't the com station manned around the clock?"

He licked his lips and puffed out his chest. "Can't afford it now that we're an owner-operated facility. If something marked urgent comes in after hours, the computer forwards an alert to my nanocom. Hey, maybe I could answer your questions over a cup of coffee?"

"Maybe later." Kama dragged fingertips down her neck to her zipper and eased it another inch lower. The tech sucked in his breath. "Is SD321-44321 one of the station's ships?"

"I've never heard of it. All our vessel codes are prefixed G132. Apart from the mail ship you came in on last night, the only deep-space ship that's been around here lately is the monthly robot supply drone, and that's still tied to the side—doesn't leave until tonight."

Kama plucked her duffel from the floor and headed for the door, more driven than ever to contact Samir. Maybe he could still catch Levine. She didn't want to think about what her boss might do to the manager.

"Hey," the tech called. "I thought you were going to try to repair the com?"

"Oh, yeah, well I can't repair what isn't there to repair, now can I?"

She gave him a wave and shut the door behind her. Then she yanked her zipper up to her neck. Levine had trashed the radio and set up a rendezvous. He wouldn't leave without his cash chip, so he must still be here. They could catch him at the rendezvous, but Samir would have to scramble.

If she couldn't use the station's long range equipment, she'd have to find some elsewhere. Maybe that floating emporium parked near the station.

She stowed her bag on her shoulder, ready with a new plan. All she needed was to borrow a ride. Reviewing her memory of the station layout, she hurried away to the runabout docking bay.

Through the door viewport, she made out two runabouts parked in the bay. She didn't see anyone. Checking both ways of the corridor first, she cracked the hatch and slipped inside. At the sound of low voices, she froze. Damn. She couldn't open the outer bay doors with men in the bay. The worrisome tone of the voices sent her digging in her bag for her amplifier ear bud.

On silent feet, she crept closer to the far runabout and peeked around it. Four miners hunched over a work table nursing coffee, ignoring the machine parts scattered before them. Kama pulled back and listened.

"Of course he's in the infirmary. Where else would he be?" one of the miners grumbled. "Once we've taken him hostage, we can call that ship of theirs and tell them to go back to whatever swamp they crawled out of. Then we'll show Mr. Smart Ass Security Man we're not just a buncha dumb fucks here in the Belt."

"Are you sure their ship is full of mercs?" another asked. "I heard he was just an inspector."

"That's what he said, but he lied. That Oasis woman called him out. If it weren't for her warning, we'd be overrun with mercs right now, I betcha. I say we move and soon, before Browning gets any big ideas about how to handle things."

Kama's breath caught in her throat. They'd nearly killed McTavish already. If they roughed him up further, they'd finish him, and it would be her fault. When she'd called his bluff, she hadn't thought about why he might be laying low, keeping his identity hidden. Nor had she realized the grievous extent of his injuries. All she'd seen was another lying, greedy corporate bastard trying to hoodwink the hardworking miners and getting the beating he'd probably deserved.

"No worries there. Browning brought that whore of his over from Maltraw's. She'll keep him busy until the money runs out." The speaker laughed, and the others chuckled with him. "Man, wish I made a manager's salary."

She edged back to the hatch. In the corridor, she broke into a jog, all thought of stealing a runabout pushed aside. She had to warn Browning. They should move McTavish, hide him somewhere. Or better yet, put him on a shuttle to the EcoMech ship or to Maltraw's as promised. Guilt and fear sped her feet across the metal decking.

Several minutes later and out of breath, Kama reached the infirmary. She stepped in without bothering to knock. McTavish lay on a cot across the room. She heard the unsteady beep of the monitor tracing his vitals, and his color hadn't improved. The medic hovered at his side. At the foot of the bed, Browning argued with a woman. Both of them broke off and turned to her.

"Who's this, Ed?" The woman's voice had a mellifluous quality that turned anything she said into an open invitation. Females might be rare in the asteroid belt, but this one would have drawn stares anywhere. The electric blue eyes were obviously cosmetic lenses, and Kama thought a certain amount of technology had gone into producing her shape. Real women just didn't look like that, even in figure-hugging space fatigues. Jet black hair lavishly streaked with pink and purple and a face that did justice to the rest of the ensemble topped off the voluptuous whole.

"Have we met?" the apparition purred with a hint of hackles rising.

"Janice Fisher, this is Ms. Bhatia," Browning said, glowering at Kama. "She's from Oasis, helping us upgrade our equipment. She arrived last night."

The claws sheathed, but Fisher didn't look any happier than Browning. She extended a perfectly manicured hand. "Welcome aboard."

Kama took it, catching a gust of a provocative perfume laced with artificial pheromones meant to drive men wild. No doubts lingered about what Janice Fisher did for a living.

"I hate to interrupt," the medic said, "but this man isn't getting any better."

Fisher leaned over to read the monitor, then planted hands on her ample hips. "Ed, if he finds out I've worked on him or what treatment I've used..."

"You can't let him die," Browning said. "You know you can't."

"I can't guarantee my treatment will save him. It's still experimental," she shot back. She jerked a thumb at Kama. "And I thought this was going to be between just you and me."

Browning ran a hand over his forehead. He grabbed Kama's elbow and propelled her out the infirmary door. "Just do it," he ordered over his shoulder, then snapped the door shut behind them.

Kama wondered what kind of 'treatment' a woman like Janice could administer to McTavish. Massage therapy maybe? She checked both directions of the corridor, expecting angry miners to pour down on them.

"Listen, you have to move McTavish. I overheard a group of miners plotting to come for him."

"They're just blowing off steam; they don't mean anything. Look, I don't have time for this. Go back to your quarters and stay there while we sort things out."

He turned to go. Kama's anger surged. She grabbed his arm, felt the heavy bulge of muscles tense. "If McTavish dies, you know EA will be looking for a fall guy, and you're the one with the prison record."

His face darkened and his lips set in a grim smile. "I'm doing my level best to keep the lying bastard alive. If we move him again, we'll kill him for sure."

"Then set guards, a bunch of them. All these men can't be blood-thirsty brutes. Some of them must have a grain of common sense and a modicum of human decency."

"All right," Browning finally said. "But you didn't see Janice in there, got it? She was never on the station."

He chugged off along the corridor, the sound of his progress marked by a long hacking cough. Kama wondered how long it would take for guards to arrive. When they did, would they be armed? How would she distinguish Browning's guards from miners bent on finishing off McTavish? She'd better take her own precautions. She ducked back into the infirmary.

Janice was just tucking a piece of electronic equipment Kama didn't recognize into a large metal box. When she moved closer to examine the contents in the heavily padded interior, Janice slammed the lid shut and locked it. The lock was high tech, something that would take Kama at least twenty uninterrupted minutes to hack. Her interest in Janice soared.

They both moved to the bedside. Kama noticed they'd stripped McTavish of his expensive suit and covered him with a thin blanket. The surprisingly muscular shoulders, exposed above the blanket, bore a plethora of overlapping purple bruises. An IV tube ran from a bag of synth-blood hung over his head down to his arm. She wondered again what he'd done to anger the miners into delivering such a beating.

"How's he doing?"

A look passed between the medic and Janice, and the medic replied, "Too early to tell."

Kama waited a beat. "You must be from that other ship? The one with all the colored lights?"

Janice looked her up and down. "Yeah, that's my ride. Is there something I can do for you?"

"I just thought it was lucky there was a doctor close by." Janice didn't flinch, but the medic's eyes widened. Kama smiled to herself.

Janice laughed. "They don't give out medical licenses for what I do, honey. The 'establishment' doesn't much like alternative treatment. Takes away from their bottom line."

"I've always been interested in alternative medicine. What do you do?"

The woman lifted a carefully plucked eyebrow in appraisal. "I place very special crystals on a select set of meridian points, and then I repeat a chant I learned from a monk in the mountains of Tibet that causes the crystals to vibrate on certain frequencies. The vibrations affect the meridian points, and the activation of the meridian points induces healing."

As a well-practiced liar herself, Kama gave the woman points for chutzpah. Her competitive nature drove her to press further and see how long it took to break down her story.

Janice spoke first. "This man a friend of yours? You seem pretty worried."

"Hell, no," Kama replied too quickly, uncomfortable that the woman had picked up on her concern. "Wouldn't catch me within a light year of a guy like this."

"Too bad. From everything I've seen—and I mean *everything*, he'd be a catch for any woman." She waggled her eyebrows. "I hear he's rich, too. But with your looks, I guess you can afford to be picky."

"He's not my type, believe me." She thrust her hands in her pockets and frowned at McTavish, remembering the handsome features from the news vids instead of the pulpy mess on the pillow.

"And what's your type? Someone who will admire your brains instead of that pretty face? That why you camouflage your assets?"

Kama stepped back. Janice had it wrong. She didn't want a man, any man, regardless of what he admired about her. She snuffed out the little spark of passion and longing catching in her chest.

How had this conversation wandered so far off track? She ought to do something more to ensure McTavish's safety; she didn't trust Browning to take sufficient measures. And she desperately needed to get a message to Samir. She didn't have time to stand around chatting.

But maybe she didn't need to go to Maltraw's.

"My boss is going to think I dropped into an alternate dimension if he doesn't hear from me soon. I'd be happy to pay if you'd use your ship's equipment to send him my regards." Kama added a pleading smile.

"Honey, you don't need me to send a message for you. Not that I don't want to take your money, mind." She tossed her long tresses with a provocative flip of her head. "Ed already brought back the part for the station's busted com. He's probably fixing it right now."

"Let's hope he has better things to do," Kama muttered, thinking of the thug-like miners in the runabout bay.

While Janice moved off to confer with the medic, she slung her bag on an empty counter beside McTavish's bed, unzipped it, and extracted one device after another. Time to plan for the welcoming party.

7

Rafe opened his eyes and turned his head toward the voices. His sense of self seemed disembodied from any corporeal form, and he thought he'd either died, or he was dreaming. A vision of salaciousness dragged a large silver trunk out the door of the infirmary while waving goodbye. Had he seen her wink at the medic?

Clicks and clatters came from the opposite side of the cot. He eased his head in that direction, not sure if he'd really moved or if only the focus of his dream had changed. The avenging angel from the com center disassembled a variety of small electronic equipment on a counter near the bed, then reassembled mixed bits and pieces from several disparate devices. Her long slim fingers moved with confidence and dexterity until she held a palm-sized stunner in her hand.

Yes, it had to be one of those dreams dredged from the subconscious where one bizarre object morphs into another impossible object. The stunner disappeared into the pocket of her unattractive gray coveralls. She glanced his direction, and their eyes met.

Apprehension flashed in those molten chocolate pools before a mask of resignation dropped over her face. Even white teeth chewed her bottom lip. Her gaze flicked to the medic on the other side of the room before returning to him. She drew in a preparatory breath like a kid at school about to admit she hadn't done her homework.

"I'm sorry." Her low voice barely carried to his ears.

"Hm," he replied, his eyes locked on hers. "I don't believe I'm wearing your boot prints, am I?"

Resignation momentarily flashed to bewilderment before her back stiffened and she pressed on. "I'm sorry I called you a liar and told the miners who you are."

He'd developed a body again, but it felt like he'd been buried alive in wet sand. His limbs lay heavy and immobile. He tried to put one foot after the other down the path of rational thought, but his mind had other ideas. The entire tableau seemed surreal. "I had long odds against on that ploy."

"I didn't think about how the miners might react. Now that they know who you are, some of them want to hold you hostage."

"Ah." He found her sincerity disconcerting. He also felt the first tickle of fear worm through his numbed brain, making him more alert. "And you feel responsible?"

She nodded.

"And you'd like to make it up to me if you could."

She nodded again, more slowly, suspicion sliding onto her face.

"We haven't been properly introduced. Rafe McTavish, Security Partners." He tried for a handshake, but the blanket weighed a hundred kilos and held his hand against the cot.

"Kamala Bhatia, Oasis."

He thought about the beating he'd received and the stunner in her pocket. He could use a friend and ally, especially an *armed* ally, if she was right about the hostage threat. He gave her his best boyish grin, always guaranteed to soften a woman's heart. "Perhaps you'd join me for dinner sometime, Ms. Bhatia?"

Those gorgeous eyes narrowed, and she went very still. "You corporate types are all alike."

His grin faltered. Then he remembered the venom in her voice when she'd busted him. She worked for Oasis, the aggressively socialistic non-profit corp and biggest name in the software industry. That explained her attitude and her obvious intelligence. They only employed the best and the brightest. You had to be a bloody genius to work for them. His hope of befriending her—and her stunner—sank into despair while his desperation amped up.

Before he could bring his wandering brain to bear on a reply, Browning barreled in the door, huffing like a bull too long fighting in the ring. He conferred in low tones with the medic, watching Rafe while they spoke. When he'd finished, he came to stand on the opposite side of the bed. His posture wasn't friendly; neither was it murderous. Perhaps he wasn't party to the kidnapping idea.

"Mr. Browning, Ms. Bhatia tells me that some of your crew still feel... hostile toward me and intend to take me captive. I believe I'd like to transfer to that commercial vessel now." He squirmed in a failed attempt to sit up and saw alarm on Browning's face.

The medic dashed to the cot, placed a restraining hand on his chest, and studied the medical monitor with an intensity that gave Rafe the willies. "Got a death wish, eh? You're flat on your back for the next twelve hours."

"Perhaps you could enlighten me about the extent of the damages?" he asked. The small movement he'd made left him exhausted, and a wave of nausea washed over him. Alarm bells ringing in the back of his head joined the ringing in his ears.

The medic's jaw flexed. After a long minute watching the monitor, he replied, "In the next twelve hours, you'll either get better or you'll die."

A chill settled over him.

"I see," he said, although he didn't. "Could you be more explicit?"

"No," the medic said. "I'll get you some chow." He spun on his heel and hustled out.

Was he so near death they wouldn't tell him? He needed to get off the station, and if he was in critical condition and defenseless while surrounded by enemies, then he'd need help. The pinging of the heart monitor sped up. He fought to slow his breathing and pulse rate, employing all his biofeedback training without effect. Time to grovel.

"Mr. Browning, please accept my apology for my earlier deception. As Ms. Bhatia so rightfully pointed out, I *am* related to the EcoMech McTavish family. However, it's also true that I left EcoMech many years ago and now manage my own company. Unlikely as it may seem, I'm simply fulfilling an inspection contract for the EcoMech board of directors. I'm not involved with EcoMech and the facility purchase, nor do I have a platoon of mercs standing ready on the EcoMech ship. EcoMech doesn't even employ my company for their security needs."

"You have a lot of experience inspecting mining facilities, Mr. McTavish?" There was no mistaking the skepticism in Browning's voice.

"Please call me Rafe. Evaluating the state of the equipment, no. But my company is experienced in forensic audits. We're quite good at rooting out fraud, embezzlement, and employee theft, as well as providing physical security."

Anger lit Browning's eyes. "So which is it? You gonna supply the forces to throw us off, or do you intend to prove we're a bunch of crooks?"

Everything Rafe said made matters worse; had to be the drugs, or maybe the bang on the head. This never happened with his clients—or women. He could talk them into anything, smooth any rough patches. It was his gift. How could it fail him now?

The smelter supervisor glared at him, stance wide, hands on hips, and brow furrowed. "Why are you looking for Levine?"

Surprise—or maybe panic—flashed in Ms. Bhatia's eyes. He sensed another minefield ahead, but saw no alternative to stumbling forward.

"The paperwork from Galaxy says he's the station manager, and EcoMech told him to expect me." Not quite the truth; he worked directly for Aaron Goldman, not the company, but he wouldn't air the Goldman family feud here. Still, any lies he told would show up on the biomonitor readings if they knew what to look for, and he needed them to trust him. He'd tread carefully.

"So he's in on the scam, along with you guys and Galaxy." Browning slapped a hand on the bed frame. "Never should have trusted the little weasel—or Galaxy."

"There is no scam, at least not on EcoMech's part," Rafe protested. "The lawyers wouldn't approve the purchase unless Galaxy provided a clean title. I'm sure the sale was an above-board transaction."

Ms. Bhatia snorted. "The miners are supposed to trust corporate lawyers? Isn't that how they got into this mess, by trusting sales contracts vetted by corporate lawyers?"

"But surely the miners had independent legal counsel working on their behalf through the incorporation and purchase. Have you contacted them?" he asked, hoping calm discussion would soothe the supervisor. "Or if you have concerns about their competency, hire a different firm to look over your contracts and tell you where you stand."

"Lawyers! Vultures feasting on the remains of corporate kills," she said.

Browning nodded his agreement. "Now we're supposed to hire a second batch to look over the shoulders of the first batch? How do we pay all these legions of lawyers? The operation's barely scraping by as it is. And what's to stop EcoMech or Galaxy from buying off our lawyers?"

Ms. Bhatia lifted a brow, daring Rafe to reply.

Was this a mining station or an insane asylum? Sure, some corporations didn't always play by the rules. He'd busted a few in his day. But to accuse Galaxy or EcoMech of bribing lawyers to win a favorable settlement? He'd landed amidst paranoid lunatics. All the more reason to get out of there if he could only figure out how. He cursed the drug haze and stress that clouded his thinking.

"Someone needs to go through your incorporation and purchase paperwork to understand what's happening," he said. "And you need to find Levine if he was your company's primary representative. Since you're headed for court, whoever looks over your documents needs to be a disinterested third party."

"I can do that," Ms. Bhatia volunteered before he could jump in with his own offer.

Rafe lifted a hand from under the blanket, glad it responded to his will. "Hold on now. If the computer system contains evidence, you need an EA representative to oversee an investigation. If Ms. Bhatia here—"

"Kama," she said.

Excellent, they were on a first name basis. "If Kama does anything to the computer before it's been formally seized by EA, whatever's on it can't be used later in court."

She blinked at him. "It'll take weeks to get an EA investigator out here. Do you really think everyone will happily wait that long?"

"I have contacts at EA. They can deputize me, and then I can help you untangle what's happened." He had to convince them he was a friend; it might save his life.

"You're in no condition to work," she said, waving a hand at his body. "You're doped to the gills, and you've had a blow to the head. Besides, you're not a disinterested third party. You already admitted working for EcoMech."

Hung by his own words, he clenched his teeth, then went on the attack. He had to win this one, had to become part of the miners' team.

"I'd be considered a third party if I'm deputized." Browning wasn't swayed, so he continued. "I'm sure you have excellent computer skills, Kama, but we're talking about business forensics, not writing a batch file to install an operating system upgrade."

Her eyes narrowed and sharp color flamed up her cheeks. She ignored him and addressed the smelter supervisor.

"How can you possibly trust someone who changes loyalties so easily?" she asked. "He's just another lying corporate drone."

The infirmary door opened, and Roshal burst through waving his nanocom in the air.

"You can call off the search for Levine, Ed. Lookit what I found on the airlock security recording."

Roshal shoved the nanocom in front of Browning who watched it with a silent scowl. Then he passed it to Kama who twisted it so Rafe could share the view. In a video clip on the three inch by four inch screen, a mousy little man opened an airlock door and stepped through, dogging the hatch behind him. Rafe could just make out the day and time stamp: 2:23 a.m. Assuming he hadn't been unconscious longer than he thought, the video footage was recorded that morning, seven hours before the EcoMech corporate yacht arrived.

"This is Mr. Levine leaving the station?" Kama said. "Where's he going?"

"The cargo drone," Roshal said. "That's where it was docked last night. It left about 3 a.m."

"God damn it," muttered Browning. "He must be guilty of something or he wouldn't be sneaking away on a cargo drone." He smacked a fist into his palm. "If I get my hands on his scrawny neck..."

Kama seemed suddenly quiet, replaying the video over again while she twisted a strand of hair in her fingers. Rafe realized he'd give a lot to know what she was thinking.

"Your com tech said the drone wasn't scheduled to leave until tonight."

Roshal flung his arms around like a windmill in a storm. "You better get a call in to EA, Ed. Maybe they can stop the drone when it hits Earth orbit. Levine has a lot to explain."

"Well, hell. By the time EA pulls their brown noses out of the big corps' asses and looks into this, we'll all be dead of old age." Browning broke into a round of hacking. "Sorry, it's my allergies."

"Let me take a look at the computer system," Kama said. "You might at least be able to freeze assets before they all disappear."

"I strongly advise against that," Rafe warned. "I don't doubt your technical abilities, but if you mess with the evidence chain, you may prevent the investors from recovering anything. Do this the right way; let me help."

"You? We should leave well enough alone until an EA investigator from Earth gets here," Roshal said.

"Well, Mr. McTavish, excuse me for saying this, but why should I take the advice of someone who lies to save his own butt?" Browning asked.

Rafe's face flushed. Yes, he'd pretended to be a lowly inspector hired by Leon, but that was only a small stretch of the truth, not an outright lie. He wasn't part of EcoMech or the mine purchase, and he had nothing to do with the rest of his family. Why wouldn't they listen?

Roshal said, "You know, Ed, if you'd taken the beating he had, you mighta lied, too."

The smelter supervisor ran a hand over his face and gave a congested cough, but then he nodded to Kama. "If you're willing to have a go with our records, I'd appreciate it."

Disappointment and frustration swept over him. Browning still considered him the enemy. He felt like he'd swallowed a brick, throat raw and stomach turned to cement.

"What about the men planning to kidnap me?" Rafe asked.

"You're safe enough here," Browning said. "I'll have a talk with the men, and they'll leave you alone."

Kama cleared her throat.

"And I'm posting a couple of guards," he added. "You're not in any danger."

Browning's pronouncement did nothing to vanquish Rafe's worries. The lump in his stomach grew heavier. "Do either of you have any information about my condition?"

"No," Browning and Kama chimed in unison.

"We're doing the best we can, but the facilities are limited. You just need to rest," Browning continued.

"I'll get on the records search." Kama scooped a beat-up duffel bag off the counter. One soft hand reached down to touch him. Serious brown eyes looked into his. "Take care of yourself, Mr. McTavish."

The stunner slid unseen beneath his palm. "Rafe," he said, surprised and heartened by her gift. "Call me Rafe."

Kama and Browning left together. The stunner, cool under his hand, provided a tiny measure of comfort. When he'd served with EA security forces, he'd always had a squad—or at least a buddy—watching his back. He'd had body armor, the latest weapons, and an overall strategy for victory. Now he had a single beautiful but distant ally, no physical mobility, and the tiny stunner as his only defense. Even his powers of persuasion failed him. He needed to retreat and regroup, come up with a plan, but how?

Roshal defended him against Browning's insinuation of cowardice. Maybe Rafe could petition him for help. Roshal drifted to the door and stopped, where he stood scratching stubble on his chin.

"Perhaps if you have time, you could stay until the medic gets back?" Rafe suggested.

The shipping manager turned to face him. "If you're bleeding out, there isn't much I can do."

Rafe glanced up at the IV pole. So, internal hemorrhage, more than a bit of speed heal could fix. That explained the movement restriction. He loosened his death grip on the stunner and focused on slowing and deepening his breathing.

"Pull up a chair. Tell me about the station. I haven't had a chance to see much of it yet. Mostly just the deck."

Roshal frowned and looked around for a chair, but there weren't any. He sauntered across to one of the empty cots and perched on the edge, making it impossible for Rafe to see him without craning his neck, which required more strength than he had. He waited for the man to speak, but all he did was squirm.

"What is it you do here, Mr. Roshal?"

"Shipping manager, second in command to Levine."

Second in command? He'd thought Browning was running things in Levine's absence. Maybe he could leverage that information, especially since Browning and Roshal seemed to disagree on what ought to be done.

"Sounds like an important position, one that keeps you busy. Have you been out here long?"

Rustling came from the cot, and Roshal reappeared in his field of vision. "'Bout three years."

"Must be tough stuck so far away from civilization. You get off the station much?"

Roshal wandered out of sight again. "I make the jump gate run once or twice a week with the ore shipments."

"That's a lot of travel. Do you get frequent flyer miles?"

He popped up at the side of Rafe's cot, puzzlement on his face. "Frequent flyer miles? I operate the station tug."

"Ah," Rafe stammered. The man seemed incapable of appreciating humor. "I thought as a manager, you had a desk job. You command the tug crew then?"

Roshal laughed. "Tug crew? You ever been to the asteroid belt before? Naw, it's just an old ore-hauling tug, not some star cruiser. I call it Ol' Betsy after a girl I almost married. Helps remind me why I stay single. So do you work for EcoMech or not? Seems like working in the family business oughta be pretty cushy. I wonder why a man would walk away from that."

Good news at last. He'd found someone who could get him off the station. All he had to do was side-step the familial interrogation and get Roshal to agree.

"I always had an independent streak." He began to feel every one of those myriad boot prints on his back and legs, not to mention the ache in his ribs. "If Levine's done a bunk, I guess you won't be operating Ol' Betsy much longer. I should think you'd be first in line for promotion to station manager."

"That kinda all depends, doesn't it?" The shipping manager squinted up at the synth-blood, tilting his head to read the label. "Huh, like I thought—out of date."

Rafe stared up at the bag, and the heart monitor missed a plink. The stuff lasted forever. Just how old was it?

"Depends?" he mumbled.

"On whether there's any station left when the dust settles." The man swept his unfriendly gaze over Rafe and shook his head. "The guys would have to vote me in as station manager, and they'd rather have Ed, assuming little ol' Independent Mining can prove it owns the place, of course. Don't know as I'd put money on that happening."

Rafe tore his eyes from the bag. "If EcoMech owns the station, it'll be up to Leon Goldman to decide."

"You think that Goldman guy would promote me?" Roshal sauntered off.

Truthfully? Leon would eat you alive. But Rafe didn't say that. "Goldman's no fool. He'll want someone who knows the operation so the station produces efficiently through this transition."

"Hmm," said Roshal from somewhere across the room. "If I'm going to work for a man, I like to meet him first, face to face. Maybe you could call him on the radio and arrange that?"

"Might be possible." Hope flickered to life. Progress at last. He felt better already. "Consider that you might make a better impression if you showed him how you'd taken command."

"Yeah? What do ya got in mind?"

"You could take me to the EcoMech ship with you, and I could introduce you to Goldman. You'd gain his favor by defusing this potential hostage situation." Rafe waited to see if his bait worked.

Roshal appeared at the foot of the cot, scratching at his rough cheek. "I can't drag that cot to the airlock. Besides, I wouldn't get too friendly a welcome home if the guys find out I helped you."

"I'm restricted only until this evening. If we go then, I can walk." A small stretch of the truth, but if he didn't get off the station, he could face another angry mob. "I'd make the risk worth your while."

"Oh?" Roshal leaned closer, showing a mouthful of yellowed, uneven teeth. "What's a trip worth to you?"

"A thousand credits?" He held his breath.

The man threw back his head and laughed. "Not enough."

"Five thousand." He could hear the desperation in his voice. "Ten."

The shipping manager sauntered toward the door. "I'll think about it."

Rafe went slack, energy reserves gone, uncertain whether he'd see another day.

8

Kama laughed inwardly as the tech charged past her out the door of the com center. A few words conveying a phony request to help Janice Fisher in the infirmary, and the man had flown from his desk like air rushing from a hull breach. She locked the door behind him and took his seat at the console. The smile slid from her face as her call to Samir connected.

Slim and muscular, dark hair touched with gray at the temples, and olive face ominous, Samir filled the view screen. "This is unexpected."

"I apologize for disturbing you outside our normal communication channels," she replied, acknowledging their unsecured line. "I wanted to let you know that I'd arrived safely. I would have contacted you sooner, but the station experienced communication issues."

One almond-shaped eye twitched. "Issues?"

"Yes, but it didn't prevent me from sending your birthday present. It's on a cargo drone headed for Earth orbit. It left here shortly after I arrived. I wasn't able to check your present's condition." She held her breath.

Samir went very still. She expected frost to form on the view screen so cold was the displeasure in his gaze. He hated complications, and she'd barely started listing them.

"Inconvenient. I'll see the package is retrieved." He smoothed the front of his immaculate gray suit with long, thin fingers.

She plunged on. "Unfortunately, your present isn't complete. Pieces are missing, and other collectors have taken an interest."

His hand stopped in mid-stroke. "Other collectors?"

Kama swallowed. Sweat moistened her palms where they rested on the console. He really wouldn't like the next news. "There's also a problem with the grant work I'm to do here for Independent Mining. Seems EcoMech claims to have bought the place, and Leon Goldman came in person to take possession. He has Rafael McTavish in tow."

The intensity of Samir's stare rocked her back from the console.

"Is Mr. McTavish aware of your presence?" he asked in a deadly calm voice.

"We've been introduced," she replied.

"It's a large station. Enjoy those parts where Mr. McTavish is not found," he ordered, his brows pulling down.

"Well, that's the thing," she said, her voice rising in pitch. "There's a bit of a shooting war going on here, and he's been taken prisoner by the miners."

His brows shot up, and then he mastered his composure. "Just tell me the rest, and quickly."

"The station ownership seems to be in dispute, which may have repercussions for our little, uh, project. I expect EA will be on the scene soon." She licked her lips. "I'd like to be gone before they arrive."

Samir tapped fingertips on his chin while he stared into space. He returned his gaze to her. "Oasis values you more than my present. Expect retrieval in the next six hours. Can you get clear of the station? I'd prefer a remote pickup."

"Wait," she said, puzzled. "Why one or the other? Why not both?"

He sighed. "It's a resource issue, some kind of maintenance problem... one that may require your consultation to fix."

Kama frowned. So they were down to one working fast transport prototype instead of two. A normal ship couldn't arrive for at least twenty-four hours, and the remaining prototype wouldn't get there any sooner if it chased down the drone first. The thought of staying on the station another day took her breath away, but she wouldn't risk failure for the Sharma Network because Levine escaped. She gritted her teeth.

"Go for the drone. I can hold on here."

Samir shook his head. "Varun won't permit it. You come first."

She slapped a hand on the console. "Like hell! If you send the ship for me instead of the drone, I quit. You can tell Varun I said so."

He stared at her, and she glared back, unblinking, until her eyes burned. He looked away first.

"All right, but stay away from McTavish and out of trouble."

☠   ☠   ☠

Every miner Kama passed on the way to the business office had some kind of weapon in his hands: lengths of pipe, hammers, laser cutters. And they all had murder in their eyes. With her delayed prospect for rescue, she felt like a tightrope walker working without a net.

She hoped Browning had those guards in place—and that they could be trusted. The stunner she'd given McTavish wouldn't stop a mob. Despite Samir's warning to steer clear of him, responsibility for the danger he faced fell squarely on her shoulders. She'd check in on him later, she promised herself. Her promise did nothing to ease her guilt.

His gibe about her ability made her hackles rise, but she'd show him. With complete access to the station's computer network, she'd make sure no copies of the contract remained for prying eyes; then she'd ferret out who Levine sold it to. And she'd find out where the money had gone, too. Money trails always led to the guilty party. The miners didn't need McTavish's help.

Kama stepped into the business office. Thick crystal portholes in the carpeted deck showed distant Jupiter and the surrounding starscape endlessly circling as the station's gravity carousel spun. The great red giant crossed the window and vanished. Bloodshot light fell dead on the pitted steel walls. Looking at all that empty void through the glass made the hairs on her neck rise.

A miniature Mongol horde marched in neat ranks across a glass-fronted cabinet near Levine's desk. More than half were painted, mounts and men lit up in vivid color and intricate detail. The rest awaited decoration. She imagined him filling the lonely hours out here, brush in hand. Like his quarters, his office was all right-angles and razor-edged folds, a desert where a speck of dust would die of loneliness.

Miss Patty sat at the desk, staring at a blank screen and dabbing tears from the corners of her eyes with a lacy handkerchief. The woman sniffled once and hid the handkerchief in her lap.

"Now what do you want?" Her voice shook.

"Browning asked me to look at your business server, and see if I can figure out what's going on."

The manager's assistant tucked a few stray strands of dyed platinum blonde hair back into the bun on the top of her head. Beneath her makeup, the worry lines and the dark circles under her eyes aged her plain face ten years. She was probably closer to seventy than the sixty or so that Kama originally thought. What brought a woman like her out here?

"That's just like Ed, making decisions without consulting anybody. He's a bully," Miss Patty said.

"I'll need an account on the system, one with administrator rights," Kama said, dumping her duffel on Levine's beat-up desk next to an archaic terminal and a delicious-smelling plate of scones.

The woman didn't budge from the chair. "I'm not sure I should give you unrestricted access, especially when Donald—Mr. Levine—isn't here to authorize it."

She ground her teeth. "I'm doing this because Ed asked me, and since Levine did a runner, I have all the authorization I need."

"Yuri's in charge whenever Mr. Levine leaves the station, not Ed. Did Yuri give you permission?"

"Yes," she lied in a syrupy voice.

"I'll need it in writing." Miss Patty's chin rose, fire in her eyes. "For the files."

Kama considered returning to her quarters and just hacking the system. It would be faster and a lot less aggravating, but the woman was bound to rat her out if she did. With EA involved, she couldn't afford the fast, easy route. What could she use as a lever to dislodge the insufferable old busybody?

"Certainly, I'll be happy to find Yuri and get permission in writing. Would you mind drawing up something that states why you delayed my access?" she asked, smiling and rolling doe eyes at the woman. "I mean, if things get violent again and the courts think that violence could have been prevented by reviewing the records sooner, I don't want to take the blame. A wrongful death lawsuit would wipe out my savings and keep me working until I'm ninety."

"Well..." The fire in the woman's eyes morphed to concern, and she moved out of the chair. "If you give me a written statement saying you had authorization, I guess that would do for now. But you need to bring me Yuri's written permission at some point."

"Of course, happy to," she replied, struggling to keep a straight face. "Now if I could just have the administrator password?"

Kama shifted a framed photograph of Levine aside to make more room on the desk. In the picture, he was a small man in a precisely creased suit, smiling nervously at the camera with his hands folded in front of him. Apart from a thin gold wedding band on one finger, he seemed completely colorless. He looked too mousy for a thief, she decided, but then, he hadn't stolen the Oasis secret; it had fallen in his lap.

Miss Patty removed the photograph and carried it to an adjoining office that wasn't much more than a cubbyhole with a desk. She scribbled something on a filmie and returned, clutching it to her chest. With a look of disapproval, she handed over the filmie.

"There's your password."

Kama could hardly believe her eyes. The old bat had written the password down instead of just telling it to her. Yes, filmie sheets could be blanked after use so their nano-substrate could be reused, but it you knew what you were doing, it was possible to retrieve what had previously been written. And the password was only six characters. She could have cracked it in less time than it had taken Miss Patty to write it down. She wondered in what century the woman received her computer training.

She flicked on the desktop terminal. While it booted, she extracted a stick drive from her duffel and attached it to the archaic machine.

"What's that for?" the assistant asked.

"Oh, uh, it has a virus checking program that we Oasis techs always run on a system before interfacing with it."

"You won't be installing that, will you? Mr. Levine is very fussy about what goes on the system. He doesn't want any downtime because some software update blocks processes or closes ports in the firewall."

Kama rolled her eyes, then reached in her bag, pulled out a pair of black silk gloves, and slipped them on. A few taps on her nanocom and she had it networked with the station system. She moved the clunky keyboard aside.

"Don't worry; the scanning software stays on the stick drive," she assured the woman. *But the seek bot won't.* She waved her hands, as though she played an air piano. A torrent of computer code ripped across the screen, and the assistant sucked in a noisy breath. *Bot uploaded, records downloading.*

Kama eyed the plate of scones, and her stomach growled. "May I have one of these?"

Miss Patty touched a hand to her cheek, eyes on the screen, and pursed her lips. "I'm sure they're stale by now."

She took that as tacit permission, stripped off a glove, and snatched a scone. It had a tender, crumbly texture that made her mouth water. Two more bites finished it. A hint of sweetness vied with the tart fresh fruit embedded in the batter.

"Ohh," she moaned, regretting all her impatience with the woman. "Mmm, they're wonderful! Did you make these yourself?"

Miss Patty's shy smile cracked her pancake make-up. "Well, yes. I bake things for our morning break most days, but with Donald... Mr. Levine not... "

"Where do you get the strawberries?" Kama asked, trying to get a berry into her mouth and keep it off the desk. "Do they really deliver fresh fruit out here?"

Miss Patty shook her head. "Oh, no. I get them from our hydroponics bay. But you must have been there already, mustn't you?"

Well, I'll be... She reached for the last scone, and crumbs cascaded down her coveralls. The woman bounced up with a wastebasket and helped brush her down.

"Thanks," Kama said, blushing.

"You made a bit of a mess of yourself, didn't you?"

She looked at the huge red hydraulic fluid stain on the coveralls she still hadn't had time to change out of and grinned ruefully. "Just a bit."

"Don't worry. It'll wash right out."

"I hope so. This is my favorite pair." She watched the assistant tidying every tiny crumb from the desk and floor and wondered whether Levine and the woman were more than co-workers. Had he shared his secrets with her?

"You do realize that Levine isn't coming back?"

Miss Patty jerked upright. "Mr. Levine is no coward, and there's no proof that he's done anything wrong. He's a wonderful manager, always very careful about his work. He'll spend hours checking and rechecking the daily reports on discovery and production, making sure he's got all the facts exactly right for the monthly roll-up.

"If anyone gets sick or injured, he makes sure they get proper medical attention over at the jump gate station, not just from that half-baked med tech we have. He takes his responsibility for the men very seriously, not like some around here. He wouldn't abandon them."

Incredulous, Kama rocked back in the chair. "But there's video of him sneaking away on an unmanned cargo drone in the middle of the night! Where was he going?"

The woman narrowed her eyes and stared down at Kama. "Maybe he was fleeing for his life."

"Fleeing from whom?" she asked, her voice rising in disbelieve.

"Ed Browning, for one. He's a dangerous man with a vile temper. Just yesterday afternoon, he was in here shouting at Mr. Levine. He nearly put his fist through the desk."

"Really?" Kama said, drawing her face into a false expression of shock and disapproval. Things were finally getting interesting, and she sat straighter. "What were they arguing about?"

Miss Patty turned her face away, color rising from her neck and disappearing under the makeup. "Oh, I couldn't say. My job requires discretion."

After ten minutes, Kama thought about putting her own fist through Levine's desk. No amount of cajoling wheedled the information from the assistant. Eventually, Miss Patty cleared the scone plate from Levine's desk and left, taking her infuriating secret with her.

Time to get down to business. She checked first to see what the seek bot had returned. Sure enough, there was the Oasis contract for a phenomenal amount of wassonite—a document that also contained undeleted comments some fool had left marching down the margins. The comments detailed a managerial debate of Oasis' negotiations with other facilities for massive amounts of the rare mineral. Oasis' competitors would kill for advance knowledge of their plans, especially for something on this scale.

She replaced the old version with a new one—minus the comments—and made sure to cover any signs of her actions. To her surprise, she found no evidence of the contract attached to outgoing mail sent by anyone on the station. Had Levine been the only honest man in the galaxy and not sought to take advantage of Oasis' mistake? Then why did he run? And what about the buyout mess? Was it really some kind of scam cooked up between EcoMech and Galaxy after all? A clammy cold crawled over her skin.

Kama turned her attention to Independent Mining's bank records. She'd expected a single account; she found two dozen. Money flowed in from hundreds of sources, swirled around through the accounts, splitting and recombining like snowflakes in a blizzard, and then gushed out again to a lengthy list of businesses and to the miners themselves as wages and dividends. None of it made any sense, except for the part that showed most of the current account balances near zero.

After six hours, she had no more idea about whether Independent Mining was a legitimate operation than when she'd started. She rocked the chair back and massaged her throbbing temples. McTavish's words haunted her. She'd look like a moorhk, a moron, a fool. She felt a blush start just thinking about admitting her failure to him.

Ready for a break, her mind drifted to the question of Levine, the Oasis contract, and the money chip hidden in his quarters. Who else might have seen the document? Curious, she pulled up the list of names with access to the business systems: Levine, Miss Patty, Browning, and Roshal.

On a hunch, she wrote a computer program, an automated bot that would seek out information elsewhere in the galaxy. If Samir found out, he'd be displeased. He had no objections to hacking, but he wanted it done his way, with deep layers of misdirection and minimal risk. That took ages. If she did it her way, she'd have an answer before tomorrow morning. A little thrill zinged up her spine as she dropped the bot into the outgoing message queue.

She sneaked out long enough to shower and wash her coveralls, with disappointing results. The giant red blotch still covered the front of them. *So much for Miss Patty's assurances.* When she turned to them, the Independent Mining incorporation paperwork and the purchase contract, ostensibly signed by Galaxy, were all a lot of legal mumbo jumbo, written so no normal human being could understand it. Her revulsion toward lawyers mounted.

By ten-fifteen, she was nodding off at Levine's desk despite her grim determination to make some sense of the business records. The hum of the station's engines driving the big cylinder's rotation provided a low level white noise conducive to sleep, and she found it irresistible. She raised a hand to stifle a yawn. She ought to check on McTavish. He could be up to anything by now.

The station alarm wailed in the quiet, shattering the silence of the station night cycle. Kama jumped, every cell shrieking with sudden adrenaline, grabbed her duffel, and leaped for the door. She ran down the corridor to the next cross junction where she bounced off Browning's muscular frame.

"What's happened?" she asked, still tensed.

Browning recovered his balance and strode off. She jogged to keep pace with him. The throbbing alarm made every hair on her body stand on end. People scurried back and forth in the corridors, shouting and yelling in confusion. Browning grabbed shoulders and shoved people in the right direction, giving brusque orders, bulldozing any complaints.

Kama lunged for his sleeve and tried again. "What's going on?"

Browning swung an angry gaze onto her. "Something's coming at us, something bigger than the usual space dust and gravel. The trajectory indicates it came from the EcoMech ship. We're evacuating the impact area. So much for trusting our friend in the infirmary."

"If the EcoMech ship launched something at us, McTavish had nothing to do with it."

Browning tossed her a strange look. "How do you know?"

"I don't," she stammered, and fought for more conviction. "But the only contact he's had with the EcoMech ship was when you were right there, so how could he?"

Browning only grunted in reply. He swung into the equipment-packed control center with Kama in his wake. External cameras projected star-dusted images onto screens all around the walls. A white-faced technician manned one of the consoles. Browning clapped a hand onto his shoulder and asked for an update. The tech winced at the ferocity of his supervisor's grip.

"It's coming through in our blind spot where Camera 3B failed," he said. "It must have started out slow enough to avoid setting off the collision alarms, then accelerated."

"How close?" Browning demanded.

"Maybe five minutes out. No more than two kilometers distant."

"Shit. How big is it?"

"Two or three meters long," the tech replied.

"Buddha save us," Browning said. "Something that size could puncture the outer skin. It might weigh hundreds of kilos. Whatever it is, it isn't just some lump of trash; it's capable of course corrections. Get the defense lasers ready."

The tech scurried to another console and tapped keys.

Kama looked on. A red light flashed above the main screen. "Defense lasers?"

Browning nodded. "To burn up micro-meteorites and small-scale debris. They usually operate on automatic, but they don't engage anything bigger than a few centimeters across. We'll need to run them manually."

"That thing's more than a few centimeters."

"No time to launch a tug or a sweeper vessel. Besides, if it's a bomb, I don't want any of our people going near it."

"A bomb?" Kama exclaimed. "Why the hell would it be a bomb?"

"How the fuck should I know?" Browning retorted over his shoulder. "Maybe that CEO of theirs wants to threaten us. Whatever it is, it's on a collision course."

"But you said the lasers don't work on things that big."

"They might poke enough holes through it to throw the goddamn thing off course." He turned to the tech. "How long until we need to hit it if we want to prevent impact with the station?"

"We're just about there now."

"Bring up the sensors and target the lasers," Browning ordered.

The tech pointed to a console, where a blurry rectangle floated around a set of crosshairs. Browning seized a joystick and manipulated the view until the object was centered in the lasers' sights, then raised a finger to the technician.

"Prepare to fire."

The tech reached for the trigger. Kama still looked at the flashing red light above the screen, trying to make out the tiny printed sign beneath it. *Ultra-high what?* Oh no! She leaped forward. "Don't fire!"

"Hey, what the—" Browning began, then stopped as Kama flicked a control.

A burst of static came over the audio feed, and then a voice, very faintly. "—Greg Nighthorse. I'm out of thruster fuel, and my oxygen is in the red. Can you hear me?"

Kama shoved the technician away from the trigger. "That's not a bomb! It's someone in a spacesuit!"

"What?! What's he doing out there?" Browning shouted.

"I don't know," she snapped. "You can't shoot him."

"At the rate he's coming, we won't need to. He'll pancake when he hits the hull. Goddamn stupid idiot!" He smacked the joystick to point the lasers away, and thumped a fist down on the console, cracking the plastic housing.

Kama grabbed his arm. "Get some men out there to slow him down. Where's the transmitter switch? Greg Nighthorse, this is Kamala Bhatia. Do you hear me?"

The reply came through a storm of static. "Hello?"

"Greg, what are you doing?"

"I'm trying to get to the station to help my uncle, Rafe McTavish."

Kama thought of the gangly teenage boy she'd seen on the monitor when McTavish had called Goldman. "Kali save his stupid ass. He's just a dumb kid. Browning, get going! We haven't much time!"

Browning jumped for the door.

Kama's hands shook on the transmitter, but she tried to keep her voice light and level. "Greg, do you have any thruster fuel left?"

"No," he replied. "My oxygen started to run out so I used all the thruster fuel I had to get here faster."

"And what is your oxygen situation now, Greg?"

"It's in the red. It's been in the red for the last couple of minutes." He paused. "Am I going to die?"

The technician waved to get her attention, pointing her to the main screen. Red LED numbers had appeared above on it, counting down from five minutes.

"We have a rescue crew coming out for you now," Kama said. "You just have to hold on a few minutes more." She shuddered as she pictured him slamming into the bristling surface of the station. His suit would be shredded, and his body smashed to pulp before decompressing and freezing at the same time.

"Are they coming in a runabout?"

"No, Greg. They're coming out in suits to get you. You're in a little close for a runabout now. You need to save your air, so I think you should stop talking." She flicked off the transmitter. "How long does it take to get people out into space?" she asked the tech.

"Five minutes," he replied, his voice dull. Kama wondered if he was afraid he'd be blamed if Greg died. By missing the light indicating the boy's transmission, he'd wasted invaluable time.

She saw movement on one of the screens showing the feed from the security camera in the main airlock. Four men, Browning among them, were throwing spacesuits on with the speed of quick change artists. She switched on the sound, and heard Browning spitting instructions and cursing like a drill sergeant through his suit-to-suit radio. In less than three minutes, they were out the airlock.

The radio crackled. "I can see them, Ms. Bhatia," said Greg, his voice quavering.

"You can call me Kama."

"Um, Kama, why do they have a net?"

She recalled some of Browning's curse-laden instructions. "Well, you're coming toward the station a bit too fast, and we need to slow you down a little before you get here."

"Oh." After a pause, he continued, "I guess I screwed up, huh?"

"Yeah, you screwed up. But, hey, we all make mistakes. We just have to bounce back." She cringed as soon as she said it.

He laughed, hysteria tingeing his voice.

Browning cut in over the suit-to-suit frequency, breathing hard.

"Hate to break up the party, but shut up and listen. Kid, we're going to accelerate toward you, catch you in the net, and hope we've got enough momentum between us to slow you down. Don't touch a goddamn thing, and don't move a muscle."

"Thank you, sir, I—"

"And don't talk either. Stupid little bastard. If we live through this, I'll kill you anyway."

With no outside video feed, Kama had to imagine the scene from the bursts of conversation she heard over the radio. Browning and his men positioning themselves, firing their suit thrusters madly to accelerate away from the station, unfurling the coarse cargo net between them. The tangled confusion as Greg hurtled into the center of the net, folding it up around him and dragging all five of them toward the station with his residual momentum. And then the shock and the curses as they thudded into the hull, winding them, bruising them, but no more.

Kama quit the control room and sprinted toward the airlock. She was a couple turns away from it when she rounded a corner and plowed into McTavish, barefoot and wearing surgical scrubs two sizes too big. He grunted and staggered sideways against the wall, pain draining what color remained in his already pale face. Behind him, Roshal looked first panicked and then guilty, like a kid caught stealing candy.

"What are you doing out of bed? Moorhk!" As he swayed, she ducked under his left arm and supported him.

"Call me names if you like, but I'm leaving the station before anyone else sets their sights on me," he replied. He sounded whispery and breathless and leaned heavily on her.

"Excellent timing. Your nephew has just arrived, I presume to rescue you." He groaned, but she didn't think it was from pain.

"Put us both back on the shuttle then," he said.

"Love to. If only he'd come in a shuttle." She felt the lump of the stunner in the pocket of his scrubs and deftly transferred it to her own pocket. He looked at her with a questioning expression. "He used a spacesuit. Apparently stupidity runs in your family."

She thought she heard him mutter a curse, or maybe he gasped for breath. She couldn't be sure.

The medic trotted up, eyes troubled, and slid under McTavish's right arm. "Not much for brains, eh?"

They staggered back toward the infirmary. Browning emerged from a cross-corridor sputtering explicatives in a torrent punctuated by coughs. A hangdog Greg followed in his wake. Three more miners brought up the rear. He spotted Kama's party and strode up to her, making a visible effort to breathe. His powerful, stubby fingers rubbed the grey-sprinkled fuzz on his head. "Touch of insanity in this McTavish clan, is there?"

Greg's voice saved her the need to reply. "Thank you so much for rescuing me. I know what I did was really stupid. I'm so sorry. You guys saved my life, and I won't forget it."

He reminded her of a younger, taller version of his uncle, right down to the cobalt blue eyes and the natural charm.

"You idiot!" the supervisor raged. "What the hell did you think you were doing out there? Don't you understand the basic principles of physics? We nearly blew you away with the proximity lasers!"

Kama began to see that Browning's anger was as much about nearly killing the boy as it was about the kid's stunt. Poor Greg hung his head in shame until he recognized McTavish. His eyes grew round. For a moment, Kama thought they'd be picking Greg up off the deck next. Miners drifted up and looked on with animosity.

Browning turned his anger on Rafe. "And where the hell do you think you're going?"

"Give him a break, Browning," Kama snapped. She purposefully moved her eyes over the gathering crowd. "He was worried about his nephew. Help us get him back to the infirmary."

Browning glanced around. "What are all you gawking at? Get back to bed before I find something for you to do."

Kama saw a look pass between Roshal and McTavish, and then Roshal jittered away. The other miners were slow to respond. A few muttered angry threats, and one spit on the deck at McTavish's feet. The muscles in McTavish's jaw tightened, but he kept walking. She gave him credit for poise under fire—even if he didn't have a brain in his head when it came to taking care of himself. The more she saw of his grit and determination, the less she wanted him hanging around getting in her way. She needed to be rid of him and his loopy nephew.

When the miners were gone, Kama called out. "Hey, Browning, maybe since McTavish is up anyway, we should send him and his nephew back to their ship."

"Good idea," muttered the medic. "Since we don't have a proper morgue."

Browning pulled to a halt in front of the infirmary door and faced them, hands on hips. "Yeah, maybe we should."

"But Uncle Rafe," Greg blurted, "I thought you were going to find out what's going on here. I mean, that's why you came, isn't it? And I'll assist you just like you said. I came to tell you Mr. Goldman ordered two cruisers of space marines from First Security. He says if the miners won't stand down, he'll take the station by force. They'll arrive tomorrow afternoon."

9

Rafe sat on the edge of the cot in the station infirmary, wondering what he'd done to deserve his current situation. It seemed a tremendous miscarriage of karma. Every inch of him *ached*. He felt nauseous, which probably meant he was bleeding internally again. His stupid, *stupid* nephew stood across the room thinking of himself as some junior spy master, and the damnably contrary drop-dead gorgeous Oasis technician had relieved him of his only weapon. Had he missed anything? Oh, yes, his helpful brother-in-law intended to turn the station into a war zone tomorrow. And Browning wouldn't stop roaring.

"I asked you, can he make it to the runabout bay?" Browning shouted a foot from the medic's face. "I want both of them out of here now."

"I can make it," Rafe said through gritted teeth. "There's nothing I want more than to be off this station."

"Great!"

Browning made to grab for Rafe's arm, but the medic blocked him. "No way. He's done walking around until I say otherwise."

"No problem," the supervisor bellowed. "I'll carry him."

"Browning, think about it," Kama pleaded. "When those mercs arrive, there's nothing to stop them from assaulting the station. Men will get injured or worse. You have to keep McTavish here while you get the place under control. They won't come aboard if they think he could get hurt in the fight. He's too important."

Wasn't she the one warning him he might become a hostage? And now she was advocating they do exactly that? Whose side was she on?

"We aren't going to hide behind some namby-pamby guy in a suit," shouted Browning, and Rafe wished he *had* a suit instead of the ridiculous, embarrassing scrubs. Or maybe fatigues and body armor.

The supervisor marched over to stand toe-to-toe with Kama. Despite his rage, she remained calm, but Rafe noticed that her hand slid into the pocket with the stunner. Cool, but prepared. If only he were going to have time to get to know her better, but he wouldn't put himself or his nephew in the middle of this fight. They were leaving the station tonight. Leon could back the yacht away and bring in a crew of professional negotiators or space marines or rodeo clowns, whatever made him happy. He didn't care anymore. He should never have taken this job in the first place. If his father's reputation went up in flames with the station, so be it.

"EcoMech won't allow the use of deadly force," Rafe said. "It would cost them too much in damage claims from the victims' families. They'll board and flood the station with knockout gas. If you keep me or my nephew here, you'll be adding kidnapping on top of whatever else Goldman decides to charge you with."

Kama glared at him. "What good is gas against spacesuits? And the mercs will answer with deadly force when the miners go at them with laser cutters and worse."

"Yeah," Browning said, whirling on him. "We'll break out the old torpedoes from the munitions bunker and greet those ships with a light show like they've never seen before."

Rafe frowned. It made his face hurt. "Torpedoes?"

"They buy decommissioned torpedoes from EA and recycle the explosive to break asteroids apart," Kama said. "The propulsion systems have been stripped."

"Don't worry, we can fix that," Browning said.

"Uncle Rafe, Mom's counting on you to help Gramps. You can't let the station get wrecked."

Rafe's chest constricted, and it had nothing to do with his injuries. The iron fist of failure squeezed his heart. The medic stood by his bedside and read his medical monitor. Rafe looked him in the eye, seething.

"Don't mess me about. How bad's the bleeding?"

"Not as bad as I thought, but not good. The treatment's been partially successful. You would have died without it, but it hasn't worked as fast or as well as surgery. The best I can do is hang another bag of blood and wait to see if the seepage stops. The more you move around, the worse it gets. You need time."

Rafe nodded. Time was the thing they didn't have. Kama was right. If the miners started a shooting war with the cruisers, the situation would quickly escalate into a bloodbath with the EcoMech yacht caught in the middle. And it would all come down on his father, who'd been hoodwinked by Leon into backing the purchase. Skyrocketing anger at

Leon, his father, and the stupidity of the whole awful situation drove him to his feet to face Browning.

"What did you find in the business records?" he demanded.

The smelter supervisor whirled on the Oasis tech. "Well?"

Her face shaded red, and she thrust her hands deeper into her pockets. "It's complicated, and I'm still working on it."

"Is that code for 'I haven't got a clue'?" Rafe asked.

She flinched under his assault, and a twinge of regret rippled through him, but it was no match for his rage.

"Here's what we're going to do. You're going to put Greg in a shuttle and take him back to the EcoMech ship. In the morning, I'm going to talk to Leon Goldman and tell him the situation is under control. I'll tell him I'm investigating your ownership claim and putting the miners' fears to rest. In return, he'll send the cruisers after that cargo drone that Levine escaped on. Do you think your men will accept that?"

Browning's face hardened, but before he could say anything, Greg stepped forward.

"I'm not going back. You said I'd be your assistant. Besides, if there's two of us here, the mercs will be even less likely to attack."

It had been a shitty day, and the dam holding Rafe's anger and frustration burst. "You're not my assistant, and you're not staying on the station. Grow up, kid. I don't need you under foot."

Shock registered on the boy's face, and then came the welling of tears that he struggled to hold back. No one spoke. Rafe felt ten times worse than he had a moment earlier and sat heavily on the cot, unable to face the damage he'd done. How like his own father he was. Shame crept over him.

"Sorry, McTavish," came Kama's soft voice in the sudden quiet. "Greg's right. With two of you here, the mercs will be less likely to attack, and the miners will be more likely to believe you're sincere about helping them. He stays."

Rafe watched the medic reattach his IV and hang a fresh bag of blood from the pole. So little time before the fuse burned down and the station exploded. He wouldn't sit helpless waiting for it to happen. "Give me access to the station's business records."

"Now?" asked Browning.

"It's the middle of the bleeding night!" Kama protested. "You need to rest."

"Now," Rafe said.

Kama came to stand by the cot. "They're a mess. It would take a team of accountants days to untangle them."

"Now," he repeated. "We're wasting time. Where's my nanocom?"

The medic fished in a drawer and pulled out the shattered remains of his device. The gauntlet was battered and a chunk of the crystal screen was missing. Rafe wanted to toss it across the room, but he wasn't sure he had the strength.

Kama set her bag on the counter and rooted around, pulling out all manner of strange electronic equipment. She plugged a stick drive into a nanocom, tapped the screen, and then pulled the drive before handing him the device and another box he thought might be a filmie encoder—although he'd never seen one quite like it—and a dozen filmie sheets.

"You can code documents onto the filmies, read them, and recode. It'll be easier than using the nanocom screen."

"You have a local copy of the records?" he asked, accusation plain in his voice.

Her face blanched, and a wary look came into her eyes. "I thought we might need to send documents off to lawyers or something, so I made a copy."

Legally speaking, it was data theft, and he considered calling her on it, especially after she'd kept Greg trapped here with him. But she had the stunner, and he might need her help later, so he let it pass. Browning, muscles still taut and face like stone, shook his head and left.

"Let's get you down," said the medic. "Prone's the safest position for you."

"Screw that," replied Rafe. "Get me some pillows. And coffee."

"No stimulants, not before tomorrow."

"You can bring it, or I can fetch it myself. Make it large, hot, and very, very black."

"Come on, Greg," Kama said. "Let's get you bunked down for the night."

She took the boy's arm and guided him from the room. The medic brought pillows and left. Rafe sagged back into them and closed his eyes. He couldn't remember ever feeling so physically drained, and now he intended to pull an all-nighter examining the station records. His anger seethed and glowed like a banked fire. He hoped it would provide him the strength to keep going.

The medic brought him coffee—small and tepid—checked his IV, and left again. Kama returned, dumped her duffel under a spare cot and stretched out. She didn't seem inclined toward conversation, which suited him fine. He ignored her and dug into the station's records.

At midnight, he knew he was onto something. By four, the scope astounded him. By five, he'd fallen into an exhausted sleep, the nanocom in his lap and filmies scattered over and around the cot.

A little after six, the rustling of filmies woke Rafe. His eyes were gummed shut, he had a crick in his neck, and his back ached. He couldn't remember covering himself with the blanket that now laid over him. He supposed he should be glad he'd lived to see another day, but 'glad' wasn't in his repertoire. He gingerly rubbed the sleep from his bruised eyes and saw Kama stowing the electronics she'd loaned him in her duffel. The filmies lay in drifts on the floor around the cot.

"Hey," she said.

He glanced around. No medic in sight. Good. He had a bone to pick with the Oasis technician, and a little blowing on the embers of his anger brought the flames back to life.

"I thought you were on my side."

She gave him a long, cool look. "What's that supposed to mean?"

"First you warn me that the miners intend to hold me as a hostage, and then you encourage them to do exactly that. Is that some kind of wacky reverse psychology?"

He floundered around trying to sit up straighter, too sore to make a proper job of it. She stepped in, lifted him under his arms, and fluffed his pillows before settling him against them. Her hair was freshly shampooed, and she smelled of lavender and spices. He felt like a helpless child, which only increased his anger.

"I can almost forgive you for keeping me here," he argued, "but you should have let the kid go back to the EcoMech ship. He's just an innocent bystander."

"Don't you see? The miners are innocent bystanders, too. They didn't ask to be swindled. Most of them invested their life savings in the buyout. They deserve justice—and safety—as much as Greg does."

"Greg isn't preparing torpedoes for launch."

"The miners wouldn't be either if you corporate types weren't running roughshod over them." Frustration edged her voice. "Cruisers full of marines? Maybe you should try talking to them like men with free will instead of slaves."

She straightened his blanket, tucking it in at the foot of the bed. He thought about thrashing his legs and jerking it loose again. Then she gathered the filmies scattered on the floor and stacked them on a nearby counter.

"Thanks for tidying up. Maybe I do need an assistant." His juvenile quip came out more bitter than he'd intended.

"Greg's a great kid. You could do worse."

Rafe's guilt over his behavior the previous evening blossomed. He hoped his bruises covered the heat creeping up his cheeks. Why couldn't he control his mouth around this woman?

"Family relationships have no place in a business environment."

She perched on the edge of his cot, and her deep brown eyes seemed to contain the wisdom of the ages. He was lost in an insane world, and they were a beacon of sanity.

"All you've done since you got here is dis your family. You deny you know them, you lie to your nephew, and when he risks his life for you, you push him away with verbal abuse. What's up with that?"

"It's a long story." He plucked at the blanket and considered how to change the subject.

"I'm not going anywhere," she said.

He was so tired; tired of the guilt and the pain. Tired of keeping it bottled up inside. Tired of being alone. He might die here, and no one would ever hear his remorse, the apology he'd never made for the damage he'd done. The walls crumbled, and the words came out unbidden.

"Years ago, George Tanaka, Aaron Goldman, and my father, Cullen McTavish, pooled their resources and founded EcoMech. They needed capital to grow, so they issued stock, but being both greedy and paranoid, they worried that someday the founding families might lose control. One drunken night while their children were still very young, they hatched a plan to inter-marry their children into each other's families to consolidate the power of future generations."

Kama's face grew troubled. "Arranged marriages? That's barbaric. How could they assure that the children wouldn't revolt when they grew up?"

A grim smile. "Brainwashing. But that's another story. My sister, Shannon, was paired with Leon Goldman, Aaron's only child. My brother, Miguel, would marry Amaya Tanaka, the elder Tanaka daughter, and I would marry Youko Tanaka, George's other child.

"But the patriarchs underestimated the stubborn streak in the McTavish line and my mother's subtle counter-indoctrination. Shannon started the whole house of cards tumbling down when she refused Leon and married a lowly contract field worker, Ben Nighthorse. Leon married Amaya Tanaka instead. My father, concerned about the power consolidation between the Goldmans and the Tanakas, decided that Miguel had to marry Youko.

"I knew it would never happen. My brother was just as stubborn as Shannon—and gay. To please my father, when I turned 16, I proposed to Youko. Instead of pleased, my father was outraged. He saw my actions as an attempt to usurp my brother. But Tanaka wanted the union, so Youko and I were married."

"At 16? You were still children."

"Not in those days. You may be too young to remember. Earth still reeled from the ice flu epidemic. A third of the population dead, another third disabled with scarred lungs and failing hearts. Earth passed the Mandatory Service Act forcing the off-planet colonies, which had been spared from the flu, to send every able-bodied colonist between the ages of 16 and 35 for a year of volunteer service on Earth, doing the crucial jobs that the disabled couldn't. EA also tried to off-load the disabled to the colonies by instituting population growth quotas. If corporate colonies didn't meet their targets, they'd lose their planetary leases."

Kama's face darkened. "And so the slave trade began."

Rafe shifted, uneasy. He'd hit a nerve. But still he plowed on. The coming horror welled in him like an unstoppable flood. "To avoid meeting their quotas by taking on the disabled, corporations offered generous stock grant incentives for children born on-planet. The founding families set the example. Two surrogate mothers were assigned to Youko and me, and Youko's eggs were harvested and fertilized. She and the surrogate mothers each received a viable fetus.

"Seven months later, my number came up for mandatory service. Youko was furious. She'd be stuck on Harvest with 'a bunch of squalling brats' while I escaped to Earth. We argued. God, did we argue, every minute we were together." He stopped. It seemed so crass to talk of his marriage this way, but he couldn't help it. He'd hidden the truth too long.

"On the morning of my departure, I rose and showered early, hoping to avoid an ugly scene. When I returned to our bedroom, it was drenched in blood. Youko lay dead on our bed, her womb sliced open. Our daughter..." Rafe's voice broke. "Our daughter lay beside her, a kitchen knife protruding from her tiny chest. I couldn't look at her like that, so small and violated. I pulled the knife from her and cradled her in my arms. I think I screamed. It's all a blur.

"I was frightened. I thought we had an intruder in the house. I went to find the surrogate mothers, who lived with us. They were dead too, butchered in their beds." In his mind, he saw them as they were the night before their deaths, not much older than he'd been then and brimming with merriment as they teased him while he packed.

"I must have set off the security alarm when I staggered out the front door. The EcoMech security chief arrived, along with my father. My father took one look around and asked, 'Why'd you do it?' That's when the interrogation began in earnest."

"He thought you'd killed them?" Kama asked, incredulous.

"I was covered in blood. So much blood. And my fingerprints were on the knife—along with Youko's."

Kama sucked in a breath and took his hand, trembling on the blanket. "She'd killed them all and then herself."

Rafe nodded, cleared his throat, blinked back tears. "The security chief cuffed me, and while he was loading me in his flyer, Aaron Goldman arrived. He went inside the house. When he came out, he vomited in the garden by the door. He listened to me and believed I was innocent. There was no ironclad way to exonerate me. Questions would always remain, especially considering the extraordinary scene in the house. He told my father and the security chief that EcoMech couldn't afford the scandal.

"Then Aaron Goldman cleaned me up, took me to the shuttleport, and put me on my flight to Earth, as though nothing had happened. All record of the surrogate mothers disappeared. The official report states that Youko had a miscarriage and bled to death alone at home later that afternoon. I haven't seen or spoken to any of my family since. I'm ashamed to face them."

"Ashamed? You have nothing to be ashamed of."

Rafe drew in a deep, ragged breath. "I failed them, failed them all: the surrogate mothers, my children, Youko, even my father. He still believes I'm a murderer. I should have seen that Youko was unbalanced, been a better husband, more supportive. I could have delayed my service or bribed my way out of it completely. Truthfully, I looked forward to being away from her. My selfishness killed them."

"Youko killed them, and you're as much a victim as the dead. Vishnu! You lost your *children*. There's nothing more painful, and you suffered that loss in silence and the company of strangers." Her eyes brimmed with tears, and she squeezed his hand. He detected an undercurrent of shared experience in her voice. It stabbed at his heart.

After a moment she said, "Your nephew loves you, you know."

Rafe laughed in derision. "He doesn't know me."

"He does. He told me about you last night when I walked him to my quarters. You used to take him for rides in your flyer when he was a toddler. You let him eat ice cream for dinner when you babysat him. He's followed your career, knows everything you've done. He worships you."

Rafe's emotions swung from despair to annoyance. He didn't want a family. He was done with them. Families caused nothing but pain. He looked down at her hand, still holding his. What would it be like if she held it forever? No, he wouldn't think about it.

"I'm a piss-poor role model. He should pick another."

"His actions speak for him. He'd never been in a spacesuit before last night, but he could see you were in trouble, and he came to back you up." She lifted his chin so he couldn't avoid her eyes. "It's called unconditional love."

"I don't deserve it."

She sighed, withdrew her hand, and rose. "Stay put. I'll be back shortly."

"Bring me coffee," he commanded, suddenly embarrassed by his outpouring.

She laughed. "Corporate types. Think everyone's a servant."

She tossed her duffel over her shoulder and walked away. When she opened the door to leave, Greg slouched in.

"Greg," she said, disapproval in her voice. "I thought I told you to wait in my quarters until I came for you."

He frowned down at her. "I'm not a kid. I can find my way around."

Kama just lifted an eyebrow and shook her head before she stepped past him. "I'm off. Keep an eye on your uncle. No elephant safaris or sightseeing tours. He's to stay in bed until the medic says otherwise."

The door closed behind her, and the room seemed to chill. Why had he shared his tale with her when he'd never told it to anyone before? He hardly knew her. But he felt a strange relief all the same.

Greg stood uncomfortably just inside the room, and an awkward silence grew. Rafe watched him twiddle a scrap of discarded medical supply wrapper between his fingers and gaze around at the half-empty cupboards like they were great works of art.

"If your mother ever finds out what you did, she'll skin us both."

Pink flooded into Greg's face. "Mr. Goldman wouldn't send a shuttle. I had no choice."

"Ah."

He'd forgotten Greg as a toddler, could hardly believe he'd grown into this gangly young man. Unconditional love seemed an unbearable burden. He remembered Kama's apology for betraying his identity to the miners. He hoped he had her fortitude and grace while he made his own.

"Look, I'm sorry for last night. I shouldn't have lied about taking you on as an assistant, and I should have thanked you for your show of concern."

Greg eased toward the bed, hope kindling in his eyes. "If you'd just give me a chance, I could be an ace helper."

"I'm sorry. I can't."

The hope snuffed out. "Then I'm screwed. I need an internship to finish my management coursework. Mom's gonna kill me."

"Mr. Goldman will take you back. Your grandfather can intercede on your behalf if necessary."

Greg turned a jaundiced eye on him. "Gramps doesn't like me that much. And Goldman won't take me back no matter what. When he wouldn't send anyone to help you, I said some things to him that I probably shouldn't have."

"Ah."

Worse and worse. It was because of him that Greg was in this hole. Family or no, the kid deserved his help. He'd do it just this once, but then he intended to retreat to Earth and keep his family at arm's length as he had before. He wouldn't risk more.

"I have some contacts at Wandermere Consortium. Are you familiar with it?"

"Well, yeah!" said Greg. "Wandermere is EcoMech's biggest customer."

"I can't promise anything, but I'll see if I can get you an internship there."

"Thanks, Uncle Rafe. If there's anything I can do for you, just say the word. I mean, while we're stuck here, that is."

Kama returned, carrying a tray of... something, and placed it on his lap. The label on a little foil block said 'Prepackaged Protein Substitute.' A half-full coffee cup sat beside it. He tore back the cover on the block. Greasy eggs, limp hash browns, and something red and unidentifiable he wasn't going near. He shuddered and took a swallow of coffee. It tasted like pond water. He forked up some bland mash and fought to avoid spitting it out.

Kama settled back on the foot of the cot, a look of amusement on her face as she watched him toy with the rations. "Something missing?"

Rafe grimaced. "Yeah, food."

She chuckled. "I'll have the chef flogged."

Kama fished in her bag and pulled out ration bars. She tossed one to Greg and tore one open for herself.

"I have errands to run, but they won't take long." She hopped off the cot and left.

Rafe watched Greg open his ration bar. "Want to trade?"

"No thanks," Greg mumbled around a mouthful of the bar. "This is pretty good."

The medic came in, followed closely by Browning and Roshal. He bustled about, checking Rafe's medical monitor and removing the empty blood bag.

"How're you feeling this morning, kid?" Browning asked.

Greg blushed. "Very well, thank you, sir. I apologize again for—"

"Forget it," Browning cut him off. "Just don't do it again on my watch. First time I've been off the station in a week—it was good to get some fresh air."

"You done with this?" the medic asked, pointing to Rafe's tray.

"Definitely," Rafe replied. The medic swept the tray away.

Roshal looked discomfited and wouldn't meet his eyes. Rafe wondered whether the shipping manager still expected his ten thousand credits, even though they hadn't reached the EcoMech yacht.

Browning, on the other hand, planted himself at the foot of Rafe's cot and stared so hard he thought the man's eyes might pop out.

"Well? Do we own the place?"

"There's good news, and there's bad news," Rafe replied. The smelter supervisor's fists bunched. "Your incorporation is legitimate. Independent Mining is an EA-recognized entity. But the buyout is a fraud."

"God damn it! So Galaxy fleeced us." Browning paced the room, smacking his fist into the opposite palm. "God damn corporations, always cheating the little guy."

"Galaxy didn't cheat you." Browning pulled up at his bedside, and he resisted the urge to flinch back from the miner's fury. "Levine's the culprit."

Roshal shuffled his feet and flapped his hands. "That little weasel can't find his ass with both hands and a map. If he's involved, he's working for Galaxy. We might as well pack it in, Ed. We can't fight big corps like EcoMech and Galaxy. I say we set some charges around the station and evacuate. When everybody's off, we blow the place. Let 'em sweep space for the pieces."

Rafe's throat closed. These guys were way beyond crazy. He'd hoped his discoveries might calm the miners, not make them suicidal.

"How do you know?" demanded Browning. "Kama said the records were too complicated to get anything from them that fast."

Rafe spread his hands, palms up. "Don't shoot the messenger. The signature on your purchase agreement read 'Hector Santos'. You signed the contract six months back, but Santos quit as Galaxy's chief financial officer over a year ago. Dead giveaway. And there's plenty of other evidence as well."

"You could be lying to cover for Galaxy and EcoMech," said Roshal, hands stuffed in jeans pockets and head twitching. "Ed, if that Oasis tech can't figure out what's going on, we need a real disinterested third party to look over the records, someone we can believe."

Rafe wondered if something contagious in the station air caused the extreme corporate distrust. Large multi-national corps were the first to rise from the financial ashes of the ice flu fifteen years earlier. True, they'd lobbied for weakened labor rights to reduce corporate costs and speed economic recovery, but that didn't mean they were all cheats and cut-throats, enslaving their workers. You'd think that, though, from talking to anyone on the station. He might not lay claim to his family name, but he'd never been ashamed of belonging to the corporate world, and he wouldn't start now.

"I've said it before, and I'll say it again: I don't have a dog in this fight. You can keep on thinking EcoMech and Galaxy are out to fleece you and lose everything, including your lives. Or you can come to your senses and look for a peaceful resolution."

The smelter supervisor paced again, his steps punctuated by hacking coughs. "Did you mean what you said about helping us, or is that just BS you're going to tell Goldman?"

"My previous behavior notwithstanding, I don't prevaricate."

"Is that yes or no?" Browning demanded.

Rafe stifled a sigh. "I'm trying to help, but I can't guarantee Mr. Goldman's cooperation."

"But you think you can get him to divert those cruisers?"

"I can argue the case for why he should. I can't promise I'll sway him." Hope sparked in him. Maybe they were finally listening.

Browning crossed his arms over his muscular chest. "You don't sound very sure of yourself."

"You wanted honesty."

"And if Goldman backs down, will you continue to help us?"

Rafe hesitated. Building the case against Levine would take months and involve both Galaxy and EcoMech as well as the miners. The costs would be enormous. Galaxy and EcoMech had the deep pockets to pay for it. The miners didn't. Most likely, they wouldn't recover a single credit, especially not with two large corporations competing for the same resources.

But if he didn't help them resolve their differences with EcoMech, a lot of people could die. God knew the miners needed someone on their side. In a strange way, he relished the coming confrontation with his brother-in-law. He'd finally settle the score for all the bullying, taunts, and beatings he'd suffered at Leon's hands while growing up, and he'd do it not with his fists, but by proving he was the smarter businessman.

"For the duration of my stay, I'll continue to represent your concerns to Mr. Goldman. I can't promise to help you pursue your legal case against Levine."

Browning turned to Roshal. "Now we know where we stand. Yuri, you better be ready in case Goldman doesn't divert the cruisers."

"Ready how?" Rafe asked, alarmed at Browning's tone.

"I can't stop the men if they decide to attack those cruisers, but I can make sure the torpedoes don't get used. If Goldman doesn't agree, Yuri will blow the munitions bunker."

Rafe gaped at Browning. He threw back the blanket and gingerly swung his legs over the edge of the cot.

"Let's get this show on the road. Take me to the com center."

Five minutes later, Rafe traversed the station, sitting on the squeaky trolley. He'd refused to let them load the cot on it again. Bad enough being dressed in the ridiculous scrubs without adding the insult of complete helplessness. They made a freakish parade, Browning walking point, Greg pushing the cart, and Roshal and the medic bringing up the rear. More than a few miners stopped to stare.

When they arrived at the com center, Kama rose from the tech's chair. Embarrassed by his attire and his transportation, he acknowledged her with a forced smile that she didn't return. She slipped into a quiet corner where she twirled a strand of hair and looked unhappy. The medic helped Rafe into a seat before the transmitter. Browning made to pull up a chair beside him.

"No offense, Ed, but I think this will go better if you're not with me," Rafe said.

Browning gave him an uncertain look before sliding his chair sideways off camera. Rafe signaled the tech, and in a moment, Benson appeared on screen looking haggard. At Rafe's request, he disappeared to fetch Leon.

Leon looked no better rested than Benson. His hair was rumpled, and a red crease marked one cheek. He wore a black silk dressing gown embroidered with red Chinese characters.

"McTavish, imagine seeing you again. I thought you were to be delivered to that cargo hauler or whatever it is?"

"That was Plan A. Now we're on Plan B. I understand you've got some security cruisers headed this way, and I'd like to borrow them."

Leon sneered at him. "If you know about the cruisers, then Greg survived his little jaunt. Tell him he'll have a long walk home. And if you want cruisers, surely you can get some of your own? Mine will be occupied securing EcoMech property."

"Sorry to hear that, Leon. You see, Levine, the station manager who's—shall we say—a person of interest in the apparent buyout swindle perpetrated against the miners, slipped off the station on a cargo drone before we arrived. Your cruisers should be ideally positioned to intercept that drone."

Rafe paused for Leon to take in what he'd said. He wondered just how badly the man wanted Levine, and why. "Of course, if your cruisers aren't available, I can ask EA to pick up the drone when it enters Earth orbit and detain Mr. Levine while the miners file their charges against him."

Leon grew still. Rafe could almost hear the wheels going around in the CEO's head. The audio went dead while Leon conferred with Benson. Rafe guessed he was asking Benson whether the EcoMech ship could catch the drone. He saw Benson shake his head.

"Why are you telling me this?" Leon asked a moment later.

"Levine is the one who cheated the miners, not EcoMech. If they can see that he's being brought to justice, they'll stand down. You can send your security forces home."

"Let the miners show there are no hard feelings against EcoMech by delivering you and Greg to me," Leon countered. "And I want the names of the men who attacked you."

Rafe stiffened his jaw. Leon wanted to hold all the cards. What was it Kama had said—treat the miners like men and not slaves? "The miners have contracted with Security Partners to assist them in loss recovery. The accommodations they've provided me are sufficient, and staying here keeps me closer to the heart of the investigation."

Leon's eyes narrowed. "Stay if you want, but send Greg back."

Rafe gave him a cold smile. "You fired him. He's not yours to order around anymore."

The CEO answered with a shark-tooth smile of his own, hard eyes glittering. "I've decided to rehire him, effective immediately."

Greg was the more valuable asset. Despite what Kama thought, no one at EcoMech cared if Rafe got himself killed in an assault on the station. But Greg was another story.

Torn by guilt, Rafe responded, "I'm sorry, Leon, he's proved too valuable an assistant for me to part with him."

Leon's smile died. "Hear me, McTavish. If I don't find Levine on that drone, I will have to assume this is all a ruse by the miners to divert my forces, and that you're being held against your will, in which case, the cruisers will converge on the station and take control by whatever means necessary."

10

"The situation here is more complicated than you realize. It's in every-one's best interest if we cooperate to find a solution," lectured McTav-ish.

Kama looked on as he spoke to the miners, pity for him vying with irritation that he'd untangled the business records when she'd failed. Mc-Tavish had read the files as though they were a children's picture book, and it chafed her. After spending most of the day alternately poring over the financials and falling asleep from exhaustion, he'd asked Browning to call everyone together so he could address them.

A partially dismantled repair drone stinking of grease occupied one corner of the storage bay. Miners crowded the remaining space, some sitting on the floor around the walls, most packed together on their feet. The climate control system struggled to circulate enough fresh air. The musky scent of their sweating bodies mingled with oil and cleaning sol-vent from patches of grime on the deck. If the meeting took much longer, she'd need a shower to wash the stench off.

He'd been talking for five minutes already, explaining his findings and assuring them that Levine would be caught by the EcoMech forces. He'd urged the miners to be patient and suggested that their best course of action was to return to their duties so they could show Mr. Goldman what hard-working and dedicated employees they were. It was all a lot of morale-boosting psycho-babble intended to put the miners at ease, and for the most part, it seemed to be working. She couldn't believe they fell for it.

Unfortunately, McTavish labored under the assumption that Levine would be found on the drone, and his capture would end the crisis.

Nothing could be farther from the truth. Samir had intercepted the drone already. Levine wasn't on it. When that information reached Goldman and the miners, it would provide the spark to reignite hostilities. She couldn't allow McTavish to cajole the miners into a peaceful outcome that depended on Levine's apprehension. The miners needed protection.

"If we cooperate, does that mean we'll get our money back?" shouted one of the miners buried in the crowd.

McTavish raised his hands in a placatory gesture. "Gentlemen, I understand how concerned you are about losing your money to Levine. I've been told many of you invested your life savings. That's a grievous blow. I sympathize. My top priority is to find Levine, and then the recovery process can begin."

"What about those security forces that CEO ordered?" cried another miner.

Kama saw her opening and jumped in. "If you don't trust the CEO, then get backup. Contact EA and ask for peacekeepers and labor negotiators. With them on the station, you won't need to worry about the security cruisers."

One of the miners in the front row laughed. "My kids'll be old and gray before EA peacekeepers get here. You think that CEO will wait that long?"

The group shouted and jeered. McTavish struggled out of the chair he'd been sitting in and stood beside her. He tossed a puzzled glance her way before opening his arms and addressing the miners.

"It's a good suggestion, but unnecessary," he said. "Mr. Goldman will keep his part of the bargain and detain Levine. In return, you'll all go back to work. Problem solved."

"It never hurts to have some extra insurance." Kama pressed. From the corner of her eye, she saw McTavish's brows draw down. "Better to be safe than sorry, isn't it?"

Browning moved up beside them. "You really think EA would respond? We're not some big corp about to have labor riots."

"I can guarantee it," she replied. "You have a contract with Oasis, and Oasis has a schedule to keep. They'll speak to EA on your behalf."

McTavish gave her a penetrating look with those disarming blue eyes, then his face became a calm mask. He took another step closer to the miners. The movement caused him to wince, but he covered it and stood relaxed and open.

"We're turning a pinhole puncture into a total blowout," he said. "If we bring in EA, they're going to ask questions about how this all started, and they're going to want the names of everyone involved. I don't think we want to go there. We had a simple misunderstanding, and we're fixing it ourselves without outside interference."

Damn, he's good. He'd used 'we' as though he was one of them, and he'd deliberately changed his body language to befriend them. While that walk forward had cost him in pain and fatigue, it had put him among them. Kama muttered a curse under her breath and thought about poking him in his broken ribs to shut him up.

"I don't know about you boys, but I don't want EA here." Browning moved to join the group of miners and faced McTavish.

Kama moved forward, too. "You'll need EA here for the investigation of the buyout fraud. The sooner they get started, the sooner you'll see your money back. And Goldman has already asked for the names of the miners involved in the assault. He won't let the attack go unprosecuted. It'll look better if you contact EA first."

McTavish gave her an openly angry look before addressing the miners again. "I'm the injured party, and I'm not pressing charges. While it's true that we want EA involved in the fraud investigation, asking for peacekeepers is overkill. Let's keep our focus on Levine and take this one step at a time."

A chorus of disparate replies came from the crowd as the miners voiced their opinions. One burly worker pushed to the front of the group to stand before McTavish. Kama tensed and slipped her hand in her pocket to cradle the stunner.

"You're stringing us along, aren't you? We're never going to see a single credit back. You just want to get your lying ass off the station in one piece."

Another miner, small but wiry, intercepted the first miner. "We're in enough of a shit hole, Grant. Back off."

With a sneer, Grant shouted, "I'll show you a shit hole, Warner."

Grant lunged at Warner, who ducked a right hook and connected with one of his own. The other miner, twice his size, shook off the blow and rushed him, arms spread to grapple. Warner raised his hands in a boxer's stance, but was borne backwards by the other man's weight. His foot slipped on a greasy patch and shot out from under him. Kama reached for his flailing arm and missed. The back of his head smashed into the edge of a work table with a sickening thud, and then he was lying flat and still on the deck, eyes closed.

McTavish was the first to kneel next to the stricken Warner, feeling for a pulse. Kama jumped to assist, her heart beating fast. She hoped the violence wouldn't spread to the others as they jostled to get a better look at their fallen comrade.

"He's still breathing." McTavish announced. His eyes locked on Grant. "You! Bring that cart in from the corridor."

In a matter of minutes, the miners had hoisted Warner's limp form onto the trolley that had brought McTavish to the storage bay. They wheeled it away with care, everyone trailing after the makeshift ambulance.

McTavish watched them go until he and Greg stood alone with her, and then his pupils dilated and one hand crept up to his ribs. She darted to his side and inveigled herself under his arm. Greg grabbed the other. McTavish sagged. She kept her arm tight around his waist and steered him to the chair.

"Uncle Rafe, are you okay? Should I get the medic?" The boy looked pasty.

"I'm good," he gasped, still holding his ribs. "It looks worse than it is."

"Liar," she said.

McTavish gave her an unfriendly glance before speaking to his nephew. "Greg, can you go to the infirmary and bring back the trolley?"

"Sure, Uncle Rafe."

He watched the boy go, eyes narrowed, before he turned back to her. The mask of friendly boyish charm vaporized, replaced by the face of a man nearing his breaking point.

"What the hell were you doing? In case you didn't know, the objective is to calm the men, not start a riot."

Durga, give me strength. "Your plan relies on that slimeball Goldman's promise not to attack if he finds Levine in the drone. He's just another greedy corporate type embarrassed because he was run off his turf. He'll want revenge and to show the miners he's boss. I don't trust him, and the miners shouldn't either."

McTavish combed his fingers through his unruly black hair. "What about me? Am I another 'greedy corporate type' that you don't trust?"

Kama swallowed hard and chewed her lip, weighing her choices. Lives hung in the balance: McTavish, his nephew, the miners. But she had Oasis' secrets, so many secrets, that were also her charge.

Did she trust him? That's what it came down to in the end, a gamble on his integrity, and she was out of options if she wanted to help the miners.

"It's not about you. It's about keeping everyone safe. Levine isn't on that drone." She drew in a deep breath. "He was never on the drone."

At first, he just blinked. Then his eyes got a faraway look and the anger gave way to an internal focus so intense it frightened her. When he'd returned to the reality of his surroundings, he asked, "You're certain?"

"No mass changes, no fluctuating oxygen refresh rates, no hatch openings since departure, which rules out a mid-flight rendezvous."

One eyebrow twitched up, and his cobalt blue eyes drilled into her like lasers. She expected him to ask how she knew all this. Instead he said, "I'm sorry I swore at you. I see now why you advocated for EA peacekeepers."

"You have to take Greg and get off the station before the miners find out."

"I've given them my word that I'll help them. I can't quit now."

"Help them from the EcoMech ship. Convince Goldman to send the mercs home. You aren't any help to anybody if you're dead." Kama thought he took her announcement rather lightly. He didn't seem the least bit worried.

"You have something more to tell me," he said at last. "Not about the drone, but about Levine."

"What?" Kama asked. What was he, some kind of psychic? She wouldn't answer, but he just waited until she had no choice. "On the first morning after I arrived, the morning Levine disappeared, someone searched his quarters."

He frowned and shook his head. "I don't follow you."

"No one could find him. They searched the station, but no one had access to his quarters. I thought—" she hesitated.

"You thought you could help them open the lock, what with your, er... exceptional computer skills."

"Yes, exactly." She hurried on. "Miss Patty was inside when I got there. I guess no one realized she could get in. I had a sense that she hadn't been there long. She'd left the door standing open."

"You think she took something?"

"If she did, it would have been small, something she could hide on her person. But the rooms had been searched, thoroughly and carefully, without disturbing anything." She reached in her pocket and pulled out the cash chip. "I went back right after Miss Patty left and found this hidden inside the vid screen frame."

McTavish took the chip with its bank logo and weighed it in his hand. "Feels like about 50,000 credits worth, and I imagine it arrived in the mail the night before we did."

Kama's jaw sagged. "How did you know?"

"Levine didn't just scam the miners. He's been embezzling from Galaxy for the past three years. He's a damn genius at creative bookkeeping. Every month, he has a cash chip sent from a Mars bank. It's pulled from the account for a shipping company, one I suspect exists only in cyberspace. It's one of the ways he's been laundering the money. They're always timed to come in on the mail ship."

"Every month?" Kama's brain churned furiously. If the cash chip wasn't a payment for the Sharma Network secret... and McTavish had found this information in the business records, the same records she'd dismissed as useless. She wanted to kick herself for her stupidity.

"I'm sorry I implied you're incompetent. That was uncalled for," he said, as though reading her mind. "Even the best forensic accountants will struggle with this case."

His apology made it all the worse. She hung her head, ashamed of her failure and in awe of his skills. She'd misjudged him when she'd thought he was only a pretty face. *But he's still a slimy corporate liar,* she reminded herself.

"You didn't tell the miners any of this."

"No. It seems a very large operation for only one man to pull off, particularly for as long as this one has lasted. Levine might have an accomplice, and I didn't want to risk spooking a potential co-conspirator. Was there just the one chip?"

"That's all I found in his quarters. He might have others stashed elsewhere."

McTavish raked his hands through his hair and frowned. "He knew the station had been sold and that I was due to arrive. If he delayed his own departure waiting for the chip to get here, why not take it with him when he vanished?"

She'd had more time to ponder the question than he had, but she'd found no answer. She was almost glad he couldn't solve the problem. She felt incompetent enough.

"He faked the video footage," she said.

"If what you say about the drone is true, I see no other alternative. Levine's a clever man, experienced at misdirection."

His cool gaze lingered on her. Reassessing, she thought. He'd trusted her with his secret. Was he sorry now? But she had bigger worries. If Levine was still hiding on or in the vicinity of the station, how would she find him before McTavish now that he knew the manager was still here?

She needed time to look for him, and she needed McTavish out of the way, or at least not also looking for Levine. Telling him about the search was one thing. Letting him in on the secret of the Sharma Network another.

"Levine may have arranged for a ship to pick him up here. Just before the drone left, he sent a message requesting a meeting. I thought the message meant a rendezvous with the drone, but if he didn't take the drone, maybe it didn't. If we can find that ship and track it, we can set a trap to catch him when he makes the transfer, assuming he hasn't already."

McTavish mulled over her statement. His color looked better, and he wasn't holding his ribs anymore. "Not a bad plan, provided he isn't already gone or we don't have to wait too long. Patience is running thin on both sides of this mess. I'll have EA run the ship's ID code. I can do that while I'm on EcoMech's ship."

Kama's hopes rose. He'd changed his mind and wouldn't be here to impede her own search of the station. "Glad you're finally talking sense. I can run you and Greg over now, while the miners are occupied with Warner."

"I'd like you to stay here and keep an eye on Greg. I know it's a lot to ask, what with the explosive situation, and I worry about leaving you in danger, but I won't be there long. If Levine is on the station, then we should set up a systematic search and set the trap for the rendezvous ship as a backup plan. I can't organize a search from the EcoMech ship."

Kama checked her anger and frustration. How dare he imply that she couldn't take care of herself when she'd been the one watching out for him. Men!

"You're not taking Greg? I thought you were the one who wanted him safely away from here?"

McTavish hung his head and studied the deck. "Let's just say I'm hedging my bets."

Her frustration crept a little higher. "Then why are you going?"

"If the financials that Galaxy provided to EcoMech were fraudulent, EcoMech can back out of the purchase. From EcoMech's side, the purchase never made any kind of sense anyway. And if EcoMech doesn't own the station, there's no reason to send in space marines or for the EcoMech ship to hang about. But I need to present the evidence to Goldman, and I need to do it face to face. Let's find Ed or Yuri and set up transportation for me."

Kama's grip tightened on her duffel strap. McTavish was the most infuriating man. Now he'd saddled her with a babysitting assignment while she needed to look for Levine. She'd have to find a place to stash the kid while she hunted.

"While you're over there, try to remember your doctor's orders: no unnecessary walking."

He looked thoughtful. "Does the 'doctor' have pink and purple hair and an enormous metallic handbag?" He shook his head. "Don't answer that. I must have been hallucinating."

They waited for Greg in silence, each lost in their own thoughts. Kama grew more concerned about the prospect of Levine being on the station. If he had the Oasis contract, how would she get to him first, and what was to prevent him from telling others? Did he have an accomplice, and if so, did the accomplice know about the contract? Maybe it was better to let the manager appear to escape, and then Samir could surreptitiously intercept. It was the kind of "wetware" problem she didn't like.

McTavish cleared his throat. "The contract with Oasis you mentioned, it's a pretty big purchase, but it doesn't seem to justify Oasis' involvement on the miners' behalf. Seems like it would be easier for Oasis to just get their shipment elsewhere."

I'm a moorhk. She wandered over to one of the work tables and pretended to examine the tools, keeping her back to him. "Oasis is a champion of the little people, not like greedy for-profit corps. They'll step in because it's the only way Independent Mining can get justice."

"Ah," he said. "And you have the authority to make that commitment on Oasis' behalf?"

Kama froze. She should have listened to Samir and steered clear of McTavish. She pushed her apprehension away and searched for an angry retort. Better keep this guy at arm's length. She arranged her face into a deliberate scowl and spun around.

"First you malign my abilities, and now you doubt my word?" she said, feigning offense and avoiding his question.

McTavish held up his hands. "Just asking."

After another moment, he said, "Probably best all around if your involvement in the search for Levine stays off the record."

Why would he cover her involvement? The big corporations saw to it that EA punished corporate espionage to the full extent of the law as an example for others. His company specialized in catching hackers like her. She couldn't figure him out, and that worried her. One more puzzle she didn't want to think about, along with what to do should she find Levine.

Greg arrived with the trolley, and they loaded McTavish. The two of them went to the runabout bay while she diverted by the infirmary. The miners had dispersed, and only Browning remained with the medic and Warner. Browning wasn't happy when she told him about McTavish's plan. He followed her to the runabout bay.

McTavish stood just outside the bay doors, back against the wall and feet splayed, like he'd fall over without the extra support. He bounced a little rubber ball off the deck, over and over in an endless rhythm, with that same intense focus she's glimpsed in the storage bay. She sensed it wasn't the ball he focused on. As soon as he saw them, he tucked the ball in the pocket of his scrubs.

"Thanks for coming, Ed. How's Warner?"

Kama wondered whether his concern for Warner was genuine or just a ploy to soften the smelter supervisor.

"He'll live. Medic's keeping him overnight just to be safe. What's this Kama says about you leaving us?"

"Can you spare a runabout pilot? I need a roundtrip to the EcoMech ship posthaste."

Ed ran a beefy hand over his face. "You taking the kid?"

Without hesitation, McTavish responded. "No, he has work to do here. Kama promised she'd keep an eye on him so he won't be under your feet."

Browning glared at him. "You gonna tell me why you want to go over there?"

McTavish flashed his endearing boyish grin, all the more effective for the sympathy vote his bruised and swollen face elicited. "A good magician never reveals his tricks. Suffice it to say I'll be working on the miners' behalf."

"You ever give a straight answer, Mr. McTavish?" Browning asked.

The grin broadened. "Rafe. Call me Rafe."

With that, he shuffled into the runabout bay where two hulking transport craft waited. The smelter supervisor followed, muttering imprecations. He cracked a hatch and helped McTavish inside, then he climbed in and dogged the hatch.

Kama and Greg watched the craft launch through the porthole in the bay door.

"What's this work your uncle wants done?" she asked, hopeful that she might be able to ditch the kid while she conducted her own station search. She took his arm and steered him away from the runabout bay.

"He wants filmie prints of the station schematics, section by section, ready for him when he gets back. He said you'd have what I needed, and if you didn't, you'd be able to get it. He also asked me to review all the airlock videos and make a list of everyone who came or went from the station the night Levine disappeared." He trudged along in silence for a moment and then said, "He said you were very resourceful. Did you know him from before?"

"No," Kama replied, puzzled. "What gave you that impression?"

"He said that if things got hairy while he was gone, I was to do whatever you told me, no arguments, no matter how crazy it sounded. He said he trusted you with my life because he trusted you with his. I thought you guys must know one another pretty well."

Kama was speechless, first with surprise, and then with fury. How dare McTavish dump responsibility for his nephew's safety in her lap! Typical corporate type, sloughing his duties downstream onto his lackeys. She resented the implication that he was somehow her boss. She'd have a word with him when he returned.

In the meantime, she'd drop Greg off in the infirmary to encode the filmies McTavish wanted and start reviewing the videos. The medic could keep an eye on him. She had her own agenda.

"Are you married?" Greg asked. "Or dating anybody?"

She lifted her eyebrows, amused that he might be hitting on her. "Did you want to ask me out?"

His face reddened. "You're really beautiful and all, but I think you're kind of old for me. I thought maybe if you were unattached, you might date Uncle Rafe."

Her amusement vanished, and the anger returned. First McTavish asks her out to dinner, and now he has this young whelp matchmaking for him. Kama rounded on Greg. "Did your uncle put you up to this?"

"Oh, no!" he said. "It's just my mom worries about him. She says he needs to stop window shopping and get serious about someone. I thought maybe since the two of you get along so well..."

Kama rolled her eyes. *Get along so well?* "I don't date."

"You don't? Not anyone?"

"Not anyone."

Greg took her denial as news that his uncle had a chance with her and grinned. She stalked to the infirmary in silence, annoyed that he'd missed the point. She wasn't going to date McTavish or any other man, now or in the future. If they knew who she was, what she'd done, they wouldn't want her.

Once she'd settled Greg with a supply of filmies and the station plans, Kama borrowed a medical scanner and headed into the bowels of the station. She dismissed the common areas from her search. If he still waited on the station, Levine would be somewhere not frequently visited and not immediately obvious as a hiding space.

She stopped in front of an access door, knelt to the deck, and pulled equipment from her bag. In a matter of minutes, she'd married the medical scanner to a signal amplifier and patched the Frankenstein assembly to her nanocom. On the tiny display, she indicated her own body readout as noise to be ignored. Satisfied that the device was ready, she stepped through the access door into the bowels of Hell.

Dripping pipe-work and tangled spaghetti-servings of plumbing and wiring lined the close, confining corridor. The rest of the station was humid enough, with two hundred angry men sweating and smelling wherever you turned, but this place was like a rainforest: dimly lit, and with mysterious bubblings and gurglings. She threw nervous glances over her shoulder, not entirely trusting the scanner to alert her if someone approached.

She picked her way down the murky corridor, stepping over exposed pipes and recoiling when condensation dripped from above. A steady stream of drips ran down into a drainage channel in the floor, trickling malodorously away into drainage holes for recycling and making enough noise to more than cover the sound of stealthy footsteps. She swept her jury-rigged scanner in an unsteady arc before her, keeping an eye on the nanocom screen and her stunner ready in her other hand.

Minutes seemed to stretch like hours as she threaded the seamy underbelly of the station checking for human readings. Her shoulders ached, tense from waiting for Levine to pop out of the gloom, armed with some sinister weapon. If he surprised and overpowered her, how long would it be until someone discovered her body? Would McTavish find her?

The long, winding corridor opened out into something else. She wiped sweat from her forehead and peered into the gloom. The pipe work through which she'd been struggling flared out away from the corridor's mouth, which was dominated by a regular network of low dark shapes, illuminated with a bluish glow. A faint sound reached her ears: low, unsteady, somehow alive. She glanced over her shoulder, then moved forward, damp hand shaking on the stunner.

She emerged into the hydroponics bay. Bright grow lights suspended over a plant table blinded her and cast deep shadows on the opposite side of the bay. Gurgling recycling vats lined up like a row of sweating servants, their glass sides streaked with condensation. They waited on a vast crowd of vegetative diners that sprawled across the grooved surface of an endless table, sucking up red hydroponic fluid from the channels like vampires at a blood bank. Her stomach seized, and her pulse pounded in her ears.

Kama unzipped her coveralls a few inches and pulled the collar away from her sticky neck. The air was so heavy it felt like walking in fog. *Jack the Ripper* rose unbidden in her mind, making her shudder. She wrinkled her nose at the cloying, fetid stench, like a huge compost heap, hot with the oppressive warmth of rotting, and then she scrabbled half crouched between pipe runs to the far end of the space.

A feeling of eyes watching grew in her chest. She played her scanner from side to side, but the display filled with static—interference from hydroponic equipment—eroding the last shreds of her confidence. She'd have to search the old-fashioned way, with no early warning system. Her hand twitched on the stunner. A quick dive into her bag produced a work light.

In a capped tank beside her, sickly brown goo swirled, stirred by knife-edged paddles; everything from waste food to raw sewage rendered down into tiny particles. Next to it stood two high-pressure steel sterilization cylinders, heating the sludge to kill bacteria, followed by a maze of pipes that zigzagged through a UV light box and ended in a monstrous covered vat where a dark red bacterial culture broke down the organics in the slop into their component parts.

She shivered. If she were to immerse her hands in that vat, her skin would slough and the muscles beneath melt inside an hour. Hydroponic cultures were fearsome things. But the cylinder lid was tightly sealed. A dozen different small pipes connected from the lid to other containers; she assumed they provided chemicals necessary to stabilize the process. She cautiously shone her light into the dark empty space between the tank and the wall.

More pipes led from the tank through another sterilizer and into an open vat of liquid, five meters across and chest high on her, its contents bright red from the dead bacterial culture, now part of the rich organic soup. Under the grow lights, it looked like a vast bowl of blood-red holiday gelatin waiting for a party of giants to partake.

A regular stream of tiny bubbles barely disturbed the viscous surface, running out from the center like spokes from a wheel. It sounded as though the tank whispered protests against the loss of its hydroponic feast to the parasitic plants. Or did she hear the whisper of voices from some dark corner? She waved her light around the cavernous space, her mouth dry.

Squeezing reluctantly between the tank and a table, she flashed her light into the space behind the tank. Still nothing. She let the light drop down the side of the tank as she squirmed to turn around. The beam picked up a shadow on the inside wall of the tank near the floor. Curious, she crouched for a closer look. Behind the glass, moving in lazy circles like kelp in an ocean current, a severed hand drifted, occasionally thumping against the wall.

Kama dropped the light. It banged on the floor and skittered away, sending freakish shadows leaping and dancing around the walls and tanks. She held perfectly still, willing her heart to slow its frantic pounding. Then she retrieved her light.

A quick search under the plant tables netted a step stool. In the murk behind the tanks, she found a wall rack holding a long cleaning pole with a pitted metal hook at one end. She planted the stool beside the open tank and mounted it.

She eased the pole into the liquid. A metallic clank from behind her made her jump and splatter fluid on the floor. She whirled around and listened. After several seconds, the noise came again, then repeated, gradually picking up a steady rhythm before stopping abruptly. She let out a breath, cursing whatever bad valve or loose fitting caused the clatter.

Taking a firm grip on the slippery pole, she thrust it across the surface, let the tip drop to the bottom of the tank, and slowly pulled it back. She felt resistance for a moment, but then it slid easily. The red glop coating her hands made her skin crawl.

Gritting her teeth, she tried again. Her hands slipped up the rod as it caught on something. Keeping a steady pressure, she brought the end closer until the pole came vertical. She heaved, trying to raise the end off the bottom, but only succeeded in wrenching it free and losing her balance. Catching herself with a quick backward step off the stool, she jumped back another step.

A figure bumped against the clear side of the tank. The thick red fluid blurred the detail, but she still recognized the bloated shape and crinkled flesh of another human being, white as a slug's belly, half-decomposed. Patches of brown hair drifted from the skull where scalp still remained, a great depressed dent marking a huge skull fracture from some heavy blow.

Kama clamped an arm over her mouth and turned away, fighting down the urge to retch. She'd found the missing Mr. Levine.

11

Rafe hoped he'd make it to Leon's ship before he puked. Nothing like zero gravity to make the stomach cartwheel. The last thing he wanted was to ask the hardboiled smelter supervisor for a barf bag. He wondered if they even had such things on the runabout. Probably not. Men who didn't have the intestinal fortitude for free-fall didn't last long on space assignments. He gripped the armrests of his chair and peered out the window.

He glimpsed the huge, blocky, ugly structure of the station, sharp-edged and perfectly defined in the vacuum of space, lit more by internal lights than by the distant sun. A vast cylinder, it spun slowly on its axis to give the illusion of gravity to those within. Other vessels littered the surrounding space; small and medium-sized ships for the most part. The number surprised him. There must be at least a dozen of them just in his field of vision. Beyond them, the silver pricks of distant suns dusted a vast, black canvas.

He couldn't understand why anyone stayed out there. The idea of living where a leaking spacesuit seal, or a tiny overlooked hull puncture killed you seemed insane. Just the thought made his muscles tense. Give him sun on his face, firm soil beneath his feet, and clean sea air to breathe. He'd take his view of Back Bay in Mumbai over this view any day. He wished he were home now, sharing a bottle of cabernet sauvignon with Barb and Ying Ying while watching the sun set over the Arabian Sea.

He spotted a single big cargo ship, its exterior painted in dazzling white with lots of exterior floodlights, hanging some distance away. It looked sleek and expensive, a stark contrast to the grimy and functional look of the rest of the place.

"What's that?" Rafe asked.

Browning glanced where he pointed. "That's Maltraw's ship."

"The cargo hauler?"

"Asteroid belt robber baron. His ship's half shopping mall, half entertainment station, and all expensive."

"Ah. Then why buy from him?"

Browning shifted in his harness. "Sometimes we need things on short notice, like the modulation board for the long range com."

Efficient inventory control measures should prevent shortages even for specialty parts like the modulation board. Rafe began to see why the station's finances ran in the red. On the other hand, perhaps Maltraw offered things cargo drones couldn't, illegal things like drugs.

"Must get pretty boring out here. Doesn't seem like there's much to do besides work. Bit like being in prison, isn't it?"

Browning's head jerked around. "Look, if you want to know about my arrest record, just ask. Don't try to waltz around it like you're pretending to make conversation. I got busted because of a bar fight. A guy came at me with a broken bottle. I gave him a roundhouse punch to the head in self-defense, and he died. His buddies lied and said I started it. I got five years on Bliss. Now you know." He returned his attention to the controls.

"It was just a metaphor," said Rafe, casting about for a way to change the subject. "It must get pretty lonely. I haven't seen many women beyond Kama and Miss Patty. I understand Kama is here on a temporary assignment. What's a woman like Miss Patty doing way out here?"

"Same as the rest of us," Browning replied. "Folks who work the asteroid field are generally folks who don't have other options. Miss Patty worked with Levine when he was at Mars Development Corp a few years back. She probably traded on their friendship to get hired by Galaxy. She's supposed to be our computer tech, although she's useless with them. She has helpdesk on speed dial and uses them for even the simplest things. That's why I applied for the Oasis grant to get some updates done."

"I don't know much about Levine, but he doesn't seem like the type to be out here either. What was his story?"

The man glanced sideways at him. "You're just full of questions."

"If you're hunting bear, it helps to know a little about them."

Browning grunted agreement. "You hear about the tunnel collapse on Mars four or five years ago? Bunch of residents had just moved in, lots of people hurt and killed?"

"I remember. Caused by faulty materials that didn't meet spec. Big scandal, but in the end, no one was held accountable, right?"

"The Mars Dev upper management came out unscathed, but behind the scenes, a lot of middle managers lost their jobs. Levine was one of them." Browning passed a hand over his face. "That's how it always works. The big guys at the top get away with murder, and the little guys take the blame."

Interesting group out here: crooked managers, incompetent computer techs, and convicted murderers. Rafe decided it was time to know them all a little better. When he got to the ship, he'd send a message to Security Partners requesting background checks on the lot.

"Oh, and that woman I saw in the infirmary when I first woke up. Who was she?"

"Medic said you were hallucinating from the speed heal." The man made some small adjustments to the instruments.

"Pink and purple hair? With a big silver box? You sure that doesn't ring a bell?" Rafe asked, beginning to doubt what he'd seen.

"Oh," Browning said, grudgingly. "You must mean Janice Fisher. She ran some supplies over from Maltraw's. Didn't want you dying on us for want of a bandaid."

"Ah," he said, certain that he'd just heard a lie. "So she's Maltraw's delivery girl?"

"She's an independent contractor. She rents space from Maltraw."

"And what is it that she does exactly?" he pressed. The smelter supervisor gave him a pained looked and said nothing.

A light on the pilot console flashed rapidly, and an alarm blared. Had Rafe not been floating against the harness already, he would have jumped out of his seat. Browning seemed unfazed, merely flicking a few switches on the console. The light continued to flash, but the alarm stopped.

"What the hell was that?"

Browning smiled, his expression more than a little condescending. "Proximity alert. See that vessel over there?"

Out Browning's window, Rafe could discern what looked like floating space junk decorated with a hundred tiny red lights defining its outline. Even from a distance, he could see the metal of the structure had been scoured and pitted with space dust, giving the conglomeration of orbs, struts, and propulsion pods a sense of ghostly abandonment.

"That's the munitions bunker. It has a broadcast beacon that sets off our proximity alarm. We're taking a little shortcut through the warning zone to get to the EcoMech ship faster."

"If it has as many explosives on board as you say, isn't it too close to the station?"

"If it was farther away, we'd have those thieves over at R. S. Steele sneaking in to steal our explosives as well as our claims," Browning huffed. "You familiar with shaped charges? How you can determine the direction the blast force will go depending on how you place the explosive?"

Rafe nodded. He was all too familiar with explosives from his time as a soldier in EA's forces.

"Well the bunker is loaded such that the blast force will go that way, blowing out the end section of the bunker." He waved a meaty hand to his left. "And the bulk of the bunker will go the opposite direction, which means the station is in the clear. We have nothing to worry about."

Too many ships, and now a large munitions bunker, all excellent places for Levine to hide. Rafe saw the scope of the search double. They should start with the ships and bunker first. Maybe they'd find Levine before they got to the station. It would be best if the miners weren't on their ships while the search progressed.

"We should have word about the drone intercept by tomorrow morning. Can you call another meeting of the miners so I can give them an update?" Rafe asked, wondering who he could use to search the ships while he talked to the men. Maybe he could borrow some of the EcoMech crew.

Browning nodded and reached for the controls. The EcoMech ship hove into view on Rafe's left, alarmingly close to the path Browning indicated a bunker explosion might send debris. After a quick call to Benson, the EcoMech captain agreed to let them dock. Browning waited in the pilot's seat, adamant that he wasn't leaving the craft. Rafe shuffled out the hatch and dogged it.

"Mr. McTavish." Benson all but saluted, not quite able to keep the concern from his face. "As you asked, I haven't told Mr. Goldman you're aboard yet."

"Thank you, Captain. I have a few messages to send, and I'll stop by my cabin for a change of clothes. I'd like Cookie to make me a large cup of his excellent coffee and bring it to me in the lounge. Then I'll be ready to see Mr. Goldman. I don't want us to be disturbed. And if you can scare one up, I'll need a loaner nanocom."

"Yes, sir. I'll see to it." Benson spun on his heel and hurried away.

Rafe shambled down the corridor to the com station and dropped into a chair before the console, thankful that he hadn't bumped into Leon or Amaya. He sent off a batch of requests, and then pushed up again and struggled to his cabin. The bed looked incredibly inviting, and he'd kill for a shower. Instead, he opened the closet and pulled out his spare business suit, a supple dark blue silk affair custom-tailored for his slim frame. He hesitated, his mind casting back to Kama's remarks when he'd first seen her. What had she said about his clothes?

With a sigh, he replaced the suit and dug his workout clothes from his bag. By the time he'd squirmed into the loose pants and pulled the t-shirt over his head, the bed was shouting his name. He ignored it, decided socks were too much bother, and slid his feet into his workout shoes.

He made it to the lounge door by leaning heavily against the corridor wall. Benson came up behind him and slid Rafe's arm around his shoulders. Together, they crossed the room to one of the armchairs in half the time it would have taken Rafe alone, assuming he'd remained on his feet that long.

Cookie followed them in, bringing a huge mug of coffee, fragrant steam rising in a cloud that made Rafe's mouth water. Even the dim light of the lounge couldn't mask the horror in the cook's expression at the sight of Rafe. The captain pulled a nanocom from his pocket and helped him strap it on his wrist. The man stared at his med bracelet, still cycling through his vitals, looked into Rafe's eyes, and swallowed before nodding his goodbye.

Rafe lifted the mug carefully, using two hands to keep it from wobbling, and sipped the ambrosia. The hot liquid scorched his throat, and the burn doubled when it hit his empty stomach. As the caffeine absorbed into his system, his headache dissipated and calm settled over him. He chided himself for not doing something about his caffeine addiction, but it helped him focus.

Leon stepped through the door of the lounge. He had dark circles under his eyes but wore an immaculate suit. He stalked to Rafe's chair and glowered down.

"You look like hell. Where's Greg?"

Breathe, think, speak, he reminded himself. "Greg's waiting for me on the station. I've come to tell you that Levine isn't on the drone."

"Then what are you doing here? I thought you'd be on the station playing your part as the sacrificial lamb and protecting the poor miners from my mercs." He strode to the bar in the corner of the lounge and poured a large bourbon.

"I've made some interesting discoveries while I've been over there, discoveries that may change your decision to buy the station." He dug in his pocket, withdrew a stick drive, and tossed it on the little table beside his chair. "You can verify my assessment for yourself."

The CEO walked back to a chair opposite, ignored the stick drive, and sat down, throwing one leg over the other. He swirled the bourbon in his glass, stopped to take a gulp, and swirled it again. "Give me the executive summary."

"Levine's been embezzling under Galaxy's nose for the past three years. None of the financials Galaxy provided to EcoMech represent the real situation with the station. That gives EcoMech grounds to renege on the purchase without penalty."

Leon froze for a moment, and then he set the bourbon on a side table. "How can you be sure Levine isn't on the drone? You seemed pretty certain he was. Or was that just a lie to keep the mercs away from the station?"

Rafe sipped his coffee. His brother-in-law hadn't given up any of his paranoia as he'd grown older. "We had airlock video of him getting on the drone. We now believe that video is fake and that Levine's hiding on the station, or perhaps on one of the ships around the station."

"'We'? So the miners know about this?"

"No, they don't." *Watch your mouth. You promised to keep her out of this.* "There's an Oasis technician on the station. She's been able to get me access to the computer system so I could recover this information." He gestured to the stick drive, hoping to divert Leon's attention from his slip of the tongue. "Levine's a damn clever manipulator."

Leon leaped from his chair and paced the plush carpet. He checked his nanocom. "It's seven now. The cruisers can be here by seven tomorrow morning. You have until then to get Greg back here. At eight, my security forces will board the station and begin the search for Levine. Any miners who interfere will be dealt with."

Rafe stopped, coffee halfway to this mouth. Had he heard correctly? "If you go in with brute force, you'll meet resistance, I guarantee it. Why take the risk? Dismiss your mercs and go home, back out of the purchase. You know it never made any sense."

"I want Levine." Leon snatched up his glass, swilled down the remainder of the contents, and went to the bar for a refill.

"Dead? Because that's the probable outcome if you insist on storming the station." Rafe set his coffee on the table by the stick drive and struggled to his feet, putting himself in Leon's path. The CEO stopped inches away. "Tell me what's going on. Why is Levine so important to you that you'll risk lives to get him?"

Leon glared, color rising, alcohol breath washing over Rafe. He waited, willing himself to stay upright despite the trembling in his legs. The man's shoulders slumped.

"When we were kids, McTavish, I beat you to a pulp three times a week. You just took it, never stood up to me, never fought back. I thought you were a coward, especially after Youko—" Leon's eyes took the measure of Rafe's unsteady body. "But when those miners rushed us, you went straight at them like some crazy warrior in a kung-fu vid. I may have misjudged you."

He stepped back and waved a hand toward a chair. "Sit down before you collapse. I'm sorry we left you behind in the airlock. I couldn't risk letting them overrun the yacht, not with Gabe on board."

Rafe lowered himself into his seat. Deep inside, a little thrill of victory kindled. He crossed his legs, folded his hands in his lap, and tried to keep the win off his face.

"I want your assurance that everything I tell you will be in the strictest confidence. You'll tell no one." Leon leaned forward. "That includes my father."

Rafe hated ethical dilemmas, and he stared one in the face. He owed Aaron Goldman an explanation, but he had to do whatever he could to stop bloodshed at the station. He heaved a sigh. "All right."

"I'm being blackmailed, have been for years. And now I think maybe the blackmailer is trying to kill me." The CEO leaned back, watching him.

Blackmail Rafe could believe. Leon's inappropriate behavior with women surfaced in the tabloids almost like clockwork, and his business practices defined sharp. But murder? Had he gone off the deep end?

"Who's the blackmailer?"

His brother-in-law laughed, a bitter, defeated sound. "There's the rub. I've spent a million credits trying to find out. Maybe I should have hired you instead of First Security."

"If you don't know his identity, how do you make the payoffs?"

"I don't. The blackmailer never asks for money. It's always 'favors' of some kind."

Unconsciously, Rafe pulled the little rubber ball from his pocket and rolled it between his palms. "What kinds of favors?"

"Hirings, firings, letters of recommendation, canceling or signing contracts, buying this station. None of them make the least sense. Some of them are probably misdirection meant to muddy the water. I've picked apart the lives of everyone involved and been unable to turn up any connections. I've sidestepped unpleasant consequences, smoothed over ruffled feathers on the EcoMech board when it impacted the bottom line."

"Until the station purchase."

The CEO nodded. "I could see from the beginning that it was a disaster in the making."

"So you arranged to set up my father to take the fall."

"Yes." Leon showed no contrition. "I've suspected for some time that the blackmailer might be trying to force me from power. I had to follow directions without putting myself in jeopardy. But when we boarded the station and things became violent, I began to rethink my conclusions. What if the station purchase was all a ruse to get me out here and kill me?"

"How could your blackmailer know for certain you'd come?" Rafe asked.

"Whoever it is, they know me, know how I operate, where I'll be."

Years of blackmail, while his brother-in-law chased a phantom. His curiosity soared. "What do they have on you?"

Leon's expression hardened. "None of your business."

"Where does Levine fit?" Rafe walked the little ball over and under the fingers of one hand and then the other, thinking that his brother-in-law's theories had some gaping logic holes.

"If he's involved in all this larceny, then maybe he has some connection to the blackmailer, maybe he has information that I can backtrack. Hell, if he can pull off all this fraud, maybe he's my blackmailer." He set his empty glass aside. "I want to question him—before he's handed over to EA. I'm sending the mercs in tomorrow to get him, even if I have to dismantle the station section by section."

Rafe wondered whether Levine would make it to EA custody if the CEO got to him first. "The miners are also quite anxious to have him. And they aren't too thrilled about your security troops."

Leon's eyes glittered. "Then I'll have to make them more receptive. Before the mercs board, I'll announce a million credit bounty for Levine unharmed."

That might keep the man from harm, but Rafe thought it might also cause the miners to turn on one another in pursuit of the bounty. And what if Levine did have an accomplice? How would he or she react? Uneasiness walked with tiny cold feet up his spine. He had to beat Leon to the station manager.

"There's a chance someone worked with him," Rafe said. "If that person fears exposure, your bounty may cause a change of loyalty."

"An accomplice?" Leon rose from his chair to pace again. "You have definite proof?"

"Nothing admissible as evidence," he admitted, "but some things don't add up."

"Not good enough. I'll take my chances finding Levine. I'm not chasing some damn ghost anymore. I've done enough of that." Leon stopped in front of him. "What will you do?"

"I'm going back to hunt for Levine and his accomplice. It's what I promised the miners." Rafe rose, careful to make sure he was steady before letting go of the chair. He looked the man in the eye. "Let's make a deal."

His brother-in-law's expression sharpened, suddenly all business. "What kind of deal?"

"If I identity your blackmailer, you'll shield my father from any fallout on the station purchase." He waited, fighting to keep his face and body relaxed.

Leon's brow furrowed and his mouth thinned. "He treated you like shit. Why do you care what happens to him?"

"Do we have a deal?" he pressed. When the CEO nodded, a sense of heaviness lifted from his shoulders. "Before I go, I'd like the personnel files you got from Galaxy."

Leon tapped a few commands into his nanocom. "Done. It's been sent to your mail."

The CEO swept up the stick drive and marched to the lounge door. He stopped in the doorway without turning around.

"Be careful over there, McTavish," he blurted before disappearing down the hallway.

Rafe accessed the ship's network on his loaner nanocom and downloaded the personnel records supplied by Leon along with replies from his earlier inquiries. He'd have another long, sleepless night ahead of him while he sifted their contents, looking not only for Levine's accomplice, but also connections to Leon's blackmailer.

His running shoes seemed to weigh fifty kilos each, and the lounge grew monstrously large. He made it to the door, but the few meters of corridor to the airlock stretched like an endless ribbon.

Benson came out of nowhere and supported him.

"Is there nothing we can do for you, sir?"

"There is," Rafe said. "Move your vessel to the other side of the station. You're parked next to the munitions bunker."

The captain's eyebrows raised. "Yes, sir."

"And it would be helpful if you could have a small communications problem tomorrow when those security cruisers arrive, something that delays Mr. Goldman from communicating with them for as long as reasonably possible. Don't put yourself in any risk of firing, mind."

"I'll see what I can do, sir."

"Rafe. Call me Rafe."

He staggered into the runabout and dropped into the copilot's seat. Browning took one look at him, blew out his cheeks, and reached over to fasten his harness. As they started the trip back, Rafe kept his attention on the nanocom, reviewing his new data and hoping it would keep his mind off the queasy way the coffee floated in his stomach. He should have asked the captain for a barf bag.

He got half-way through the folder on Janice Fisher before his eyelids felt too heavy to keep open, which shouldn't have been possible in zero gravity where they weighed nothing. Interesting. He'd think about that just for a minute...

☠   ☠   ☠

The bump of the runabout setting down on the deck jolted him awake. Browning helped him stumble out of the craft. The medic and Yuri waited outside the bay with the trolley, and he had to admit that he was glad to see it. As he eased down onto it, a tall, blond miner walked up. He held an icepack over his nose, and blood streaked the front of his shirt.

Browning glowered at him. "Swede! What the hell happened to you?"

The miner waved an arm down the corridor. "We were watching soccer on the vid in the rec hall. Some of the boys backing Juventus got a bit out of hand, and the next thing I knew a fist landed in my face. I hightailed it out of there on the double."

The medic lifted the ice bag and examined the miner's nose. "Not broken, lucky for you." He returned to the trolley and pushed it forward.

The smelter supervisor swore under his breath. "Yuri, see that Mr. McTavish gets back to the infirmary safely."

"Hey, Swede, who's ahead?" Roshal asked. Rafe thought he saw a sneer form under the big miner's ice bag.

"Aerosaurs. Your good friends from Caligo are up by two. Babangida scored both."

The shipping manager looked like he'd bitten into a lemon. "Babangida? Shouldn't even be playing," he mumbled.

Rafe gestured at Roshal's bright yellow shirt, with its detailed black and green reptile logo. "I thought you were an Aerosaurs fan."

The man snorted. "I back winners. Caligo were odds-on for the win, but I had a tip from one of Caligo's physios. He said Babangida was gonna miss the final with a back injury."

"Guess you were tipped wrong, huh?" Rafe said, but got no reply.

The group walked in silence away from the runabout bay.

"Take me to the admin office," he said, thinking of the work ahead sorting through the personnel records and background checks. It seemed an insurmountable task in his present state. Maybe with the trappings of a work environment around him, he could stay awake long enough to get through it all. Fatigue weighed on him like a suit of chainmail.

"No way," the medic replied. "You're headed back to the infirmary for dinner and a good night's sleep."

"I have work to do, and I can't do it in bed," Rafe protested.

"Read my lips. Rest or die."

"I'll sit still, I promise." He saw the stern look on the medic's face. No concessions there. "Can I at least have a table in the infirmary?"

"You do what the medic says," Browning ordered. Shouts, jeers, and banging came from a cross corridor. The smelter supervisor hurried in the direction of the noise, Swede trailing in his wake.

"Just what I need, more customers," muttered the medic. "Yuri, can you get our friend here back to the infirmary? And don't let him near the admin office." He abandoned the trolley and ran down the corridor after the two departing men.

Yuri replaced the medic behind the trolley. It lurched forward, nearly toppling Rafe and sending a lancing pain through his chest. He gasped and clutched at the side of the trolley.

"Sorry about that," the lanky shipping manager said, voice devoid of any apology. "I would have taken you to the EcoMech ship if I'd known you were going."

"It was a spur of the moment idea," he said. If the man thought he could still hold Rafe up for a ten thousand credit transport fee, he was delusional.

"Us guys started talking while you and Ed were gone. You got a point. We've decided to go back to work. If we own the station, we'll be making some money, and if we don't, EcoMech will have to pay our wages. Either way, we win."

They pitched around another corner, passing so close that the trolley clipped the wall. Rafe snatched his hand back from the edge just in time to prevent it being banged, and another pain streaked through his chest, stopping his breath. He began to doubt he'd make it to the infirmary and wondered whether the shipping manager drove his space tug with the same carelessness, God forbid. Maybe he should be glad he hadn't fled the station with Roshal.

Collecting his thoughts while he shifted to stabilize his balance, he considered the man's words. If the miners returned to work, all those ships would scatter into space, and one of them might have Levine aboard. He couldn't let that happen. In the morning, Leon would announce his search. He just needed the miners to hold tight until then.

"There's no doubt in my mind that EcoMech is the rightful owner of the facility, and as the CEO of EcoMech, Mr. Goldman has asked that the miners wait to resume work," he temporized. "That's what I'll recommend."

"What? I thought you said we needed to show Goldman what good workers we are. How we gonna do that sitting on our butts? I bet he's pissed about his welcome, and he's gonna fire us all."

They stopped at a lift. When the door slid open, Roshal drove the trolley in hard, smacking it against the back wall. Rafe's head spun and his vision fuzzed around the edges. He wished the medic were in the lift with him instead of the lunatic currently driving the trolley. Afraid he might topple off and worried about his sudden dizziness, he eased onto his back and braced his feet high up the wall. The blurry edges receded, but the bruises on his back screamed their complaint. This had become the trolley ride from Hell.

"Hey, you don't look so good," the shipping manager commented.

He snatched his feet off the wall and got them braced on the floor of the trolley a split second before the man rattled it out of the lift. The corridor they'd come into looked familiar, and he breathed a sigh of relief. Only a short distance more to the infirmary.

The miners needed their paychecks, and they needed something to do to keep them out of trouble, but he had to keep them close. He hated saying it.

"The best thing for the miners is to follow Mr. Goldman's instructions. Everyone should wait on the station until he sends orders."

"Yeah? Well, the guys aren't gonna go for you flip-flopping like that. They're gonna think you're a turn-coat, that you sold out to EcoMech, especially after you ran off to Goldman's ship. What do think they're gonna do if they decide they can't trust you?"

Rafe felt again the beating delivered by the angry miners and thought about Greg waiting for him in the infirmary. Had he made a terrible mistake keeping the boy on the station?

12

"*Vishnu!*" Kama murmured, and leaped up from the spare infirmary cot.

McTavish lay on his back, knees bent to fit on the trolley, eyes closed, faint sheen of perspiration coating his pasty skin, looking as dead as a living person could look. At her oath, his eyes opened, and he grinned at her despite the pain and fatigue on his face. Roshal watched while she and Greg helped him into bed.

"Didn't we have a chat about you taking care of yourself?" she admonished.

His grin broadened, and he held up his arms. "Look, Ma, no new bruises!"

Roshal ambled over to peer at the dozens of filmies taped to the wall beside Rafe's cot. Kama wished he'd clear out. They couldn't talk with him hanging around, and anyway, he gave her the creeps.

Browning barreled into the infirmary, invectives flying. The medic followed, oblivious to the torrent of swearing.

"God damn idiots! They oughta know better than to start throwing punches," the smelter supervisor grumbled.

Kama didn't know what he was on about, but from the thunderous look on his face, she wasn't about to ask. The last thing she wanted was to hear about more violence on the station. She'd be glad when she got back to Earth and away from all the testosterone-driven aggression. Just give her a little climate-controlled cubbyhole by herself with a connection to the Net, and she'd be happy.

Browning stopped by Warner's cot. "How's he doing?"

"Still sedated," the medic replied. He checked McTavish's med bracelet, then hung another bag of synth blood.

"Ohh!" Kama sassed. "Dinner!"

The medic lifted an eyebrow in disbelief. "No, Miss Patty'll bring dinner directly."

If she makes anything half as good as those scones, we're in for a treat. Then she remembered Levine's body floating in the tank and the tubing leading to the strawberry plants growing on the tables. She put a hand to her mouth and swallowed her rising gorge.

Browning crossed the room to stand beside Roshal, staring at the wall covered in filmies. "What's all this mess?"

"Art project," McTavish said. Kama stifled a laugh.

The shipping manager said, "Looks like the blueprints for the station. What do you need those for?"

"Since my friend won't let me out for a tour, I've gone the virtual route." McTavish waved at the medic. The man shot him a dirty look and pushed the trolley out the door.

Roshal looked at McTavish like he didn't quite believe what he heard, or maybe didn't understand. He sauntered over and stared at the unconscious Warner a moment, and then strolled out without saying goodbye. Kama shivered. The smelter supervisor waved his farewell and followed.

"Don't forget my table!" McTavish called. He waved at the filmie display. "I see you've been busy. Well done."

Greg rushed forward with a stick drive. "Here's the list you asked for. When will we start the search?"

His uncle looked distinctly unhappy. "Mr. Goldman's security forces will be conducting the search tomorrow morning."

Kama sucked in a breath. "I knew he couldn't be trusted. He'll barge in here, guns blazing, and we'll have a riot on our hands."

McTavish gave an ironic laugh. "More like bank account blazing, but we'll still have a riot. He plans to offer a one million credit bounty for Levine if he's brought in alive."

"A million?" Greg breathed. The boy got a starry-eyed look. "Will I be allowed to search?"

Rolling her eyes, Kama realized it wouldn't matter anyway. No one would collect, but a snipe hunt of epic proportions might keep McTavish busy while she tracked alternate prey.

"I think our focus is better placed on finding Levine and his possible accomplice before Leon's forces arrive tomorrow," he said.

She sighed, wishing he'd just keep his mind on Levine while she smoked out the killer and probable partner. She needed to ensure the silence of anyone who'd seen the Oasis contract. She didn't need to dodge 'Mr. Security Partners CEO' every step of the way.

"What about the rendezvous ship? Who owns it?"

He snorted. "No one. It doesn't exist."

Kama chewed her lip. Another false trail. She thought it might be, after finding Levine's body. She'd hoped it would keep him busy longer, though.

"So who do you think it is?" Greg asked. "You must have suspects, right?"

"Yeah," his uncle replied. "About two hundred suspects. But probably it'll be one of the managers who have access to the business system. Miss Patty is my pick. As Levine's assistant, she'd have to be blind, incompetent, or both not to know what was happening. And she could open Levine's quarters. Everyone will have to be checked, of course."

Miss Patty. Kama saw the logic. The station manager wasn't a big man, and for all her age, the assistant seemed strong enough to bludgeon Levine and dump the body in the hydroponic vat. With administrator rights on the system, she had easy access to the Oasis contract. Tension crept up Kama's back and stole into her neck.

"How do you intend to do that in the next twelve hours?" she asked.

"Old-fashioned paperwork," he replied, resignation coloring his voice. "I have the personnel files for all the employees, and I had my company run background checks. If someone just brings me a table, I can get started."

Kama wanted those files. She tamped down her frustration and worked to make her own voice even. "You're dead on your feet. Why don't you have a meal, and then get some rest? I'll start through the files, and if I find anything interesting, I can wake you."

McTavish gazed at her for what seemed an eternity. His eyes looked right through her façade to the devious, scheming corporate spy beneath, she was sure of it. She fought to keep her breathing slow and regular like she'd trained to do. He wouldn't spook her with anymore of those near-psychic blasts of insight. She was prepared this time.

The boyish grin split his face, and charm oozed from his very pores. "I appreciate your offer, but I pledged my help to the miners, even if takes all night."

"Then at least let me help you. Divide and conquer, you know." She smiled, hoping it didn't look as phony as it felt.

"I can help, too, Uncle Rafe. What are we looking for? Arrest records and stuff?"

A gentle tapping rang against the door to the infirmary. Kama went to open it, her hand slipping into the pocket with the stunner. Miss Patty hovered outside, pushing the trolley, which was laden down with covered platters and tableware. The smell of fresh baked bread wafted on the air. *Speak of the devil.* With some trepidation, she beckoned the woman in.

Miss Patty gave McTavish a smile broad enough to crack her pancake makeup and stopped the trolley beside his cot. "Mr. McTavish, I must apologize for the reception you've had. The medic mentioned that you aren't eating very well and asked if I could fix you something special. I know that prepackaged station food is appalling, so I brought you something I hope you'll find more palatable."

His eyes lit up. He inhaled long and hard, vacuuming up the scent of the bread. "Miss Hertzog, your dedication to your company is an inspiration to us all."

"Oh, please, Mr. McTavish, everyone calls me Miss Patty."

The assistant produced two white linen napkins from the pocket of the frilly apron she wore, handed one to Greg, then tucked the other into the collar of McTavish's t-shirt, smoothing it against his chest while she looked into his eyes. He gazed back, smiling like a fool, and struggled to sit straighter.

"Thank you, Miss Patty. Please, call me Rafe. I'm sorry we don't have a proper table. I've asked for one, but sadly, it hasn't arrived." He waved imperiously at his nephew. "Greg, there's a conference room just down the hall. Maybe you could bring some chairs for the ladies?"

Showing enthusiasm equal to his uncle's, the boy scurried from the room. The old woman turned to Kama.

"I'm sorry Ms. Bhatia, I only brought enough for the men, but maybe you want to run to the dining hall while I'm looking after things here?" She began lifting covers on the platters.

Kama seethed. No way would she leave Miss Patty alone to have a confidential chat with this rich playboy. He had the kind of deep pockets to pay well for Oasis' secret, should the woman possess it. And she might be a killer, too. McTavish wasn't in any condition to defend himself from an attack.

"Don't worry about little ol' me. I have a protein bar in my pack." She opened her duffel and scrounged. No protein bars.

"You've brought a veritable feast," McTavish observed. "I'm sure we'll have enough to share."

His radiant smile overwhelmed Miss Patty's scowl. The woman responded by bringing him a spoon and a small bowl of red liquid. Greg banged through the door with two chairs.

"I've brought two kinds of salad dressing," the woman said. "You can decide which you'd prefer."

Salad? Sure enough, on the trolley, a large bowl of greens topped by some kind of protein cubes, tomato slices, and pepper rings rested beside a platter of warm, fragrant French rolls, a carafe of a thick pinkish liquid, and a covered plate. Her stomach seized as the image of the bloated corpse floated across her mind.

Miss Patty spooned up a dab of the liquid and held it before his mouth. "This one's a strawberry vinaigrette."

He opened for her, like an infant being fed by his mother, and she inserted the spoon, a sly smile on her face, her eyes gazing into his. A drop of the dressing slipped down his chin. She dabbed it off with the napkin. His brows drew together, and he hummed his pleasure before smiling back. Kama stared, opened mouthed, at the woman's not-so-subtle seduction techniques. What was she after?

Bowls were swapped, and the sampling ritual repeated with something the woman claimed was buttermilk dressing. McTavish moaned like he experienced an orgasm, and Miss Patty glowed.

Kama ground her teeth. Wasn't he laying it on a little thick? Sure the woman would be more cooperative if she thought she'd made a friend, but really! That Miss Patty couldn't see through his exaggerated charm insulted women everywhere.

Greg hung over her shoulder, oblivious to his uncle, eyes only for the spread on the trolley. Unable to resist, the boy grabbed a plate and reached for the salad bowl.

"Greg, manners," warned McTavish. "Miss Patty, you'll join us, won't you?"

"Oh, no, I had my dinner hours ago. This is just for you." She smiled and fluttered her eyelashes.

McTavish beamed at the woman, and then gestured for Kama to help herself.

She gagged and covered it with a cough.

"I'm, uh, kind of on a diet." She hadn't seen any wheat growing in hydroponics, had she? "I'll just have one of these rolls. They smell fantastic."

The old assistant glared at her with disapproval. "You really need a more balanced meal to stay healthy. I'm sure they'll have something you'd like in the dining hall."

Kama snatched a roll and backpedaled from the trolley, "I had something earlier."

"So *that's* where you were all that time," the boy said, reproach in his expression.

McTavish's hungry gaze swiveled from the repast to her like a compass to a lodestone. But the pull of the food seemed too much for him, and he turned his attention back.

Miss Patty buttered two rolls, put them on a plate next to a heaping mound of salad awash in the buttermilk dressing, and handed it to him. He dug in with gusto, making mewling sounds as he forked it down.

"Nothing like real, fresh-baked bread," he said, gesturing with a half-eaten roll. "Yours?"

Miss Patty lifted her brows. "Why yes, I make them the old-fashioned way, from scratch. I'm surprised you could tell."

"Uncle Rafe's a gourmet cook," said Greg, spewing crumbs.

Well, if he's used to eating raw oysters and dead snails, maybe he won't mind where the nitrogen came from to grow the salad. Kama's whole body twitched as she thought about how much Levine's decomposing body looked like a slug.

"And what a delightful salad. I thought hydroponics mostly produced protein bases, and algae for oxygen replenishment," he said. He'd turned the charm up at least a hundred megawatts. Kama expected Miss Patty to ignite any minute.

"We started growing our own vegetables because it costs so much to get them delivered. I look after them between shifts, because I enjoy cooking and have a bit of a green thumb. It's messy, though—I'm always getting that awful red hydroponic fluid on my clothes, but it washes right out." She looked at Kama's stained coveralls and giggled, although Kama couldn't imagine why, then hitched herself up to sit on the edge of McTavish's cot.

"Where did you learn to cook?" he asked, staring with rapture into the old woman's face.

Kama dragged her eyes from the nauseating spectacle and feigned interest in the filmies that papered the wall. She whistled a little tune, trying to drown the sounds of the crisp lettuce and peppers snapping between his teeth. Would Levine's bones still snap, or had they turned spongy by now? No, she wouldn't think about it.

"Oh, I'm self-taught mostly. My mother passed away when I was quite young, and I had to cook for my father. I used to help him run his business," she said.

"Really. You're a woman of many talents," he said, placing one hand on top of hers where it rested on the covers. "I imagine you brought great comfort to Mr. Levine."

Miss Patty jerked, the smile freezing on her face, and Kama covered a snicker. Had he meant to imply she was sleeping with her boss? He'd been doing so well, using the same psychological ploys that he'd used on the miners in the storage bay meeting. A few more gaffes like that and he'd get nothing from the woman.

"As assistant to the manager, I always felt it was my job to see that Mr. Levine had decent food to eat. How could he do his job if he didn't get proper nutrition?"

"I hope Mr. Levine realized what a gem you are, Miss Patty. I couldn't get along for a day without Barb, my executive assistant. Why, she practically runs my company. It's always the assistants who do the really important work—making sure monthly reports get done on time, collating production numbers, making sure the employees get their vacation days."

Kama wondered if Barb was a figment of his imagination. No, she was probably some hot babe in a tight skirt and low-cut blouse who sat at a desk in his outer office buffing her nails. Corporate types always seemed to keep a squeeze handy around the office. It disgusted her.

Miss Patty fluttered like a moth in torchlight. "Mr. Levine used to write the monthly reports. I only converted the daily totals to monthly figures, and then he'd take it from there. My duties are more along the lines of supply chain. You know, keeping track of provisions, notifying Mr. Levine if we're low on anything. That kind of thing." Then as though she'd downplayed her contribution too much, she added, "Of course, I did all those other things when I worked in my father's business. My father was disabled, and I shouldered responsibility for much of the business operations."

"Why, you are a wonder, Miss Patty. Did he suffer from ice flu complications?" he asked.

"No, he was injured in an explosion at a construction site. He owned a demolitions company and passed away just before the flu hit." She heaved a sigh and made cow eyes at him.

"You must have been a great help when the miners decided to buy the station," Kama interjected. "Since you'd know about contracts and whatnot."

McTavish swiveled her direction, as though he'd forgotten her. She batted her eyelashes at him, and he blinked, surprised, which gave her an idea. Maybe she could throw him off his game sufficiently that he wouldn't wheedle a confession from Miss Patty.

"What kind of a question is that?" the assistant asked, her voice shrill.

"Kama just meant that with your experience running a business, you must have been an invaluable advisor," McTavish soothed, drawing the woman's attention back to him. "I'm sure Mr. Levine tricked you the same as he tricked the men. He had quite the knack for juggling the books."

Kama glared at him, but he didn't notice, still engrossed with the remains of his salad. Miss Patty went to the trolley and poured nectar into a glass, which she gave to McTavish before perching again on the edge of his bed, hip to hip with him. Greg, who'd inhaled his salad and rolls, fetched nectar for himself and Kama. She took a cautious sip. It tasted heavenly, like thick peach lemonade.

McTavish took a swig of his drink, and more moaning sounds issued from him. "Lovely, Miss Patty, just lovely."

The woman lifted the corner of his napkin and wiped a skiff of lemonade from his upper lip. He grinned, placed a friendly hand on her shoulder, and she leaned closer.

Kama growled to herself. This had to stop. She couldn't risk Miss Patty spilling the beans. She casually reached for her zipper and slipped it down several inches. *Let's see McTavish stay on track now.*

"It's warm in here, isn't it?" she said, trailing a hand slowly down her throat and onto her exposed chest. McTavish glanced her way, then did a double-take. She arched her back and put a hand on her thigh, while drawing in a deep breath that lifted her breasts against the fabric of her coveralls. His eyes widened infinitesimally, and a knowing little smile played around his mouth.

"You know, I'm not very familiar with the station or the mining business," he said, returning his attention to Miss Patty and infuriating Kama. "Your help could be just what we need to figure out this mess. Mr. Goldman and I would certainly appreciate your advice."

"Yes, but would they follow it if you bothered to give it?" Kama said, switching tactics. "You know these corporate types. They think they know everything."

Miss Patty drew back and put a hand to her mouth. "Mr. Goldman? I heard a rumor that he won't allow anyone to return to work. Is that true?"

"Well," he replied, fumbling for words, "he's, uh, working on some insurance requirements that need to be in place before work starts again."

Ah, ha! Another little glitch in his patter. Kama considered her next move with growing enthusiasm. This could be fun.

Worry caused a cascade of creases in the old woman's forehead. "The men say he intends to fire everyone. Does he?"

"Men always get so macho over incidents like this," Kama commented. "He'll have to fire everyone to save face."

Miss Patty half-turned toward her, mouth open, and Kama mentally credited herself with a point. But McTavish was quick. He took the woman's hand in his. He had a sweet, puppy-dog look on his face, nearly irresistible even for a hardened liar and manipulator like Kama.

"Don't worry yourself unnecessarily. Mr. Goldman's a smart businessman. He'll want the station to operate efficiently through the transition in ownership, so, no, I don't think he has any intention of firing anyone."

The woman nearly swooned. Kama felt Miss Patty slipping through her fingers. He could charm a hungry lioness into rolling on its back for him. She prepared another salvo.

"I wouldn't be so sure, Miss Patty. You know how untrustworthy powerful men can be," she said, putting heart-felt concern in her words. When he looked her way, she reached up and pulled the band from her hair, then tossed her head to shake it loose. Her thick hair tumbled around her shoulders. His hand fell from Miss Patty's, and he rubbed it along his thigh.

"I don't have a lot of options, do I?" the assistant whined, alternately looking from one to the other with a frown while they ignored her. "I can't afford to be unemployed, and it wouldn't be easy to find another position."

Miss Patty touched his hand, and his eyes tracked back to her. "I can't very well ask Mr. Levine for a job recommendation, now can I? Would you help me, Mr. McTavish? You've been so wonderful about volunteering to help the men."

He sipped his drink and licked nectar from his lips, his gaze sneaking over to Kama before settling on the assistant. "You know how grateful Mr. Goldman and I would be for any help you could give us, don't you, Miss Patty?"

"Have you met Mr. Goldman?" Kama asked, carefully modulating the disbelief in her voice. "He doesn't seem like a very appreciative boss. He sounds a bit like mine. 'Kama do this, Kama watch that, Kama wait here.'"

Kama lifted an eyebrow and gave him a haughty look. He smothered a laugh. Yes, he knew who she was talking about, and he'd taken it as a joke. *Joke my ass.* She crossed one leg over the other and pumped her foot up and down, considering her next move. He ran a hand through his hair and flashed his own cheeky smile her direction. The room seemed warmer, and she sipped her drink, trying to cool off while he struggled with his composure.

"I met him just for a moment when he first boarded," Miss Patty replied. "He didn't seem very friendly."

Too late, McTavish jerked his head around to the assistant and seemed unable to recover his train of thought. A finger traced around the rim of his glass.

"I've worked these kinds of cases before," he said, and cleared his throat, his brows drawing down in concentration. "A highly placed supervisor abuses his privileges, his relationship with those he manages, and when he's caught in an act of fraud, those beneath him are afraid to come forward, concerned that they'll become embroiled in his crimes."

Color drained from Miss Patty's cheeks. He didn't seem to notice, his gaze roaming back to Kama, who responded by smiling sweetly. He rattled on, like he delivered a well-rehearsed lecture to a group of students at a police academy.

"In complicated cases like this one, the employees who assist the investigation are granted immunity from prosecution. Law enforcement is more focused on landing the big fish and not on those who may have inadvertently helped the criminal."

"Is that right?" Kama rose, determined to wrest the last vestiges of control from him. She could taste her victory, and it was sweet. She set her glass on the trolley and stood next to a trembling Miss Patty. She lifted her chin, threw her shoulders back, and rested a hand on one hip. "Because by all the news accounts I've seen, whistleblowers are treated quite badly."

It must be a trick of the light. His eyes were larger and sparkled, and his color seemed markedly improved. *Such beautiful eyes.* He hadn't realized his defeat yet. That must be why he looked so pleased.

Miss Patty slid off the bed, unnoticed, taking his empty dishes with her. The ridiculous napkin looked like a bib on a small child, and he was no kid. His muscular torso stretched the fabric of his t-shirt, which arrowed down to a slender waist and flat stomach. No, not a kid at all.

Kama slid the napkin off his chest, her fingertips brushing against him. He plucked it out of her hand and wiped a crumb from the corner of her mouth, that queer little smile playing across his lips again. She breathed a little faster.

"Mr. Levine was always a wonderful manager to work for. So kind and caring with everyone." The old woman's voice climbed in pitch. She clattered the dishes against the trolley. "I don't know anything at all about any fraud."

A flicker of worry crossed his face a moment later, and he glanced the woman's direction, puzzled, like he'd missed something.

"Wow, Miss Patty," Greg said. "That looks great! What is it?"

"It's molten lava cake." The assistant handed a plate with a small, rounded chocolate mass on it to the boy. "I'm afraid I only prepared two."

Chocolate. Kama's lips parted as Miss Patty passed the second cake by her and into McTavish's hands. No, she had a job to do. Now wasn't the time to be distracted by food. Her stomach rumbled. *Traitor.*

He may have failed to convince the woman to confide in him tonight, but she needed to ensure he didn't' get a second chance. He *had* failed, hadn't he? What made her think that? She couldn't remember. Regardless, she should get the assistant off the station and into Samir's hands. Her boss would soon find out what the woman knew.

"Have you thought about applying to Oasis?" Kama asked. McTavish cut into the gooey cake, and dark chocolate syrup oozed out. He smiled, first at the cake, and then at her, his eyebrows waggling. She grabbed the edge of the bed, resisting the urge to drag her finger through the syrup.

"Oasis would never take me," Miss Patty replied. "I'm not a computer programmer."

McTavish plunged the spoon in again, slicing off a bite of cake and popping it in his mouth. He groaned and licked his lips, smearing them with chocolate. Kama turned her back on him, but that put Greg, spooning up his own luscious dessert, squarely in her line of vision. From behind her, she heard McTavish smacking his lips. A faint keening sigh escaped her.

"We hire more than computer programmers. We have lots of different positions in the company, and I'm sure we'd have one just right for you," she lied, unable to take her eyes from the boy's fast disappearing dessert. There must be something wrong with the climate control. The room seemed unusually warm.

Miss Patty stopped fussing with the platters on the trolley. "You'd recommend me?"

"Of course. We working women need to stick together, and Oasis is a wonderful place to be." She rejoiced, but hid it with a serious expression. She had the old biddy right where she wanted her. "I can even offer you a free ride."

Fingertips touched her forearm, and she turned. McTavish waved the plate of half-eaten cake at her, and her mouth watered.

"Want to share?" he asked.

Without waiting for her reply, he scooped up an enormous spoonful of cake and aimed it for her mouth. She leaned forward and crammed it all in, sucking hard on the spoon to get every drip of syrup off as he pulled it out. That's when she noticed the crafty look in his eyes and froze.

"Does Oasis still screen all its prospective employees with psychological tests and biometrics interviews?" he asked, all innocence.

Kama choked on the cake.

"Biometrics interviews?" Miss Patty asked. "What are those?"

"They hook you up to a med scanner while they do the employment interview," he said, giving Kama an impudent smile. "It works like an old-fashioned lie detector test, only it's much harder to fool."

A platter crashed to the floor.

13

What the hell happened?

Practiced as he was at deflecting the unwanted attentions of women, he'd failed to prevent Kama from beating—no, *seducing*—her way through his defenses and scrambling his brain. He'd lost Miss Patty when, by now, she should have been gushing her confession. Why was Kama so intent on getting the woman away to Oasis?

Rafe swung his feet off the cot and stood in front of the filmies. For the first time since his arrival, he felt almost human. He still had plenty of aches and pains, but a trickle of energy coursed through him. He didn't know whether to credit the coffee, the nap, the excellent meal, or that last bag of blood hanging empty on the pole. Or maybe it was Kama. *Damn, she was hot when she wanted to be.*

He scratched the rapidly growing stubble on his chin and peered at the blueprints, then located the showers—right next door to the infirmary. It looked like a long night ahead. A shower would help him stay awake; maybe a cold shower. He unhooked his IV and shuffled to the door.

Then he pulled up and shuffled back. Still unconscious, Warner lay on his cot, breathing slowly. Rafe took a couple of pillows and stuffed them under the blankets of his own cot, mimicking the shape of a sleeping body. He dimmed the lights, hoping his ruse would give him time to complete his shower before Kama found out what he was doing. He was sure she'd be back, even though he didn't understand why she hung around.

The hallway was clear. Keeping a steadying hand on the wall, he crept to the shower room door.

Inside, he found soap, shampoo, towels, and a packet of depilatory cream. Apparently, injured miners weren't trusted with real razors. He stripped out of his workout clothes and unstrapped the nanocom from his wrist, finding exactly how many muscles still didn't extend to their full range, but feeling stronger and much less sore than earlier in the day.

He turned on the shower and smeared the cream on his face while the water warmed up. Then he stepped into the hot water and let it stream down over his aching body. The bruises made unattractive splotches of purple and green across rigid muscles, which gradually relaxed under the gentle, steaming massage of the shower. He groaned in satisfaction as the water worked its magic.

Judging that he'd left the cream on long enough, he ducked his head under the water and lathered the shampoo into his hair. He winced when he touched the lump from the blow that had mercifully knocked him unconscious in the docking bay. Wriggling his toes in the puddle of water forming at the drain, he slapped his feet down, delighted with the splash.

"All right, Mr. Kelly, time to get out of the rain before you fall down and hurt yourself again."

He whirled to face Kama, then just as quickly turned away. "How long have you been there?" he asked, face burning.

"Long enough," she replied. "But I promise I'll turn my back while you get dressed if you do it sitting down." From behind him, he heard the rattle of a stool sliding across the floor and the thump of a towel landing on top. When he looked, she faced the door. At light speed, he snatched the towel, made a bad job of drying his legs, and pulled on his pants.

"Who's Mr. Kelly?" he asked.

"Not a fan of old movies, I see," she chuckled as she advanced on him. She'd zipped her coveralls firmly against her neck again and replaced her hair tie. She still looked gorgeous. He sucked in a breath through his teeth, not at all confident he could keep his mind on business.

"Gene Kelly was a famous dancer, oh, a hundred or so years ago. He sang a song and tap-danced on a rainy street. And he was better dressed than you."

She pushed him down on the stool, grabbed a towel, and rubbed his hair. He winced when she hit the tender place on his skull.

"Sorry," she apologized.

"I'm not completely helpless, you know," he grumbled, pretending he didn't enjoy her attentions as she started again, more gently. The scent of lavender wafted off her, and he drank it in, a twinge of desire purring to life in him. She finished with his hair and stroked the towel down his back and arms as gently as if handling a baby. His body responded while his brain screamed about how inappropriate the timing was. *Focus.*

"The pillows didn't fool you?"

"You have more lumps."

He laughed openly, giving up any hope of resistance to her charms. "Too true, I'm afraid."

She was reaching for his t-shirt when a loud clatter in the infirmary next door stopped her. She opened the shower room door, and then a thunderous roar shook the walls and knocked her against the doorframe. Smoke rolled over her in a hot, acrid cloud.

The blast wave, damped by the distance, was still enough to rattle Rafe's stool. *Plastic explosive,* his ear told him, not an accident. A station alarm blared out, raucous and insistent. He snatched up the t-shirt from a puddle on the floor, pulled it over his head, and made for the door.

The corridor outside was filthy with smoke and dust, and the infirmary door hung halfway off its hinges. From the infirmary came the crackling and snapping of flame and the clatter of falling debris. Kama sat on the floor, one hand pressed against her head, a bloody smear on her cheek. Rafe crouched next to her, paying no heed to the stab of pain in his ribs. He ran his fingertips over her scalp, searching for the spongy depression of a fracture but finding none.

She levered herself up as shouts of alarm and the sound of running feet approached. Browning rounded the corner, closely followed by Roshal and half a dozen miners. They lurched to a tumbling halt as they saw Rafe and Kama, then the smoke bursting from the ruined infirmary.

"What the hell's going on?" Browning roared.

"Bomb!" Rafe shouted back. "Someone blew up the infirmary!"

"Fucking EcoMech!" someone yelled. "Bastards are attacking us again!"

Browning approached the ruined door, one hand shielding his face from the heat beyond. "Everybody out!" he shouted. "There's a hull breach in there, and this bulkhead's compromised! We need to seal off this corridor!"

"Wait!" Rafe shouted. "Warner's still in there! He could be alive!"

Browning yelled to the men. "We have to seal this corridor! That whole outer wall could collapse!"

Rafe shook his head and lunged forward. "Be ready to seal the corridor when I come out! I need two minutes!"

Browning stared at him in disbelief. "You're crazy!" the big supervisor shouted. "You can barely walk!"

Rafe turned and caught Kama's eye. "Look after Greg for me," he said, then plunged into the smoke and fire.

He held the front of his t-shirt over his mouth, and crouched low to avoid the smoke. The heat was stifling, and he felt the cooling water leaching out of the shirt with each passing second. It was dark in the infirmary—the emergency lights must have been blown out—and he shuffled his way forward by dim firelight. The back of the room was still in flames, a roiling orange mass thrusting out from a blanketing cloud of smoke.

His foot caught on something soft and giving. He tumbled forward, his knee smacking painfully into the deck, and he took an unguarded breath. Coughs wracked his body as he took in a lungful of smoke, each hacking convulsion grinding at his injured ribs. His vision swam, and he grabbed a fistful of drying fabric to breathe through. In his head, he heard the seconds ticking away—Browning wouldn't give him more than the two minutes.

Rafe reached down to disentangle his foot, and his hand met wetness and the horrible sponginess of meat. He found himself clutching the ragged end of a severed leg. He retched and flung it aside, swallowing the foul taste of vomit, then turned to press on. Warner was a black man, and that—thing—was white.

The adrenaline that had thrown him through the door drained away. He was going to die, an idiot to the last. His hands trembled, the pain in his ribs increasing. He clutched at his chest, letting the shirt fall away from his mouth. Somewhere ahead, in the darkness, a piercing whistle rang out, the whistle of air escaping into space.

The heat of the fire rushed over him as he tried vainly to choke down each agonizing cough. His vision blurred, and he wondered if it would be the searing fire or the icy cold of space that killed him. Suddenly, he was back in the nightmare, the hideous, never-forgotten scene of Youko's death, in another endless, blood-soaked room, lashed by the flames of demons and his father's scorn, his whole being reduced to a single, taunting thought—you aren't good enough; you should have done more.

He crawled, his hands encountering scorching metal, ashes, and fragments of shattered glass and plastic. He swept them aside, along with another gobbet of dismembered flesh—still not Warner's. He kept the layout of the infirmary in his mind. The cot hadn't been more than a few feet away. There it was! He ignored the burning in his fingertip as he touched the scorching metal frame. The blanket was not on fire, and Rafe grabbed the edge and flung it up over the top of the cot, where Warner's insensate shape still lay.

He seized the wounded man by leg and arm, and hauled him up onto his shoulders, staggering underneath the weight. He hefted Warner's uncooperative bulk and took a first, shuffling step away from the fire. Wind tugged at Rafe's clothes as the whistle of the widening hull breach dropped rapidly in pitch. A low, ominous groaning of fatigued metal reverberated over the whistle. One pace at a time, one foot in front of the other, he forced himself toward the door.

"There he is!" someone cried, and Warner's weight slid from his shoulders. Hands grabbed his arms and legs, and a swarm of men hoisted him long enough to run through a rapidly closing bulkhead door. They set him with care on the deck, and Kama speared between them to crouch by his side. He coughed and rubbed his stinging eyes, insanely overjoyed to see her.

"I got him," he said, grinning.

"*Moorhk*," she muttered. Her smoldering eyes raked over him before settling on his med bracelet.

His grin broadened. She cared. A thrill raced through him. He struggled to get his feet under himself. A dozen miners' hands reached down and pulled him upright. They slapped his back or squeezed his shoulder. Gone was the sullen hostility. They looked on him with respect and admiration.

"Let's go! Let's go!" Browning shouted, pushing through the growing crowd of miners. "We've got a hull breach. Man your stations! Yuri, get your tug and bring a replacement hull section from storage. Where's my welding crew? Suit up! The rest of you start closing bulkheads on both sides of this section and on the floor above. Move!"

Browning and Roshal led the miners away at a trot. The medic crouched over Warner, who lay on a blanket. Swede and another miner looked on. The smell of burnt flesh hit his nostrils.

"How is he?" Kama asked, looking away from the hideous melted husk on the deck.

"Burned pretty bad." He waved at Swede. "Hold the packs in place. Dammit, I can't work like this! I need another med kit! He's lucky to be sedated. But he'll come around in about an hour, and I haven't got anything to give him. These burns are more severe than I'm qualified to deal with."

"Can we ship him to the jump gate hospital?" Kama said.

The medic shook his head. "He'd die long before he got there."

"Do what you can for him until we get back," Rafe told the medic. He pulled Kama aside. "You said you could fly a runabout?"

"Yes," she said.

He detected hesitation in her voice, but he saw little choice. Warner needed help, and he wasn't keeping Greg on the station another minute. He ought to get Kama off, too.

"Where do you want to go?"

"Maltraw's. Warner needs help, and I want Greg out of here now," he said, walking away.

She jogged to catch up to him. "I'll get Greg and meet you at the runabout bay."

She ducked into the shower room, emerged with her duffel, and sprinted away. Rafe shuffled his way through the dimly lit station, warning lights still strobing at every intersection until he reached the runabout bay. Within a minute, Kama and Greg joined him, out of breath. Greg looked pale and frightened, but at least he was unharmed. A little tension released in Rafe's shoulders. Together, they crossed the deck and climbed into one of the craft.

Kama stowed her duffel in a storage bin and took the pilot seat. By the time Rafe had his harness buckled, she was looking over the controls. She licked her thumb and scrubbed it over a couple of the control labels, cleaning grime from them. They didn't seem any more readable for her efforts. She keyed a switch, then another, with no result.

"You do have a pilot's license, right?" he asked.

Kama pressed a button beneath a vid screen, which filled first with a splashy logo, and then with a menu. She touched one of the options. He thought it looked suspiciously like the option for an instruction manual.

"This isn't the model I usually fly." She glanced his direction. "Don't worry, I'll get us there."

Dense text filled the screen. She flipped to the next page, flipped again. Pages rushed by in a blur while she squinted at them. When she reached the end, she sat back, took a deep breath, and placed her hands on the console. He swore he heard her muttering a checklist as though reading it while she brought the runabout to life. With the final press of a button, she opened the bay doors and coaxed the craft out. After a bump and a screech of metal, they cleared the station.

"Sorry," she murmured.

"And what model do you usually fly?" he asked, his stomach already starting to roll as they became weightless.

"I have several hundred hours at the controls of an X311."

She goosed the thrusters, and Rafe was pressed back into his seat. "I don't think I recognize that one. Who makes it?"

From the seat behind him, Greg hooted. "Uncle Rafe, don't you play *Galaxy at War*? The X311 is what Henderson uses to transport his squad for planetary missions."

14

Kama's hands shook at the controls. Piloting the runabout didn't worry her; she'd done hundreds of hours in various simulators, and she'd just memorized the flight manual for this one. What made her hands shake was the close call in the infirmary. Someone wanted McTavish dead. She had to convince him to leave the station.

"I can take the medical supplies back. You and Greg should wait at Maltraw's and get Goldman to pick you up there."

"I'll contact Captain Benson to pick up Greg, but I'm going back to the station." McTavish looked decidedly green and clutched the armrests. "You should go with Greg. Or stay at Maltraw's for the time being."

"That blast was meant for you. You can't take the risk. Next time, you might not be so lucky."

"Next time Levine comes at me, I'll be better prepared."

Kama stared at him. "Levine? You don't think you were attacked because you represent the big corporation about to throw the miners off their station?"

"No one on the station is more rabidly anti-corporate than you, and if you haven't seen the need to blow me to Kingdom come, why would they?"

"Be serious," she said. In her mind, she saw him emerging from the smoke of the infirmary, Warner on his back, and shuddered. All the management types she'd met would have run the opposite direction. He was a genuine hero. Or maybe just insane.

"Levine as the bomber is the only choice that makes sense." McTavish ran the back of his hand over his mouth. "Maybe I can draw him out before Leon's men board."

"Make yourself a target? Are you crazy?"

He wouldn't know who to look for, but it sure wouldn't be Levine. She had to get him off the station. And if she did, it would make her search for the killer that much easier.

While they crossed to the cargo hauler, McTavish radioed to the EcoMech ship. Over Greg's protests, he arranged for his pick up at Maltraw's.

Viewed from the runabout on approach, Maltraw's ship was a standard, three-for-a-credit cargo hauler. The owner had put lights and a flashy white exterior on it, but it was only a skin deep cosmetic treatment. That skin was pitted and holed, marked with the craters of interstellar dust, little more than another floating warehouse underneath.

Kama turned on auto-dock for their approach, hoping to avoid a repeat of their clumsy departure from the station.

Once they were secure, the airlock hissed open, and bright, pinkish light poured out around them. She hauled open a pair of doors, and led them through into a cargo bay, jam-packed with goods. The place sold everything she'd expected—clothes, books, games, chocolate, liquor, pornography.

A man approached. He carried himself with a swagger, a gold ring set with diamonds on his right hand, and a thick gold chain around his left wrist. One ear was bedecked with half-a-dozen ruby studs. Costume jewelry quality, like the skin-deep glitz of the ship.

"Name's Maltraw, Jay Maltraw. Welcome aboard. What can I do for you folks this evening?" He extended a hand.

"Captain Maltraw." McTavish took the hand, flinching under the grip. "Rafe McTavish."

Maltraw glanced at Kama and Greg, and then raked his gaze over McTavish's grimy, blood-encrusted clothes. He sniffed. "The little missus burn dinner?"

Kama didn't see the humor, but a hint of a smile played over McTavish's face. "I'd like to see Janice Fisher."

"Well and wouldn't I love to show her to you, but she's off shift now. Maybe you want to do some shopping and have a bit of refreshment while you wait?" A pair of crafty hazel eyes looked Kama up and down.

She wanted to spit in his face.

"We're in a bit of a hurry," McTavish said. "If you could please ask her to see me immediately, I'd make it worth your while."

"I see." Maltraw narrowed his eyes. One bejeweled finger tapped his lips. "I suppose I could ask her to start early, but her fee will of course be somewhat higher. And if it's a threesome you want, that'll be triple."

"Shiva take you," Kama muttered.

McTavish plastered that charming smile on his face and said, "A chat will do. Be a good fellow and call Ms. Fisher."

"A chat you say? That'll be one hundred credits."

Kama goggled. "A hundred credits to talk?"

"I'll need some other items as well. Let's say I authorize five thousand credits, and you can charge up against that," McTavish said. "Can you call Ms. Fisher now?"

Maltraw registered surprise, then scrambled for his order pad. "Yes, sir, Mr. McTavish. Happy to do business with you. If you'll just enter your account information there and a thumb print."

The merchant tapped a few times on his nanocom, and they all waited for Janice. When she arrived, she seemed to writhe instead of walk between the rows of goods. Fierce turquoise eyes gave McTavish a guarded look, while she tossed masses of blue hair with streaks of neon green and orange back from her shoulders. Her musky scent arrived before her. Greg's eyes widened, and his mouth popped open.

"What can I do for you, stranger?"

"Jay, if you wouldn't mind, I'd like to speak with Ms. Fisher alone." McTavish waited for Maltraw to disappear into his inventory before continuing. "Dr. Fisher, Rafe McTavish. We've had a rather bad accident on the station. One of the miners has been severely burned and all the medical supplies on the station destroyed. The medic is overwhelmed. We need your expertise."

All the sexual posturing dropped away, and Janice crossed her arms. "I'm not a doctor. I'm sorry you've wasted your trip. Jay has some medical supplies, but that's the extent of what we can do for you."

"You *were* a doctor, researching tissue regeneration *in situ* before you ran afoul of the pharmaceutical companies. Given that I'm not a corpse, I believe you've retained your skills."

Janice scowled at him. "Doesn't matter who I used to be. I'm not risking prison for practicing medicine without a license, even out here in the cesspit of the solar system."

"I appreciate your situation, but a man's life is at stake. To compensate you, I've opened a generous tab with Jay, on which I'll expect to see billing for your 'standard services' for both the treatment you provided me and for Warner, the injured miner. His condition is grave; we need to hurry."

Fisher pursed absurdly pouty lips. "You don't take 'no' for an answer do you, Mr. McTavish?"

"I'll say," Kama whispered.

McTavish grinned. "Rafe. Call me Rafe."

Janice trotted off to gather her medical kit, and McTavish wandered the aisles pulling out clothing, a coffee maker, and a bag of gourmet coffee. Kama added half a dozen ration bars to his pile. McTavish raised an eyebrow.

"I'm a little short. You don't mind getting those, do you?" she asked.

Maltraw rang up the purchases. A moment later, Janice arrived with her silver trunk.

"Look, McTavish, you shouldn't go back," Kama said, hoping he might be reasonable this time. "It's too dangerous."

"Just as dangerous for you," he replied. "When Leon's security forces board in the morning, things could go sideways in a hurry. And there's a killer loose on the station. It's not safe there. Wait with Greg on the EcoMech ship."

She grabbed his arm and faced him, toe to toe.

"No one's trying to kill me," she said, angered by the implication that she couldn't take care of herself and determined to change his mind.

"Do we know that for a fact?" he said, voice rising. "Perhaps they were after two birds with one stone."

"Get a room, for God's sake," Janice commented, halting their argument. They both stared at her, struck dumb. McTavish recovered first.

"Let me help you with that, doctor."

He grabbed Janice's trunk and dragged it toward the airlock. Kama watched him go, fuming. What was she going to do now? Maybe she could ask the doctor for something to drug him with. Yeah, that should do the trick. Then she'd tie him up with a fancy ribbon and ship him back to Goldman before he got himself killed. She tramped into the airlock behind them.

☠ ☠ ☠

Back on the station, they found the medic set up in a conference room, Warner stretched out on the table. Fisher walked over to her patient, checked his stats on his wrist monitor, and swept her eyes over him.

"Holy Mother of God," she breathed. "I can stabilize him, but then he'll need transport to the jump gate station hospital facilities, or maybe even to a med station in Earth orbit. It doesn't look good."

"How soon can you ship him out?" McTavish asked.

Kama held her breath. Somewhere on the station, a killer lurked, a killer with Oasis' secret. Running Warner to the jump gate would be a perfect way to escape.

"Can't say for certain. We'll know more in the next twelve hours, if he makes it that long." She unlocked her trunk and began extracting equipment.

McTavish led the way into the corridor carrying his bundle from Maltraw's. The emergency lights no longer flashed, and the corridor was wrapped in a dim night silence. Exhaustion plain on his face, he looked first left and then right.

"Which way is the infirmary?" he asked.

"This way."

He shuffled along, occasionally grimacing, until they reached the corridor outside the infirmary. Soot grimed the floor and walls, and the stench of burned chemicals and burned flesh hung in the air. They stood by the infirmary door, crumpled and hanging crooked from its frame, a black hole beyond its gape. Kama fished a work light from her bag and shone it inside.

"You should wait out here." McTavish took the light from her and stepped through.

She followed him in. Glass shards and twisted metal littered the floor. Glass-fronted cabinets hung open, their contents shattered and burned. McTavish pointed the light at something on the floor and crouched beside it. He picked up a length of plasteel and held it to his nose.

"Table leg—with plastic explosive residue on it."

He wiped his hand on his pants, then rose and moved forward, flashing the light across the floor. It stopped on another leg, or at least part of a leg. It still had most of a work boot on an all too human foot. Not far away, the light picked up a shattered torso, half-dressed in a loud tropical-print shirt. The torso was mostly intact, pallid white under the jellied bloodstains, arms broken and bent. It stopped at the waist, a vast jagged wound spilling entrails onto the tiled floor. McTavish checked the shirt pocket. Kama sucked in her breath and covered her mouth.

"Go back out," McTavish ordered.

"That's Davy Todd. Or it was. He wore that shirt while I worked on his prospecting ship." As the light swung away, she spotted a second body. "And that's probably Juan Rodriguez, his partner."

Despite the horror, Kama heaved a sigh of relief. Todd and Rodriguez must have been Levine's accomplices, must have killed him and dumped his body in hydroponics. She'd need to search their ship to be sure they didn't have a copy of the Oasis contract, and then her job here was done.

"Can we go now?"

"Not until I find answers." McTavish, swinging the light her way, returned to her and placed his hands on her shoulders. "You don't have to do this."

She trembled under his touch and swallowed hard. "What are we looking for?"

Resigned, he swung the light back to the floor. "The charge was made from plastic explosive. You can heat it, freeze it, take a sledgehammer to it, even throw it on a fire if you want to, and it won't blow up. It only goes off if you put a current through it. The detonator may tell us something about the device, or at the very least, provide evidence that will convict Levine of murder."

"Levine? But it was Todd and Rodriguez in here with the bomb."

McTavish bent down, sifted through debris, and plucked something from the floor. He held it in front of the lamp. "Yes, strange that they'd be in here when the blast went off."

"What's that?" she asked.

"Part of the device. If they planned to leave the bomb in here with me, they needed a way to set it off. Timer, remote detonator, something like that." He dug something out of a melted chair-back. "Here's more. Looks like part of a remote detonator. Just a radio receiver, basically, tuned to a particular frequency. You send a signal from any radio transmitter and off you go."

He crossed to where his cot had been. The floor was gouged beside it, and the ceiling above marked with a rosette of blackened insulation.

"This was the point of detonation. Next to the cot. I'd asked for a work table, and they brought one. They set it down here..." He meandered around, examining the patterns of blast damage.

"They meant to leave the table, and then blow you up," she said. If he hadn't sneaked away to the shower... "But their detonator malfunctioned and went off early?"

"It doesn't add up," he said frowning at the blast marks. "We've got two miners skilled in the use of explosives, using a substance they're intimately familiar with, accidentally blowing themselves to bits in an attempt to kill me and possibly you, too."

"Accidents happen," she said.

"Neither of them is carrying a transmitter," McTavish said.

Her earlier sense of relief snuffed out, suffocated by a creeping chill that made the hair on the back of her neck stand up. If she'd told McTavish about finding Levine dead, would Todd and Rodriguez be alive now? She had to find a bolt hole for the two of them, and then she had to tell him the truth, all of it, before anymore lives were lost.

Their search of the infirmary completed, Kama led him through the dim corridors, avoiding sections where she thought they might encounter miners. She stopped outside Levine's quarters, checked to be sure no lurking watchers observed them, and pressed her ring to the lock. She hurried McTavish through the door and locked it behind them.

He wandered through to the bedroom. Kama heard the shower running. Unbidden, the memory of his naked body arose; those firm, well-defined shoulders, lean muscular back, tight buttocks, shapely legs. *He must be hot in the sack.*

What was she thinking? He was the CEO of a Fortune 1000 company, a charmer, a manipulator extraordinaire. Definitely not her type.

Definitely. She was in the middle of a mission gone horribly wrong. And now she needed to tell him her dark secrets before more people died, not add her name to his list of bimbo conquests. Her head ached. She dived into her duffel and extracted equipment, trying to put him out of her mind. She had data to review, a killer to find, a mission to complete.

Hooking a black box to Levine's vid screen, she set her gloves on the plasteel coffee table and sat on the couch. She used her nanocom to access the station network and tunneled through to the message queue. Her bots had returned victorious; she had financial data on Levine, Roshal, Browning, and Miss Patty.

Now all she needed were the files off McTavish's nanocom. It, too, was tucked away in the duffel, rescued from where he'd abandoned it in the shower room. She pulled it out. The smell of soap and coffee washed over her, and she twisted around, startled. McTavish stood behind her.

"Excellent, you found my nanocom. You wouldn't have a coffee cup in there, would you? I'm afraid I didn't think to pick one up."

He was dressed in baggy tan cargo pants and a denim work shirt, the top several buttons open to expose muscled pecs and curly black chest hair. He'd padded up undetected on bare feet. His sparkling eyes swept over her equipment.

Kama dug her travel cup from her bag and handed it to him. He shuffled back to the bathroom and returned to sit gingerly on the couch beside her, a steaming cup in his hand.

"What's all this?" he asked.

"Just some stuff I use." Kama took a deep breath, afraid that if she didn't tell him now, she'd lose her nerve. "Levine's dead. His body's hidden in hydroponics."

His blue eyes fixed on her. He seemed speechless and took a slow sip of coffee.

"I found him while you were gone. Someone caved his head in." Her hands formed hard knots in her lap. "It wasn't Levine who tried to kill you."

His expression became guarded. "You weren't going to tell me, were you? You were going to let me keep looking for him. Why?"

Kama squirmed. She was good at lying. Why couldn't she just make up a story? But he'd know if she lied. He was a damn psychic. "I think the killer may have found something that Oasis lost and would like to have back."

McTavish settled into the couch. "Lost?"

"Fumbled is a better description, sent to Levine by mistake a week ago."

"Ah. Unfortunate." He sipped the coffee again. "Can you tell me what it is?"

Kama gritted her teeth. "A time-sensitive document of great value, but only for another seven days."

"So it's small, electronic, easily hidden, easily transported. Who might find this document to be valuable?"

"Someone of means who wanted a substantial return on their investment."

McTavish snorted. "Someone like me, for instance, a rich playboy? And here I thought it was my masculine charm that kept you hovering."

She glared at him. "You're a successful security professional; I was concerned you might get to the document before me. This isn't a joke."

His expression turned serious. "Sorry. I'm easily distracted. Do you think it's possible that Leon Goldman might be the buyer?"

"Goldman." She hadn't thought about him since McTavish arrived, but of course he'd be exactly the kind of buyer she'd imagined. And he was right here at the station. "Has anyone from the station contacted him? Did he say anything about Oasis?"

"He has other things on his mind." McTavish stared down at his coffee, frowning. "It seems like we're in this together for better or for worse. What I'm going to tell you is in the strictest confidence and can't end up in a file somewhere."

So he knew who she really worked for, and he still trusted her. Her heart thumped a fast staccato rhythm, unexpectedly happy. Foolish. She had commitments to Oasis, and she'd tell them whatever he said. But maybe this time, she wouldn't. Maybe she could keep some information back.

"Tell me," she said.

"I was hired by Goldman's father to find out why Leon insisted on buying this station, and I have. He was blackmailed into it. He doesn't know his blackmailer's identity, but he's convinced that Levine could tell him who it is. The blackmailer doesn't want money; the objective seems to be to get Leon thrown out on his ear. As bad as the financials are on this place, the purchase will do it."

It was Kama's turn to sink back into the couch, stunned by McTavish's revelation. So his masquerade as an inspector wasn't for the benefit of the miners but was part of some family feud at the highest level of EcoMech management. "Hence his determination to board the station with those mercs of his. I suppose we should retrieve the body."

"We should leave it until an EA forensic team arrives. There's one based at the jump gate station. They could be here in six hours."

She grimaced and pushed away the vision of body parts separating as the corpse was pulled from the vat. "He's, um, in a hydroponic tank... dissolving."

"Ah," he replied, nose crinkling. "No wonder you didn't want salad.

So the longer we wait, the more forensic evidence we lose."

"What will Goldman do if he finds out Levine is dead?"

"Same as us—go after the murderer."

"And the miners? How will they react?" Her stomach tied itself in a knot. With no target for their anger, they might turn on McTavish.

He sighed. "Who knows? Yuri said they wanted to go back to work, something I'd suggested they do, and I when I nixed that idea, he warned me that they might retaliate."

Surprised, she stared at him. "So the infirmary blast might not be the work of the murderer but just a bunch of pissed-off miners?"

"I don't think so. Another beating would have finished me without risking Warner's life. The bomb was meant to kill me and hand investigators the two perps on a platter. If the infirmary wall had given way—as I think it was intended to—the evidence to contradict that theory would have been lost in the blow-out."

He shivered and went for a coffee refill. Her mind wandered to his arrival beating. He must know who his attackers were. Why hadn't he fingered them to Goldman or EA? Maybe he worried that the men had friends who'd come after him, and he'd file charges when he got clear of the station.

"We have until morning to sort out who killed Levine," he said, returning with his coffee. He sucked the stuff down like most people breathed air. "After that, the place will be crawling with security forces. You can bet that if Leon gets his hands on Levine's accomplice, he won't end up in EA custody. I can't let someone go free after committing three murders. I think we keep the body quiet for the time being."

"Someone fiddled video on the last night we know Levine was alive, and only three people had high level permissions to do it: Roshal, Browning, and Miss Patty," she said, glad they wouldn't be fishing the corpse out of the vat themselves.

"The video edits could have been done by Levine before he was killed. Maybe he thought he could hide and flee later. Nonetheless, Yuri, Ed, and Miss Patty are also the people most likely to have known about the fraud." He logged on his nanocom. From the corner of her eye, Kama made note of his password.

"I asked Greg to review the airlock video footage and make a list of all the arrivals and departures from the station from early evening the day before we arrived until nine the next morning when we docked."

He scooted across the couch until his hip and shoulder touched hers, and he held the tiny nanocom screen so she could see it. He smelled of new clothes and soap, and his body radiated heat like a blast furnace. She tensed at his contact and ignored her quickening pulse. She was a creature of intellect and did her best to deny her own baser instincts, but she had an uphill battle while sitting next to his sensual body.

She forced her eyes to the nanocom screen, which displayed a list of time-stamps followed by names and links to video clips. McTavish started at the top of the list. In the first clip, a fire-breathing hag in an Oasis' jumpsuit stepped off the mail ship ready to kill someone or fall asleep standing. She watched her video-self silently converse with Browning, while Miss Patty hauled away the mail trolley in the background. She wished McTavish weren't seeing this footage. *I look like Ganesh's ugly sister.*

"That's the ship I came in on," she said. "It delivered mail with the cash chip. If we assume that only Levine would hide the chip in his quarters, then we know he was still alive at this time."

McTavish opened a file time-stamped 1:15 a.m. The footage wasn't great—none of it was—but they couldn't mistake Browning's hulking figure as he entered a docking bay, squeezed through the airlock hatch, and swung it shut behind him, leaving the station.

"Greg made a note about this clip. He says he can't find another clip where Browning returns, but Browning met us when we docked."

"Interesting," Kama muttered.

"Yeah?" he said.

Kama gave him a grim smile. "When Browning rescued Greg, he said that he hadn't been off the station in a week."

"Ah. Food for thought."

McTavish scrolled through the list and opened another file. This time, the window showed the familiar footage of Levine's scrawny figure sauntering into the airlock and slipping through, never to be seen again.

"Greg's put another note in about this one. I think we'll need to see it on something bigger than the nanocom screen."

Kama took the nanocom from him and plugged a device into the output port. Levine's vid screen came to life, displaying a larger version of the image on the nanocom. She could see that Greg had manipulated the video clip to illustrate a point.

The area next to the airlock expanded to fill the screen, hazy and unfocused at first, then abruptly pinging into sharpness. The panel displayed station time, seconds ticking lazily away. The vid zoomed in again, until there were only two things on the screen—the clock next to the airlock door as Levine made his escape, and the time-stamp automatically pasted onto the video by the recorder.

"They don't match. They aren't even close," McTavish noted. "Someone used some old footage of Levine leaving the station days or weeks ago and pasted it into the footage of the night he disappeared, covering up what was really there from one-thirty to three-thirty in the morning."

"Browning must have returned sometime in that window, which is why your nephew can't find the video."

She opened a new video file. Same dull airlock shot, empty and inert. They read Greg's notes.

"This is video from a different airlock camera the same night that Levine disappeared, taken about eleven-thirty."

The video zoomed in on the clock next to the airlock door. Big, foreshortened numbers ticked along, this time matching precisely the video time-stamp in the corner. Tick, tick, tick, went the airlock clock. And then the figures stopped, frozen at the same time while the video time-stamp ticked onwards. For twenty seconds it went on, the airlock clock frozen while the video time-stamp ticked further out of sync with each second. Then, abruptly, the airlock clock jumped, bridging the gap to match the video time-stamp, and both ticked on as if nothing happened.

Kama exhaled slowly. "Does that mean what I think it does?"

"Someone tampered with it," McTavish said. "They pasted the same frame over and over again into the original footage, covering something up."

"But what?" Kama wondered. "Someone arriving or leaving? Who?"

The next video in the queue showed Roshal and her leaving to fix Todd's mass spec, and then the shipping manager coming out of the runabout bay, followed by Davy Todd, Juan Rodriguez, and herself. A dozen more closely bunched files showed the stampede of miners returning to the station, probably as a result of Browning's orders.

Kama poked the nanocom and opened the final file.

"Skip this one," ordered McTavish, reaching for the nanocom.

"Why?" she asked, moving the device out of his reach.

"It's my arrival with Leon; it won't be useful. Shut it off," he repeated, his voice irritated.

What had McTavish done that instigated his beating? It must be something he didn't want her to see. Perhaps he was embarrassed about how he'd behaved. But she wanted to know which of the miners had done it. Curious, she let the file play on.

A different scene—the station's spacious main docking bay. Browning, Miss Patty, and Roshal stood in a line, facing McTavish, Greg, Goldman, and another man she didn't recognize; a secretary or assistant from his downtrodden appearance.

This camera was better than the others. Their clothes, especially Roshal's stained yellow shirt, stood out jarringly against the grey metal and peeling paint of the dingy backdrop. She'd barely realized the videos were in full color before, but here the image was clear enough to show the sweat trickling down Browning's forehead. Mouths moved silently, and bodies tensed.

Greg wandered away from the main group, and his face turned up-ward, staring into the camera with a bored expression. McTavish looked sharply off-screen and shouted something. He shoved his boss and the assistant back toward their own vessel. Then he lashed out like a snake, snatching the boy back and flinging him toward the airlock.

He charged the first two attackers who rushed on camera, weapons swinging, and took them down. His speed and grace amazed her, hands and feet blurring with a professional, deadly economy of movement. She watched, open mouthed, shame casting it's shadow over her.

She'd thought him a desk jockey, a pretty face born with a silver spoon in his mouth, a smarmy corporate type whose own behavior trig-gered the miners' attack. But he'd done nothing, said nothing to pro-voke them. In the video, a consummate professional pulled his punches, tempered his strikes, temporarily disabling when he could have killed; a humanitarian facing a murderous mob.

Kama couldn't imagine how he'd been so badly hurt—until he sacrificed his defensible position to rescue Greg, only to be jumped from behind. His attackers swept over him like hyenas falling on a downed gazelle. The hatch swung shut, abandoning him to the pack of predators, and he disappeared under the kicking, clubbing mass.

The enormity of how she'd misjudged him burned through her, leav-ing her throat raw, chest constricted. She'd thought him a helpless fool, a dandy, beaten senseless by a few burly men who didn't like how he'd greeted them. He'd proved himself a biblical David set upon by a host of Goliaths, and he'd defeated them in the end not with his fighting skills, but by his forgiveness, his willingness to help them despite how they'd punished him, his heroic rescue of Warner. Tears filled her eyes.

Beside her, McTavish stared at the screen. His knuckles were white on the coffee cup, and his breathing sounded ragged. He jerked to his feet and headed to the bedroom with hurried strides.

She'd been an idiot. Why hadn't she listened when he'd asked her to stop the video? He didn't need to be reminded of a beating like that, nor of his abandonment by his brother-in-law. He deserved—and had—her respect. Her hands clenched in her lap. *Moorhk, moorhk, moorhk!* What had she done?

When he returned, he looked exhausted and slumped at the far end of the couch, huddled in on himself.

"Are you okay?" she asked. *Dumb. Of course he isn't.*

He stared at the coffee table and nodded, nothing like okay. She slid along the plastic couch until she sat a hand's breadth from him, wanting to comfort him but uncertain about whether he'd accept it.

"I'm sorry," she said, the words sticking in her throat. "I've been dead wrong about you. I made assumptions based on stereotypes instead of looking at the man in front of me. And now I've wounded you further by playing the video. You deserve better."

To her surprise, his distress worsened. What kind of brainwashing had his family put him through that after all he'd done, he still thought he was inadequate? When he didn't look at her, she punched his shoulder. That got his attention.

"*Moorhk,* you're supposed to be a gentleman and say you forgive me."

His eyes registered bewilderment, and then he gave her a sheepish grin that didn't quite cover his torment. "Sorry. I'll try harder to be an evil corporate bastard in future."

She heaved a sigh, glad to see his sense of humor recovering, even if his hands still shook. "Time for the heavy lifting. Only two hundred files; no problem. I wish we had more time."

"Captain Benson will try to stall the security forces, but it won't give us more than an extra half hour."

Kama chewed her lip. "We need more than that if we're going to delve into the background of everyone on the station. Maybe I can delay the cruisers at the gate if they haven't come through already."

She checked the time on her nanocom. Not yet midnight. She'd make it if she hurried. Samir wouldn't like it. Hastily organized missions had high risks of exposure. And if he found out that McTavish knew about their capabilities—well, too bad. She coded a message and dropped it in the queue for immediate transmission.

"How can you stop them?" McTavish asked.

She flashed him an evil grin. "The jump gate is about to have an issue with its computer systems. They'll have to stop all incoming and outgoing jumps until the problem gets resolved."

McTavish gave her an incredulous look. "But their systems are impregnable. Besides, you can't take down the jump gate just to stall Leon's cruisers. Think of the havoc that wreaks for thousands of people who depend on the traffic getting through."

"How does a little inconvenience for thousands weigh against catching a killer? I don't know how you do the math, but for me, the choice is clear."

"And the person doing the nobbling? How much is twenty years in prison worth?" he argued.

She glared at him and passed a stick drive. "I'll need a copy of your files to work with."

He frowned back, but provided the files.

She pulled on her gloves. "System security here isn't great, but the place isn't exactly crawling with hackers, either. I'm going to look over the files on the crew just to be safe, but I still think Browning, Roshal, and Miss Patty are our primary suspects because of the computer access level required. You can start with the three of them."

"We have a lot of ground to cover. It makes more sense for both of us to focus on the suspects of greatest interest."

She plugged the stick drive into her nanocom and lifted her hands. The first file opened on the vid screen, drawing McTavish's attention. With a twitch of her right hand, she adjusted the page size and line length. Then she set the page speed to one page every ten seconds and focused on the screen, gradually speeding up until she'd halved the time, and halved it again.

"You're not really reading those, are you?" he asked.

Kama flicked her little finger to pause the display. "Yes, of course I am. Otherwise, what would be the point?"

"But..."

"Follow along on the vid." She rattled off the first two paragraphs of the text without taking her eyes off him. "Satisfied?"

"Speed reading *and* photographic memory. You really know how to make a guy feel inferior," he grumbled. "*Please* tell me you occasionally need help opening jars."

He reached in his pocket and pulled out a small rubber ball, which he rolled between his palms while he read his first report.

Kama returned to her own reading. They couldn't afford to overlook someone. Todd and Rodriquez didn't seem like killers, and yet they had to know the table was rigged to explode. Too risky to have them handle it without being in on the plan. Maybe she could find a link between them and the killer.

A thumping noise, rhythmic and annoying, brought her to a halt. McTavish was hunched over the coffee table, reading from a stack of filmies. He bounced his ball next to the pile, caught it, bounced it, caught it. She went back to her own reading, trying to block the irritating sound, but it was late, and she was tired.

Kama stopped her display again, timed the bounces, and snatched the ball in mid-air, setting it out of his reach on her end of the coffee table and giving him a pointed stare. He mumbled 'sorry' and went for another cup of coffee.

He'd been back perhaps half a minute when she felt the jiggle begin. He bounced one heel against the floor, a fidget that shook the whole couch. Without stopping her reading, she placed a hand on his knee and held his foot down. He mumbled another apology.

A minute later, he was flicking the corner of the stack of filmies with his thumbnail. She heard a sudden crack and a broken triangle of filmie caught her eye as it skittered across the coffee table. He glanced at her, smoothed the filmie, and then shuffled it to the bottom of the pile.

He picked up her travel cup and went back to reading. In less than ten seconds, he'd snapped the lid off the cup, pressed it back, and snapped it off again.

"McTavish!"

"Sorry," he murmured, setting the cup aside.

"And stop apologizing."

"Sorry. Sorry." Pink climbed up his cheeks. He looked like a small boy scolded by his teacher.

Kama sighed. "Maybe you should try cutting back on the caffeine."

His color mounted. "It's not the caffeine. I have, uh, some attentional problems... and, um, some issues with hyperactivity."

She stared at him. Then she laughed. "You're ADHD. Well that explains a lot."

He shaded into brilliant scarlet and refused to meet her eyes. She realized too late that he was genuinely ashamed and felt guilty for laughing at him. Without thinking, she tousled his hair. His head snapped up, his expression uncertain.

"The ball isn't a toy, is it?" She picked it up and handed it back.

"No. It's a conditioned stimulus used in conjunction with biofeedback training to help me increase beta brainwaves so I focus better." He gave her a sad smile. "And it keeps my hands busy so I don't destroy things unconsciously."

She waggled a forefinger at him in mock sternness. "Roll it, juggle it, but don't bounce it."

"Deal." He grinned, and her breath caught in her throat. She hated to admit it—that grin was growing on her.

They passed another half hour in silence while Kama finished reading the personnel files for the two hundred miners working at the station, and McTavish juggled his ball and studied the three managers' records. She did a quick run through the managers' files just to be sure McTavish hadn't missed anything. When she'd finished, she stood and stretched.

"Anything interesting?" he asked.

"About what you'd expect out here. Lots of arrest records for petty charges, and a few with more serious convictions. Davy Todd was at Mars Dev when Levine first started there, but only for a short while. No one on the station worked with our prime suspects or Levine before they came here. I didn't see any indication that anyone made videography a hobby. What about you?"

"Browning is every manager's worst nightmare—great at his job but unwilling to manage up to company goals, and he has a conviction for manslaughter, although he claims it was self-defense. He also lied about being off the station, which doesn't make a lot of sense. You'd think he'd want everyone to know he has an alibi."

"And he argued with Levine the day I arrived, according to Miss Patty," she said.

His interest sharpened. "What about?"

"I don't know," she said. He raised a brow. "I don't. Miss Patty wouldn't tell me, the infuriating old gossip. Maybe you can charm it out of her."

He laughed and ran a hand through his hair. "I think you put the kibosh on me charming her any further, although I admit I'm still not sure where it all went wrong."

She laughed with him, feeling lighthearted despite their grim situation. "And I'll never spirit her away to Oasis, either, thanks to you. You cheated."

"So did you!" he protested, his eyes crinkling with his grin.

He picked up the filmies. "Roshal hasn't held a supervisory position before, and I can't understand why he has that role now, given his performance since I arrived. No video background. The night Greg arrived, he was more than willing to take me to the EcoMech ship if I paid him ten thousand credits, so no loyalty either."

"So that's where you were going," she said. "That's highway robbery! Would you have paid him?"

He shrugged and shifted uncomfortably. "Yes."

Ouch. She'd blundered into painful territory. "Finally a modicum of common sense. I was beginning to wonder whether you possessed any. Get on with it, then. What else did you find?"

"Miss Patty has no qualifications to be here beyond a one-week computer training course she took nine years ago and her experience in her father's business, which isn't saying much. When he died, creditors seized the business before she could file bankruptcy, not that there were any assets left to protect. Then she went to Mars Dev." McTavish drained his coffee cup.

"She's guilty of something." Kama tapped a forefinger on her lips. "She ran like a scared rabbit after you mentioned immunity from prosecution."

He picked up his ball and bounced it against the tabletop. "Yes, but guilty of what? Nothing in the business records implicates her in the fraud, so it's not like we have proof of wrongdoing. Unless she's really the top man, she ought to be eager to come forward given a promise of immunity. It's too bad we don't have financial data on our suspects, but we don't have enough evidence to request a warrant."

The financials! She'd forgotten about them. But what would McTavish do when he saw them? A chill coursed through her. That data stepped over the invisible line into 'provably illegal.' If he reported her, she'd get a minimum twenty year sentence. If anyone found out he knew she had the records and he hadn't reported her, they'd both go down.

She held her breath, flexed her hands, and Levine's bank records appeared on the vid screen.

He glanced at the screen, then stared and went very still. Tension burned in her shoulders while she waited for his next move. He said nothing, just rolled his ball in his palms and stared unseeing into space.

"Maybe you want to go for a coffee refill," she offered, her voice cracking. He'd have deniability if he did.

He snapped back to awareness and scrutinized her. The room seemed to spin and fade, his intense blue eyes all that remained of the physical world. After an eternity, he turned those beacons away from her and squinted at the screen. "Bump the font size up."

She did as he asked, her shoulders loosening, and then began scrolling through the data. Like any smart embezzler, Levine's bank account showed no unusual activity. Most of his credits were shunted to his ex-wife. He'd laundered the embezzled funds by other means, and she'd start tracing those in the morning.

Miss Patty received regular payments from R. S. Steele, Independent Mining's nearest competitor in this sector of the asteroid belt, most probably in exchange for some kind of business information about Independent Mining's activities, Kama guessed. No wonder Steele keep beating Independent Mining to the best asteroids. Her mouth went dry. A company like Steele, already conducting espionage, wouldn't hesitate to buy the Oasis document.

Roshal owed money everywhere, including over 45,000 credits to two separate banks for loans he'd taken out. Perhaps that was why he'd agreed to take McTavish to the EcoMech ship despite the problems it could cause him on the station. What was he doing with all the money?

And Browning had his salary delivered to the station in a cash chip, a good indicator he was spending his wages on something illegal, although they had no indication of what. Interestingly, a month earlier, he'd paid five thousand credits to a med station in Earth orbit. She wondered what medical condition would warrant that kind of expensive care and not disqualify him for employment in space.

Worn out, Kama stripped off her gloves and tossed them on the table. She pulled off her boots, dug a ration bar from McTavish's sack, and slumped back, putting her stocking feet on the coffee table. McTavish placed his bare feet beside hers.

She waved her ration bar at him. "Want one?"

"No thanks." He looked like she'd offered him snake venom.

"Now we know why Miss Patty has a bad case of the guilts," she said, tearing open the ration bar and taking a bite. "And there's something fishy about Browning spending a wad at a med station. I can't imagine allergy treatment is all that expensive."

"But no smoking gun of embezzled funds." He slipped the ball in his pocket and passed a hand through his unruly hair.

"Too bad your ball isn't crystal instead of rubber."

A tired smile curved his lips, and he rubbed bloodshot eyes. "Maybe we need to try a new approach, but I'm too exhausted to think of one."

"I bet if I suggested we have mad passionate sex here on the couch, you'd find you're a lot less exhausted than you think," she said.

He jerked to an upright position, and his eyes widened.

She chuckled. "See, it works every time."

He laughed and slumped back beside her. "Unfortunately, it's not my brain you're waking up."

"Pity, especially since you're in no condition for that kind of activity." Not that it mattered. She and McTavish had no future. A little pang of sadness shot through her.

"At least we had dinner together," he said, deadpan, but his eyes danced with amusement.

Kama glared at him in mock anger. "Focus. We have a killer to catch."

"Trying." He held up his hands in surrender.

"What's the connection between all the brouhaha here on the station and Goldman's blackmail?" she asked.

"If the financial reports that Galaxy supplied to EcoMech had been accurate, then Leon would have looked like a fool for buying the place. He's avoided that by laying the decision to purchase at my father's doorstep, so if the plan was to force Leon out, he's already foiled it."

"Oh, McTavish, tell me you didn't take that beating to rescue your toxic father." She took his hand in hers. It was as bruised and battered as the rest of him.

He closed his eyes and continued, doggedly remaining on task. "But the reports Galaxy had weren't accurate. The station is better positioned than they knew. If Leon's blackmailer wanted to replace him at EcoMech, what better way to start the new job than to turn around Leon's failure? To do that, they'd have to control the embezzlement, or at least be aware of it so they could blow the whistle at the appropriate moment."

Kama tensed.

McTavish slit his eyes open and looked at her. "What?"

"We read it all wrong." She sat up, letting his hand go. "There's a takeover in progress already. We just didn't realize it. We didn't understand the relationship."

He frowned at her. "What takeover? What relationship?"

"Did Amaya want to marry Leon?" she asked, excitement spurring her forward.

He stiffened. "What's this got to do with the station?"

"You said all the marriages were arranged. Did Amaya want to marry Leon and play the trophy wife, or did she want something else?" She saw pain in his eyes but pressed on. "Amaya's been buying up EcoMech stock. Not directly, but through layers of holding companies that aren't easily linked to her. We thought it was some kind of stealth power play on the Goldmans' part to gain more control of the company without attracting attention. If the public knew they were buying up stock, share prices would climb. But it's all been hidden in normal day-to-day buying and selling through several shell companies, so no one's noticed. And the money must be coming from the embezzlement. That's why we can't trace it."

"We?" His voice held a sharp edge.

Kama turned away and tidied her gear, loading it back in her bag. She should have kept quiet, sent a message to Samir instead of blurting to McTavish. Some secrets were too important to share. The depth of snooping she'd just hinted at was a thousand times worse than hacking the banks.

He grabbed her arm and turned her to face him. She saw the anguish she'd stirred up and regretted causing it, but she also saw strength and determination.

He took her hands in his, his grip gentle but firm. "I need your help. I need you to trust me. Don't tell me more than I need to know, but tell me what you're talking about. Please, help me."

Kama thought about Levine's body floating in the hydroponic vat, and then about the millions of crippled and poverty-stricken humans huddled on Earth. If Oasis' plans leaked because she helped McTavish, those poor masses would be doomed, caught in the trap of economic slavery for the rest of their joyless lives. But if Oasis partnered with EcoMech and EcoMech management proved unstable, then Oasis' plans might also fail.

So much pressure, so many unknowns; who could be trusted, who couldn't. Her insides twisted in knots. She stared at his hands, battered and bruised, and she had her answer. *Battered and bruised in defense of others.* She took a deep breath.

"Oasis has made a technology breakthrough that will change human society across the galaxy. But it's of such a scale that we need partners with deep pockets to develop it with us. We've been researching potential corporate candidates to determine their suitability. That's how we uncovered the information about Amaya buying up EcoMech stock. We never considered that she might be working without Leon's and Aaron Goldman's knowledge. It's clear there's no love lost between Amaya and Leon, but we thought their common interest in EcoMech would keep them together. We may have been wrong."

McTavish let go of her hands and rose to pace the room. The ball came out of his pocket, and he bounced it with each step, oblivious to everything around him. After several minutes, he stopped in front of her.

"Tell me more about the money."

"It's not coming from any of the Goldmans' bank accounts. The holding companies get cash infusions, and then that's used to buy stock."

"How much?"

"A hundred million and climbing."

"Shares or credits?"

"Credits."

McTavish resumed his pacing, the ball now striking the floor in double time. "It's too much for the station and not enough for a takeover. So what's she up to?"

"Too much, not enough?" Kama made a grab and caught his ball.

"The embezzlement and buyout haven't netted more than twenty million in the three years Levine's been here, which is a lot less than what she's spent. And a hundred million credits won't buy enough additional shares of EcoMech stock to give her control." His brows drew down. "Unless she has other shareholders to back her. I wonder whether Leon's search for the blackmailer included an investigation of Amaya. God knows she must have some dirt on him."

He paced again, hands raking his hair. "No, no, it still doesn't add up. Amaya wasn't on the station to kill Levine, and the whole employee buyout blew the embezzlement scam wide open."

"Maybe the accomplice and Levine got greedy and decided to free-lance? Maybe Amaya didn't know about the buyout swindle?"

McTavish dropped onto the couch. "Too many questions. I need to run this by Leon. We're assuming that he doesn't know about Amaya's stock grab, but he's so paranoid, not much gets past him."

"If Amaya is part of this, she'll never come to justice, nor will the accomplice," Kama said, her voice flat. She wondered if she'd made a mistake trusting McTavish to help her find the killer and recover the Oasis contract. After all, these people were his family.

He took her hand in both of his. "I promise you that I'll do everything I can to see that the killer is convicted in a court of law and that Oasis' secret is kept."

The question she'd wrestled with since she'd found Levine's body tingled on her tongue; she had to ask it. "And if those two things are mutually exclusive?"

15

Rafe reached through a fog of fatigue and a blinding headache to his beeping nanocom on the bedside table. It read 6 a.m. He fumbled it into silence and rolled to look at Kama on the other side of the bed, happy to see she'd slept through the alarm. What a sight she was, curled in a ball under the blanket like a slumbering angel, albeit an avenging angel who scared the daylights out of him.

After a ferocious argument in which each of them insisted they'd be the one to sleep on the uncomfortable couch while the other took the bed, they'd finally compromised by agreeing to share the bed, each on their own side, with a no-man's land between them. He wanted to strip off her blanket and her coveralls and ravish her body, but that desire warred with another: to run like hell, frightened by the depth of his loneliness and his need for her.

Focus. Leon would know by now about the infirmary explosion, courtesy of Greg. He would also know that his security cruisers weren't coming, assuming Kama had really delayed them. He didn't doubt her ability to arrange such a feat; in all his years of security work, he'd only once gone up against a hacker with half her skill, and that one got away.

He'd always been suspicious of Oasis. They were a bit too 'big brother' to be trusted, but he'd never guessed at their reach before seeing her in action. Shutting down jump gates at five minutes' notice? That meant having either agents or perhaps a software virus standing ready for such a contingency. Who thought about doing those kinds of things? His only answer was *terrorist organizations*, and that scared him worse than sharing a bed with Kama.

He sat up and shoved his sockless feet into his running shoes. He thought about brewing coffee, but dismissed the idea. It might wake her.

In the corridor, he didn't go far before he encountered other station inhabitants. Some greeted him with a curt nod, others with open welcome. He responded in kind, all the while remembering that he had a target painted on his back, and he wasn't sure why. Was the killer simply trying for maximum chaos while Levine's corpse rotted in hydroponics, or had he done something to attract the killer's attentions? Surely asking for a table wasn't a capital offense?

He found the com center after a couple of wrong turns and asked the tech to contact the EcoMech ship. When his brother-in-law appeared on the vid screen, Rafe didn't think his face looked much better than his own reflection in the mirror had. Certainly Leon wasn't any better rested.

"Well, McTavish, I understand you've become a popular guy on the station. Do you have anything to report?"

"I need more time, and I'd like to have a private discussion with you as soon as possible."

Leon sat straighter, his alertness sharpening. "I can't hang around out here forever. I have a company to run. I'm coming aboard the station this morning, and I expect you to smooth the way. I'd like to address all the miners, and when I'm done with them, we'll chat."

"I recommend against that. The station still isn't safe. You'll be a sitting duck with the yacht docked here, and you have your family's safety to think about." Rafe glanced at the com tech, aware that everything he said would be spread through the station minutes after he left the room.

"Then we won't dock. I'll come over in a runabout."

"With a bunch of security goons? You won't be welcome here."

"The cruisers have been delayed. They won't arrive until late this afternoon. I'll bring six crew members with me for escort. The miners can't possibly object to a group of harmless crewmen."

There it was: validation that Kama shut down the jump gate. A chill wiggled up his spine, and he shifted in the chair. Now wasn't the time to think about the Oasis technician.

With his comments about a bunch of harmless crewmen, Leon was sending assurance that he'd be far from helpless. Every man serving on the EcoMech yacht had special forces training. They were probably better fighters and more reliable than the rent-a-cops on the cruisers. If he couldn't convince the lunatic CEO to stay away, he'd have a private word with the escorts, alert them to the danger they faced.

"All right, I'll set up a meeting for ten."

"Make it eight. Time is money, McTavish." Leon cut the connection.

Pain throbbed behind his eyes, and marched with jack-boots down his neck. *Great, just ninety minutes to get the miners together.* Could Browning assemble everyone that fast? On reflection, maybe it was better to organize the meeting quickly, before the killer had time to think up a deadly plan to use against his brother-in-law. Worry multiplied like rabbits, driving him to his feet. He'd better get moving.

"Any idea where I can find Ed Browning this morning?" Rafe asked the com tech.

"I think he went to check on Warner."

Rafe trudged through the station, occasionally stopping a miner to ask for directions. He wished he'd had more chance to study the blueprints before they'd been destroyed in the infirmary. He felt naked and exposed already. Adding 'lost' to the list didn't bolster his confidence.

Outside the conference room, the stench of bodily fluids and charred flesh rode the air like smoke in a forest fire. Inside, Browning and Janice conferred in one corner while the medic hung a fresh bag of fluids for Warner. Janice had dark rings under her eyes and the posture of someone too long on duty. Browning broke off the discussion to join Rafe at Warner's side. Janice approached from the opposite side of the table.

"How's he doing, doctor?" Rafe asked.

"It's Janice now, Mr. McTavish. He made it through the night. He should be ready for transport by this afternoon if his condition doesn't worsen." She eyed him up and down. "I hear you were the one who pulled him out. Maybe I should take a look at those burns on your hands."

"I'm fine," Rafe replied. "It looks worse than it is."

"Liar," Kama called from the doorway.

She sauntered over to join Janice, and Rafe's heart sped up. He became aware, too late, that he was grinning like the village idiot and wrenched his attention back to Janice, who watched him with an amused expression.

"You two a matched set?" Janice asked.

"Nah," Kama said, her nonchalance belied by the spark of challenge in her eyes. "I'm his minder. He can't be trusted out on his own."

The doctor and the smelter supervisor exchanged a look, like they shared some private joke, most probably at Rafe's expense, and internally, he squirmed.

Kama glowered at them both. "What's the plan for Warner?"

"If he's stable, Swede will run him to the jump gate hospital late this afternoon," Browning said. "The medic will ride along to monitor him."

Rafe thought he saw a shadow of satisfaction cross her face. He turned to the smelter supervisor. "Ed, Mr. Goldman would like to address everyone on the station this morning at eight."

"He still planning on landing a bunch of mercs?"

"He'll bring six crew members with him as an escort, and come in on a runabout," Rafe said.

"Since he owns the place, I suppose we're stuck with him, but I'm not taking responsibility for anything that happens. Hell, I don't even know if I have a job here anymore."

Browning stalked out to arrange the meeting.

"So what'd you do to Todd and Rodriguez that they wanted you dead?" Janice said.

"Nothing," Kama snapped, folding her arms and frowning. "He's had the shit kicked out of him for no reason whatsoever, and he doesn't deserve it."

Rafe glowed. He may have arrived with no friends, but he had a fearsome ally now. They'd take the killer down together, and he'd make sure the Oasis document was safe. He owed her that.

The doctor arched an eyebrow, chuckling. "Down, girl. I'm just the friendly neighborhood quack, not your competition."

Nonplussed, Kama shifted her frown to him. He wiped the smile from his own face and turned to Janice.

"Did you know Todd and Rodriguez well?"

Both carefully plucked eyebrows lifted. "Discretion is my watchword, honey. I don't go around flashing my client list, even when clients are no longer among the living. You do know that Rodriguez had a wife and two kids back on Mars?"

"No, I didn't know that." A pang of sympathy lanced through his chest. "I'm sorry to hear it. I was just wondering who their friends were, who they hung out with. I didn't mean to pry into whether they were your clients."

Janice gave him a shrewd look. "You think someone was in on the bombing with them."

"I'm trying to make sense of why they died. It seems such a waste. If I knew more about them..." He waited, the silence in the room filled only by Warner's labored breathing and the beep of the medical monitor.

The doctor's lips thinned. She caught the medic's eye and jerked her chin toward the door. He left, muttering something about a second breakfast and days until departure.

"Juan and Davy spent their time—and a lot of money—with Jay, not me. Jay and Davy used to be partners in a prospecting ship three or four years ago."

This was information that should have been in the background reports. Rafe glanced at Kama. Her eyes flickered, as though she read something.

"The *Soledad*?" she asked. "It was owned by some investment firm, not Maltraw and Todd."

"That's the one," the doctor replied. "It was supposed to be the start of a fleet. They made decent money, but Davy couldn't hang onto his, whereas Jay saved to invest in something better—or at least that's how Jay tells the story. So they split and let their backers take the ship. Davy came to the station, and Jay bought the emporium."

"What was it Davy spent his money on?" Rafe asked, feeling like they might finally be making progress.

"Bad bets. He wasn't as addicted to gambling as that Yuri Roshal, but he always seemed to find a few more credits to flush down the toilet on long shots. Jay'll be pissed that he died. He owed a good sized tab."

So now we know where Roshal's money goes. Rafe leaned closer and dropped his voice. "Sounds like he was losing more than he earned. Any idea where the money came from?"

Janice turned away and fiddled with Warner's IV. Then she checked his monitor. "I don't like to speak ill of the dead."

Rafe rubbed his chin. He'd have to be careful about what he said. The doctor and Browning were too close, and Browning remained a prime suspect. He couldn't reveal anything he didn't want the smelter supervisor to also know. At least Kama seemed content to let him take the lead, and he thanked his lucky stars for that.

"Juan's wife and kids don't deserve to be without a husband and a father. If someone talked him and Davy into getting involved, that person should suffer the consequences, too, don't you think?"

The doctor grimaced. "There's no justice in this galaxy, no balancing of the scales. Good people die, bad people walk free. There's nothing I can do about it."

"Yes, there is," Kama said, stepping closer, her face so fierce that Janice moved back. "It's because good people believe they're powerless that justice has become a joke. But it doesn't have to be that way. You can take a stand, right here, right now, and make a difference instead of making excuses."

The force of Kama's passion made his toes curl. His admiration of her soared, along with a burning desire to know her better, spend more time with her—maybe the rest of his life, if she'd have him.

Cowed, the doctor refused to meet her eyes, and addressed Rafe instead.

"I don't know anything for sure, but Jay implied Davy and Juan might be tagging asteroids to make extra money on the side."

"Tagging asteroids?" He shrugged. "Sorry, I thought that was their job?"

"Out here, most prospectors are independent contractors. They sell their finds to the highest bidder. That's all very well for companies like Steele or Galaxy, but it means the little guys like Independent can't get the better rocks because they can't outbid the big corps. So the smaller companies don't use contractors. They pay their prospectors just like regular employees, based on the hours they work instead of the finds they make.

"But some crooked hourly employees still sell their better finds to companies like Steele on the sly. If they locate a quality asteroid, they'll tag it with one of Steele's beacons and report to their own company that it was worthless. They get paid for their time by their company, and they paid by Steele for the tag."

The amount of fraud being perpetrated at the station astounded Rafe, and after nine years running Security Partners, he thought he'd seen it all. *I need to open a branch office out here.*

"Did you tell anyone at the station about your suspicions?" he asked.

"Not Ed, if that's what you're asking," Janice replied, her words encased in ice.

"What about Levine? Did he know?" Kama asked. "I heard he and Todd were friends from their Mars Dev days."

"Beats me," the doctor responded. "I didn't go to the station, and Levine never came to the emporium. He didn't approve of Jay's operation."

"And Yuri? Were he and Davy friends?" Rafe said.

Janice laughed. "Pull the other one. No one is friends with Yuri. You seen that stupid yellow Aerosaurs shirt of his?" When he and Kama both nodded, she continued. "Eighteen months ago, the Aerosaurs had a big match against the Wandermere Poseidons for some interplanetary soccer championship. Yuri told everyone he was backing Wandermere, and because he knows his sports, most of the station followed his lead.

"The Aerosaurs ended up walking the game—turned out they'd poached Wandermere's star player just before the match—and the guys all lost their money. But not Yuri. He'd lied to everyone to drive up the odds because he'd known all along about the switch and backed the Aerosaurs. He's been wearing that shirt ever since, just to rub the guys' noses in it."

Rafe exhaled through his teeth. It was a wonder they hadn't had more murders out here with the amount of cheating, swindling, and fraud going on. The sense of forward progress dissolved into a morass of tangled connections that led nowhere and everywhere. They'd never get to the murderer at this rate, and time was running out.

Janice insisted on applying burn ointment to his hands before letting him leave. She also waved a med scanner over him and seemed surprised at the results. When he asked how he was doing, her only reply was, "Better than I expected."

He and Kama wandered the corridors until they arrived at a mess hall a third full with miners. Kama made a cup of tea for herself and took a seat at a table well removed from the others. Rafe looked over the breakfast choices, settled on a bagel and cream cheese as the least disgusting, and hoped the coffee was drinkable. By the time he'd joined Kama, she'd torn the wrapper from another ration bar and was munching it while she typed something on her nanocom.

"What are you up to?" he asked.

She glanced around. "Chasing the money."

"Ah." They ought to let EA do that, but he doubted that anything he'd say would stop her. The cream cheese had the consistency of half-hardened glue, but without the appealing aroma. He spread it on the stale, dry bagel and took a bite. One was enough. He put it aside and tried the coffee, which proved weak and bitter. His stomach growled loud enough for Kama to notice. She pulled another ration bar from her duffel and slid it across the table without looking up.

"Now aren't you glad you bought these?" she said.

Grudgingly, he unwrapped the bar and nibbled at it. It wasn't quite as bad as he remembered from his days in the service, and infinitely better than the bagel. He couldn't wait to return to Mumbai and cook himself a decent meal. He washed the bar down with the bad coffee and thought about what he'd say to Leon.

If the CEO knew about Amaya's stock purchases, then the idea of a stealth takeover went out the window. But if he knew nothing of what his wife was up to, it put Amaya squarely in the picture as the blackmailer. They should be looking for connections between Levine and Amaya, he realized. Or Amaya and anyone else on the station.

"Kama, do you have the records Oasis dug up on Amaya?"

She smiled. "I wondered how long it would take you to ask. Samir's already looking for links to station personnel. If he turns up anything, he'll let me know immediately."

Rafe frowned. "I thought we discussed the confidentiality of the information I shared with you."

Kama laughed. "Samir's response was much the same when I told him you were helping with my inquiries. He asked—facetiously, I assume—whether he should send a formal contract with mutual non-disclosure statements for both sides to sign and wondered what your rate would be. He's very budget conscious."

"Who is this Samir?" he asked, suddenly worried that he'd trusted her with too much information.

"He's my boss, and he's not at all happy about you, either, if it makes you feel any better." Amusement danced in her eyes. "Nothing will end up in Goldman's file that wasn't already there."

Irritation made his aching head pound harder. "How can you be sure?"

"Because Oasis' security system was my second hacking conquest. I can remove anything Samir adds, and he knows it. He'll respect my request to keep things off the record."

Rafe's irritation grew. "And Samir's boss? Will he be told? It's not just files I'm worried about. People talk. Leaks have a way of developing."

She sighed. "Perhaps you should check your own files if you want assurance. Security Partners must have a dossier on Samir Ganguly."

The air in the mess hall seemed suddenly thinned, as though all the oxygen had whooshed out in a hull breech. *Samir Ganguly, rumored to be the real head of Oasis security, the man behind the official public puppet listed in Oasis corporate brochures.* Security Partners had a dossier all right, as did EA; a very thin dossier with lots of supposition about events he *may* have been involved with, planned, and carried to completion, and without one shred of proof. Some people wondered whether he even existed.

Not only real, but Kama's boss. His handiwork leaned toward the macabre. She didn't seem the type to be working with someone like Ganguly.

"Why do you do it?" he asked.

She looked at him with serious brown eyes. "Someone has to. EA politicians are owned by the corporations and do nothing to curb corporate power. Law enforcement is contracted out to more corporations and works to protect corporate interests, not the people.

"A culture that values greed and profits above human welfare surrounds corporate executives, making them blind to the pain their decisions inflict. Should a man with the moral strength and courage to look beyond the bottom line, to resist the temptations of boundless wealth and power, rise in the corporate structure, he'll be booted out by the board of directors, lest others follow his example."

"And stealing corporate secrets keeps the corporations in check?" Rafe said, anger overtaking his concerns for her affiliations. He resented her sweeping generalizations. He was a CEO, and he wasn't some evil bastard trampling on the little people. "I expect you make good money selling what you steal. Or do you donate it all to charity?"

She snorted. "You're familiar with SinoChem and the bad press they've had lately?"

"Vaguely. A whistleblower inside their company released internal documents showing they knew their new pesticide caused a rise in birth defects, but they released it anyway." He frowned. "You had something to do with that?"

"Easier to blame a whistleblower than to admit you don't know how the information leaked. Because the documents leaked, a class action suit has been started against them that will benefit the handicapped children harmed by their product." She took a sip of her tea. "Surely you saw the news vids of the thirteen year old girl working in a shoe factory in Brazil who was beaten to death by her floor supervisor for asking for a toilet break?"

"Yes, I remember it." The footage had brought tears to his eyes.

"It came from an internal security camera positioned to stop employee theft." She watched him, her face cold and immobile. "When a week passed and the company that owned the factory did nothing to acknowledge the death or punish the manager, I made sure the video reached the news media. Their share prices plummeted. They're now the target of a takeover by a company with more respect for workers' rights."

Rafe shifted, uncomfortable under her gaze. He wondered how many employees would be made redundant by the takeover, but he sensed thin ice. "No matter how noble your cause, it's still wrong to steal the information."

"No," she said, her mouth turning down. "It's illegal, but it isn't wrong. We agreed to help one another, McTavish. To trust one another. Have you changed your mind?"

Rafe swallowed, thinking he was in way over his head and hoping she didn't lump him with the corporate types she'd described. He took good care of his employees, treated his customers fairly, and made regular charitable donations to worthy causes. Of course he watched the bottom line; after all, he was a businessman. That didn't make him Satan's second cousin, did it?

"No, I haven't changed my mind." He stood. "If we're going to meet Leon when he docks, we better get moving."

In the corridors, the miners moved toward the storage bay where Leon would address them. Rafe and Kama walked the opposite direction, toward the runabout bays. When they drew close, he stopped. Browning, Roshal, and Miss Patty waited near the bay door.

"When Leon announces the bounty, there'll be a stampede instead of an orderly search. Maybe it would be best if you were already in hydroponics and could divert everyone away from the body," he suggested. "I'll stick with Leon. Our killer won't want to approach and negotiate a sale for the Oasis document with an Oasis representative looking over Leon's shoulder."

Rafe received a simple nod for a reply and continued to the bay door. He heard Kama's soft footfalls retreating down the corridor and wished she didn't have to go.

Browning had changed into a decent, long-sleeved shirt that covered his prison tattoo, a pair of slacks, and well-worn dress shoes recently polished. Roshal had traded his hideous Aerosaurs t-shirt for a threadbare pea green work shirt, blue jeans, and scuffed boots. Miss Patty wore another of her old-fashioned frilly dresses.

Rafe noted that while she was over sixty and female, she was strongly built. Levine was a little guy. Rafe imagined her hoisting the man's body into the hydroponic vat. She could do it, he decided.

They heard the outer bay doors close. A few moments later, the door before them opened. Cookie, clearly the squad leader for this assignment, and three other crewmen stepped through into the corridor. While Cookie did a quick visual check of the station personnel for weapons, the other three dispersed in both directions of the corridor. When Leon emerged, one of the remaining crewmen joined him. The other stayed behind to keep an eye on the runabout.

"Mr. Goldman, I'm Edgar Browning." He offered his hand.

"Let's skip the formalities, shall we?" said Leon, ignoring the hand. "You have the workers assembled?"

"Yes, sir, in one of the storage bays." Browning dropped his hand and glanced at Rafe, who shrugged in reply.

"Lead the way."

Rafe caught Cookie's eye and flicked a hand. Cookie nodded, passed barely perceptible hand signals to the other crewmen, and hung back while the group moved down the corridor. When they were out of earshot, Cookie and Rafe fell in behind them.

"Last night, a killer tried to take me out with a bomb," Rafe told him, voice low. "I believe the three people with Leon are the prime suspects, but whoever it is, he or she is not above using hired help. Keep your perimeter well back, watch for suspicious packages. You know the drill."

"You think they'll try for Mr. Goldman while he's here on the station?" Cookie asked, face grim.

"I wish I knew, but we can't take any chances." They both lengthened their strides. "And Cookie, there's an Oasis technician on the station. She's helping me with the investigation. Consider her my second."

"How will I recognize her, sir?"

Without thinking, he said, "She's the most intelligent and beautiful woman in the galaxy." Cookie looked perplexed, and Rafe stumbled on, trying to recover his composure. "She's also the only other woman on the station besides Miss Patty, the one walking with Mr. Goldman."

"Yes, sir."

On the long walk to the storage bay, Leon set a brisk pace, and Miss Patty scurried to keep up. Browning puffed along like a steam engine with a leaky boiler and made no attempt at conversation with his new boss. Roshal sauntered behind on his long, loose legs, hands jammed in jean pockets. Rafe found the pace to be too much and gradually lost ground. His ribs still ached despite Janice's miracle cure for his internal bleeding.

Roshal looked back, saw him lagging, and waited.

"Say, Mr. McTavish, did you speak to Mr. Goldman about how I tried to help you out?" he asked in a low voice. "I know I didn't get you over to his ship, but that wasn't my fault."

"Sorry, Yuri, I haven't had an opportunity. I'll be meeting with him later, though."

They walked in silence. Rafe glimpsed the storage bay ahead.

"When do you think he'll let us go back to work?" the shipping manager asked. "We got customers asking where their ore is, and we all need our paychecks. Mr. Goldman won't want to lose paying customers, will he? Maybe you could speak to him? Speed things up?"

"I can't make any promises, but perhaps I can have a word," he said, his side aching.

Roshal ambled through the storage bay door, and Browning waved his arms at the assembly. "Men, this is Mr. Goldman, CEO of EcoMech, the new owner of the station. He'd like to say a few words."

Leon stepped in front of the men, looking like a lion deciding which zebra to cut out of the herd. "As you know, I sent a security detail to intercept a cargo drone believed to be the escape vehicle used by your former manager to leave the station."

The miners waited, tense and glowering. Leon's security squad watched the crowd, hands in bulging pockets where Rafe suspected they kept stunners. The miners were unarmed, but plenty of potential weapons lay around the storage bay if another riot began.

"I'm sorry to report that Mr. Levine was not onboard." Leon waited while the voices of the men rose in surprise and anger and fell again. "I have reason to believe that Mr. Levine never left the station, that he is still here, hiding."

The noise level climbed, and Browning waved it down. "Mr. Goldman, we searched the station from top to bottom when Levine first went missing, and we didn't find him. What makes you think he's still here?"

"Someone set off a bomb in the infirmary last night. I believe that Mr. Levine was behind that action. In fact, I believe that so strongly that I'm going to give every one of you the day off with pay so you can search the station again." The men groaned and rolled their eyes. "And to see that you're properly motivated, I'm offering a one million credit reward to the man or men who bring me Mr. Levine unharmed."

The roar of the crowd was as deafening as a rocket launch. Leon raised his hands and, gradually, the men quieted.

"I want to be absolutely sure no stone is left unturned, no nook or cranny left uninspected. You'll search in pairs, and you'll report in to me about where you've searched as you complete an area. You'll find me in the administrative offices."

With that, Leon stalked from the bay, his security detail scrambling to deploy around him. The miners streamed out in a rush, jostling and shouting as they stampeded through the corridors. When they'd passed, Leon ordered Browning to direct him to the admin section. In a few minutes, they'd reached Levine's office. Cookie and one of the crewmen went inside, while the others spread out in the corridor.

Leon turned to the three managers and waved at Levine's workstation. "Get me the station schematics on screen."

After some hesitation, Miss Patty sat at Levine's desk and accessed the terminal. Her hands shook. When she'd brought up the station plans on the monitor, she popped off Levine's chair like a Jack-in-the-box.

"Can I bring you anything, Mr. Goldman? Some coffee?" she offered. He nodded, and she hurried away.

"McTavish, you stay. Everyone else out," Leon commanded. "And close the door."

Leon took a seat behind the desk, and Rafe pulled up a visitor's chair, grateful to sit down. The CEO rocked back, his bulk dwarfing the desk chair, his stubby fingers beating a tattoo on the edge of the desk. His eyes drilled into Rafe.

"What have you got?"

"I need the files from your investigation. I can't work in the dark."

"You just tell me what you've found, and I'll be the judge of whether your information is relevant. What have you learned about Levine? Do you have any proof of an accomplice?"

Rafe checked his rising temper and kept his voice level. "Two men died in the attack last night, and a third man, who is in no way involved in anything, hangs by a thread. The sooner we sort out what's going on, the better off everyone will be."

Leon sat straighter. "Greg didn't tell me about any fatalities."

"He didn't know. I found the bodies after we returned from Maltraw's."

"Who were they?"

"Todd and Rodriguez, two prospectors. They delivered the bomb to the infirmary." Rafe saw the dismembered bodies in his mind and shivered.

"You think they were Levine's accomplices?"

"No, I think they were sacrificed to draw suspicion away from the person who really planned the bombing. Leon, we're not dealing with just blackmail anymore. The bombing was premeditated murder, and the bomber didn't care whether innocent people died in the blast. That kind of callous disregard for human life puts everyone on this station in jeopardy."

"But why did Levine try to kill you?" Leon said.

"Possibly because I was going through the business records. Maybe there's a clue to where the money's gone, or something that identifies who Levine worked with. I don't honestly know. I didn't see anything there that would be immediately useful, but maybe I missed something. Maybe our mad bomber thought that the embezzlement against Galaxy hadn't been detected yet and wanted to delay discovery. No one on the station knows about the embezzlement. They're aware only of the buyout fraud."

Leon rocked back in the chair again. "I can think of an alternative reason to kill you that directly relates to the blackmail."

"What?"

"Your mother's trust fund. It controls nearly thirty percent of EcoMech's shares, and you have complete control. If those shares fell into hands other than yours, the Goldman family shares wouldn't be sufficient to prevent a takeover."

Rafe frowned. "You and your father have enough allies on the board to stave off a takeover even if the Madison Trust shares were sold."

"You've never taken Security Partners public, so you don't have the experience of dealing with shareholders. Business allies stay that way only as long as you serve their greed. They'd shift their allegiance to Satan himself if they'd get larger dividends."

"But why come after me now?"

"Because in the past, you've kept your distance, haven't voted your shares in any elections, been indifferent to whether EcoMech succeeded or failed. But suddenly you're here with me, poking your nose into places where you're not wanted. If the objective is to oust me and you're seen helping me, you become a threat, a roadblock to be removed."

Rafe raked his fingers through his hair, taking in this disturbing new perspective. It seemed surreal. But it gave him an opening. "Leon, are you buying up additional shares of EcoMech stock as a countermeasure to this blackmail?"

The CEO's eyes narrowed. "Why do you ask?"

Rafe shrugged and pretended indifference. "If I were in your position, I would, maybe in my wife's name—or perhaps through holding companies to keep the purchases quiet and prevent the price from rising."

"No, I haven't been making stock purchases." He laughed ruefully. "Amaya's been 'diversifying our portfolio' by purchasing old paintings. Bunch of rubbish as far as I can see, but as long as they hold their value and keep her quiet, I don't care whether we have the cash or the canvases."

A knock at the door interrupted their conversation. Miss Patty came in carrying a tray with a pot and cups. A plate of blueberry muffins, sugar packets, and a tiny carafe of cream filled the remainder of the tray. The wonderful smell of coffee overwhelmed the stale, moist odor of the station air. Rafe wanted to grab the pot and toss the entire thing down his throat. Behind Miss Patty, a pair of miners waited for Leon's permission to enter.

"Anything else, McTavish?" Leon asked, waving Miss Patty to put the tray on the desk.

"I need those files, Leon."

"You're not getting them." Leon poured a cup of coffee and waved the two miners in. "Now, I have a search to conduct."

Rafe left the office right behind Miss Patty, who continued down the corridor, moving quickly. Roshal was nowhere to be seen. Off searching the station, no doubt. For someone with his proclivity for gambling, the million credit reward was a jackpot worth betting on. Unless he was Levine's accomplice. Then he might be building his next bomb.

Browning stamped back and forth not far from the office, running his hand over his face and looking like he wanted to hit something.

"I have a question for you," the smelter supervisor said. "What the hell am I supposed to be doing? That asshole won't even speak to me." Browning glared toward the office. Two more miners brushed by, reporting in to Leon.

"He's a jerk. Ignore him," Rafe replied without thinking.

Browning looked askance. "I thought you were the peacemaker, the glib guy who always had the appropriate words to hand."

Rafe gave him a half smile and hurried away. He needed to get to Kama, tell her what he planned to do next.

The search was the most disorganized and inefficient he'd seen. Men rushed everywhere occasionally muscling one another out of the way to be first into a room that had probably already been searched by half a dozen others. Spacesuits had been pulled from storage closets and tossed on the floor. Any bin large enough to contain Levine had been emptied, leaving mounds of equipment piled on tables and chairs. He heard men crawling in the ventilation ducts and wondered how long Leon would let the search continue.

When Rafe reached hydroponics, he found Kama standing by a large vat of gelatinous red liquid. She flashed her work light into the space behind the vat and waved off a couple of miners, then moved along to shine the light around another vat. Rafe saw wet splashes of red hydroponic fluid around the cuffs and up the sleeves of her coveralls.

"McTavish!" she hissed. "You're supposed to be keeping an eye on Goldman."

"How'd you get all that fluid on you?" he asked, keeping his voice down. Every little sound seemed to reverberate through the area.

She glanced around to be sure they were alone. "He's turned into a floater. I had to weigh him down. Did you talk to Goldman?"

Rafe wondered briefly what she'd used to sink the body but decided he didn't want to know. He kept underestimating her ingenuity and perseverance, and chided himself for it.

"Leon has no idea Amaya's buying stock. She fed him a line of bull about buying Old Masters. He did have a suggestion for why someone on the station might try to kill me that I hadn't thought of."

"You don't look very happy about it."

"He thinks by coming here with him, the blackmailer has assumed that I've got his back. If I throw the voting shares I control in with the Goldmans', Leon becomes invincible."

"And that would quash any plans Amaya has for a takeover," Kama said. "I'm glad I don't have your family."

Four miners entered in a noisy hurry and rummaged through the area. Two more entered from the opposite direction, saw the crowd, and turned away.

"Leon won't give me access to his information, and I couldn't ask him directly whether he'd included her in his investigations without revealing that we suspect her. I don't suppose you have access to his and Amaya's personal files?"

She lifted an eyebrow. "What, you think we've hacked everyone in the galaxy?"

He held his hands up in surrender. "Just asking."

She sniffed dismissively. "We haven't been able to breach the EcoMech corporate firewall, and EcoMech rarely hires our techs. We'll succeed eventually, but not today."

"Ah." He noticed that he was no longer amazed by her startling— and illegal—responses. "I suspect that the files are also encrypted. They'd take time to break, and time's something we haven't got."

"Well…" Kama said, "if I can get a bot onto their network, I can trap their passwords, as well as steal a copy of the files. Then we don't have to crack encryption. Do you have access?"

"No, not to corporate. I'm relaying from outside their firewall when I use my nanocom on the ship."

He reached in his pocket for his ball, found it empty. Where had he left it this time? Kama produced it from her own pocket with a flourish that made him blush. Did she know him that well already? He bounced it on the deck while he considered options. More miners traipsed through, but he ignored them. She pretended to search around the vats again. When the men left, she rejoined him.

"I'm going to the EcoMech ship to talk to Amaya. If she's behind this, maybe I can convince her to give up the accomplice in exchange for not telling Leon she's behind the blackmail."

"But—" Kama looked decidedly unhappy.

"I know, not the ideal resolution. I don't believe Amaya would be a party to murder. I think your guess that Levine and his accomplice started to freelance with the mine buyout scam is correct, and the accomplice is murdering to cover the tracks. If we can get the killer and find your contract, it'll be better than getting nothing, which is what we have at the moment."

He raked his hands through his hair, not liking where his thoughts were going. "I think we should hedge our bets, in case Amaya doesn't cooperate. Give me that bot of yours."

"How will you get it on the network?" she asked.

Rafe felt queasy, but he saw no alternative. "Greg must have an EcoMech corporate account. I'll ask him to upload it."

Surprise crossed Kama's face before she hid it. She knelt on the floor, spread a square of metallic cloth on her bag, and pulled on her gloves. Her fingers flexed, and a line of text appeared on the cloth. Her hands waved and flicked. She looked like she was conjuring magic by drawing runes in the air, and huge blocks of computer code streamed by in a blur. In a few minutes, she slipped a stick drive in the port of her nanocom, made a few simple movements with one hand, and then handed the stick drive to him.

"There's your bot. You're sure you want to do this?" she asked.

"No, I'm not," Rafe replied, the thought of asking Greg to engage in criminal activity weighing like a dark shroud on his soul. "You'd better go sit on Leon while I'm gone."

She glared, slit-eyed. "I don't do lap dances, so how am I supposed to explain why I suddenly have to be in the office?"

Rafe grinned. "If you can take down a jump gate, I'm confident you can break that terminal he's using."

Rafe made for the runabout bay. He bumped into Swede on the way and persuaded the big, blond miner to be his pilot. The man seemed thrilled to give up the search for Levine.

Fifteen minutes later, they'd docked with the EcoMech ship. Swede remained behind in the runabout. Captain Benson greeted him at the airlock and agreed to have someone bring first a mug of coffee, and then Amaya Goldman to the lounge.

He seated himself in Leon's favorite corner chair and sipped the coffee while he rehearsed what he would say. His hands shook, and the hot liquid didn't sit well in his stomach. He'd avoided Amaya for fourteen years, and would gladly have gone the rest of his life without confronting her. He knew he wouldn't find forgiveness. He just hoped she'd confess quickly and bring an end to the hunt for Levine's killer before more lives were lost. If she did, he could skip loading Kama's bot on the EcoMech network and making Greg party to corporate espionage.

The lounge door opened, and Amaya stood silhouetted by the bright corridor light. When she'd located him, she closed the door and crossed the lounge to stand before his chair. She seemed unsteady, and Rafe wondered if she'd been drinking. She looked gray and doughy.

He scrambled to his feet.

"Amaya, thank you for seeing me. Please sit down." He gestured to a nearby chair, hand trembling.

"You murdered my sister, and now you ask me to sit with you."

"I'm very sorry for the loss of Youko. I feel responsible, like I should have done more, been more cognizant of her state of mind." His heart thumped in his chest, and he struggled not to slide into the nightmare flashback of Youko's death. "But I didn't kill my wife. She committed suicide."

"She may have been legally married to you, but she was never your wife. She wouldn't allow you to touch her." Amaya's flat, dead eyes squinted, and her hand fumbled for a chair. She lowered herself to the seat with caution.

Her words struck like a hot knife plunged into his heart. Rafe took his own chair. "We all suffered from the folly of our fathers. We all had dreams crushed by their craving for a business empire to be passed on through the generations."

"You selfish, small-minded little man. I married Leon and sacrificed my future to fulfill my father's commitment so Youko wouldn't have to. Miguel set her free. Her spirit soared on wings of happiness. She would have her dream to be a model, to live her own life, find her true love." Her voice shook, harsh with bitterness. "And you burned those dreams to ash. You made my sacrifice meaningless.

"What dreams have you lost, Rafael McTavish? What sacrifice did you make? You shrugged off your familial obligations and enjoyed the freedom denied to the rest of us."

The depth of her hatred startled him. He'd known nothing of her feelings, how his attempt to honor his father's commitment had nullified the purpose for which she lived. A tsunami of guilt flooded through him.

"I'm sorry. I didn't realize... Like you, I tried to do as my father asked—"

"Your father never asked you to marry my sister. You took it upon yourself to propose, against his wishes."

"I wanted to please him," he stammered, short of breath.

"He despises you. You'll never please him."

Rafe gripped the arms of the chair, the truth in her words flaying his soul. He gave up any hope of reconciling with her.

"Did you know that two miners are dead and a third in critical condition as a result of a bomb?"

"What do you want from me?"

"Someone's gone to a lot of trouble to maneuver Leon into buying this station. The purchase makes sense only if he's supposed to fail, to be disgraced and weakened so that he can be replaced."

"Aaron was a blind fool to make him CEO. My husband likes to boast about his power, likes to make employees cringe while he bullies them, but he takes little interest in understanding the complexities of running EcoMech." Her voice rose in pitch. "My son will have nothing to inherit if something isn't done soon."

Rafe wished he'd thought to turn up the lights. Amaya's face was half hidden in darkness, making it difficult to read.

"I remember when we were kids, you were always the one studying business courses, reading the latest management journals, following the markets while the rest of us talked about becoming pilots and engineers and vintners. Is it time for your ascendance?"

She sat immobile, watching him. "You've never taken the least interest in what happened at EcoMech."

"And I still don't," Rafe said with heartfelt sincerity.

"Perhaps if you had, EcoMech wouldn't totter on the brink of insolvency. But you ran from your responsibility to the company as well as to your family."

He ignored her dig, and pushed on, desperate to be out of her presence. "I know you've been quietly buying stock without his knowledge. I think you're behind his blackmail, using it as a tool to weaken him before you make your move. It all adds up to a takeover. Have you decided to replace him, Amaya?"

He waited for her to respond. When she didn't, he continued. "You're just as deserving of the CEO position as Leon, and in truth, you'd probably do a better job. I wouldn't stand against you if you sought the position."

She pulled a silk handkerchief from her pocket and coughed into it. "If you're uninterested in EcoMech, why do you care what happens here?"

"The killing has to stop. I don't believe you're involved in the deaths. You're not a ruthless murderer willing to take out innocent bystanders. I think your agents on the station have gone rogue. I need their names."

"But you already know the station manager is behind the fraud."

"Levine is dead, killed by an accomplice who's been helping him in the scams. That same accomplice planted the bomb that killed the other two miners. I want the name of that person. If you'll tell me who worked with Levine, I'll say nothing to Leon." Rafe took a deep breath. He'd put his cards on the table. All he could do was wait.

Amaya rose and tottered to the bar. She pulled out a bottle of water and drank half in careful sips before leaving the remainder and coming to stand in front of him.

"You're very clever, Rafael, just like Leon. But I don't know who helped Levine. I dealt only with him and didn't know he had a partner or anything about the buyout swindle. I, too, was duped." She regained her chair. "You're sure Leon doesn't connect me to his blackmail?"

Rafe's heart sank. He wanted this nightmare to be over. "That's not my impression."

"What will you do now?"

"Go back to the station and keep looking for the killer."

"Will you tell my husband about my plans?" she asked.

"Honestly, I don't care what happens to EcoMech, as long as my father isn't caught in the crossfire. If you agree not to tell Leon that Levine's dead, I'll say nothing about your activities." He rose. "Thank you for seeing me. I know it's long overdue, but please accept my sympathies on the loss of your sister."

He crossed the lounge and exited into the corridor, rolling the ball in his palms, every muscle in his body aching. Did he believe Amaya? She'd seemed willing enough to admit to blackmailing Leon, so she didn't fear prosecution. She couldn't reveal the accomplice's name without implicating herself in the murders, assuming that she knew it. If, as she said, she'd been duped by Levine and his accomplice, she probably hadn't heard about the Oasis contract. That should make Kama happy. He couldn't sort the truth from the lies, he realized. He couldn't trust Amaya.

Rafe rapped on Greg's cabin door. After a long wait, the boy answered.

"Uncle Rafe! Is Mr. Goldman back, too?" He gave an apprehensive glance down the corridor.

Rafe slithered past him and shut the door. "I need your help with something."

Greg backed across the cabin and refused to meet his eyes. "I'm not sure I can work for you anymore, Uncle Rafe."

Puzzled, Rafe wondered whether the boy was still angry about being sent back to the ship, or whether Leon had said something to poison Greg against him. Or had he overheard Amaya refer to him as a murderer? All his reasons for avoiding his family came rushing back, but he needed help getting the bot on the EcoMech network.

"I'm sorry if I got you in more trouble with Leon by keeping you on the station."

Greg's face flushed. "It isn't Mr. Goldman. Mom found out what's been happening here. She's really pissed. She said you have a brain disorder, and I shouldn't trust your judgment, that you'd get me killed. She said I couldn't hang around with you anymore.

"Is that true? Do you really have a brain disorder? Because I don't see how you could do so well and all if you were crazy. I think she just doesn't want me around you because then maybe I might leave EcoMech, too."

Rafe's face heated. So Shannon's maternal instincts had kicked in, and she'd warned Greg off. Did she say he was some demented madman?

"I do have a brain problem. I'm easily distracted, I fidget a lot, and I tend to act without thinking about consequences. It's a condition called ADHD."

He sat on Greg's bunk and motioned the boy to join him. "Your mother's worried that I'll make an impulsive decision, which might put you in harm's way. From her perspective, her fears are justified. I did a lot of stupid, dangerous stuff when I was a bit younger than you."

"Is that why you're in the security business? Because you're addicted to the adrenaline rush?"

Rafe gave a rueful laugh. "Soldiers addicted to adrenaline are soldiers who die young. I never wanted to be a hero. But I believe society should provide safety and justice for everyone, and that's why I'm in the security business."

Greg frowned. "So you're not crazy? But if you're brain damaged, how did you become so successful?"

"I pulled one dangerous stunt too many, and as punishment for my delinquency, I ended up on a garraweed burn crew for six months with your dad as my crew boss. He taught me that being ADHD was no excuse for anything. I had to learn to compensate for my deficits, and eventually I did." Rafe smiled at the memory of tall, quiet Ben Nighthorse, a fair man with endless patience and an iron determination to set him on the right track.

"Wow! I feel sorry for you. I hate working for my dad."

"I hope one day you realize how lucky you are to have him. Without his intervention, I'd probably be dead by now."

Greg considered for a moment. "What do you want me to do?"

"I want you to give me your EcoMech credentials, and then I want you to leave the cabin for a minute."

Greg's eyes got round. "Are you hacking into EcoMech?"

"It's better if you don't know. If anyone ever asks, you can say you had no part in it."

"But I will have a part in it if I give you my credentials." Greg wiped his palms on his trouser legs and frowned at the floor. "Is this what Mom meant by impaired judgment?"

Rafe snorted. "Maybe it is. I'm sorry, Greg, I shouldn't have asked."

Feeling defeated on all fronts and wondering what he'd do next, he walked to the door. Greg shuffled behind.

"Uncle Rafe, why do you need to hack the EcoMech network?"

"Levine's dead. Kama found his body hidden in hydroponics. Two more crewmen were killed in the infirmary blast last night. Leon and Amaya are neck-deep in the fraud that's been going on at the station, but they won't share their information with me. I'd hoped that what they know might help me find the killer before anyone else gets hurt. I have some software that can retrieve their files if I can get it on the network, but it's totally illegal. If I get caught, I'll do hard time. That's why I'd want you to deny involvement."

"But if it's illegal..." Greg's brows pulled down, and he jammed his hands in his pockets.

"Sometimes you have to do the wrong thing to do the right thing," Rafe said, running a hand over the back of his neck and wishing things weren't so complicated. "It seems to me that keeping anyone else from harm is worth the risk of getting caught pilfering the Goldmans' files, but I can make that decision only for myself. I can't make it for you."

Rafe reached for the door, but Greg put up a hand to block him. "After Mom did her rant about you, Dad gave me some of that mystic Native American advice of his. He said, 'If Rafe asks for help, listen to his heart, and then you'll know what to do.'"

Rafe laughed. "He used to tell me that stuff, too. I had to grow up a lot before I figured out what most of it meant."

"Yeah, I never understand it." Greg grinned. Then the grin faded. "But maybe I get it this time. I'm not a very good liar. If anyone asks what I knew, I'd have to tell them everything, so there's no point in you trying to protect me. You may as well let me upload the software."

Rafe's conscience nudged him, wondering whether he was unfairly trading on the boy's worship of him. He hoped that if things went sideways, Greg's membership in the EcoMech founding families would protect his nephew. He drew the stick drive from his pocket and handed it to Greg.

"Log on, access the stick, and then start the file."

Greg took the stick drive and plugged it into the port on his nanocom. "Hey, do you think if we get caught they'll let us share the same cell?"

Rafe gave the boy a disparaging look and opened the door. Once he got back, he'd see what the files from Leon and Amaya held, and maybe he'd finally catch a break. In a minute, he was in the runabout headed for the station, enveloped in a black cloud of doubt and depression.

16

Kama unzipped her coveralls enough to give a modest look at her cleavage and waited for the shouting. On cue, she heard Leon roar. She smiled briefly, and then put on her serious, helpful-technician face before hustling down the corridor toward the admin office. One of Goldman's guards stepped into her path, but another closer to the door flagged her on. Goldman stood at Levine's desk scowling down at the monitor.

"What the fuck's wrong with this terminal?" he growled.

Two miners waiting by the door backed out, leery of the CEO's tone. Kama breezed past them to stand beside Leon. It took all her will power not to punch him in the gut. She hadn't forgiven him for his abandonment of McTavish in the airlock and wanted to get even more than anything in the galaxy.

The monitor intermittently turned to static before clearing to display the station schematics. Leon shifted his gaze from the recalcitrant monitor to Kama, and his unpleasant expression softened.

"Who're you?" he asked, voice rude and demanding.

"Kamala Bhatia, Oasis technician."

She pursed her lips and stared at the monitor as though she were trying to suss out its aberrant behavior. Her little disrupter program had been written in haste, without testing, but it seemed to be working admirably. She wished she'd thought to ask McTavish what Goldman knew about computers; she didn't want to set off his BS detector when she explained what was 'wrong' with the terminal.

"Oh, yeah, McTavish mentioned you." Goldman leered. "He didn't tell me you were pretty. Must of been keeping that to himself."

"It's a pleasure to meet you, sir." Kama showed more teeth in her smile than she ought to, but Goldman didn't seem to notice. His eyes ventured no higher than her cleavage. The depth of her hatred grew, and the hackles rose on the back of her neck.

"You can call me Leon. Here, have one of these muffins," he said, sliding the half empty plate across the desk and edging so close that their shoulders brushed. "They're pretty good."

Would someone who set off a bomb to kill McTavish think to poison Goldman? Kama decided to pass on the muffins, just in case.

"I think we're having some network interference. Maybe a cable got damaged by the infirmary explosion."

"Cable?" Leon asked. "I thought these things ran on a light beam network."

Oops. He knows more than I gave him credit for. "If the explosion damaged the shielding on a power cable, it could be leaking EM interference and disrupting the light network."

"Oh, yeah, I see what you mean," he replied.

Kama smothered a laugh. He didn't have a clue what she'd just said, which was a good thing, since it was utter nonsense. She slipped around him and crossed to Miss Patty's desk, then sat down and started the terminal. Leon sauntered over and stood behind her. The terminal frizzed and pulsed in time with the one on Levine's desk.

"Yep, seems to be a network disruption. I'll see if I can isolate its location."

She tapped away on the keyboard, opening the business server's I/O performance logs.

Leon leaned over her shoulder and placed a hand on the desk, perfectly positioned to get a look down her coveralls. She gritted her teeth and scrolled through the logs as though they would tell her what the problem was. She felt Goldman's hot breath on her ear and fought to keep herself in the chair while she silently cursed McTavish for putting her in this position.

"It'll be lunchtime soon. Would you care to dine with me?"

Kama remembered McTavish's proposal for a meal when they'd first met. What was with these corporate types? Did they think every woman was a cheap date? Feed them and they'd fall into bed with you?

But McTavish wasn't a corporate type, she reminded herself, and dinner with him had proved more entertaining than she'd thought possible. She stifled a grin.

"Oh, thanks ever so much, Mr. Goldman, but I brought my lunch with me, and I wouldn't want to abandon my post until I have this issue traced and fixed."

"You think it will be long?"

Leon brushed a loose strand of hair back from her face. She considered biting his finger and wished she'd slapped on a dash of eau du road kill before she came in. Too late now.

"Mr. McTavish mentioned that you had your family with you on this trip."

Leon grunted agreement. "My wife and son are on the corporate yacht. But my wife isn't feeling well. She's had health issues ever since her volunteer service. She worked on jump ships in the days before they realized the dangers of jump field exposure."

"Oh, I'm so sorry to hear that. It must be hard for you to see her ill all the time." Maybe if she could keep him on the subject of his family, he'd behave, but she doubted it. He was a lecherous cad.

"Yes, it is hard. Of course I want to be loyal to her, but a man has his needs, too. You understand that, don't you, Miss Bhatia?"

Goldman placed a hand on her shoulder.

The conversation seemed to be plummeting downhill into territory Kama preferred to avoid, and revulsion tightened her muscles. Could she roll the desk chair over his foot? Back it into his groin? Would he kick her out of the office if she did?

"I love children," she said, trying to turn the conversation to safer ground. "Tell me about your son. What's he like?"

Goldman straightened. "Gabe's a chip off the ol' block. He's smart, handsome, well-mannered; everything you could want in a kid. When he gets a little older, he'll be a real heartbreaker. The girls won't be able to keep their hands off him."

Kama glanced up at him, surprised to see him gazing at his nanocom instead of her. Who would have thought?

"That's him," Goldman said, thrusting the nanocom in front of her and flipping through a series of photos. "You know, I came home the other day, and he showed me a robot he'd built himself. It fetched my slippers. Yeah, he's going far, lots farther than me. He's going to open new worlds, not get stuck behind a desk all his life."

"You don't want him to follow in your footsteps at EcoMech?" she asked, puzzled. Weren't the founding families all about dynasty building?

"Sure, some day, but before he does, he needs to sow his wild oats, have some excitement and adventure in his life. When he's older, he can settle down and take over the company." Goldman spoke with adoration. "After all, I'll be running EcoMech for a long time yet. Hey, you want to see some poetry he wrote? It's pretty good."

Kama waited while he brought the text up on the nanocom. She had little appreciation for poetry, but at least what Gabe had written managed to rhyme. She tried to display some enthusiasm, but it didn't matter; Goldman was enthralled with his son and paid no attention to her.

She marveled at the depth of the CEO's feelings. She'd never thought about corporate types being fathers who loved their sons. She reminded herself that Goldman had shared the same horrible upbringing that McTavish described. Brainwashing? Clearly he wanted his son's childhood to be far different from what he'd experienced, and she admired him for it, something she'd never thought she'd feel for a man like Goldman.

"Hey, you know about electronics," Goldman said. "I worry that somebody might try to snatch Gabe, so I want to get a tracking chip implanted. Not just one of those things they put right under your skin. Those are too easily removed. I want a deep plant chip, one that broadcasts long range. But I worry about side effects, you know? I've heard that the chips can corrode, and that it might not be good to expose him to the energy waves they put out. Don't want to stunt his growth, if you get my meaning. What do you think of those chips?"

"Not a lot of long-term data on health effects yet. The stronger ones have only been on the market for about five years. Occasionally they migrate after implantation and end up somewhere they shouldn't be, but—"

Kama eyes widened, and her breath caught in her throat. She knew how to identify Levine's killer.

"Excuse me, Mr. Goldman. I think I've figured out where the cable problem lies. I'll just go along and check it. Your terminal should settle down in a few minutes."

She rushed past Goldman and into the corridor. As she jogged toward the runabout bay, she punched a few commands into her nanocom to cancel the disruptor program and noticed that her bot had already started relaying files from the EcoMech network. So McTavish had gotten Greg to upload it. That surprised her. He seemed like such a law and order kind of guy. Well, she'd sort through them later. Right now, she needed to find McTavish.

She'd nearly paced a trench in the floor outside the runabout bay by the time he returned. As soon as he emerged, she grabbed his arm and dragged him down the corridor to a deserted airlock. She pulled him inside and shut the hatch.

"What did Amaya say?" she asked, bouncing from foot to foot.

McTavish shook his head, weariness slumping his shoulders. "She said she had contact only with Levine. She doesn't know who the accomplice is. You were right. She didn't know about the buyout scam. It was something Levine put together on the side."

Kama smiled broadly. "I've figured out how to trap the killer."

McTavish stared, open mouthed. "When did you figure this out?"

"It was something Goldman said. He was talking about getting a tracking chip for his son. A few years back, it was possible to get chips that could not only be used for ID and for tracking, but also to store and access other important data like bank records."

"What's that have to do with trapping the killer?"

"We'll put it around the station that Levine had one of those chips, and we'll say that I'm putting together a tracking device that will pick it up. We can suggest that he may have kept his accounting records for the buyout scam there, which is why we couldn't find them on the station computer system. The killer will have to go after the body to be sure that there isn't any incriminating evidence on the chip. All we have to do is wait in hydroponics to see who shows up."

"Brilliant!" McTavish grinned at her. "We'll have to wait for Leon to give up his search and leave. As soon as he does, I'll make the announcement. I should have brought a weapon back with me. Maybe I can get something from Cookie."

His gaze dropped to her chest and lingered. "How'd it go with Leon?"

Kama gave him a cold stare and tugged her zipper up. "Fine, once we got on the subject of his son. Now you run along and finish your babysitting assignment. I'll go see if I can find something relaxing to do, wrestle a crocodile or something. Oh, and the files started to arrive."

McTavish frowned and ran a hand through his hair. "I wish you'd thought of your trap before I had Greg upload that bot."

"Yeah, I know. I wish I had, too." She opened the hatch. "If it makes you feel any better, I can guarantee that the only security service that's ever come close to catching me won't be on the case this time."

She gave him a wink, laughed at his consternation, and strode off down the corridor. She didn't relish returning to hydroponics, but they couldn't afford to have Levine discovered now.

While she waited with the body for the search to end, she reviewed the new files. She started with Amaya's. The woman had exchanged a lot of mail with art dealers and auction houses. Most notable by its absence was any correspondence with Levine or with anyone else on the station.

Kama did a quick search of the thousands of files in her download and found no mention of the station in any of them. Maybe Amaya was as paranoid as her husband and kept her incriminating evidence off the EcoMech network. If that was the case, she'd have to chase it down elsewhere. Not a job to be done in an hour or two while body-watching. She'd just started on Leon's files when McTavish arrived.

"Leon's gone back to the yacht. When the cruisers arrive this afternoon, he'll begin the search again using his security people," he said. "Time to make our announcement to our suspects. It's noon now. Should we tell them it'll take two hours to prepare the equipment, and then we'll begin the search?"

"Make it an hour. I'd like to have the killer in custody well before the mercs arrive." Kama watched him closely. "Once we have the killer, then what?"

"Depends on what the killer knows about your contract. Making someone disappear for seven days and then reappear to be handed over to EA isn't easy."

"Five days. We've pulled the schedule in."

McTavish walked his ball in and out through his fingers. "I assume you have a suggestion?"

"An Oasis ship is waiting nearby. They'll pick up our prisoner and transport to Earth, but they'll have engine trouble along the way that will delay their arrival." Kama waited, holding her breath.

McTavish frowned. "Please understand that I trust you. But your boss, Ganguly, has a reputation that makes me uncomfortable. How do I know the killer will make it to Earth alive?"

Kama scuffed a boot toe on the deck. She shared McTavish's concerns, but she couldn't tell him that. "With Goldman involved, this is going to be a high profile case. I think Samir will find it more expedient to deliver the prisoner intact than to cover some kind of transport accident."

"Leon won't want the killer transported by Oasis. He'll send his cruisers after the ship." McTavish pocketed the ball. "In Samir's situation, I know what I would do with the prisoner if I thought I was in danger of being boarded."

"I can guarantee that the cruisers won't catch our ship," Kama said.

McTavish bowed his head, studying her boot as she moved it back and forth. "I can think of half a dozen ways they can do it. I don't want to expose Oasis' contract, but this killer has to be brought to justice in a court of law. I see the odds of that happening with the killer in either Leon's or Oasis' hands as zilch."

She really could guarantee the cruisers wouldn't catch the Oasis ship, but she'd revealed enough Oasis secrets to him already. "What's the alternative?"

"I contacted EA yesterday. A ship's on the way. It should arrive the same time as the cruisers. The commander's a friend of mine. He'll be parked here three or four days doing his investigation, and he'll keep his prisoner in solitary. That's the longest delay he could agree to."

His eyes met hers, and his uncertainty mirrored her own. He'd withheld this from her when they'd talked in Levine's quarters. On the other hand, he could have waited to tell her until after they'd apprehended the killer. She trusted him, but not EA. The killer had to be Oasis' prize, no matter what it took.

17

"Hey, Mr. McTavish!"

Swede jogged toward Rafe, who eyed Kama, wondering what she was thinking. She hadn't agreed to turn the killer over to EA, and that concerned him.

"Mr. McTavish, we got an urgent message from the EcoMech ship," the big blond miner said. "Someone named 'Amaya' contacted us. She says you need to get over there right away. Your nephew's been hurt. I can take you now."

Rafe's throat constricted. "What happened? How badly is Greg injured?"

Swede gave an apologetic shrug. "Sorry. The com tech took the message."

He needed to get to the ship, see to Greg. But would Kama wait to set their plan in motion with the EA ship bearing down on the station? He didn't think so. If he left now, she could face a killer alone. He couldn't let her do that. What if something happened to her? His hands spasmed into fists.

Kama stroked his cheek, a gleam in her eye that confirmed his suspicions about her intended actions. "Go take care of your nephew. I can hold the fort. Family first."

Rafe's concern for her vied with his worry about Greg. What could have happened to the boy? Was it his fault? He squeezed her shoulder, not happy to leave her behind, and hurried after the miner.

Swede had the runabout powered up and off the station in record time. Rafe barely noticed his queasy stomach. The fifteen-minute journey and docking procedure seemed to take far longer. Before they'd settled, he'd thrown off the seat harness and started for the door. He passed through the airlock into the main companionway.

Amaya, standing by the lounge door, beckoned to him. It crossed his mind that Greg should be in his cabin since the ship didn't have an infirmary. Why would he be in the lounge? Behind her, Gabe slipped stealthily into the room, like a cat burglar sneaking in a second-story window.

When he'd nearly reached her, Amaya disappeared inside. He followed her, and she closed the door behind him. The place was as dim as ever, and it took his eyes a minute to adjust. Amaya moved unsteadily to stand near Leon's favorite corner chair, where Leon slumped, a bourbon glass on the side table as always. He didn't see Greg. Was his nephew dead, and she hadn't wanted to tell him over the com?

His chest seized, and he hurried toward Leon. The CEOs head drooped, hands slack in his lap. Rafe's off-hand dueling dagger protruded from the man's chest. A trail of blood ran down his shirt front, across his trousers, and onto the fabric of the chair. Rafe stared, not believing his eyes.

"You thought you were so clever. You thought you could murder my sister and get away with it because you are a McTavish." Amaya's voice carried to him, barely above a whisper.

Rafe tore his eyes from Leon to look at Amaya, a deadly zip gun in her grasp. She steadied herself against a chair with her other hand but still swayed as though a stiff breeze buffeted her.

"A pity I never thought to blackmail Leon into relinquishing the CEO position to me. I could have replaced him much sooner, ensuring the company remained strong and viable while waiting for Gabe to take his rightful place at the helm. Do you know what the blackmailer had on my husband?" she asked.

Rafe coughed, found his voice. "No, Leon wouldn't tell me."

"Oh, well, he had many indiscretions, but they will pass with him. Gabe's future is all that matters." Amaya chuckled. "I'll be rid of Leon, and you'll take the blame. As the new CEO of EcoMech, I can ensure the investigation doesn't include any forensic evidence that disputes my version of the facts, just as Aaron Goldman covered for you in the death of my sister. How ironic that only today you thought I didn't have killer instincts."

Some warped, sad part of Rafe agreed with her—he should pay a price for Youko's death. But he also thought about Kama, alone, facing a killer. He couldn't die without helping her. He had to think of something, had to survive long enough to tell someone about the danger she faced.

Amaya extended the zip gun, shaking badly. Rafe was one step too far away to disarm her before she fired. In a blur, Gabe flashed from behind a couch and shoved his mother aside. Amaya toppled against the chair she'd used for support, rolled onto the seat, and bounced to the floor. The zip gun slid off into darkness. Gabe stared down at her, horrified.

Rafe moved in quickly, prepared to restrain her. Her eyes rolled back in her head, she convulsed once, and then she lay motionless. He couldn't find a pulse.

She shouldn't be dead. She hadn't hit her head on the way down, or even fallen hard. What was wrong with her? He started CPR, desperate to save her. Fear doubled his strength as he pumped her chest.

"Mother?" Gabe said.

Rafe nearly told him to go for help, then he reconsidered. She'd murdered Leon. How much harder would it be on Gabe to see his mother go through a protracted trial and on to a death sentence? Maybe it was better if it ended here. He stopped the CPR and checked again for a pulse. Nothing.

He stood and put an arm around the boy, his own heart pounding. "I'm sorry, Gabe."

"I killed her," Gabe whispered. "I shouldn't have knocked her down. I'm a murderer, just like her."

"That's not true."

Rafe tried to hug Gabe, turn him away from the sight of his dead parents, but the boy fought like a tiger. He ran across the lounge and plunged into the corridor screaming, "I killed her!"

Rafe ran after him. Gabe made it to his cabin and locked the door. He raised his hand to pound, but motion in the corridor caught his eye.

Benson and two crew members came into the corridor from the dining room, drawn by the commotion. Rafe thought about the scene in the lounge: Amaya dead on the floor and Leon with the dagger in him. The captain wouldn't let him off the ship without conducting a thorough investigation. He didn't have time to answer questions.

With a creeping sense of déjà vu for turning his back on another death room, he walked away down the corridor toward the airlock. The hairs on the back of his neck crawled with a will of their own. Every step he took felt wrong. He couldn't run away again, but he had to. Greg's door opened, and the boy emerged into the corridor.

"Walk with me," Rafe ordered, taking him by the arm and marching him toward the airlock. "Don't look back. I have to get to the station to help Kama."

"Can I come?"

"No, you have to stay here. Stay with Gabe. Don't leave him. Leon and Amaya are dead."

Greg's head jerked toward him. "What? How?"

"Captain Benson may think that I did it. As soon as I know Kama is safe, I'll turn myself in. But for now, Gabe needs you, understand?"

"Mr. McTavish," Benson called. The captain's footsteps sped up behind them.

Rafe gave Benson a wave and stepped through the airlock. He transferred into the runabout and nodded to Swede, who began undocking.

"How's the nephew?" Swede asked.

"False alarm," Rafe replied. "Let's get back."

They'd cleared the yacht and were well on their way back to the station when the radio crackled.

"Station runabout, this is Captain Benson. Return Mr. McTavish to the ship at once."

Swede glanced at him, pointed to the radio. "What's that about?"

"Probably Goldman wants to ride my ass about something. You know these corporate types, always bossing people around." How much would Benson be willing to say over an open channel? Rafe hoped not much.

Swede wiggled a finger up and down on the transmit button. "EcoMech ship, this is Runabout 1. You're breaking up. Repeat, you're breaking up." Swede grinned and flicked the radio off.

"Guess that'll show 'em."

Rafe prayed there wouldn't be armed escorts waiting for him when they reached the station. He knew Benson would send his own people as quickly as he could scramble them.

They were on final approach to the runabout bay when an alarm went off. Red lights flashed across the control console. Swede flipped on a display. It looked like a snowstorm.

"Holy shit! Where'd all that come from?" he muttered. His hands played over the controls, silencing the alarm.

"What's wrong?" Rafe asked.

"It looks like a serious meteor shower passing through, but we haven't had warning of one. Must be something wrong with the sensors."

Swede piloted them into the bay. Rafe skipped out the door and into chaos. Alarms wailed, and the emergency lights flashed. The corridors were deserted, and he said a quick prayer of thanks.

"What the hell's going on?" Swede said. He jogged away.

Rafe hurried the opposite direction, hoping he could remember how to get to hydroponics. No point bothering to take the long way around. There was no one to see him. He made a wrong turn, doubled back, and found his destination.

Dusky light left the bay barely visible. Only a few weak safety lights illuminated the recycling vats, and none shone on the long table of shadowy foliage now in night cycle. The foul smell of the place overwhelmed him; a rotting odor mingled with the scent of the vegetation.

Someone was growing herbs. He identified rosemary, probably fresh cut by Miss Patty. He heard the bubbling of the vat fluid, the intermittent hiss and click of valves opening and closing, the dripping of condensation all around, water trickling away through the floor collectors. He couldn't see Kama. Sweat formed on his brow, and he edged forward. Was he too late?

As he neared the vat holding Levine's body, he smelled basil and then a faint trace of lavender. Behind him, a muffled clang echoed through the room. He slipped between tanks into shadow. Light blazed into the bay as the hatchway opened, and footsteps squeaked on the deck.

"Uncle Rafe?" came Greg's voice. "Are you down here?"

Rafe watched the lanky silhouette tiptoe into the dark bay. The boy was alone. Rafe sprinted forward, clapped a hand across Greg's mouth, and shoved the hatchway closed with the other, uncertain whether the killer was somewhere in the bay.

Yanking his nephew into the shadows, he whispered furiously in his ear. "What the hell are you doing here?"

"Helping you," he whispered back, voice choked with fear. "Captain Benson sent a bunch of guys to look for you. I told them I knew where you'd be so they brought me along, but I led them to the other end of the station and gave them the slip."

Rafe grabbed his arm and twisted it to see the boy's nanocom. It glowed faintly, displaying the date and time along with a list of waiting messages.

"They can track your nanocom's location. Get out of here now. Lead them somewhere else."

He steered the boy back to the hatch, but before they reached it, the latch mechanism whirred. He shoved Greg deep into the shadows near the wall and backtracked down the bay toward the vat holding Levine's body. A footstep boomed on the deck, and light flooded around him before he could hide.

"Stop right there, Mr. McTavish," Cookie called.

Cookie and his assistant edged toward him between the tables of vegetation and the recycling vats, weapons pointed and ready. And not precise, civilized stunners either. The crewmen carried combat shotguns; twenty shells each in semi-automatic disc magazines, and two muzzles that looked like the Black Hole of Calcutta as they pointed unwaveringly at Rafe's chest.

Low-velocity buckshot wouldn't poke holes in the station hull, but he tried not to imagine the pretty patterns his guts would make on the bulkhead if either pulled the trigger.

"Cookie, I can't come with you right now. I'm trying to catch a killer.

I promise, I'll turn myself in as soon as this is over."

Cookie's aim didn't waver, but his fellow wiped a sweaty palm on his pants before returning it to the blue steel of his shotgun barrel. "Let's do this nice and easy, Mr. McTavish," Cookie said.

Rafe kept both hands open and away from his sides. He wrinkled his nose and backed slowly away, closer to the lavender and rot of the tanks. Somewhere back there Kama lurked with her stunner, his only hope of remaining free. The two crewmen followed, keeping their distance.

"Are you alone?" Cookie asked, eyes scanning the bay.

"I sent Greg away. This is nothing to do with him."

"We gotta take you in, Mr. McTavish," Cookie said. "You know I like you, but we'll take your body back if we have to."

Rafe glanced to either side and kept backtracking. What range would a stunner have in this humidity? His back smacked up against one of the plant tables, the warm wet surface slippery under his touch. *Far enough?*

"Can't let you take my body anywhere, Cookie. I'm liable to need it."

"We can figure this out," Cookie promised. "On your knees, hands behind your head."

She better be watching... Rafe thought, and lowered himself slowly onto his knees.

Cookie jerked his head at his compatriot, then slung his shotgun across his broad back and fished out a plastic quick-tie.

"Keep me covered," the big crewman instructed his assistant. "Now, Mr. McTavish, don't go giving us any trouble."

Rafe flexed his fingers. When Kama took the second guy, he'd move on Cookie. Any moment now...

Nothing happened. No stunner flash, no thud of a falling body, no wavering of the shotgun barrel. Just Cookie's meaty hand grabbing his wrist. In that moment, he realized that Kama wouldn't help. She wanted the killer for Oasis, and she'd sacrifice him if necessary. A shrapnel mine detonated inside his chest, shredding his budding love to pieces.

Then the silence was broken.

"CHAAAAAAAAAAAAAAAAAARGE!!!!"

Greg came hurtling out of the shadows, arms outspread and head down, shrieking like a banshee. With a crunch, the lanky teenager's head cannoned into the small of the assistant's back and bounced off. The assistant looked in amazement as the boy tottered with unfocussed eyes, then toppled like a sapling cut off at the roots.

Body armor, Rafe thought. *Ouch.* But he had no time for sympathy. He swung a vicious uppercut into Cookie's groin and flung himself backward under the plant table.

"Shit! Get him!" came a pained roar from Cookie.

On hands and knees, Rafe scurried up the bay closer to the vat with Levine's body and the faint smell of lavender, threading his way through a jungle of pipes. A shotgun roared, and buckshot rattled against the metalwork a few feet away like gravel flung at glass. Rafe rolled to one side and ducked into a dark crevice under an overhanging table.

"Dammit! Where did he go?"

"Watch your back—he's a slippery bastard!"

Rafe heard boots pounding on the deck plates as the two crewmen ran forward. They stopped perhaps twenty feet from him, too far away to rush them. From a prone position, he could see their booted feet, their stances screaming their readiness to kill.

With desperate caution, Rafe drew his ball from his pocket and flipped it farther down the row of tables. It twanged off a table leg. Cookie's assistant hurried ahead, but Cookie held his position, his legs twisting as he swept his weapon over the length of the tables, watching his assistant's back.

Rafe cursed his luck under his breath. Couldn't Leon have gotten some doughnut-eating rent-a-cops instead of these guys? They knew he wasn't armed, that his best chance lay in ambushing them both together hand-to-hand, and so they were keeping their distance from one another. Break cover to drop one, and the other gets the drop on you. He crawled on his knees, keeping his shoes off the noisy metal deck, sliding out from under the table to crouch on the far side.

The only way he could take them both would be to knock Cookie out with a single blow and reach cover before the other guy blew his head off. He flexed his hands and tightened his leg muscles.

With a fizz and crackle, a stunner fired from between two vats farther down the recycling line. Cookie's assistant fell to the deck with a clatter. Energy surged through Rafe so suddenly he thought he'd burst, flooding him with new hope. A grin split his face. *She didn't abandon me.*

Cookie swung toward the blast, and Rafe took his chance, leaping onto the table. His shoes skated across the slimy tabletop and tangled in the plants. Instead of the planned graceful sliding arc onto Cookie's back, he fell well short. He rolled as he hit the deck, and his ears rang as Cookie's shotgun sent a torrent of buckshot inches over his head.

Rafe came in low and kicked out the man's knees. Cookie went down hard; the shotgun skittered away under the plant table, and his breath rushed out with a whooshing sound. Rafe leaped on top of the bigger man and swung a fist for his jaw. Cookie blocked his swing and jammed an elbow into Rafe's healing ribs. Paralyzing pain streaked up his side. Cookie flipped him sideways onto the deck and rolled on top, cocking his hand back to deliver a smashing blow.

"Freeze or I'll shoot!" Greg shouted.

Rafe and Cookie both stopped. Greg stood nearby, the assistant's shotgun awkwardly in hand, pointing somewhere vaguely in the direction of the two men's heads. The kid's eyes were dazed, and the black circle of the shotgun barrel weaved.

"Put it down!" Rafe and Cookie howled together.

"Don't worry, Uncle Rafe, I'll save you!" Greg slurred.

Out of the darkness, Kama rocketed into Greg, knocking the gun barrel into the air. The gun roared and buckshot pinged against the ceiling before falling like rain. The recoil propelled Greg backward, the gun flying from his hands and falling into the hydroponic vat with a dull splat.

Cookie watched, open mouthed, fist still raised high over Rafe's head. Rafe reacted first, smashing the heel of his hand into Cookie's nose, and connecting again with an elbow to the jaw that sent the crewman sprawling.

Rafe scrambled up and flung himself onto the plant table, sliding across the ooze and plants on his belly, going for Cookie's discarded shotgun on the other side. He landed in a roll that put him back on his feet. Cookie vaulted the table and tackled him waist high, taking them both down, but the man couldn't maintain his grip on Rafe's slimy clothes. He scuttled to his feet and lunged for the shotgun, but the crewman grabbed his ankle and dumped him back to the deck inches short of the weapon.

The pain in his ribs exploded, taking his breath away. Cookie was on him in a flash, cranking his arm up behind his back. Rafe felt him fumbling for handcuffs. From the corner of his eye, a blur of Kama leapt from the table, her boot aimed at Cookie's head. He heard a thunk, and the crewman's weight fell away.

Rafe rolled over, coughed, and clutched his ribs. "What took you so long?"

"*Shiva*, McTavish!" she said as she crouched next to him, stunner in hand. "Is there *anyone* who doesn't want you dead?"

He rolled to his knees and checked Cookie's pulse before pulling a plastic tie from the man's pocket and securing his hands behind his back. He retrieved the remaining shotgun and scooted back over the table, drenched from head to toe in hydroponic fluid and trailing mangled bits of vegetation. Together, he and Kama hoisted a dazed Greg from the floor.

"I'm sorry, Uncle Rafe," the boy mumbled, rubbing at his bruised head.

"You did okay." Rafe clapped the boy on the shoulder.

Kama grabbed the feet of Cookie's stunned assistant and hauled him into the darkness behind the recycling line. They regrouped near the vat holding Levine's body.

"What the hell's going on?" she demanded. "Why are Leon's goons after you?"

Before Rafe could answer, Greg jumped in. "There's been a huge explosion. Uncle Rafe, you must have heard about it on the runabout radio. It happened a few minutes after you left the ship. Our runabout got hit with some of the debris when we came to the station."

"Explosion?" Rafe replied in a whisper. "What are you talking about?"

"The explosives bunker went up. There was all this radio chatter that Levine was hiding out there, and everyone wanted the reward. Miners went out there in their ships, in suits, and then—kaboom."

Rafe listened, horrified. A booby-trap, it had to be. A diversion to turn all prying eyes away from the station. The killer must be coming soon.

"McTavish," Kama breathed. She trailed her fingers through the hydroponic fluid smearing his shirt, and then examined her own stained coveralls. "I know who it is. Hydroponic fluid washes out, but hydraulic fluid doesn't. It's—"

"What's that?" Rafe held up a hand. Just on the edge of hearing, a low hum sounded. "It's not coming from the corridor or the crawlspace."

He squinted into the gloom, then pointed to a small, round portal set into the end wall, half hidden by tangled plant growth. "There's an airlock back there. It's the pressurization pumps." His body tensed.

"Greg—get into the shadows and stay there. Kama, stay with him."

"Wait a min—" she protested.

"No time for arguments," Rafe insisted. He hefted the shotgun. "Whoever comes through that airlock isn't going to be playing games. That stunner of yours won't do spit against someone in a full spacesuit."

Breathing lightly and ignoring the tears starting in his eyes from the biting pain in his chest, he crept forward and pressed himself against one of the hydroponic tanks. He peered between the bay's encroaching clutter, managing to get a view of the airlock door. The hum of the pressurization pumps ended with an abrupt click.

The crank on the hatch turned, and the door swung open. A figure stepped out, stripping off a spacesuit helmet and gloves and dumping them in the airlock. Yuri Roshal, face alive with nervous tics, peered into the gloom. The shipping manager pulled a weapon from his belt and looked around the bay, twitching and jumping at every click and gurgle from the machinery, keyed to breaking point.

Roshal took two nervous steps into the hydroponics bay, and then froze, head swiveling. Rafe held his breath, deliberately not ducking back so his movement wouldn't attract Roshal's attention. He checked the safety catch on Cookie's shotgun with his thumb. He couldn't make out what weapon the lanky tug pilot held, but he doubted it was anything so civilized as a stunner.

A flash of movement caught his eye. With a cat's stealth, Kama moved past him. In the universal code of soldiers everywhere, Rafe flicked her an angry hand signal. *Hold in place.* He didn't want Roshal spooked. Best to catch him in the act of extracting the body, when he'd have to put away his weapon to drag Levine's inert mass out of the cloying fluid. Kama ignored him, and slunk out of his sight, moving in the direction of the airlock. Roshal moved forward, closer to the vat.

Behind him, Rafe heard a moan and a crash, then Cookie's assistant staggered into the aisle. Roshal leapt like a startled rabbit, handgun coming up. The assistant stood in plain view, unaware of the shipping manager. Something flashed, a crack sounded, and then a red rosette blossomed in the assistant's groin. He toppled backwards.

Rafe advanced toward Roshal, threading between the recycling equipment. Another shot rang out and a pipe near his shoulder spewed an acrid liquid in response. There, outlined in the safety lights around the main hydroponic vat, stood Roshal, handgun now pointed at Kama, who stood five feet away, a length of pipe raised to strike. Rafe ducked behind another vat.

"Weapon down and out in the open, missy!" Roshal shouted. "Right now, or you die!"

Rafe choked down his fear and tried to get a bead on Roshal. Kama blocked most of her captor's body, and the shotgun was not a sniper's tool. She pitched the pipe to one side and raised her hands.

Roshal grinned. "Thanks. That makes it easier." He cocked the pistol.

Rafe fired. The shotgun roared and kicked back into his shoulder, and the pellets ripped out the glass side of the vat in a vast snowstorm of splinters. Blood-red fluid gushed out in a tidal wave, sending Roshal flying off his feet. Kama went down too, as thousands of gallons of fluid battered into them. A man-sized, bulbous something slid out with it, splattering on the floor—Levine's half-dissolved corpse.

Rafe barreled out into the open, all his abused muscles working to get him a bead on the fallen murderer before he could regain his feet. Too late. Roshal had lost his pistol, but he grabbed Kama's coverall's collar and held a knife at her throat.

Rafe skidded to a halt.

Roshal's face twitched like a madman's. "Nice try, McTavish," he laughed, backing toward the open airlock door and dragging Kama with him. Her eyes glowed with fury. He dug the knife-tip in deep enough to draw blood, then seized a spare spacesuit and flung it into the open air-lock. "Want to rush me now? Not good odds."

Rafe kept his shotgun raised as the murderer backed away. "Turn her loose, and I'll let you go."

Roshal pulled Kama into the airlock chamber. "Nah," he said, and swung the hatch closed.

Rafe ran forward as the locking wheel spun. He pounded on the unyielding window, watching helplessly as Roshal slammed her head into the wall, then flung her to the floor and hammered his boot into her belly. She curled in a ball while the shipping manager seized his helmet and gauntlets. He thumbed a control, and the whirr of the extraction pumps started.

Rage, frustration, and cold fear swelled in Rafe. He punched the intercom control. "Where do you think you're going to run to, Roshal? Two security cruisers and an EA patrol boat will be here in hours. Do you really think you'll beat them to the jump gate in your little tug?"

Roshal grinned. "They'll be kinda busy cleaning up after that little mess I made of the explosives bunker. I'll give myself about six to one against. Not great. Better odds than she's got, though." He shoved the spare suit toward Kama. "Put it on."

She shook her head, and Roshal laughed. "Suit yourself. Hold your breath if you want to."

He pulled on his helmet. Rafe wrenched at the locking wheel, but the door wouldn't open until the cycle completed. Kama scrambled desperately into the suit, pounding at her ears as the air pressure dropped.

"Roshal!" Rafe roared. "Damn you, open this hatch!"

Roshal only bent down and shoved the helmet over Kama's head, then kicked her over onto her stomach and used a tool belt to tie her spacesuited hands behind her.

"Don't think so," he said, tossing the knife aside with one clumsy gauntlet. "Why don't you go tell your nice friends in their shiny cruisers that I'm carrying something valuable? Wouldn't want me to break anything, would we?" He thumped the airlock release control, seized Kama by the belt, and pulled himself out of the station and out of sight.

"Damn it!" Rafe swore, punching the control to start cycling the airlock again. Pumps whirred once more as the chamber began to refill with air.

Greg stood beside him, eyes wide. "What are you going to do?"

"Get in a suit and get out there after them." He snatched the remaining suit from the rack and shoved his legs in.

"I'll come too."

Rafe shook his head. "Get help for the injured man, and get Benson to send a runabout after us."

"But—"

"No arguments, soldier. Follow orders."

The lock finally pressurized, and the inner door hammered against the wall as he jerked it open. Rafe lunged inside and hit the controls to cycle the lock, still fastening seals on his suit. Then he waited impatiently for the light by the hatch to change from red to green and the hatch to crack open.

His breathing echoed in his ears, the only sound in the universe. But for the stars outside the hatch, everything else was black and empty, a billion miles of loneliness on every side. Ahead, Kama and Roshal were tiny shapes in the unfillable dark, the angular shape of Roshal's tug a barely-visible silhouette beyond them.

He oriented himself toward the dwindling figures and jumped off. His hands and fingers felt cold; not, he prayed, from a leaking cuff seal. He reached to the control panel on his chest, flipped on the master switch for his thrusters, and put his thumb down on the thruster control inside his glove. He accelerated away into the nothingness, using half his fuel in a mad burn. But out in the endless cold, he sensed no movement. He could as well have been floating motionless.

Details of the figures ahead became clear; Kama's arms bound behind her, her motionless legs, the barest hint of a line or tether binding the two of them together. Roshal was still, his posture relaxed. Of course, he would have spent thousands of hours in suits, would know them intimately. Both he and Kama faced the tug; no sign they knew they were pursued. Rafe touched his thrusters again.

Roshal was closer now, maybe two hundred meters ahead. With the mass of two people and only one set of thrusters, he'd accelerated much more slowly than Rafe. But he'd had a long start, and the tug was too close.

Rafe's suit beeped at him, warning him of his marginal fuel state. He had barely enough propellant to slow to a halt, let alone enough to return to the station. He would either guess right and make it to the tug, or he'd drift forever.

He watched Kama lift her knees toward her chest. In a contorted move, she extended one leg along the tether that passed from her waist to Roshal's. Her leg moved in a circle, wrapping the line around it and bringing her closer to the murderer one twist at a time. When she'd closed the distance between them, she jerked the wrapped leg toward her chest and extended the other. Her maneuver slammed her foot against Roshal's oxygen recycling tanks. Admiration mixed with terror gnawed hungrily at Rafe's guts.

Roshal fired his maneuvering jets to turn toward her, but the shortness of the tether prevented him from reaching her. Like a crazy yoyo, she rebounded to the end of the tether and snapped back again, aiming her next blow for the back of Roshal's helmet.

They spun now, in a soundless slow motion dance growing ever closer to the tug. Roshal fumbled at the tether attached to his belt. In a moment, he'd loosed the catch, and Kama spun away alone. Vapor puffed from Roshal's thrusters, and his approach to the tug slowed. But Kama, no longer harnessed to him and unable to switch on her own thruster control, continued ahead at an alarming pace.

Rafe gulped air, breaths gasping in his ears. This was madness. She was too close to the tug, and he was low on fuel. His fingers caressed the thruster control. The thrusters flared, silently, and Roshal's silhouette grew larger much faster.

They were no more than a thousand meters from the tug now. Roshal's thrusters flared again, and he turned to meet Rafe's charge, a laser cutting torch extended in his hand. As the suit beeped Fuel Critical warnings in his ears, Rafe groped at the tool belt for a weapon, anything. Nothing. With meters to go before they joined, he touched his thrusters and altered course. He shot past the shipping manager, just out of range.

Ahead, Kama plunged on toward the tug. Rafe began braking with what little fuel he had left, slowing his speed to match hers. His fuel gave out as his fingers grasped at her suit. He couldn't find a purchase, and he slipped past, panic freezing his brain.

The loose end of the tether whipped against his shoulder as he slid by her. He clung to it, pulled himself closer. They tumbled on toward the tug while he found the thruster control switch on her chest, flipped it on, and threaded his arms around her back. They didn't have time for him to release her hands. He glimpsed her fearful eyes through the visor. If she braked too hard, he'd lose his grip and crash into the tug by himself. If she didn't brake hard, they'd both be smashed on the tug.

Kama fired the thrusters, correcting their spin. Then she fired a series of short bursts, each one threatening to rip her from his arms. He couldn't see the tug before them, but he saw Roshal, gliding in behind them, still wielding the laser cutter. Rafe's blood pounded in his ears.

Kama made a final prolonged burn, and at the last moment, re-oriented them so her body cushioned their impact against the station. They hit hard. Her eyes squeezed shut from the pain. He grabbed onto a handhold by the tug's open airlock and prevented them from ricocheting back into space. Her suit went slack, and he felt rather than heard the hiss of air leaking. Her mouth opened, gasping. Her eyes looked into his, and he saw her confidence in him. Then she looked beyond him, and terror sparked.

Rafe jerked them sideways, yanked loose the tool belt binding her hands, and shoved her into the open airlock. He hit the control to cycle it and turned to face Roshal who, laser cutter at the ready, glided silent and deadly toward him.

Roshal raised the cutter to bring it down in a slashing movement, and Rafe pushed off, catching the man in the midriff with his shoulder, his hand reaching for control of the cutter. They tumbled backward through blackness. Roshal reached across Rafe's back, trying to shut off his air supply. He wrapped his legs around the miner and reached over to twist loose the cuff seal on the hand that held the laser cutter. Escaping air carried frozen condensation sparkling across the vacuum.

Roshal panicked and let the cutter go. It tumbled away behind the shipping manager, its bright beam marking its lazy motion. Rafe, seeing the danger, hit his depleted thrusters to no avail. Before it drifted out of range, the cutter sliced a razor thin line up the back of Roshal's suit, his raised arm, and the tip of Rafe's gloved finger. The man convulsed between Rafe's legs. Blood spewed from his mouth and covered the helmet faceplate.

Rafe released the lifeless miner and grabbed his leaking glove, trying to pinch off the missing tip. The air in the suit thinned, the chill of infinity sliding in to join him. He had no thruster fuel left to return to the tug. In a few minutes, he'd be dead. He wished he'd turned on the suit radio earlier when he'd had an available hand. He wanted to say goodbye to Kama. He'd had so much more he wanted to say to her.

18

Kama punched buttons to recycle the airlock and open the outer hatch again. She cursed at the bulky space suit as she pulled herself up the tug's companionway to the cockpit, banging damaged air tanks on the ceiling and overhanging cupboards in the weightless environment. She had to shrug out of the suit to fit into the pilot's chair, wasting more precious time. She skipped the safety harness and hooked a foot under the seat to hold her position.

Somewhere out there, McTavish faced Roshal alone and unarmed. She couldn't see either of them out the tug's front windows. Where the hell were they? She had to help him, but she had no familiarity with the tugs controls.

Her eyes played over the dash. All she needed were the thrusters. How hard could it be to find thruster controls? None of the switches and buttons were labeled.

Well, then, trial and error. She flipped a switch and wiggled the joystick in front of her. Nothing happened. She tried another switch and the cabin lights shut down. *Moorhk,* she cursed herself. *Get it right.* On her third try, she felt the tug respond with a tiny swing right. *Thank Lakshmi.*

As the craft came around, she spotted two suited figures about a hundred meters away. She nudged the tug forward. One of the suits spun spread-eagled. The other drifted, back to her, hands out of sight. She couldn't tell which of them was McTavish. She gave the thrusters another little spurt.

When she got closer, she could see the rupture up the back of the spread-eagled suit, and her heart seemed to stop beating. The body rotated, and she saw the obscured faceplate, still unable to recognize a face. Then she remembered that McTavish was out of thruster fuel. If the other suit were Roshal, he would have used his thrusters to come to the tug by now, wouldn't he?

Kama edged the tug sideways toward the second suit. Since McTavish couldn't come to her, she needed to make contact, but if she hit him too hard, she'd just send him spinning farther away. She decided catching him might be the better bet. She maneuvered the tug past him until it was immediately in his path and rushed back the companionway.

A quiet thump, followed by scrabbling sounds, echoed along the side of the tug. Through the port in the hatch, she saw McTavish pull himself into the airlock, holding both hands together. His motions seemed slow and weak, and when his hands drifted apart, she spotted the hole in his glove. She slapped the controls to start the lock cycling, urging it to hurry. When it finished, she swung open the inner hatch and charged through.

McTavish looked blue through his faceplate, his eyelids fluttering. She ripped at his helmet seals, her hands shaking, and pulled the helmet loose. He took deep, ragged breaths while she stripped the remainder of the suit off. Their eyes met and his arms wrapped around her, holding her so close she couldn't breathe. She hugged him back, her eyes filling with tears. He was as cold as a snowman. After an eternity, she pushed him to arm's length.

He beamed at her, and she felt like she stood at the brink of a cliff staring into a bottomless canyon. He was on the verge of saying something, speaking words that could never be taken back, words she wanted to hear with all her heart. She mustn't let him. He was a cop, and she was a thief. *Shiva*, they'd destroy one another.

"Okay, McTavish. Why were Goldman's goons after you?" she asked, stopping his next words. The glowing happiness in his expression dimmed, and pain stabbed at her soul.

"Amaya killed Leon with my dagger. That's why she made up the story about Greg being injured, to lure me back to the ship and pin Leon's murder on me. She intended to kill me and make it look like self-defense, but Gabe intervened. Then she just... fell down and died. I tried to revive her..."

Kama struggled to take it in, but it all seemed too fantastic. "So she was behind all of this, and when it looked like her plan might fail, she killed Leon instead?"

"No, that's the crazy part." McTavish shook his head. "She admitted that she lied earlier. She wasn't Leon's blackmailer, didn't know about any of it. I think she hatched the plan to kill Leon while I talked to her. Maybe she was worried that I'd tell him about her takeover plot."

"But why the pursuit?"

He avoided her eyes. "I had to get back to help you, and they wouldn't have believed I was innocent, not with my dagger buried in Leon's chest. I left without telling anyone what happened."

"Leon dead from your weapon, and you fled the scene. They may not listen to Gabe even if he can exonerate you. Let me take you to the Oasis ship until we know how things stand."

His gaze swung up, fierce. "I won't run away this time. When we get back to the station, I'm turning myself over to Captain Benson."

She wanted to beat her fists on his chest, tell him what a moorhk he was. Instead she said, "All right, if that's what you want. But first, we search the tug."

Kama put a hand on a grab bar and pulled herself into the corridor. "You take the back, I'll start up front."

"Wait a minute," he called, trailing her from the airlock. "What was that business about hydraulic fluid and hydroponic fluid?"

She anchored a foot on a rail and pointed to the stain on her coveralls. "This is hydraulic fluid. No amount of washing takes it out, believe me. I got this stain the morning after I arrived while working on Todd's prospecting ship. When Roshal came to take me back to the station, I noticed a similar stain on that Aerosaurs shirt of his. He claimed it was a hydraulic fluid stain too, and he'd gotten it the night before while working on his tug."

McTavish rubbed his temple, frowning. "But there wasn't a stain on his shirt the last time I saw it."

"Exactly. Miss Patty assures me that hydroponic fluid washes right out."

"Ah," McTavish said, his expression clearing. "He got hydroponic fluid on his shirt getting Levine into the tank, and then he lied about it."

She gave him a smug smile. "Elementary."

McTavish floated down the companionway and disappeared into a compartment at the back of the tug. She heard him opening doors and rifling through things, and went forward to begin her own search, thinking about what might happen to McTavish if she took him back to the station. The man had principles, she'd give him that, but she couldn't turn him over to Benson. His freedom hinged on the testimony of a kid, and who'd listen to a traumatized little boy? She'd alert Samir to expect a passenger.

Ten minutes later, she'd worked her way back to the airlock again without finding anything. The far end of the tug was suspiciously quiet. She glided along the corridor and found McTavish in a tiny bunk space, his back to the door and a sheaf of filmies in his hands. She floated up behind him undetected and read over his shoulder.

The top filmie had an Oasis letterhead, the first page of the Oasis contract, all the comments visible in the margins. He flipped through the pages and shook his head in exasperation before moving to the next set of documents in the stack.

"You found something."

McTavish jerked and drifted around to face her. He folded the contract in two and held it out.

"This is yours, I think." He watched her stuff the filmies in her pocket.

"Thank you," she said in a small voice.

He grinned and thrust the rest of the bundle at her. "More interesting reading. Bank statements, Levine's, but from a long time ago. And these look like purchase orders and supply invoices from the same period. Mars Development letterhead, no less. Incriminating evidence that holds Levine partially responsible for the Mars Dev tunnel collapse some years ago, where he also seems to have run an embezzlement racket.

"But here's the kicker. This" he held up another filmie, "is a confession from Levine stating that he was blackmailed into running the embezzlement here on the station—but not by Roshal. Roshal was just an unknown blackmailer's on-site enforcer. Later Roshal made Levine work the buyout scam, but my guess is his boss didn't know about it. There can't be two blackmailers. Levine and Leon had to be blackmailed by the same person.

"Then there's this." He hoisted a plastic bag between his thumb and finger, condensation on the sides obscuring the contents.

Kama took the bag, queasily guessing what it contained.

"Levine's thumb. *Ew*," she said after closer examination. She passed it back to him. "That's how he got in to search Levine's quarters. But why try to kill you with a bomb? He could have just waited."

"As long as we were all chasing a ghost across the galaxy, Roshal didn't have to worry about leaving behind forensic evidence. But when he saw the station schematics on the walls of the infirmary, he must have thought we were at least suspicious that Levine hadn't left the station despite his elaborate false trail. Since he didn't find the cash chip in Levine's quarters, he knew Levine had a storage location that he'd been unable to discover. The last thing he wanted was a search to turn up either the body or the storage cache, which might have contained another copy of Levine's confession." McTavish made for the corridor. "We'd better get back. They'll need the tug for rescue operations."

Kama led the way to the cockpit. This time she skimmed the operations manual before setting out. When she turned on the radio, it buzzed with rescue chatter.

McTavish listened, and his face grew grim.

"I should have thought about how Roshal might respond to a trap."

"You aren't responsible for the carnage here any more than you're responsible in Leon's and Amaya's deaths."

She worked out rendezvous coordinates for the Oasis ship. Would he notice they were going the wrong direction to return to the station? Would the cruisers pursue them? McTavish deluded himself if he thought a court would take the word of a child over the evidence of his dagger—undoubtedly with his fingerprints on it—used as the murder weapon. Add his estrangement from his family, and he had no one in his corner. It might be wrong to run, but better that than prison.

She made a slow turn and started away, moving through darkness, her soul abysmal. He'd be on the run, and she'd never see him again. Or he'd clear his name and return to his company, and she'd still never see him again. So ironic—he didn't even know they both lived in the same city. While they might both call Mumbai home, they would never move in the same circles unless it was him coming to arrest her.

McTavish, who'd seemed lost in thought, leaned toward the window. "Kama, please don't take this as an insult, but aren't we going the wrong direction? I think the station is over there."

She stared straight ahead. "I can't take you back there. It's too risky. What if they don't believe Gabe? What if he tells a different story? Leon Goldman's dead. What do you think his father will do, welcome the prime suspect with open arms?"

McTavish sighed. He took her hand from the controls and held it in his own. His fingers were warm and soft, and he gave her a quiet smile.

"I appreciate that you're trying to protect me, but unless you intend to keep me prisoner forever, I'm going back. The more you delay my return, the more guilty I look."

"You did nothing wrong. You shouldn't have to defend yourself," she protested.

He laughed. "I did plenty wrong; illegal access to bank records, uploading your bot to the EcoMech network, never mind the half-truths and outright lies."

"So why stop now?" Kama asked, not sure she wanted to hear the answer.

"I did those things because I couldn't see any other way to save lives, not because I lost faith in the legal system. Running away now doesn't save anyone, not even me. I know; I've been there. You don't believe in the system, but I do. I'm asking you to trust me. It'll be okay."

Trust him. Not something she would have done three days ago; not a rich corporate playboy from an elite family. But now, those weren't the words that came to mind when she thought of him. She thought of words like *self-sacrificing, compassionate,* and above all, *trustworthy.* Sadness swallowed her whole.

"You'd better be right," she said. She withdrew her hand from his and changed their heading.

"Call the station. Let them know I'm coming," said McTavish.

19

Rafe wanted to scream and pound his fists on the control console, frustrated by the pointless and wanton destruction slipping past the window. Undamaged ships crisscrossed the space around the station rescuing survivors. Kama steered clear of the larger debris, but smaller bits pinged off the tug's hull, filling the interior with a sound like temple bells tolling for the dead.

The EcoMech ship was now docked to the station, along with other smaller ships he guessed were unloading injured. The security cruisers and the EA patrol boat responded to the station's distress calls, reporting they were closing fast.

As the tug swung around on its own docking approach, he could see broken antennae and hull punctures on the end of the station nearest the blast. Crippled prospecting ships drifted nearby. Even Maltraw's ship, partially shielded from the blast by the bulk of the station, had some of its lights knocked out. It moved steadily away from the station, like a whale leaving a beached mate. He hoped Janice wasn't on it. They'd need her skills.

Kama opened a transmission and announced their impending arrival. Browning instructed her to dock with the other ships at the far end of the station where the cargo haulers usually arrived.

Together, they walked to the hatch, and Kama faced him, worry clouding her eyes.

"It's not too late. I can still get you out of here," she said.

It occurred to him that if she were right and he ended up in prison or worse, this might be his only chance to kiss her, but that might seem too much like goodbye, and he couldn't face the thought of never seeing her again.

"I think you still owe me a dinner—a proper dinner, somewhere nice," he said, managing a shy smile and feeling like a fool. To his ears, it sounded like the dumbest pickup line he'd ever heard, and he wondered why he could never say the right thing around her.

She stared, blinked, and then slapped her forehead. "*Moorhk!* At a time like this, all you can think of is food?"

But he thought he saw both amusement and admiration in her face before she turned away to open the hatch. She stepped through and vanished, yanked out of his sight. He heard her string of Hindi invectives and pitied whoever grabbed her.

He followed, hands in the air. A circle of crewmen ringed the hatch, stunners ready. Men grabbed his arms, wrenched them behind him, and forced him to his knees while they secured his wrists with handcuffs.

The sights and sounds in the bay pummeled him. Injured men littered the floor. Screams of pain echoed against the crates and boxes pushed aside to make room. Farther down the wall, another ship offloaded more wounded. Janice and the medic moved among them, triaging a holocaust.

Captain Benson came forward to stand before him. He signaled the guards to get Rafe on his feet. They did it none too gently. He hadn't made any friends by eluding Cookie. He hoped Cookie's assistant had survived.

"Mr. McTavish, I'm arresting you on suspicion of the murders of Leon Goldman and Amaya Goldman."

Rafe's eyes swept the room, taking in the suffering. He had to do something. "Captain, the station has no medical supplies. What do you have available?"

Benson glanced around him and frowned. "These are serious charges. What do you have to say in your defense?"

"Nothing that can't wait. Maltraw's ship may have additional supplies, but he's pulling away. How quickly can you get a runabout over there? Do you have anyone with medical training on your crew? The station staff are overwhelmed."

When Benson didn't reply, Rafe continued, "The dead won't get any deader. It's the living who need your help, and they need it now. Throw me in the brig, I don't care, but don't turn your back on these people. They are, after all, EcoMech employees, too."

The captain surveyed the sea of wounded again. His frown deepened, but he began issuing orders to his crew, sending some of them away to fulfill Rafe's suggestions. Rafe shuffled his feet, trying to suppress the urge to fidget. The guard on his right tightened his grip and gave his arm a jerk that sent a lance of pain through his ribs, making him wince.

Kama shook off her own guard and leaped forward to stand toe to toe with his keeper.

"Knock it off," she said. "Or I'll see you're charged with police brutality."

Her guard grabbed her arm. She whirled on Benson.

"And I'll have this bozo charged with sexual assault if he doesn't unhand me. Can you afford the lawsuit, Captain? Because Oasis can. They get very unhappy when their employees are mistreated."

"Kama," Rafe warned. "They're just doing their job. Let it go."

"Uncle Rafe!" Greg hurried across the bay, Gabe in tow. Both of them threaded their way between the bodies scattered over the area, his nephew's expression displaying shock and dismay at the sight around them. The younger boy seemed oblivious to it all.

"Mr. Nighthorse, take Gabe away from here immediately. He's not to interact with Mr. McTavish," Benson ordered.

"Not until you've heard Gabe out," Greg replied.

"Kama, get them out of here," Rafe said. "Gabe's had enough horror for one day."

Gabe looked up at him, and he saw a familiar, untouchable calm masking the anguish of pain and loss, the same calm he'd seen in the mirror when he'd first arrived on Earth after Youko's death. Then Gabe approached Captain Benson, head up, but too serene. *He's in shock. He ought to be crying his eyes out.*

"Captain Benson, please release my uncle. He hasn't done anything wrong. He didn't kill my parents." Gabe's voice wavered. "My mother killed my father before he entered the room, and I'm responsible for my mother's death."

"Gabe, that's not true. You didn't kill her," Rafe protested.

"Then how did she die, Mr. McTavish?" Benson asked.

The boy needed comforting, not an interrogation. Rafe bunched his fists in the cuffs. "Captain, Gabe's just lost both his parents. Perhaps this could wait until later and a less public venue?"

"Fine with me," snapped Benson. "Take him to his cabin. One guard inside, one outside, and keep him cuffed until we've left the station."

"No!" Gabe shouted. "It's me you've got to lock up, not him. I did it. I pushed her down, and she died because of it. He tried to help her, but he couldn't."

The boy threw himself at Rafe, wrapping arms around his waist. Rafe wanted to hold him, take his pain away. He felt helpless, and Benson was making him more angry by the minute.

The medic sidled up to the group, looking harried. "Look, you folks, you're arguing over how many angels can dance on the head of a pin. I did an examination like Captain Benson requested. No one killed that woman. A brain scan shows she died of an aneurysm. She was a walking corpse for about the last half hour of her life. Now can you please either start helping us or get the hell out of the way?"

Benson glared at the medic, and then at McTavish. "Why did you run?"

"I didn't run. I was pursuing Yuri Roshal, the man who murdered three people on the station, the same man who blew the explosives bunker and injured all these miners. I surrendered to you as soon as I could."

"Yeah," said Greg. "And it was Roshal who shot your crewman, not Uncle Rafe."

"That's right, Captain," said Cookie, who stood nearby, his nose swollen and both eyes blackened. "I'd just come around after being knocked out and saw a man in a spacesuit shoot John. Then the same guy took a shot at Mr. McTavish and tried to kill this lady." He nodded at Kama.

"Please let him go," pleaded Gabe, face buried in Rafe's shirt.

"Well, Mr. McTavish, since there appears to be overwhelming eye witness testimony to refute your involvement in any of this... this..." Benson threw up his hands. "I release you from custody."

Cookie drew a knife from his pocket and sliced through the plastic cuffs. Rafe gathered Gabe to him, hugging the boy close.

"Did you hear what the medic said?" he whispered. "It's not your fault. You did the right thing. You saved my life. You're a hero. Your dad would be very proud of you."

Gabe's eyes misted, and he nodded uncertainly. Rafe's heart shattered. Empty platitudes weren't enough. The boy needed so much more. He hoped Gabe could let go of the guilt, something he'd never achieved.

"Greg, get Gabe back to the ship," Rafe said. He watched them go, tears stinging his eyes. Then he cleared his throat and turned to Benson. "Are the security cruisers here yet?"

"They've just arrived, sir," Benson replied.

"Good. Get one of them docked. We'll be transporting wounded as quickly as we can get it loaded."

He threaded his way through the miners on the floor, seeking out Janice. Kama trailed after him. The doctor wrapped bandages around a miner's arm, a grim expression on her face. The flesh of the arm looked freezer-burned, and the miner moaned in pain.

"How many critical?" he asked.

"Lord, I don't know. I've lost count." She gestured toward the far wall. "All of those over there."

"We'll have transport here in about fifteen minutes. They'll have another medic or two and extra supplies. Send anyone who's critical in the first wave. If we need to, we can send a second batch on the other cruiser. Then you need to disappear for a bit."

Janice looked puzzled. "Why's that, cowboy?"

"We have an EA ship incoming. I don't think the commander will appreciate the kind of 'diversion' you offer."

She laughed. "Thanks for the warning, McTavish."

"Tell me something, Janice. How bad off is Ed? Should he be headed for the hospital, too?"

"None of your damn business," Browning boomed from behind them. "Can't stop sticking your nose in, can you?"

Rafe spun around and lifted his hands in surrender. "Just asking."

"Ms. Bhatia, if you're done with my tug, I'd like to have it back for rescue operations," Browning growled. "I need it out there moving the space garbage away from the station. We have enough holes already. Where's Yuri anyway?"

Kama put a hand on Browning's arm. "He's dead, Ed. He's the one who blew the bunker and killed Todd, Rodriguez, and Levine."

"Levine! He's dead, too?" Browning wiped a hand over his face. He looked around at the carnage and said, "Looks like you got things under control here, McTavish. I gotta get back to the command center."

Rafe circulated through the men, helping where he could. He knelt over one of the miners, applying ointment to a laceration. Kama tugged his sleeve and pointed. The security cruiser had docked. Its commanding officer walked into the storage bay and lifted his eyebrows at the scene in front of him. Rafe and Kama approached him.

"Commander...?" said Rafe, extending his hand.

The commander ran his disapproving eyes over Rafe's stained and bloody clothing and didn't take the hand. "I'm looking for Mr. Goldman. I see his ship is docked here."

Kama edged forward, probably to give the man a swift kick, but he stopped her with a hand on her forearm. She glared at him, but he remained calm.

"Mr. Goldman is dead. I now represent EcoMech's interests here. We have a large number of critically wounded who need immediate transport to the jump gate hospital. I want your people to get them loaded on the double. Our medical staff will show them who to take."

The commander stared in disbelief. "Our contract is with Leon Goldman, not the riffraff on this station, and we're here to quell labor unrest, not play nursemaids. On whose authority do you represent EcoMech?"

Rafe fought to answer. After fourteen years disavowing his family, he choked on the words. Kama reached out and squeezed his hand, and his eyes flicked sideways to her. He took a deep breath, drawing courage from her touch.

"On the authority of Aaron Goldman, Chairman of the Board, and on behalf of my family. I'm Rafael McTavish."

The commander paled and squinted at his face. "*The* Rafael McTavish? Of Security Partners?"

A spark of pride ignited at the commander's recognition. It was his own hard-earned reputation the man responded to, not his familial allegiance.

"That's correct. If you'll get these people loaded, I'd like them to be at the jump gate in six hours."

"But, sir, we'd have to run beyond maximum safe speed to cover the distance that quickly," the commander protested.

"EcoMech will provide a thousand credit bonus for every man that arrives at the hospital alive." Rafe knew he had no authority to say such a thing, but he didn't care. He wanted the injured miners to get the best treatment possible, no matter the cost. If he had to, he'd pay the expense out of his own pocket.

"I'll see to it, sir."

The commander sketched a salute he seemed compelled to make and hurried back to his ship. Moments later, mercs poured into the bay. They did a double-take when Janice began ordering them around, but they complied. Two medics from the cruiser conferred with her about the condition of their new patients, and then they were gone.

The storage bay quieted. Rafe ran a hand through his hair, sticky with dried hydroponic fluid. He'd claimed that he was Aaron Goldman's representative here, a tenuous claim at best. It was time to pay the piper. He had to inform Aaron of Leon's death and all that had transpired. He looked around for Kama, but she'd vanished.

He walked through the deserted station corridors. Most of the remaining miners were busy outside the station, clearing up debris, patching the hull, or repairing damaged ships. He hoped the long range com still worked. If not, he'd have to use the one on the EcoMech yacht. When Aaron heard about events, Rafe wasn't sure he'd still be welcome on the ship, or even on the station, since it was also EcoMech property. He might have to take Kama up on her offer of a ride, assuming she hadn't already left. She'd be safer if she had, but he prayed she hadn't. He didn't know where she lived, how to contact her.

The com tech put his call through, and when it connected, he left the room, giving Rafe privacy. He dreaded the coming conversation. Aaron Goldman's maid answered the call. She refused to put him through, saying Aaron couldn't be disturbed. In the background, he heard Aaron's voice asking who she talked to. At the mention of Rafe's name, he dismissed the maid and took the call.

Aaron, a small normally dapper man in his seventies looked like a corpse reanimated in a lab. Dark circle shown under his eyes, his cheeks hung flaccid, and his eyelids drooped. *He's in shock and maybe on meds.* Benson must have already informed him of Leon's death.

"Rafe, thank God. If you're calling me, then I take it you're not in custody."

Surprised by the man's concern, he said, "I'm sorry for your loss, sir. I don't know what you've heard, but I didn't kill Leon."

"I know that," said Aaron, irritation tingeing his voice. "I told Benson he had it all wrong, but he just kept on about it being your dagger and how you'd left the ship without saying anything. I told him if you'd left the ship, it was because you had a damn good reason. Was it Amaya?"

"She wanted to be CEO."

"She's always been unbalanced. I should have done something about her. How's Gabe?"

Rafe thought he must be dreaming. This wasn't the conversation he'd expected. "He's in shock. He feels responsible for his mother's death, even though I assured him he didn't kill her. He'll need professional help when he gets home."

"That bitch. Bad enough she killed my son, but now she's damaged my grandson." Aaron lifted a glass, popped a pill in his mouth, and washed it down.

"Are you okay, sir?"

"Yes, yes." He sipped again and set the glass aside.

"We've had an explosion here at the station. I've taken the liberty of organizing transport for the injured to the jump gate hospital. I invoked your name to get the cooperation of Leon's security forces. I also promised them a bonus if they performed above spec."

"I'm sure you did what you had to do for the injured. Your actions will go a long way toward helping us should anyone file damages. Did you get to the bottom of Leon's strange behavior?"

This hardly seemed to be the time for the discussion, but Rafe didn't see a way to dodge the question.

"He was being blackmailed. It's been going on for years, and he'd been unable to discover who was behind it. He thought the objective might be to drive him out of EcoMech. The mining station purchase was another of the blackmailer's demands."

Aaron sat straighter. "Did Leon tell you what the blackmailer had on him?"

"No, he didn't share that information." Some of Aaron's tension dropped away, and Rafe wondered if he already knew about the blackmail, or at least guessed what Leon had been blackmailed about.

"Could it have been Amaya?"

"She denied it before she died," Rafe said. "I believe her."

"If someone blackmailed Leon so they could replace him at EcoMech," Aaron said, "then I'm in something of a quandary. All the most likely candidates for the CEO position are now suspect."

His eyes narrowed. "I want that blackmailer, and I want someone as CEO that I can trust to safeguard Gabe's inheritance until he's old enough to take up the mantle. Most men ambitious enough to keep EcoMech on course would never give up the position when Gabe's ready. But you would."

It took Rafe a moment to realize what Aaron had said. "You can't mean for me to become EcoMech's CEO. I have my own company to run, and I doubt the EcoMech board would consider me a suitable candidate."

"Of course they'd accept you. You've more than proven yourself while building Security Partners. And it's the strongest position from which to smoke out the blackmailer."

"I can't argue with that," he said, imagining himself strolling the EcoMech corporate campus with a target pinned to his chest. Aaron had to be crazy with grief.

"It's important to reassure the shareholders quickly that EcoMech will remain in capable hands, or stock prices will plummet. I'd like to announce your appointment this afternoon when I announce Leon's death."

Rafe wiped moist palms on his pants. Associating with Greg at the station or telling a commander he was a McTavish was one thing. Facing his father at board meetings was quite another.

"I'm sorry, Aaron. I understand how important the company is to you, but I think your loss may be clouding your judgment. You know I can't come back to Harvest."

"EcoMech's always been one big family, Rafe. I looked after you and your brother when you two got in trouble, and now I need you to help my grandson. If something happens to me, I want to know you'll be looking out for him. I want to know he'll receive Leon's legacy, my legacy, as we both intended."

Aaron had always been like a father to him, he realized, more so than his real father, and he owed a debt for that. Sweat beaded on his brow and trickled down his ribs. He'd told Kama he wouldn't run anymore. If he meant it, now was the time to step up.

"I'm honored that you'd consider me as Leon's successor, and I accept your offer."

The chairman nodded his acknowledgement. "I'll get a contract drawn up."

"Things are a mess here. I'll need a day or two to straighten them out. Would you prefer that I send Gabe back with Leon's remains immediately? I can find other transportation for myself."

"I don't want Gabe out of your sight until you deliver him to me. He's all I have left, and I want to know he's safe. Bring my son and my grandson home when you come."

Aaron cut the connection, and Rafe slumped back in his chair. What had he just done? Had he lost his mind? He didn't want to be CEO of EcoMech. Gabe was only eleven. He'd be stuck on Harvest for years. But he couldn't back out now. With deep regret, he made another call.

When the vid cut in, Rafe saw a raw-boned blonde woman with a buzz cut whom he'd clearly woken from sleep. He cursed himself for not checking the time in Mumbai first.

"RM? Why are you calling in the middle of the night? And what are you wearing?" his assistant asked, rubbing her eyes and wrinkling her nose in disapproval. She looked at him more closely and snapped to attention. "Is that blood on your shirt?"

Rafe looked down at himself and realized what a sight he must be, hydroponic fluid and blood stains smearing his chest, face bruised. When he looked up, a smaller female Chinese face crowded the screen with Barb's, alarm plain to see.

"Sorry, I didn't realize the time. I didn't mean to wake you two. I'm fine."

"You don't look fine," replied Ying Ying. "You in trouble again?"

"Barb, I need to ask you for a favor," he said, ignoring Ying Ying's question. "I know the timing isn't good with the baby due next week, but I'd like you to take over as Security Partners CEO."

She blinked at him. "You know I'm happy to fill in if you want to take some time off."

Ying Ying squinted at Rafe. "How long you want Barb to cover for you?"

Rafe shrugged. It had to be done. "Twelve to fifteen years."

"What you do, grand theft? Twelve to fifteen about right for that," Ying Ying said.

Rafe laughed."Thanks for your unwavering support. I wanted you to hear it from me before Aaron Goldman makes the announcement tomorrow. Leon Goldman's dead. I'm taking over as EcoMech's CEO."

Both women stared. Barb responded first. "Are you sure about this, RM?"

"Honestly? No. But I have an obligation. I'll continue as Security Partners' owner, but you'll be running the show. If any of our customers squawk, let me know, and I'll do what I can to reassure them."

His two best friends looked at him with sympathy and concern. A pang of loneliness shot through him, and he realized he'd deluded himself when he thought he had no family. Maybe they weren't related by blood, but he'd built a new family on Earth. Now he was leaving them behind. The real cost of his decision steamrolled over him.

"Ying, send me whatever I need to sign so Barb has the authority to cut checks against the business accounts. And remember you're supposed to be on maternity leave. No long hours at the office."

"You not my boss now. You don't tell me what to do," she sassed, then became somber. "We going to miss you, RM. You come back visit us whenever you can. Baby needs to see his godfather."

Rafe nodded, too choked to speak, and cut the connection. In a daze, he wandered out of the com center, uncertain of his next action. He reached in his pocket for his ball before remembering that he'd tossed it away in hydroponics. At least he could remember where he'd lost it this time.

Tie up loose ends. Put one foot in front of the other and get it done. His stomach reminded him of his meager breakfast, and now he'd missed both lunch and dinner. Thinking of food reminded him of Miss Patty. He'd start with her.

He didn't find her in the admin offices. Not surprising considering the chaos on the station and the time. He trooped to her quarters and pressed the call button next to the door. It opened to reveal Miss Patty in one of her characteristic frilly dresses.

"Mr. McTavish, what can I do for you?"

"I apologize for the lateness of the hour. May I come in?"

She stepped back and waved him through the door. To his surprise, her quarters were as spartan as Levine's. From the way she dressed, he'd expected doily covered furniture and knickknacks littering every surface.

She noticed the way he looked around and blushed.

"It isn't much, is it? But with the price to transport goods, I haven't been able to decorate."

Then what are you doing with the money from R. S. Steele? He waited while she seated herself on the only armchair and took a seat on the couch.

"Miss Patty, during the course of my investigation, it came to my attention that Mr. Levine was also embezzling money from Galaxy Mining. Did you have any knowledge of that?"

She wrung a handkerchief between her fingers. "No, Mr. McTavish, I knew nothing about that, or about the mine buyout. Mr. Levine seemed an honest and decent man. I was as much taken in as the others."

"It's also come to my attention that mining surveys conducted by prospecting ships from this station have been making their way into the hands of a competitor, R. S. Steele. Do you have any information about that?"

Miss Patty's hands went to her heart, and fear settled over her face. Then the matronly facade crumbled, and she wept openly. "Yes, I sold the surveys," she sobbed. "What else could I do? Mr. Levine told me he wanted to retire. When he retired, I'd lose my job too, and I'd never get another as good. I'm too old."

"And you needed the money?" Rafe asked.

She sniffed. "My grand-niece is a surrogate mother on Bliss. She's already had six children for them, and Ellie's never been strong. She would have died trying to carry another child, but they insisted she fulfill her contract or buy it out. I had to do something. I'm sorry."

"I'm sure you know by now that Mr. Levine is dead."

A fresh welling of tears flooded Miss Patty's eyes.

"I believe you know something about the night he was killed, but you withheld the information because you feared your thefts would be detected. Tell me everything," Rafe said. "I want every detail."

She lowered her handkerchief. "I sent the reports to R. S. Steele in the mail each month. Since it was the mail delivery day, I stayed behind after Mr. Levine left the office to transfer surveys to a stick drive. I put the stick drive into the mail bag and delivered it to the mail ship. I took the incoming mail back to the office, and then I went to bed."

"And then?"

"I woke up later, and I realized that I'd left a list of the reports I'd been copying on Mr. Levine's desk."

"What time was this?"

"About half-past one in the morning, I think," she said. "So I left my quarters and went down the corridor to the office to get it, but when I got near, I heard someone. I thought it must be Mr. Levine working late, so I decided to go back to my quarters."

"Did you hear anything else?"

"A few minutes later, I heard footsteps and a kind of squeaking noise from the direction of the office."

"Squeaking?"

"Yes, I think so. Like a door that needed oiling. I couldn't hear very well—it was only for a few seconds, then it faded away."

Roshal, using the damnable trolley to move Levine's body to hydro-ponics. If Miss Patty had discovered him, would he have killed her, too? Perhaps more to the point, if Miss Patty had told Rafe this sooner, could he have prevented Roshal from killing or injuring so many others? He pushed himself to his feet with a heavy heart.

"And the fight Ed had with Levine? What did they argue about?"

"I don't know for sure. Something about that woman, Janice Fisher, and how much Ed was seeing her." Miss Patty watched him, trembling. "What's going to happen to me now?"

Rafe faced her with resolute eyes. "Whatever the reason, larceny is a serious crime," he said. "I can't just let it lie. I'm confining you to your quarters until EA can be contacted to begin legal proceedings. I'm sorry."

Rafe left Miss Patty's quarters and headed back to the storage bay to find Janice Fisher. He'd been in the new job less than an hour, and already he hated it. He felt like Death's messenger, bringing bad news to one and all. Before he'd become CEO, he could overlook the problems at the station, but now they'd landed smack on his plate.

He found Janice clearing the last of her patients from the storage bay, sending them back to their quarters with instructions to return for rechecks in the morning. She and the medic looked beyond tired.

"I wanted to thank you, both on behalf of EcoMech and from me personally, for helping out. You saved lives," Rafe said.

Janice gave him a wry grin and wiggled her hips. "Wait to thank me until you see my bill."

He tried to return her smile and failed.

"You look like you just lost your best friend," she said. "Did you and that sassy Oasis technician break up? This is the first time I've seen you two apart since I met you."

Rafe thrust his hands in his pockets and rocked on his heels, thinking of how badly he'd wanted to talk to Kama on the tug and how she'd deflected him. "We weren't together exactly."

"No," she laughed, "but you both want to be."

Taken aback, Rafe goggled at her, which only made her laugh more.

"Honey, she's got the hots for you, she just won't admit it, especially to herself. You have to see past all that intellectual bullshit she shovels and look into her heart."

Focus. His love life—or lack of one—wasn't why he'd come. Why did he have to be so distractible?

"About Ed, he's pretty sick, isn't he? He told us he never left the station the night Levine disappeared, but the security cameras say otherwise. I think you're his doctor. What are you treating him for?"

Fisher's face turned to stone. "Look, maybe I'm not licensed anymore, but I've never stopped being a doctor. That information is privileged."

"Thanks, Janice, I can take it from here." Rafe jumped at the sound of Browning's voice behind him.

"I just got the message from corporate—that's EcoMech corporate—telling me you're my new boss, so I guess now I have to answer your damn questions." The smelter supervisor stood, hands on hips, a challenge in his eyes. Fisher shot him a warning look and moved away to pack her trunk.

"Last month you visited a med station in Earth orbit for a physical, only the guy described on the form is about three centimeters taller and a hundred kilos lighter than you," Rafe said. "Did Levine discover your report was fake? Is that why you argued?"

Browning's chin jutted. "My lungs are scarred from ice flu. I've always been able to cover by taking meds and staying fit, but lately that hasn't been working so well. Janice helped me get some experimental treatment. I haven't improved enough so I could pass a company physical yet, so I bribed a doctor to give me a good report. Levine found out, and we argued. But in the end, he agreed to give me another month to see if I could meet requirements. Now you know. As soon as my people are safe, you can have my resignation."

Browning rolled his shoulders and marched out without waiting for a reply. Janice, so warm and funny moments earlier, gave him a doleful look and followed.

Rafe stood alone in the storage bay, listening to the echoes of their footsteps fading away to nothing. His forlorn gaze traveled around the gray, uncluttered space. So neat, so empty. So like his future.

20

"He's done *what*?" Kama exclaimed.

"Yeah!" Greg exclaimed. "Isn't it great? Old Man Goldman convinced the board they should make Uncle Rafe the new CEO. He's taking over at EcoMech, and I'm going to work for him."

After a night tossing and turning, she'd spent the morning trying to write her report to Samir, but at mid-morning, she was less than half done. She couldn't get her mind off McTavish long enough to finish the cursed thing. Like some knight in shining armor, he'd ridden into her life and knocked all her beliefs into a cocked hat.

Then Greg arrived at her door with a filmie: the Oasis contract—without the comments—and it was signed Rafael McTavish, CEO, EcoMech.

"I don't understand," she said. "Why would he do that?"

Greg prattled on, something about press conferences, but Kama didn't pay attention. Emotions ran rampant through her like mutinous rats scurrying from the dark corners of her heart: anger that McTavish had made himself a target, fear that his goodness and honesty would be consumed by the temptations of power at the helm of EcoMech, and overwhelming desire to be at his side to protect his body and soul.

"Where's your uncle now?" she asked, interrupting Greg's litany of McTavish's glorious qualifications.

"He's in the admin offices with Bob Coleman, his assistant."

Kama snatched her duffel off the bunk and rushed out. As she neared the admin section, she rounded a corner and crashed into Browning. He rolled like a ship in heavy seas, but his eyes lit up at the sight of her.

"You headed for the office?" he asked.

"Yeah. How's it going?"

Browning shook his head. "Not good. Five dead, with Levine and Roshal, I guess. One man died on the way to the jump gate medical facilities, and two others are hanging by a thread, plus Warner. Twenty or thirty others injured, but they'll make it. The doctor at the jump gate says the numbers wouldn't be even that good if McTavish hadn't commandeered that fast cruiser. I've never seen a man quite like him. He's a real soldier. And he got rid of that EA patrol boat in a matter of hours. Almost makes me wish I'd still be working for him."

"You're not staying?" she asked, distracted from her anger by Browning's sad expression.

"I can't pass the company physical. As soon as things settle here, I'll be on my way. And that won't take long. He's got Goldman's assistant filing insurance claims already. He says EcoMech will cover the medical expenses for anyone injured in the explosion. It'd take me a month to straighten all this mess out, and I'd probably do half of it wrong.

"He's also got Miss Patty under house arrest. He says she's been selling our surveys to the competition to buy her grand-niece out of a surrogacy contract. I kind of feel sorry for her, going to prison at her age. She won't last a month." Browning ran a hand across his brow. "I better get going. Still a lot of cleanup to do."

Kama watched him walk away, the anger in her gut doing a tango with fear. Had she misjudged McTavish? Now that he had a big, new promotion, did he care about the people on the station? Did he care about her? She stormed on toward the admin section.

When she reached the admin office, she didn't bother to knock. McTavish sat at the desk wearing a white dress shirt open at the collar and sleeves rolled up to reveal fading bruises on his muscular forearms, gray slacks tailored to his slim frame, and incongruous workout shoes. Like a chameleon, he blended with the business-like surroundings of the office, and it tossed fuel on the fire of her fear.

Which was the real McTavish, the one who'd helped her recover the Oasis contract and brought Roshal to justice, or this corporate type running an empire in his shirt sleeves? Was the new power he'd wield already going to his head, tainting his soul?

He had his back to her while he took a vid call on his monitor. At the other end of the call, a blonde woman Kama instantly identified as a merc by her size, bearing, and haircut listened. From his tone of voice, Kama gathered they were close. The woman's eyes held a sadness she seemed determined to disguise.

"I'll be in town every four to six weeks on business. If you and Ying Ying don't mind, I'd like to keep sharing the house with you," McTavish said.

"No problem, RM." Her eyes looked past him, and her expression became guarded. "You have company."

McTavish glanced over his shoulder and flashed Kama a warm smile before turning back to the woman on the screen. He didn't seem concerned that Kama overheard the conversation, and somehow, his casual behavior enraged her further. He should have a guard on the door. He should be taking his security seriously.

"Barb, I'd like you to meet Kama Bhatia. Kama's been helping me here. Kama, this is Barb, my former assistant and the new CEO at Security Partners."

Barb? *This* was McTavish's assistant? Not a bimbo buffing her nails but an Amazonian lesbian he'd just promoted to run his company? Kama wasn't sure what to think about the housemates business, but she knew now she'd barely scratched the surface of who McTavish really was. Her stomach turned to an inferno.

Barb's eyes narrowed. "Isn't she an Oasis tech?"

Kama didn't bother to hide her pride. Here was a woman with intelligence, one who knew a predator when she saw one.

McTavish glanced back again before answering, his expression apologetic. "Yes, but it's not a problem."

Barb looked off-screen. "Thiti, place a level three quarantine on RM's network account and start a deep security audit of our systems." She turned to McTavish. "I'll let you know when I have the press conference arrangements finalized."

He straightened in his chair. "There's no need—"

"Take care, RM. We'll talk later on a secure channel." She cut the connection.

McTavish spun around and rose, offering Kama the visitor's chair, his cheeks coloring. "I'm sorry about that. Barb gets a little..."

"Rabid about Oasis," Kama finished for him, dumping her duffel on the chair and remaining on her feet.

McTavish blinked at her sharp tone. He seemed at a loss for what to say next. Kama heard movement behind her. She glanced over her shoulder at a man sitting at Miss Patty's desk. This must be the assistant Browning mentioned. She gave McTavish a pointed look and jerked her head toward the door.

"Bob," McTavish said, "can you please take a break?"

Bob scooted away from his desk, smiled at Kama, and left, shutting the door behind him. McTavish closed the distance between them, joyful exuberance lighting his face.

"You look—"

"Angry?" Kama growled. "Moorhk! What do you think you're doing?

Have you become a corporate drone overnight? How can you fire Browning? He's a good man, but with his record and health issues, he won't find another job. And what about Miss Patty? Does she deserve prison for trying to buy her grand-niece out of slavery? What options did she have?"

"But—"

"And you!" she said, voice rising. "What were you *thinking*? That you'd make yourself the next target of Leon's blackmailer and be some damned hero?"

McTavish studied the floor. His jaw muscles flexed. He took a deep breath, then another. When he looked at her again, all the joy had vanished.

"What would you like me to do, Kama?" he asked, his voice flat and dull.

It hit her then. He didn't want to be CEO. She could see the resistance, the pain in his eyes. And she'd just twisted the knife with her anger. She wanted to take back her words, to hug him and make him see he wasn't alone, but before she could move, he'd slumped into his chair. He didn't need a lecture, she realized. He needed her help.

"I'm sorry," she said, moving her duffel and pulling the chair close to his. "I didn't consider what a difficult transition this must be for you. When I'd heard you'd taken the job, all I could think about was the danger you'd be in. Whoever blackmailed Leon won't give up. They'll be more desperate now that their plan has failed. Think about it. They've waited patiently for years to get to this moment. And now Aaron Goldman's swapped out their patsy for a smart, savvy security guy. You can't assume they'll play nice."

"I didn't take the job to find the blackmailer," he said. "I took it to safeguard EcoMech so Gabe can inherit. He's as much a part of my family as Greg. I owe Aaron Goldman that much."

"This wasn't a personal grudge—Leon's blackmailer wants power. Whoever he is, he won't care about your motivations; he'll just want you gone."

Then she saw it, a way for them to be together for at least a while longer. Her spirits soared. She could help him find the blackmailer, and maybe while she was at it, she could keep him on track, help him deny the temptations of power. With an honest man at its helm, EcoMech could be the partner Oasis needed to drive development of the Sharma Network. And she could be the Oasis liaison. But first, she had to know that he hadn't changed, had to be sure she could sway his thinking.

"We have to find whoever did this—before they come after you."

"We?" His eyes met hers, and she saw a spark that fueled her own rising excitement.

"You can't do this alone, and you can't trust anyone at EcoMech.

You need someone in your corner, someone watching your back. We know more now than Leon did when he chased the blackmailer. And we have the best resources in the galaxy to work the problem. We can find this person if we work together."

"You'll come to Harvest with me?" His enthusiasm changed to concern. "When you say 'resources,' you don't mean Samir, do you?"

Kama laughed. "Let me handle the resource issue. You just make sure you have good security in place when you get to Harvest. Maybe you should take a few of your own folks from Security Partners, people you know you can rely on to have your safety at heart." She raised a questioning hand. "Now what are you going to do about the miners and the station? You promised to help them."

McTavish sat back, blew out his cheeks. "No clue. EcoMech isn't run anything like Security Partners. If it weren't for Bob telling me what to do, I'd be completely lost."

"This isn't about EcoMech." She couldn't hand him the solution. He had to find it himself. He had to care enough to help these people he barely knew. "The miners don't want to be part of a big company. They want to own the station."

"Yes, but they have no way to buy it," he protested. "It'll be years before they see any settlement from the fraud investigation, assuming any funds are recovered. To make it worse, with the Oasis contract in place and the embezzlement at an end, the place is worth more, making it harder for them to buy. And what makes the most sense for EcoMech is to sell as soon as possible. EcoMech is an ag company, not a mining company. It's a mess and not what I'd wish for the miners, but I don't see what I can do about it."

He might look like one of those uncaring corporate types, but he wasn't thinking like one. He was as dissatisfied with the situation as she was, and it made her heart sing. He just needed to be more creative about solving the problems.

"Let's pretend you're going to sell the station to Independent Mining. What do they need?" Kama prompted.

McTavish sighed as though she asked the impossible, pulled his ball from his pocket and walked it across the tops of his fingers, his eyes losing focus. "They'd need ten percent of the purchase price, say fifty million credits down, and that would still saddle them with stiff payments, more than the station can support and pay them wages. It wouldn't leave anything for the necessary repairs and upgrades."

"That's the standard corporate acquisition approach," she said. "Run the numbers again. How could they do it for less?"

His brows pulled down and his concentration intensified. The ball wove in and out of his fingers, moving gradually faster. "They can't own the place outright. They just don't have the capital. They need a partner, one with deep pockets to share the cost and lessen their debt load."

"Assume a partner. What do they need to bring to the table?" She waited while he leaned forward to bounce the ball between his feet, attention in another place, far from the here-and-now of the station.

"Minimum of twenty-five mill and a bank willing to carry the contract. No, a bank won't want the risk. They'll need a venture capital group backing them, but even one of those would be hard to find."

McTavish caught the ball in his fist and looked at her. "It's a pipe dream. They can't raise that kind of money. They have nothing left to draw on."

"Find the solution first, and then worry about implementation details. If Independent Mining continues, Browning could keep his job, couldn't he?" she asked.

"That would depend on the health regulations Independent Mining implements, but for his own sake, he needs treatment whether it's a company requirement or not. If their company gets a decent health insurance plan, his medical costs would be covered."

"Good. I'll have Browning call a meeting of the miners late this afternoon so you can update them." She struggled to keep the smile off her face. He was doing so well. But the difficult one was still to come. He was a stickler for law and order. "That just leaves Miss Patty to sort out. What will you do about her?"

McTavish looked confused. "Wait, I'm not sure how you think we've sorted out the problems of the station and Browning. The miners don't have the funds or the investment partner they need, and without Independent Mining, Browning doesn't have a job or health insurance."

Kama sighed. "You're a smart guy, McTavish. You'll figure it out. Now about Miss Patty?"

"She broke the law. Justice has to be served," he said, his back stiffening and his face defiant.

"How is justice served if Miss Patty goes to prison?" she shot back.

"How is justice served if she goes free?" he countered, anger edging his voice. "We're a society built on laws. Break the laws, and you'll be punished."

"Let the punishment fit the crime. Prison is the wrong punishment. You can find a more fitting one."

McTavish bounced the ball hard, once, twice. "Damn it, Kama. I can't make everything perfect. I'm not that guy."

She stood up and ruffled his hair. "Think about it."

He opened his mouth to speak, closed it, remembered his manners and scrambled to his feet.

She left him standing there. As she slipped through the door, she heard the ball hit the deck. She resisted the temptation to skip down the corridor grinning.

Stopping at the deserted com center, she hoped the tech was busy somewhere else and not among the injured or dead. She opened a connection to Oasis. After a moment, a thin, elegant man with golden skin like tanned leather appeared on screen. His white hair was swept back from a high forehead and widow's peak, and his nearly black pupils seemed to see through everything they focused on. He wore an impeccable, understated black business suit.

The man smiled when he recognized her.

"Kama, it's good to see you. Samir tells me you've done well on your assignment. Will you be coming home for a visit? Your mother will ask when she hears I've spoken to you."

"Hello, Varun. Tell her things are up in the air, but I'll try to come by soon," she replied. One eyebrow flinched, or at least she thought it did. "I wanted to discuss the Sharma Network with you, specifically Oasis' plans to bring on partners."

Varun's lips moued. "Recent events have upset our plans. We weren't entirely pleased with the idea of including EcoMech in the Sharma Network even before the death of Leon Goldman. Now with all the churn and a relative unknown at the helm, EcoMech is not an acceptable candidate to join us. It's a pity; it will delay development by a year at least."

She leaned forward. "You couldn't be more wrong. EcoMech has exactly the leadership we want to partner with. Rafael McTavish is an honest, trustworthy man who shares our goals for humanity."

There was no question of Varun's eyebrows lifting this time. "Is this Kama speaking? Kama who hates corporate executives above all else?"

She ground her teeth. "You don't have to rub it in. I've learned my lesson. All corporate executives are not the same, especially not this one. He's risked his life to help the people here, and he protected our interests, too."

"You seem quite taken with this McTavish." When she didn't rise to his bait, he said, "I will consider it."

"That's not good enough," Kama replied. "McTavish is about to take his first actions as CEO at EcoMech, and they won't be popular with the board. If he's to avoid repercussions, he has to offer them something for appeasement. It's important that he be in a strong position because I believe that the same person who blackmailed Leon Goldman will come after him. It's in Oasis' best interest to see that he succeeds and continues to lead EcoMech through our partnership."

"And so this appeasement offering is to be our request that EcoMech join the Sharma Network." Varun stroked his chin with long, thin fingers, perfectly manicured. "I can't extend such an offer without first seeing what McTavish is capable of, without taking a measure of the man."

Kama smiled. She had him where she wanted him. "Then be here in six hours and see the man in action for yourself. I guarantee it will be worth your time."

Varun's eyes narrowed, and he gave her a smile that bordered on a grimace. "You've sharpened your negotiating skills. All right, I'll come to the station."

"Safe travel, Varun. I'll see you when you dock."

21

Rafe claimed the side of the oval conference table farthest from the door. He'd refused to do another meeting in a storage bay. He and the board of Independent Mining would sit at a table and negotiate like businessmen.

Footsteps announced the first arrival, and Rafe waved Bob Coleman into the seat to his left. He wanted Kama at his right hand, but there was no sign of her. He hoped she'd be pleased with his solutions to the problems she'd posed. God knew the EcoMech board wouldn't be happy with them.

At precisely four, the miners filed in, more of them than Rafe expected. Browning took the seat directly opposite, and other miners sat nearby or stood along the wall behind him. Kama was the last to enter, accompanied by a tall, slender, white haired man dressed in the same kind of anonymous Oasis jumpsuit that Kama wore and a tattered baseball cap at odds with his otherwise flawless grooming.

Rafe eyed the stranger. Some aura or inward strength of character—more than just his anonymity—attracted the attention of others. Conversations stopped, eyes followed him until he passed. The man made him uncomfortable.

He tried to catch Kama's eye to direct her to the seat by him, but she steadfastly refused to look at him. She and the aristocratic tech took two seats next to the wall, leaving the seat to Rafe's right empty.

Her companion turned clear black eyes on Rafe, looking him up and down in a non-threatening, but somehow disconcerting way. He'd never seen a more knowing gaze. He felt as though he'd been stripped bare and put on public display, with all his physical and moral faults showing for the world to see. He squirmed in his seat and reached to check the straightness of his tie before remembering he wasn't wearing one.

"Gentlemen and Kama, if everyone's here, let's get started," Rafe said. "I won't beat around the bush. I'm aware that Independent Mining would like to own this station. However, your company doesn't have the financial resources to purchase it outright."

Grumbles came from the miners standing against the wall, and he could hear his words repeated in the corridor where the muttering grew louder. Browning waited, stone-faced. Kama calmly contemplated the tabletop, looking like a cat that just stole the cream. The old tech seemed unimpressed. Well, this was just the warm-up, and what did he care what some old tech thought? But Rafe squirmed again anyway.

He nodded to Bob, who handed filmies across the table.

"This is a business projection of the likely outcome in the event that EcoMech accedes to your request for another employee buyout, on the assumption that you're able to raise sufficient capital.

"Now, for those of you who find reports like this as dull as I do, I'll summarize. It's doomed. You have no money, no credit, and no invest-ment experience. The facility's equipment is outdated, and now large sections of it are also damaged. You'll saddle yourself with vast debts just getting control of the place, and within twelve months the banks will foreclose and leave you with nothing. And that's a best case."

Browning's brow furrowed, his eyes darkened with anger, and his lips drew into a thin line. The rumbling in the hallway grew louder. Kama hadn't even looked at her copy of the presentation.

Her unusual companion flipped through page after page in quick succession. Rafe wondered how much of the complex business proposal a mere tech would understand. The old man's penetrating stare returned to Rafe, a hint of mystification crossing his strong, handsome features, before he glanced sideways at Kama who remained serenely—no, *su-premely*—confident. His expression cleared, and he met Rafe's eyes.

"Mr. McTavish," he said, in a dark baritone that demanded silence, "I believe you have something else to show us."

Rafe narrowed his eyes. *Who was this guy?* "You're right, I do have another proposal."

He nodded to Bob, and the assistant passed another round of filmies across the table.

"Assuming that Independent Mining can raise the necessary twenty-five million credits needed for a down payment, EcoMech will sell you half of the station, keeping half ownership for itself." He swept his arm around the room. "Given the condition of the station, you need a partner, one with deep pockets that can put its financial weight behind repair-ing, upgrading, and marketizing the station. EcoMech retains fifty-one percent of the operation; you, as Independent Mining, own forty-nine percent."

Browning's eyes narrowed. "How's that any different from just working for EcoMech? It's the same thing, except we take more of the risk. I get what you're saying about the need for a partnership, but we want the controlling interest."

"You have very little experience in the world of business," argued Rafe, thinking that the EcoMech board would throw him out for selling the miners forty-nine percent and lock him in an asylum if he gave them control. "You could piss the place away in a year through nothing but inexperience. Then where's EcoMech's investment?"

"EcoMech will have seats on the Independent Mining board," countered Browning. "Send us someone who knows what they're doing, and we'll listen to them. Educate us. We can learn just as well as you."

Rafe considered Browning. He'd thought the smelter supervisor would drive a hard bargain, and he was right. They'd make a decent businessman out of the man yet.

But first, he'd make sure the miners knew what they proposed to bite off.

"Go into this with your eyes wide open. This proposal has holes big enough to fly a shuttle through. It has best-case assumptions at every turn. You need to start producing ore of a better grade right away, but keep costs... well... virtually nonexistent. It'll take incredible hard work and even more luck to make this a reality. Every man who signs on will have to give it everything he's got and be risking everything he owns. It's not a deal for the faint-hearted. It doesn't come with any guarantees. And you'll still need the twenty-five mill down payment."

Browning's face split in a big smile. "Well, Mr. McTavish, I have news for you. I just got the message an hour ago. A group called the Madison Trust has decided that we're a worthy charity project, and they've given us a grant for twenty-five million credits to be used for facilities acquisition. I have no idea how they heard about us or who they are, but we sure aren't going to look a gift horse in the mouth."

Rafe did his best to look surprised by the announcement. It had taken him most of the afternoon haggling with the lawyers to get the payout from his mother's trust arranged so quickly. Kama's eyes met his across the table, and the hint of a smile curved her lips. The elderly gentleman stared at her, not completely hiding his astonishment despite his obvious effort.

"Congratulations, Ed," Rafe said. "Keep in mind that your grant will be sufficient for your down payment only. The station needs upgrades and repairs, and as half owners, EcoMech will expect Independent Mining to pay a fair share. You'll be on a very tight budget."

Ed's smile grew larger, something Rafe hadn't thought possible. "We've got that covered, too, Mr. McTavish. Right after we got the message from the Madison Trust, we got a message from something called the GAW Foundation. They've given us a grant for thirty million credits to 'fix the place up' as they put it. You'd think it was raining money today."

It was Rafe's turn to be amazed. Kama stifled laughter; amusement danced in her eyes. The tech transferred his stare from Rafe to Kama, a resolute look on his face. He leaned back in his chair, and crossed his arms over his chest, gazing at the ceiling. Then the ghost of a smile played around his lips, and Rafe thought the tech might be resisting the urge to laugh, too. What did they both find so amusing? And what the hell was the GAW Foundation?

"Okay," he said. "The miners take fifty-one percent, EcoMech gets forty-nine. EcoMech's legal team will draft the documents and send them for your review."

After a moment of silence, one of the miners in the back row said, "That's it? The place is ours?"

Browning shook his head, mirth shining from his eyes at the vast understatement. "Yeah, boys, that's it. The place is ours."

The room erupted in a roar, taken up by the miners waiting in the hall. Everyone rose from the table. Rafe reached over and shook Browning's hand. In the crowd, he glimpsed Kama slipping out the door with her companion. When the noise in the room died down some, Browning turned to Rafe. "I think this calls for a celebration tonight. Can you stay for it?"

Rafe thought about what awaited him back on Harvest. "Sure, why not? Bob, would you tell Captain Benson we'll be delaying our departure until midnight?"

Bob nodded, grabbed filmies from the table, and threaded his way through the crowd. The men gradually funneled out, taking their celebration into the station.

Alone in the conference room, Rafe slumped in his chair, exhausted. The board wouldn't be happy. EcoMech wasn't in the investment banking business, but they'd essentially be holding the loan for the buyout by allowing the miners to make the purchase over time instead of requiring them to find a bank to back them. He didn't care. He'd done the right thing. That's what mattered.

Browning could keep his job, and with better health insurance, he could get the medical help he needed. Rafe would have to find Miss Patty. He had a solution for her, too. He'd done it, just like Kama said he would. He felt wonderful. He wished she were here with him to bask in the glow of victory.

At the sound of footsteps, he looked up. Kama and her mystery companion came around the table to stand beside him. Kama set a mug of steaming coffee at his elbow. He looked into her face, blinked, and looked again. Radiant light seemed to pour down on him from her whole being.

"Mr. McTavish, are you all right?" The mystery companion had a strong hand on his shoulder.

"Yes," Rafe stammered, wrenching his eyes from Kama. He struggled to rise from his chair.

"No, don't get up," said the tech, seating himself. Kama placed a mug of tea by his elbow. "Kama tells me you've had some pretty serious injuries over the past few days and need to rest."

"I'm fine," Rafe said.

"Liar." Kama took a seat on the opposite side of the table and grinned at him.

"I understand that you're aware of Oasis' plans to develop an exciting new technology." The tech sipped his tea. His black eyes gazed past Rafe's body into his soul.

"I'm aware that Oasis is contracting for large quantities of minerals used primarily in the building of jump gates," Rafe said. He wanted to check with Kama, afraid he might be saying too much, but he felt like he didn't dare take his eyes off the tech. "I don't have any details beyond that. I do know that jump gates are impossibly expensive to build, which is why the only ones in existence are owned by Earth Authority, the only entity large enough to be able to afford them, and since they're controlled by Earth, all outlying jump gates connect to a dedicated partner gate in Earth orbit, where EA taxes the buggery out of everyone who uses them."

"You don't disappoint, Mr. McTavish. That's precisely the issue, isn't it? All jump gates must be one of a pair, each dedicated to maintaining its own end of a wormhole, each requiring billions of computations per second to keep the gates synchronized and the wormhole open. All that investment in materials and labor to create an unwavering road between two points with no ability to take a turn in a different direction.

"But suppose for a moment that jump gates didn't come in dedicated pairs." The tech's soft voice became almost hypnotic, like a storyteller spinning a fantastic tale. "Suppose instead, a jump gate in orbit around a destination could, at will, connect to any other jump gate in the system; for example, Harvest could be connected to the asteroid belt today, Mars tomorrow, and Oasis the day after."

The enormity of what Rafe had seen in the Oasis contract dawned on him. Kama was right. If Oasis had the ability to create the kind of non-dedicated jump gates that the tech described, it would change humanity. The colony worlds would no longer be shackled to Earth and constricted by the EA tariffs for every gram of cargo that passed through.

They could trade freely, one colony to another directly. New worlds with lower traffic volumes could share a single terminal gate in Earth's solar system, making it cost effective for corporations to invest in expansion. EcoMech's board would kill for that kind of gate in Harvest's orbit.

"Excuse me," Rafe said, "but have we been introduced?"

"Ha! Told you he'd get it," Kama laughed. "Rafael McTavish, CEO, EcoMech, allow me to introduce Varun Sharma, Chairman, Oasis. Well, I'll leave you to it." She gave Rafe a wink that set his heart racing, and sauntered out of the room.

"Chairman—" Rafe spluttered. He tried again. "Chairman Sharma, what brings you to this part of the galaxy?"

"Like you, Mr. McTavish, I've been hoodwinked and manipulated by Kama," answered the chairman with a smile. "She indicated that EcoMech under your leadership might make a suitable partner to join Oasis in the founding of the Sharma Network, a series of dialable jump gates initially shared between existing colonies but eventually used to open new destinations. I had reservations before meeting you, but I believe her assessment of you is correct."

He leaned forward and looked Rafe in the eye.

"We have a prototype gate functioning in Oasis orbit now. We intend to place another here in the asteroid belt, and should we partner with EcoMech, we'll place one at Harvest."

Rafe frowned, mulling this over. "Just three gates? Then one will stand idle while the other two operate. That doesn't seem efficient."

"Very good. We don't propose that your gate stand idle. We already have one partner—the Wandermere Consortium. Four gates, each alternating between the other three. Do you think your board would be interested in such an offer?"

"Yes, sir," Rafe replied, awestruck. *Wandermere, EcoMech's largest trading partner.* Remembering himself, he added, "Provided, of course, the terms of the agreement are fair and equitable."

The chairman nodded. "I'll leave a preliminary gate proposal with you before I go. It will give you something concrete to show your board when you return. The lawyers can work out the details at their leisure.

"There's another matter I feel we need to discuss," the chairman said. "Kama tells me you have a disturbing habit of putting yourself in harm's way. She believes you're in danger from whomever sought to replace Leon Goldman. My security chief agrees with that assessment."

He seemed suddenly like a shark cruising for its next meal, a deadly force not to be messed with.

Rafe swallowed and looked him in the eye.

"It's something I'll pursue when I get to Harvest. I made a promise to Aaron Goldman, and I'll keep it."

"I don't approve of Kama getting mixed up in EcoMech's internal problems." He gave Rafe a hard look. "But neither are we able to stop her when she makes up her mind about something. Since Oasis has a grudging interest in the fortunes of EcoMech—and Kama an interest in you—I've agreed to provide support as she sees fit. Don't abuse the privilege."

"No, sir. Thank you, sir." Kama was coming to Harvest with the chairman's blessing? Rafe's spirits soared.

The chairman rose from the table. "One other word of advice, Mr. McTavish."

"What's that, sir?"

"Keep your wallet close."

Rafe didn't like what the chairman implied. "You think Kama is after me for my money?"

The chairman laughed. "Are you familiar with the game Galaxy at War?"

"Only in passing," Rafe admitted.

"You and I are probably the only ones in the galaxy who aren't playing it. Kama wrote it seven years ago, and she writes a new version yearly on her annual vacation. She holds the rights and allows Oasis to distribute it for a small—very small—percentage of the profits. She also holds about a hundred other patents, most of which net her additional income. Were she to have accumulated her earnings over these past seven years, her wealth would dwarf yours, even with your Madison Trust taken into consideration. She makes more than four billion credits a year. Do you know what she does with all that money, Mr. McTavish?"

"No," Rafe said, wondering why the chairman was telling him this. If what he said was true, wouldn't he be worried about someone chasing Kama for her money and not the other way around?

"*She gives it all away.* She lives in the storeroom of her computer school in the slums of Mumbai when she isn't on assignment, sleeping on a mat on the floor, her only source of water an outdoor tap. Some weeks, she doesn't have enough money to buy food and depends on the generosity of others to feed herself, or simply starves. The duffel she carries contains all her worldly possessions."

"I don't think I understand," he said, trying to imagine Kama in such impoverished surroundings and failing. "What does this have to do with me?"

The chairman grimaced. "Because, Mr. McTavish, she's also very good at convincing others to give away *their* money—as you've so recently experienced."

The murky became clear. *Twenty-five million from the Madison Trust to help the station.* He grinned—and saw the approval hiding under the chairman's gruff exterior. "And the GAW Foundation?"

"GAW—Galaxy at War," the chairman said.

"Ah." He couldn't help laughing.

"Consider yourself warned. Now I must be off."

"You're leaving?" asked Rafe. Then, puzzled, he added, "When did you arrive?"

"I came for the meeting. I'll be leaving as soon as I finish my discussions with Mr. Browning." The chairman picked up his empty mug and moved toward the door.

In his head, Rafe did the math. "You came all the way from Oasis for the meeting? How could you have known about it in time to get here? No vessel travels that fast, especially when you have to cycle through two jump gates in Earth orbit."

The chairman turned, a twinkle in his eye. "Kama warned me that you were perceptive. I believe you have an arrangement with her, something along the lines of 'ask me no questions, I'll tell you no lies.' I commend you for it." The old shark bared his teeth in a dangerous smile and glided out of the room.

☠   ☠   ☠

A few minutes later, he was knocking on a door. After a very long wait, it opened, revealing a disheveled Miss Patty, face puffy and eyes red.

"Good evening, Miss Patty. May I come in?"

She dabbed at her nose and stepped back, motioning him inside. Two battered suitcases, their sides bulging, stood by the door. A third, half-full bag lay open on the bed.

"I suppose you've come to take me away. I hope you'll let me forward my personal belongings to my grand-niece. I don't have much—" She sniffed, eyes brimming.

"Miss Patty," Rafe said sternly, "what you did, you did with the best of intentions, but it was still illegal."

A little sob escaped her. "I know what I did was wrong, but it was the only way to save Ellie's life. If I'd had any other options, I wouldn't have stolen those reports. But I couldn't let my grand-niece die for lack of money. I didn't keep a penny for myself."

"Do you really mean that?"

"Oh, yes, Mr. McTavish. I'm not a crook. If I could have found another way to pay back the loan—" She closed her eyes, hands still at her sides. "But what's done is done. I'll go quietly."

"Good. I'm glad to hear that." He pulled a filmie from his pocket, unfolded it, and offered it to her. "This is a contract for your services. It requires you to teach cooking skills to surrogate mothers on Earth. In essence, I have personally bought your debt and negotiated a cash settlement with Galaxy for the damages you caused them, in return for which they've agreed to release you into my custody and not press charges with EA.

"Most of your wages will go to pay off your debt to me, but you'll have some money left over, and the opportunity to take additional work if you so desire. I won't lie to you—it will probably take you the rest of your life to pay back what you owe, but you won't be destitute. If you agree to it, you'll need to have your things on the yacht before we leave at midnight. EcoMech will provide you with a furnished apartment in Mumbai."

Miss Patty stared open mouthed at the contract, and then at Rafe. "Is this a joke?"

"No joke, Miss Patty. I'm offering you a chance to make restitution. A better one than prison offers, I hope."

She flung her arms around his neck and squeezed hard, making him wince. Remembering herself, she jumped back, face flushed. She placed her thumbprint on the contract without bothering to read it.

☠ ☠ ☠

The party started around seven. Someone rigged up a music player to an old intercom system, and hard dance rhythms rocked the facility. Mountains of food covered tables in the mess hall. Hydroponics and the EcoMech yacht galley would be pretty empty for a while, Rafe thought. Cases of beer appeared from somewhere and nestled in ice baths. He recognized the logo as one bottled on Harvest and guessed it was part of the yacht's stash. He shagged one and popped the top.

The main cargo bay next door served as a dance floor for miners gyrating wildly to the pounding beat. It reminded him of African tribes preparing to go to war with their neighbors. All this group lacked were the spears and the sense of rhythm. Pressed into one corner, Greg and Gabe looked on. The older boy surreptitiously passed his can of beer to the younger, who took a sip, then spewed the beer from his mouth. The expression on Gabe's face was priceless. Rafe hoped it was a first sign of recovery.

Browning appeared at his shoulder, an open beer already in his hand, the lascivious Janice Fisher gracing his arm. The short, squat, bear of a man grinned from ear to ear as he looked out on the dance floor and took a swig.

"Thank you. I know you're taking a big risk, gambling on us, but you won't regret it. We'll make this place into something you can be proud of."

Rafe dragged his eyes from Janice and replied, "I believe you will."

He saluted the manager with his beer can and took a swallow. Ed returned the salute with his own can and threw back a slug, smiling broadly until he began wheezing.

"Too much dancing, I guess," Browning said, gasping for air.

Janice watched him, her fingers feeling for the pulse in his wrist. From the deepening concern on her face, she didn't like what she found. Another man would have malingered to attract her attentions—Browning seemed angry at displaying weakness.

"You know, you're a partially owned subsidiary of EcoMech now," Rafe said. "We'll want to be sure that the men employed here have adequate health coverage, so we'll be including you in our umbrella policy. You should be able to get a cloned-lung transplant a month or so after coverage kicks in. You'll pay a substantial deductible, of course, but I expect you can get a loan to help."

Janice's face lit up, but Browning just blinked at him. "We never had coverage like that with Galaxy. Are you sure you aren't giving me preferential treatment? Because if you are, I won't take it. It isn't fair to the rest of the guys."

"EcoMech takes care of its people, Ed. Well, it does now, anyway. They get the same benefits as you. Of course, you're only a partially owned subsidiary—as facility manager you'll have discretion to hire your own medical staff." He tilted his beer at Janice.

Browning's broad grin returned. "Okay, then." He wrapped a beefy arm around Janice's trim waist and moved off into the crowd, but not before the libidinous doctor planted a kiss on Rafe's cheek. He laughed and waved her away before she could see his face flushing.

He spent three more hours roaming through the party rooms, hoping to find Kama. He hadn't seen her since his meeting with Sharma, and wondered if she'd left with the chairman. Would she take off without saying goodbye? His heart ached at the mere thought of never seeing her again.

By eleven, he was dead on his feet. He said his goodbyes to Browning and Fisher and made his way back to the ship. A crewman ushered him to the executive cabin. Leon's and Amaya's things were gone, and his own limited kit was neatly stowed in the closet.

He crossed the hall to check on the boys, finding them engaged in a game of cards. Gabe was frighteningly quiet, responding to Greg's cheery conversation with blank stares and tiny movements of his head. He'd have to talk to Gabe in the morning, make sure the boy was okay. Rafe backed out of their room and collided with Kama in the hallway.

"Well," he said, overjoyed to see her, "I was beginning to think you'd left the station already."

She pointed to the open door of his quarters. "Is this your cabin? We need to talk."

She grabbed his wrist and dragged him inside, closing the door behind them.

"I need a job. A job on Harvest. Somewhere near you, but not too close. Do you understand?"

"You want to be undercover?" he asked, thinking that he had other more important topics to discuss with her and so little time.

"Yes, precisely. Samir will chase connections outside EcoMech. I'll be the inside man."

"Ah. You'll still be working for Oasis then, not for EcoMech?"

He could hear her teeth grinding as her jaw moved subtly back and forth. "From Oasis' point of view, I'd be the technical liaison for the Sharma Network project, but I'd prefer a lower profile while we track the blackmailer. Perhaps a systems analyst consultant or something."

"Hm," mused Rafe, his pulse thundering in his ears. This was the moment he'd waited for, and he wasn't letting her get away again. "The only open position I can think of is that of CEO's wife."

Emotions cycled across her face: surprise, joy, worry tinged with fear. Then she shut down and stepped back. "Be serious."

Rafe stepped forward and took her hands in his. "I am. I love you, Kama. I want to marry you. Come live with me on Harvest."

Kama swallowed. "I can't be your wife. I can't be anyone's wife. It wouldn't be fair. You know what I do. Someday, I'd go out the door, and I wouldn't come back. Someday, someone will catch me, and I'm not about to stop."

Rafe's spirits sank. He didn't want to go to Harvest without her. He needed her, loved her, and he thought she loved him, too. He looked in her eyes, those fiery pools of chocolate, and listened to her words.

"The poor need a champion to fight for them. Otherwise, no one's there to check the greed, the power..."

Her voice gradually rose, becoming more strident as she lectured on, but Rafe wasn't sure she was still talking to him. What had Janice said? *Look beyond what she says and into her heart.* The same advice Ben had given Greg. When he looked deep in her heart, he saw her love looking back, despite her denials and intellectual avoidance, and he rejoiced. He smiled at her, and the more he smiled, the more confused she became until she stuttered to a halt.

"I'm going to keep asking you to marry me, and eventually, you're going to say yes," he said, aware of her soft, warm hands in his and never wanting to let them go. "I don't care how long it takes."

Kama pulled her hands away but remained so close he could feel her body heat. She seemed both perplexed and pleased, and—finally—at a loss for words. She thrust her hands in her jumpsuit pockets, scuffed the toe of one boot on the floor. It took her a moment to find her voice, a casualty of the war between head and heart.

"You don't know me. When—if—you do find out about me, you may not like what you learn."

"I know that a background check turned up seventeen Kamala Bhatias ranging in age from two months to seventy-two years and none of them are you."

"Only seventeen?" she muttered. "There should have been twenty-three."

Rafe laughed, curious about how Barb could have missed the additional aliases but dismissing it. She hadn't had much time to do the research.

"Is Kamala Bhatia your real name?"

"It's my true name. I use others depending on where I am."

"Then I know all I need to know about you." He could see her reticence. "I don't care about your past. I care only about our future together."

Her lips pulled into a thin line. "I'll come as your minder. You attract trouble like a stagnant pond draws mosquitoes. Someone has to watch out for you."

Rafe wanted to crush her to him and never let go, but he sensed her need for space and checked himself. He drank in the smell of her, the look of her, and tried to make it be enough for now. Every fiber of him ached for her.

"That's good enough for me. Welcome aboard. We leave in—" he checked his nanocom, "twenty minutes."

"No," she corrected, "*you* leave in twenty minutes. I'm waiting for my relief to arrive. After all, Oasis promised to help here, and the miners certainly need it. Then I'm going home to visit my family and pack a few things."

"Ah," replied Rafe, recognizing a lie tangled up in the litany and wondering what she was really up to. He grappled with his own disappointment that they weren't traveling together. She was already headed for the door. He trailed behind her, desperate for a goodbye kiss but afraid she might reject him if he attempted it.

"Perhaps I should pay a visit to Oasis and meet your family?"

Kama's rich laughter rippled like wind chimes, filling the tiny cabin with warmth. She popped open the door and stepped through.

"You already have," she said, eyes flashing amusement. "Varun Sharma is my stepfather."

She strode off down the corridor, duffel slung over her shoulder. Rafe stood in the doorway, mouth agape. As she disappeared, he started to chuckle. Then he laughed out loud.

Also by K S Ferguson

Hostile Takeover

In the sequel to *Calculated Risk*, Rafe and Kama's pursuit of Leon Goldman's blackmailer takes them far from Earth, across space to the frontier colony world of Harvest, where EcoMech's downtrodden contract employees struggle against an ecosystem which does not welcome visitors.

After fleeing Harvest as a teenager, newly-appointed CEO Rafe McTavish is ill-prepared to face the ghosts of his past. But face them he must if he's to save EcoMech from the ruin wrought upon it by his predecessor's folly. The company is near-bankrupt, its employees are a whisker away from violent revolt, and somewhere out there is a murderous blackmailer who will stop at nothing to unseat Rafe.

Once again, Rafe's only ally is part-time programmer and full-time corporate spy Kama Bhatia. It doesn't take her long to find something very rotten at EcoMech: corporate espionage perpetrated by a hacker more skilled than any she's ever seen. She's torn between her desire to help EcoMech's oppressed underclass and her promise to support Rafe. And the hacker is on her trail.

With Chairman Aaron Goldman's support, Rafe battles to get traction on EcoMech's problems. But when Aaron is murdered and Rafe's father becomes the prime suspect, corporate politics soon escalate into open war. Can Rafe and Kama dodge the bullets and unmask the killer before Rafe and his family fall victims to a murderous hostile takeover?

For more information, visit http://www.ksferguson.net.

Also by K S Ferguson

Touching

Madness

Light bulbs talk to River Madden; God doesn't. When the homeless schizophrenic unintentionally fractures a dimensional barrier and accidentally steals a gym bag containing a million dollars, everyone from the multiverse police to the local crime boss—and an eight-foot tall demon—are after him. Can he dodge them long enough to correct his mistakes and prevent the destruction of three separate dimensions? If he succeeds, will the light bulbs stop singing off-key?

For more information, visit http://www.ksferguson.net.

Excerpt: Touching Madness

1

My feet sped over the jogging path beside the river, a madman in hoodie, jeans, and backpack, racing toward the setting sun. Winds of change gusted behind my eyes, and the world tilted off kilter. The ribbon of asphalt that lead back to Centralia, Kansas city center disintegrated into a storm of silver glitter. *Aw, hell. Another psychotic break coming to a neighborhood near me.*

The Dark Place sucked me in. Fire peeled back my flesh until my skin melted away. Then muscles scorched, enveloping me in a sickening stench. Heat bent my bones, shattering them into a thousand shards. Only my hysterical thoughts remained. Songs of demons wailed in my consciousness, and I wondered if this time I'd go permanently insane. Maybe I already was.

"Not real," I chanted, clinging to sanity through the hellish pain. "Not real, not real."

The tattooed runes that circled both my wrists itched worse than a million spider bites. Clouds of nightmares scudded away from hideous fairytale trolls, giant two-headed snakes, and a three-headed dog. They all fled from an enormous demon I thought might be Satan himself. He strode on cloven hooves through a landscape of fire and crystal and inside-out structures that couldn't possibly exist, where up was down and down was up, but none of that mattered because the creatures inhabiting the space simply ignored gravity.

"Not real. Survive. Done it before, do it again," I whispered as I streaked through the aberrant landscape.

After what seemed eternity, another onslaught of blinding silver glitter whirled around me. Like a kaleidoscope being twisted, the glitter showed first a late autumn pasture, then a dark, rain-swept alley, followed by an apocalyptic cityscape, all soot-covered ruins. One of them was real; the others not. Which one?

"Please let it be the pasture," I prayed. "I like cows. Cows are nice."

A bruising thump against my chest signaled the return of sanity. It could have been worse—I could have landed on the asphalt of the rainy alley instead of the garbage pile. Cannon blasts of pain throbbed through my head, a trickle of blood ran from my nose, and my heart raced. I waited. Right on cue, my stomach arrived, twisting in contortions that made me retch.

I rolled over on a mountain of garbage-stuffed plastic bags surrounding an overflowing dumpster that backed up against a two-story brick building, typical of the style in Centralia's older downtown district. Yep, garbage collectors out on strike again. Lucky me. The rain turned to sleet, and I shivered, my toes and fingers aching from the chill. Despite the cold and the need to get up, I lay there unmoving, too exhausted to make the effort.

Down the alley to the west, a single light above a door marked *Soo Ling's Chinese Take-away* struggled valiantly against the darkness, and I took stock, just to reassure myself that I was intact. Two feet, long toes. Two scrawny white legs none the worse for wear. Hip bones jutting against skin, stark ribs you could play a tune on. Thin arms, dark blue wrist tattoos still itching like mad. Male body parts intact, not that I had any chance with girls. What woman would date a psychotic schizophrenic who woke up naked in alleys wondering where he was and how he'd gotten there?

"Don't go there, River," I said. "Think survival. Clothes first."

Why did I always end up in the buff after a damn break? What the heck did I do with my clothes while I was crazy? How long was I loony? It had been sunset when I left reality, and now it was pitch black—maybe a different day. Was I even in Centralia? Once I'd awoken halfway across the country from the town I'd been in before the break, but I couldn't remember how I'd gotten there.

Across the alley and off to the east, the back wall of another brick building shimmered with a coating of silver sparkles. Shadows moved where the wall should be, and glimpses of the darkening cow pasture overlaid the broken city. I shivered again, the smell of my burning flesh still clinging to my memory.

"Not real."

As I gathered the strength to rise, the demon stepped through the shimmery wall. I sucked in freezing air and choked. He looked even bigger than he had in the Dark Place, all of eight feet. Fur or dense black hair wrapped the legs and hips above his cloven hooves. Chest and arm muscles bulged under ruddy skin. The fingers ended in long, sharp talons. His face looked like a bull's head. Curly mountain goat horns graced each side of it, and a third, stumpy horn stuck up off the top of his skull like a stubborn cowlick. Glassy black eyes looked straight at me, while little puffs of smoke whispered from bovine nostrils with each powerful breath.

"Not real," I reminded myself uselessly, because he sure *seemed* real, and my nervous system responded like he *was* real. Generally, my demonic hallucinations took the shape of three-foot tall gargoyles that crossed the edges of my vision, disappearing when I turned to look, not huge suckers like this one, standing in plain view. *Damn, what a fine imagination I have*, I thought as I tried to breathe normally. Too bad I didn't have paper and pencil handy. A sketch of him would sell for a couple of bucks to the Goth kids who hung around the park.

The demon turned his massive head toward the west end of the alley up past Soo Ling's, as though listening for something. Then he twisted it to the wall he'd just stepped through and listened again. Big streams of smoke snorted from his nostrils, and the corners of his mouth curved in a smile. *But cows can't smile.* With a last look at me, he trotted off to the east. His hooves clip-clopped against the asphalt as he receded into the darkness. My lungs drew in a deep breath at last.

"Stop staring at things that aren't there, River," I advised myself, "and get some covering before you freeze to death."

Plenty to choose from, a veritable scrounger's feast. I picked up the garbage sacks one after another with a connoisseur's eye, inspecting each for holes and the ripeness of their contents. Finding nothing to my liking, I minced over to another mountain of bin bags burying a second dumpster beside Soo Ling's door. I wouldn't go east toward the sparkly wall. Something about it called to me in a way I didn't like.

The first time I'd woken up naked after a psychotic episode, I looked for help before I covered myself. Six delightful months in a mental ward convinced me I'd always wrap in *something* before venturing into the world. Cops were much less sympathetic to the mentally ill than to a homeless twenty-something who passed for sixteen and dressed in garbage bags while he claimed to have been mugged for his clothes.

I found a lovely cinch-style bag that, with the bottom torn open, made a knee-length skirt I could tighten at my waist. It smelled mildly of rotten vegetables. Over my head, the light bulb sang *Frosty the Snowman* off-key while I shook harder. I hated light bulbs. Tone deaf the lot of them. I scrubbed at my scalp where a hundred thousand tiny ant feet did the Cha Cha in waves.

"Not real," I growled. "No ants." But the feet danced on undeterred.

I completed my glossy, all-black ensemble with a second bag in which I tore head and arm holes. I tried not to gag on the odor of sour milk emanating from the plastic, but at least it protected me from the biting wind. If only someone had tossed out a pair of trainers and a watch cap, I'd be in heaven. Thank goodness my tattoos no longer itched.

I was scrounging for a final bag to use as a hood and cape when the alley blazed with light. I pulled back into the darkness beside the dumpster, assuming a passing squad car had turned its spotlight toward me. The light went out, and I heard people, real ones. Or at least I thought they were real.

"Gear up," a gruff male voice ordered. "Keep the noise down so we don't attract a black-and-white. We don't want the local precinct on our case, and remember—no witnesses. Stun whoever you see whether they're a talent or not."

"Yes, sir," two voices answered in unison, one male, and one female. Both sounded young and excited. Oh, joy, overeager trainees out to prove how tough they were. Not a good night for the denizens of the streets.

"And don't get too close to the fracture. It's a big one. Sammie, you have the cuffs ready?"

The chipper female voice replied, "Yes, sir."

I peeked around the edge of the dumpster, expecting to see a patrol cruiser. At the mouth of the alley to the west, a floating stone tablet six inches thick and maybe seven feet across hovered above the pavement. Hieroglyphs ringed its edges, pulsing with faint light. A little mushroom thingy rose up a couple of feet in the center, and a large dog that wasn't quite a dog sat with its front paws resting on the mushroom cap. *Impossible*, I thought. *It's a police car.* The light bulb above the restaurant door began to hum the *Dragnet* theme.

An escapee from a costume party stood on the stone platform beside the dog. He wasn't any taller than me, maybe five foot eight, but probably weighed twice what I did. He wore a ludicrous ankle-length gold lamé robe and a matching hat that belonged on a Roman Catholic cardinal. He had a tall, softly glowing staff in his right hand, and he tapped it on the edge of the platform in time with the pulsing light. Outside my psychotic breaks, I didn't normally have such large and complex hallucinations. I worried that I might be losing it.

Three silhouettes advanced on me. I could barely make them out in the darkness of the alley. Two tall and one rather short, they wore all black—berets, uniform shirts, loose pants, and soft shoes. The clothing didn't look right for regular officers. Berets on city cops? No shiny badges or buttons? Maybe they were SWAT?

Oh, hell! My throat closed. Had I wandered into the middle of a drug bust? Or was some suspect holed up in one of the buildings along the alley, maybe with a hostage? But where were their rifles? They swung flashlights and carried what looked like plastic wands from a magic shop. The wands were too thin to be either billy clubs or cattle prods, both of which I'd experienced during my fifteen years on the streets.

I eyed the dark alley behind me as tingling fear climbed up my spine. I needed to either get out of there or hide. Sometimes I saw imaginary things; sometimes I saw real things differently from how they were. Whoever these people were, my brain thought they were a threat, or I wouldn't visualize them as cops. Johnny Law was no friend of mine.

Garbage bags rustled across the alley. A lightning bolt leaped from a wand and cracked against a dumpster near the sound. A calico cat screeched and tore away into the darkness. I ducked low. The after-image of the bolt burned on my retinas and my knees shook.

"You'll never live that one down, Griff," the female officer laughed.

"That's enough," the older officer said. "Griff, identify your target before you shoot. Unnecessary weapons' fire attracts attention we're trying to avoid."

They were too close for me to sprint away. Besides, the sparkly wall was down the alley. I eased back, intending to wedge myself between the dumpster and the building, where my attire would camouflage me nicely. I was doing great until I brushed against a loose bag, and it rolled down the heap to crash on the asphalt. Oops.

"What's that?" the one called Griff asked, pointing his wand my way.

"Sammie, take lead," the older officer said. "Watch your tracker. If the talent's running hot, back off. You don't want to get sucked into a new fracture."

Footsteps pattered along the alley, and flashlight beams swung my direction. I crouched among the bags, uncertain whether to raise my hands and come forward. I opted to hunker lower and put a bag on my head.

"Meow," I crooned, doing my best cat imitation.

A flashlight beam passed too close for comfort, and someone waded through the trash, kicking it aside. A clicking sound tapped faster the closer it got to me. I held my breath, my heart pounding like a demented drummer in a heavy metal band. I had my back to the wall and no place to go. My pursuer reached the dumpster and stopped not three feet away.

"It's okay," Sammie's soft female voice assured. "We've come to take you home. You'll be safe now."

Home? How would she manage that when I didn't have one? But her voice: so kind, so caring. No one had spoken to me that way before. No one had made me safe—not even Jimmy—through all the years. Something inside me ached.

"Whoever it is can't understand you, Sammie. They're crazy, remember? Just stun 'em and get the cuffs on so we can get out of here," Griff grumbled. "Wish we'd worn our slickers."

"We're looking for a lost human being, one who deserves respect and dignified treatment, not some feral animal," she replied.

"Get your minds on the mission, or you'll both be on report," the sergeant ordered. "Can you see the talent? Is it male or female?"

"Can't tell," she said. "Seems to be buried in the trash."

Sammie stood in the dim pool of illumination from Soo Ling's light and swept her left arm in front of her. Dark hair pulled back into a short ponytail accentuated her oval face. Thin brows angled down in concentration over exotic Asian eyes, a cute button nose, and a narrow, pouty mouth. All she lacked were pointy ears to make her an elfin princess.

The clicking came from a black lump on her wrist. Her arm pointed my direction, and the clicking grew louder and faster. The young cop moved to back her up.

"Come on out," she soothed. "I won't hurt you." She took a step forward.

A deafening boom ripped from the east end of the alley, blasting her sideways against the metal container with a sickening thud. She slumped on the bags in front of me.

Three cloaked men looking like Harry Potter wannabes strode out of the darkness down by the sparkly wall. I could see only half their faces under their hoods. Banana-shaped... *somethings* in their hands pointed at the cops. *There must be a Halloween party in the neighborhood,* I thought. *Or maybe it's a full moon and all the crazies are out.*

One of them extended his banana gun, and a second boom followed the first. The young male cop flew backward and slammed down on the pavement. My blood turned to ice. Voices shouted, and streaks of electricity arced from the third cop's wand toward the new arrivals. The new guys continued their forward march unfazed, long black robes swaying with their steps.

"Retreat!" ordered a parrot voice, complete with clicks and whistles. It came from the cruiser at the end of the alley.

Feet ran toward the patrol car, followed by another ear-splitting boom. Blinding light flashed, and the black robes stopped. One of them chuckled.

"Enough," said another, walking toward the cop who now lay deathly still in the middle of the alley. "Take the DC's tracker and find the talent. He's still here, or the collection team would have been gone already."

The chuckler waded into the garbage. When he reached Sammie, he knelt beside her and unstrapped the black lump from her wrist. It was too big for a watch—more the size of a cell phone. He extended it in my direction, and the clicking became a blur of static, like a Geiger counter.

"Found him," he called to his compatriot. "This DC's still alive."

"Finish her and get the talent back to the fracture," the first black robe replied.

Finish? As in *kill?* Where the hell was her sergeant? What about the officer with the dog at the patrol car? Why weren't they helping their fallen comrade? Fear squeezed my chest. I couldn't let this happen and live with myself, but I was unarmed and useless in a fight. She seemed so nice, so caring. He pointed his sonic banana gun at her. As I tensed to spring, the third black robe screamed.

The demon towered behind the third black robe, his nostrils billowing smoke and his talons planted deep in the man's head. He extracted his claws and licked globs of shiny white goo from them while the man stood paralyzed. My stomach flip-flopped, and I shrank lower.

The demon bent close and whispered in his victim's ear. His victim fired his weapon, and the chuckler's head ripped through the back of his hood, splattering blood, brains, and scraps of fabric on the wall above me. The edge of the shock wave blew my garbage bag hat off, and my ears ached from the sound.

The first black robe fired at the demon and his prey, and the poor guy burst like an overripe watermelon dropped from a great height. The demon roared, uninjured, his heavy bull nose wrinkling to bare pointy un-cow-like teeth.

This couldn't be real. I might see gargoyles, but I knew they didn't exist. Neither did eight-foot demons or banana guns that shot killer sonic waves. The demon took a step toward me, his eyes intent on the female officer.

The back door of the Chinese restaurant opened, and a wizened old Asian man shuffled through, garbage in hand. He saw the chuckler's body and stopped. Then he looked at the remaining black robe and dropped his bag, oblivious to the demon clopping toward us. So Black Robe at least was real. I'd sort out the demon later.

I rose from the garbage, scooped the cop onto my shoulder, and pushed through the open door. Thank goodness she was small, probably not more than ninety-five pounds soaking wet, which she was. The old man grabbed my arm and tried to toss me out, but I shrugged him off.

"Muggers!" I screamed. "Gang fight! Lock the friggin' door!"

As I charged through the kitchen, I heard the door slam behind me. I plunged into the main seating area, thinly sprinkled with staring, open-mouthed customers. Downtown Centralia—if that's where I was—didn't have a lot of nightlife. They'd probably get charged extra for my entertainment value. A boom echoed from the kitchen as I reached the front entrance, followed by the crash of the back door hitting something. I hoped the old guy had gotten clear.

I snatched a trench coat from the rack by the door, exited, and made a right, half jogging, half staggering past the restaurant windows with Sammie on my shoulder. Amazing how a good jolt of adrenaline could increase strength. Another boom and the window glass exploded, spraying me. My bare feet slid on the sleet-coated sidewalk. My legs burned, and my back bowed lower with every step. I gulped air and stumbled faster toward the end of the block, but I knew it wouldn't be fast enough, not carrying the cop. I couldn't leave her. Black Robe wanted her dead.

Storefronts dropped away, replaced by a corner parking lot with an attendant kiosk standing by the far exit. I race-walked across the lot to the kiosk. To my relief, the little building was unlocked. I plunked her on the floor as gently as I could, dragged on the too-big trench coat, and stepped out, closing the door. A city bus rolled past on the cross street and pulled over at the corner to pick up a passenger. I ran like hell for the bus stop.

Black Robe arrived at the parking lot in time to see me leap onto the bus. His banana gun fired, the side of the bus near the front dented in, and half the windows burst. The driver stared, first at the windows, and then at me.

"Mugger!" I shouted. "Drive!"

The bus lurched forward, dumping me on the floor. I looked up into the face of a thirty-something businessman sitting behind the driver, and fear looked back. His bloodless face matched the white dress shirt under his business suit. He clutched a fat blue gym bag to his stomach and glanced over his shoulder where wind whistled in the broken windows.

Someone huddled on the floor between the seats about halfway down, and a striking blonde woman hunkered in a seat near the back. She wore a waitress uniform, and despite the glass speckling her clothes and hair, peered down the aisle at me with such confidence and intensity that it scared me. *Lunatic*, I thought. *Thrill seeker.* She probably gawked at road wrecks.

"Stay down!" I yelled, scrambling to my feet to look out the back. Black Robe pounded past the kiosk without glancing at it. I squatted beside the driver, thrilled with my brilliant planning. Crazy didn't mean stupid.

The engine roared for a block, and then the driver backed off as he approached a red light.

"Keep going!" I shouted. "Go, go!"

Another boom took out the back window and the bus driver's head. Gore splattered the windshield. The driver's headless body slumped onto the steering wheel. The bus wobbled along the street. I swore. What a fool I'd been to gloat over my cleverness.

I hauled the dead driver's torso back with one hand and spun the steering wheel with the other, my knuckles white on the wheel. I kicked his foot from the accelerator and pressed down with my own. We flew around a corner too fast, clipped a parked car with a screech of metal, and zig-zagged on down the street. As we crossed our second intersection, a car t-boned us. The bus spun like a ballerina on the icy street until it crashed into the front window of a carpet shop.

My shoulder smashed against the windshield. I looked around, trying to get my bearings. The businessman had thumped his forehead against the driver's seat and appeared dazed. He'd dropped the gym bag beside his shiny dress shoes. A gym bag meant workout clothes, and no one wore dress shoes in a gym, did they? We'd only gained a block or two on Black Robe. If I was going to lead him away from the cop lady, I needed shoes. My feet ached from the cold.

I slammed the door control open and snatched the gym bag. The damn thing was heavier than I expected. I didn't have time to worry about it. Sirens wailed in the distance, and running down the center of the street barely a block and a half behind came Black Robe. No time to dig out shoes.

I vaulted from the bus and sprinted along the sidewalk, trying to keep parked cars between Black Robe and me until I could get around a corner. Black Robe's gun thundered once, rocking me with a near miss and setting off a cacophony of car alarms. I hurtled south at the next cross street, my shoulder blades crawling in expectation of another shot.

I headed though a business district toward a seedy residential neighborhood where I could give my pursuer the slip once I'd led him far, far from the police woman. She'd be safe. I'd be a hero. I smiled, regaining my confidence. Then I remembered the dead bus driver. My fault. My hands clenched on the handle of my stolen bag, and I ran faster.

Turning another corner, I pulled up under a street lamp and peeked back. Black Robe labored on at a dog trot, tiring badly. My feet were killing me. I needed shoes, and now I had time to put them on. I dropped the gym bag on the sidewalk and unzipped it.

No shoes.

Just stacks and stacks of money.